POLITICAL FICTIONS

ALSO BY PATRICK BOUCHERON

The Power of Images: Siena, 1338

France in the World: A New Global History (editor)

Machiavelli: The Art of Teaching People What to Fear

Trace and Aura: The Recurring Lives of St. Ambrose of Milan

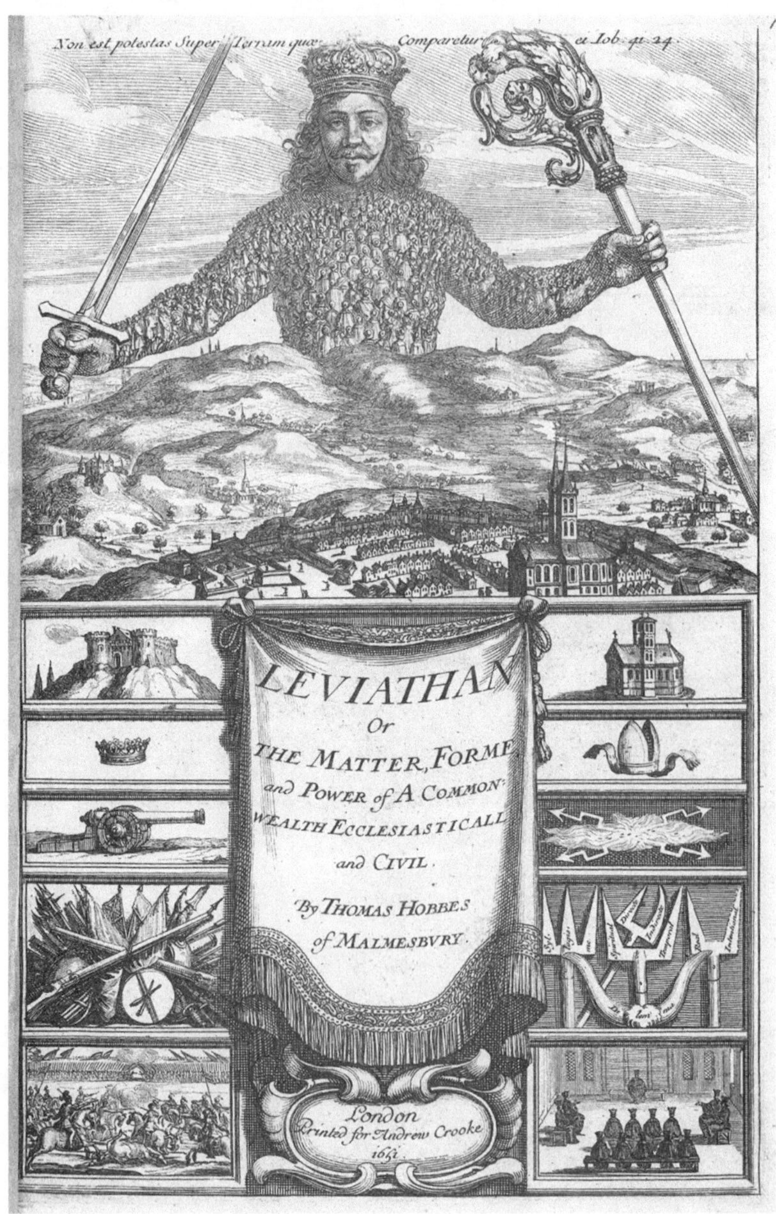

Frontispiece from the 1651 edition
of Thomas Hobbes's *Leviathan*

POLITICAL FICTIONS

From the Middle Ages to the "Post-Truth" Present

Patrick Boucheron

Translated from the French by
Willard Wood

OTHER PRESS NEW YORK

This text is based on a series of lectures given at the Collège de France between January 10, 2017, and March 21, 2017.

Edited with the helpful assistance of Elisabeth Schmitt

Production editor: Yvonne E. Cárdenas
Text designer: Julie Fry
This book was set in Arno and Trade Gothic.

10 9 8 7 6 5 4 3 2 1

 Printed in the United States of America on acid-free paper. For information write to Other Press LLC, 267 Fifth Avenue, 6th Floor, New York, NY 10016. Or visit our Web site: www.otherpress.com

Library of Congress Cataloging-in-Publication Data
Names: Boucheron, Patrick author
Title: Political fictions : from the Middle Ages to the "post-truth" present / Patrick Boucheron ; translated from the French by Willard Wood.
Description: New York : Other Press, 2025. | "This text is based on a series of lectures given at the Collège de France between January 10, 2017, and March 21, 2017." —Title page verso. | Includes bibliographical references.
Identifiers: LCCN 2025015931 (print) | LCCN 2025015932 (ebook) | ISBN 9781635423754 paperback | ISBN 9781635423761 ebook
Subjects: LCSH: Machiavelli, Niccolò, 1469–1527. Principe | Hobbes, Thomas, 1588–1679. Leviathan | Political science—Philosophy—History | Storytelling—Political aspects | Politics and literature—History
Classification: LCC JA71 .B586 2025 (print) | LCC JA71 (ebook)
LC record available at https://lccn.loc.gov/2025015931
LC ebook record available at https://lccn.loc.gov/2025015932

PREFACE

WHAT GOVERNS US? At a time when our attention is likely to be absorbed by the distressing sight of loud and violent leaders strutting on the political stage, at a time when our democratic defenses seem on the point of surrendering to the authoritarian subversion of grotesque but eminently dangerous political figures, the only question worth asking is: By what are we *really* governed? By what, not by whom. Because one of the most common tricks that tyrants use is to pretend that, through their antics, they stand with the people, a people they define in vague and imperious ways. The trap can then be snapped shut: If you are unable to dispel the gravitational pull exerted by this invading body that, as it gradually expands to fill the available space, slowly dissolves the very idea of the body politic, then you are preparing to obey.

No need, then, to hold forth at length on the psychology of

tyrants: it most often repeats, in trite and dreary terms — even when systematically making use of surprise effects — the typological traits that classical authors defined long ago. Did they not say that dictators, despite their shouts and vehemence, are called "dictators" because they always allow their behavior to be dictated by those whom they pretend to subjugate? But if the dictator is dictated to, it's certainly not by anything that is said to him explicitly — there is no convincing him of anything, he is deaf to all criticism, possibly even to all praise. No, what dictates to him is rather what political society says itself, against its own will, creating the necessary space for the set of stories, values, images, and partially imagined memories that we propose to call "political fictions" here.

Political fictions therefore refer to what already pervades in advance of any exercise of political power, even one that appears extraordinarily disruptive. They pervade *in advance*, that is the main point, and I'll return to it. They do so all the more effectively the more they stay hidden and unnoticed. In this they are the opposite of myths, which function only if they are endlessly retold, and they also differ from ideologies, which demand to be constantly trumpeted. But they borrow the narrative form of myths and the ambition of ideologies to reflect an entire worldview. When we talk about political fictions here, what we will mean is the imaginary institution of societies, to use Cornelius Castoriadis's term.

Since the Middle Ages, this imagined collective identity has expressed itself through a configuration of stories — one such is the Eucharistic metaphor and its monstrous inversion as the cannibalistic ruling power, to name one of the main plot narratives discussed in the pages that follow. But it can also be expressed in images, a form in which a fable's movement is arrested — such is the case of the famous frontispiece of Thomas Hobbes's *Leviathan*, which will stop us in our course at length also, quite literally since the image is understood here as an instance of immobilizing thought, of halting the flow of fiction, which in itself produces a visual event. In the case of both stories and images, it is a question of grasping the conditions for political embodiment, that is, the articulation between the fictive person of the king and his mortal body. Put in those terms, in the language of political theory, it can seem highly abstract. But it is patently clear to all of us today that the question of bodies politic, referring both to the leader who incarnates a public office and the people he represents, is one that is highly concrete and relevant today. Whence the need to think on the question historically, without bringing it back to a somewhat lazy analysis of the elements of language belonging to what we call today *storytelling*.

When we say "since the Middle Ages," then, we intend it not only in the historical sense — "from the Middle Ages to the present day" — but very much in an archaeological sense. The challenge is to focus on the active part of our past, the part that is still alive in our contemporary world and all the more powerful for remaining quietly buried. To bring it to light is therefore to expose it to our critical view, so that we aren't played by it. Such, I hope, is the liberating scope of this archaeology of modern government, a few of whose more salient aspects I propose to examine in this work. In trying to cast light, for instance, on our current anxiety over the scarily effective rhetoric of alternative facts, we note a strange familiarity with the odd, albeit fascinating, scholastic acceptance of the orthodoxy of the implausible. Probing this resemblance may allow us to stop wasting our time in outrage at the flimsy and absurd pronouncements uttered in a continuous stream by the leading figures of the post-truth era and grasp their paradoxical logic. We'll understand at the same time that the contemporaneity of our archaisms is a kind of haunting.

This, briefly, is the kind of historian I will try to be in the coming pages: a medievalist who, believing that all history is contemporary, tries to throw light on its shadowed aspects with a controlled use of anachronism. One might also read this book as an essay on the texture of time, whose weft can be distended to show unexpected distances and discontinuities or, on the contrary, crumpled to show unnoticed overlaps and superimpositions of contemporary phenomena. We may better understand the nonhomogeneity of time since undergoing the unique experience of Covid-19, an experience that was both universal and discontinuous, since we lived that separation simultaneously, together and apart. Time folded in on itself, bringing certain distant things close and, conversely, making the familiar strange. Perhaps we are paying the political price today for not having truly thought through that moment when our historical condition was put to the test.

If I talk about the years 2020–2022 here, it's because the unconsidered epidemic confusion of the times stands opaquely between the moment in 2017 when I gave the lectures that compose this book and the moment of its publication in 2025. A passage of years, and a passage also between languages: lectures that were originally delivered in French, then transcribed under the shaping hand of Elisabeth Schmitt, here appear in an English-language text, thanks to Willard Wood's admirable translation effort, ably seconded by Yvonne Cárdenas, Judith Gurewich, and the team at Other Press. From 2017 to 2025 and from one language to another—a double distance that requires some explanation from me. And it is all the more paradoxical for having exacerbated a distancing of the nearby when the point was to bring us closer to what is far away.

I should probably start by telling the English-speaking reader as simply as possible that the place from which, in 2017, I spoke about the past to the present was the Collège de France. I have had the good fortune to teach at this unusual institution since 2015. Founded in 1530, it has always vaunted itself as a place that offers unfettered and disinterested knowledge, free of charge. Nothing constrains what one says there, to a public that has no other expectation than the satisfaction of its curiosity. The concept is simple, but in these times when knowledge is marketed, and threats to academic freedoms are mounting, it seems almost extravagant, almost scandalous. Yet students and colleagues listen to you lecture, some in the lecture hall itself, and a far greater number remotely, since all lecture courses and seminars are posted online in openly accessible audio or video form. It's important not to disappoint those who collectively hold your discipline's knowledge and expect you to defend its rigor and autonomy. But it's also incumbent on you to speak to those who, arriving from other horizons, expect history to enter into conversation with what I'm tempted to call the poetry of knowledge.

This presents you with three obligations. The first is never to repeat yourself, and to teach the research that is currently in process. The second is to make an effort to share your erudition, but without trying to simplify everything. The third is to understand that the only way to show yourself worthy of an institution founded on freedom of thought is to take every liberty with it. While the Collège de France's motto is *Docet omnia* (Everything is taught), it is not a capitulation to the temptations of encyclopedism: not every discipline is taught there, but those that are are taught in every way possible. If I make that distinction, it is because it informs the narrative progress of the text to come, which advances less by demonstration than by an association of ideas, by assonance and diversion. "Teaching what we don't know, that is called *searching*," said Roland Barthes in his inaugural lecture at the Collège de France, marveling at his license to "dream his research out loud."

This may be why the motif of the dream, from Jules Michelet to King Louis VII of France, plays such a large part in the pages ahead. The reader will find cheek by jowl the Virgin Mary's cloak and Charlie Chaplin's moustache, Napoleon Bonaparte and Sultan Baybars, Thomas Aquinas and Harry Potter. This diversity of tones and references makes each lecture a unit, with its own dramaturgy, its theory plotlines and narrative rebounds, trying also to demonstrate by example (the *exemplum* having been a brief and edifying form in the Middle Ages) what a political fiction might be, or more accurately what it does. No attempt has been made to reconfigure these lectures into a more classical form, the decision being instead to present them as they are: lectures, anchored in place and time, performed, which is to say *addressed* to the men and women who were there, on that day.

Why then claim to transform them into a book, and what is at stake in this transformation? This question is one I considered from the very first lecture, as the reader will discover. If the scruples I raised were eventually set aside and I conceded to the friendly pressure of Judith Gurewich, it was precisely because the double distance that I cited — from 2017 to 2025, and from spoken French to an English-language text — is maybe capable of reviving interest in this project, due to the unanticipated effects of an update. To understand these, it's worth considering a few contextual elements.

The first are personal. In 2017, I was starting my second year of teaching at the Collège de France. My first, in 2016, was devoted to laying out a long-term research project on the memory of Ambrose of Milan. It was already an archaeology of the theological and political foundations of modern governments, and already an examination of the relation between the arts of governance and those of storytelling. The title of this course was "Memories, Fictions, and Beliefs: The Long Middle Ages of Ambrose of Milan." But the substance of it had already been worked on well before I came to teach it at the Collège de France — and could therefore be suitably turned into a book in 2019, translated in 2022 by Other Press as *Trace and Aura: The Recurring Lives of St. Ambrose of Milan*. The course I gave in 2017, therefore, was the first to be conceived in strict contemporaneity with its being taught at the Collège de France. I imagined the series (as I would consistently do with my subsequent courses) as the first panel of a diptych, with the second — also announced in the first lecture, and forthcoming from this same publisher — devoted more specifically to the Italian *novellistica*, or short stories, which in the wake of Boccaccio's narrative revolution professedly offered "Stories of Tyranny" (this was the title of the second panel).

Furthermore, the year 2017 also corresponded for me with an accentuation (or should I say aggravation?) of my role as a public historian. In January 2017, as I started delivering the present set of lectures, a book of which I was the general editor, *Histoire mondiale de la France*, was published to considerable public notice, exposing me to occasionally violent debates; and when the lecture series ended in April of that year, I turned my attention to preparing the texts that, broadcast on the France Inter public radio channel in summer 2017, became another book—the English-language editions of both (*France in the World: A New Global History*, 2019, and *Machiavelli: The Art of Teaching People What to Fear*, 2020) were also issued, I should note, by my faithful US publisher, Other Press.

I bring up these elements of personal context only because they are consonant with another circumstance of altogether global import. The breaking news on January 20, 2017, was of an astounding episode in the history of the United States in the world, an episode that would send shock waves around the globe, unexpectedly giving currency to the art of teaching people what to fear. With the inauguration of Donald Trump, the forty-fifth president of the United States, came also the consecration of alternative facts. People understood, though still confusedly, that the exercise of power no longer had to concern itself with truth. Once reality might no longer serve for denial, a vast field of possibility was opened to ruling powers that were unjust, violent, and out of control. This subsequently became quite clear. From the moment that one advocates an unlimited right of speech cut off from any political accountability, the very notion of truth goes out the window. We are still at that point today, stunned but unable to do anything about it.

Rereading these lectures today, I am better able to grasp the effects of this shattering irruption of historical violence into political fictions. Inevitably I reacted as a historian, that is, protecting the objects of the past from assault by the arrogance of the present and not allowing them to be contaminated by our emotions and affects, however legitimate they might be. But what kind of historian would I have been had I simply gone about sealing off the doors and windows of my area of study from the din of the world? I needed also, as a public historian, to objectivize it — that is, to set it at some distance while never losing it from sight, facing it squarely. And precisely because the times were urgent, precisely because the depressing spectacle of a frenetic present threatened to damage our freedoms, it was necessary to safeguard the independent time needed for research, slow down the pace, linger over an image, allow oneself to be guided by one's curiosity, go astray, get lost, and find one's way. Not capitulate to current affairs in order to remain contemporary: such is the silent struggle that animated, I understand it better today, this conceptual work.

But if I understand it all better today, it's that I am rereading the lectures later and in another language than my own — again this effect of double distance. Because, with the unpredictability of history, this research project on political fictions in Europe's medieval societies crossed the Atlantic a first time in 2017, which gave it an entirely unexpected American dimension. I was subsequently asked to present my work in several US universities, starting in 2018: at NYU, the University of Chicago, Brown, Harvard, Stanford, and UCLA.

The project of the present translation grew out of those engagements. And in an astonishing doubling of the wiles of history, this translation is appearing at a moment when Donald Trump, the forty-seventh president of the United States, is implementing actions for which these political fictions were perhaps a prefiguration.

This is no doubt the salient fact: my starting hypothesis was not just to conceive of fiction as a narrative form of political thought, but as a thought experiment that puts to the test the very notion of truth. In other words, it is a question of "inducing truth effects by means of a fictional discourse," in Michel Foucault's words: Considering history through its political fictions therefore comes down to bringing into view "a politics that doesn't yet exist starting from a historical reality." Consequently, it is fiction's anticipatory power that is going to be examined in the pages that follow. And that is why this first volume ends with an analysis of the relations between the foreshadowing impact of political fictions and their function as parodies, somewhere between pastiche and postiche.

It will be up to the reader to decide whether these thoughts are now outdated, in a world where Volodymyr Zelenskyy became president of Ukraine in 2019 after having played the lead character for three seasons in *Servant of the People*, a political fiction, as a television series understands that term. Zelenskyy played the comic role of a person who, unexpectedly and partly by chance, is elected president of

Ukraine, and he ended up performing that role, putting on the costume that his part required. Political reality was nothing more than a fiction that lent itself to the theater of the real. But since Russia's invasion of Ukraine on February 24, 2022, the former comic actor Zelenskyy has worn a different set of clothing, the clothing of a war chief, thereby revealing the strange and profound kinship between political dissidence, the European tradition of parodic Jewish theater, and the tragic meaning of history.

As to the historical meaning that might be given to season two of "Trump in the White House," which is currently afflicting the whole world with seemingly unforeseeable chaos, it is not my place to say anything at all about it here. Does the brutal evidence of pure oligarchic domination render meaningless the subtle theological and political analyses that draw on the narrative strength of fiction to shed light on modern governance? The advent of the oligarchs brings to mind Don DeLillo's prophetic novel *Cosmopolis* (2003), in which a New York golden boy looks from his limousine at the display of financial data scrolling overhead at Times Square, "information made sacred, ritually unreadable," while crowds gape at the symbols, prompting this scathing utterance: "Money has lost its narrative quality the way painting did once upon a time. Money is talking to itself."

It may be just as simple as that. And if that's the case, we need have nothing more to do with the political fictions discussed here, part of a history that is securely past. A second season is neither a replay nor a continuation: history does not repeat itself, and if it sometimes stutters, it's not necessarily, *pace* Marx's maxim, as parody. For we now know that the burlesque in no way precludes violence. And we also know that tyrants need to be taken seriously, even if their words need not be taken literally. At the moment of danger, therefore, one may not be wasting one's time entirely to look deeply into history, even at what's apparently farthest from us. We gain much more than a diversion or respite: the courage of truth.

LECTURE 1, JANUARY 10, 2017

"Each Epoch Dreams the Following One"

History is "this effort of laborious dreaming by which we raise ourselves from night to day, from death to life" — Lorenzetti's Siena: a woman who "is dreaming beforehand of those yet to come" — The tyrant's mask, the face of division — Politics of ugliness and politics of fakeness, the parodic and the prosthetic — Guy Debord's *The Society of the Spectacle*: more a prophecy than a description — The tyrant allures by his power to create a narrative — What is fiction? Artifactual theories and the risks of panfictionalism — A political fiction is "a narrative form of political theory" — Foucault: "Man does not fully know what he is capable of thinking; fiction is there to tell him"

IN INTRODUCING MY SUBJECT, and to lay the theoretical groundwork for what I'll try to construct in front of you, I will hold off arriving too quickly at a definition — the definition, if it comes and when it comes, can only come later, when it wants to. In introducing my subject, then, I realize that I am and remain a thorough beginner. And this gives me a feeling of comfort, of consolation. Let's just say I'd like to hold on to the babbling, terrifying grace of the beginner for a long moment.

Beginning, or rather, starting anew. That was, I think, the key phrase of my previous series of lectures in 2016: How to start anew? Looking back on it, the whole long train of thought devoted to the memory of Saint Ambrose was a way of approaching the political art of beginning again. What, in my book *Trace and Aura,* I called "the long Middle Ages of

Ambrose of Milan" was that ancient time (the Middle Ages) when an even more ancient memory (the fourth-century Ambrose of Milan) kept stubbornly returning to haunt the present, a past that repeatedly started all over again, was transformed as it started again, but also relaunched and transformed the political times.

This active, energetic back and forth between the past and the present is in fact the opposite of a tradition, which saddles the present with an insistent past, stubborn and inert. It's the opposite of a past that won't go away, and our discussion dealt with passages, struggles, reminiscences, ghosts, promises — all the things that Walter Benjamin dreamed of, in fact, in his *Arcades Project.* This back and forth of forms, then, is a political configuration, which is to say the conjunction of several political fictions. "Memories, Fictions, Beliefs": that was the title of the last set of lectures. Focusing on the middle term, the one on which the triptych hinges, "fictions," we may simply be trying to answer the question: Of what we remember, what do we take to be true?

To leave it with this overly rhetorical transition wouldn't sit well with me. Claiming a logical connection where there are only suspect links, blurry uncertainties, and dubious bifurcations would be misleading. What's disloyal, what's truly obscene, is to give a lecture series as a display of intellectual fluency, apt connections, conceptual successes. Avoid those who claim success and listen rather to those who grope for words to tell of their difficulties, failures, blind alleys, approximations and discuss these with sufficient force that when the tragic sense of history looms, you aren't driven to despair.

There might be two ways of giving a lecture series: One is the way that I tried to follow in 2016, describing the difficulties that arise in writing a book, an impossible book (maybe), in that it aimed to be a book of passages. The second is the way that I will try here, describing the difficulties that occur in transitioning from one book to another, in making a passage for oneself, or rather as in *The Arcades Project*, in tunneling out the *collective interior* that, for Benjamin, puts the inside outside and the outside inside — as a Parisian *passage* or shopping arcade does, that glass world of the nineteenth-century bourgeoisie that creates not so much a covered street as an intermediary time and space between domestic living rooms. And if Benjamin characterizes this space as "like a dream," it's because his whole book was meant to crackle with a great blaze ignited by a single spark, a phrase of Jules Michelet's: "Each epoch dreams the following one." Benjamin quotes this famous aphorism of Michelet's several times, notably in his 1935 "Exposé," originally written in French to introduce his plan for *The Arcades Project*.

A sidebar here, if I may. Benjamin is often cited as quoting Michelet. But in his 1931 essay on Karl Kraus, Benjamin asserts that "every quotation is a summons." We therefore need to go back to Michelet's text and summon the original. Michelet's phrase comes from a set of notes entitled "Avenir! Avenir!" They were written in 1842, a crucial year for the historian, both in his life and in his work, as his journal attests; at the end of the year he would write *Le peuple*, an important inflection point. And he witnessed an upsurge, elicited by the threat of death. Michelet was sitting by his wife, who was dying. "Yesterday, as I sat by my bed, I saw her make an effort to open her eyes." It was she, at the moment of danger (which we know to be the Benjaminian moment), who revealed to him the movement of History itself: "this effort of laborious dreaming by which we raise ourselves from night to day, from death to life." And here Michelet returns to the phrase "each epoch dreams the following one," a phrase he'd put at the head of his feverish notes. This is how he returns to it: "Each epoch probably dreams *in just this way of the following epochs*... Our forefathers from the earliest ages of man *dreamed us*, no doubt with feelings of sympathy... Let us dream those yet to come, let us love them prospectively, and may their lives (God grant them joy!) console us for our own."

End of sidebar. Passing, then, from one book to another by the second, more adventurous and uncertain way. So where is this passage? I'm looking for the exit that will allow me to escape from an earlier book. I'm wanting to free myself from the hold that an image had over me, an image that was also a political fiction, free myself from the political force of a gaze that brought a world into being. This world, painted by Ambrogio Lorenzetti in 1339 on the walls of the Sala della Pace (Hall of Peace), in Siena's Palazzo Pubblico, was a dream vision of social reality.

"Peace," detail from *Allegory of Good Government* by Ambrogio Lorenzetti, 1338 (Palazzo Publico, Siena)

It was true because a woman dreamed it, dreamed it in a state of peace, and this woman was Peace. It was perhaps a memory she had started to believe in to ward off her fear of the future, but we who look at her stand on an equal footing with her. We are her contemporaries since we look at her looking at us. We see her as Benjamin saw Michelet ("each epoch dreams the following one"), wondering at the prophetic power of the past. And what she sees, what we see alongside her, is not necessarily the past but an opening onto a version of the present. We need to keep in mind not just the actualizing power of fiction but its anticipatory power. What in French we call *politique-fiction,* that is, speculative or dystopian fiction focused on social and political issues, reflects the belief that fiction might allow us to anticipate the future, to tell it ahead of time. In which case, it's possible that she, Peace, "is dreaming beforehand of those yet to come" — us, if you like.

But as those who have seen the frescoes on the walls of Palazzo Pubblico know, this vision of a peaceable city under just government is not the only image on Siena's walls. The future can present other possibilities as well, some of them considerably more troubling. Lorenzetti painted a configuration, which is to say he laid out a set of political fictions, available for use in collective decision-making. He teased apart different possibilities at a moment when political categories were melting down and becoming confused to form an ideological haze, a moment when many were expressing their disenchantment with civic values and their belief that the signoria could well be the continuation of the commune by other means, that its authoritarian power might in any case be something to envisage, a possible way forward, even a desirable one, given the hidden attraction that authoritarian power exerts.

Because Tyranny also has a face. He stares at us from the adjoining wall — Peace turns her back on him, but she's seen him, she can't not have seen him, and she'll never see things the same way now that she has seen him. He has shifty eyes, I grant you, a baleful expression, a pale countenance — not a prepossessing figure. We can stare at him but not imagine him. He's got a mug more than a face. Look at his fangs, his horns. In writing about this pallid mask in *The Power of Images*, I said

"Tyranny," detail from *The Effects of Bad Government* by Ambrogio Lorenzetti, 1338 (Palazzo Pubblico, Siena)

that "everything disaggregates, everything separates," which still strikes me as accurate: This is the face of division, in the sense that its deformity expresses the contemporary passion (a wholly political one) for dividing people because one has lost the ability to see them together. For we now know that we have to confront what the historian Wendy Brown has called "the desire for walls," this drive to isolate, to divide, to build an inside protected by barriers, raised even as sovereignty is waning. But what I no longer think today is that it's a mask. In fact, I think it's the opposite: I think that Lorenzetti has unmasked tyranny, that he has painted here the face of a tyrant at the moment when a more attractive mask, no longer in view, has been whisked away, perhaps by the tyrant himself.

Film still from *Limelight*, Charlie Chaplin removing his makeup

THE CLOWN FACE is one that we can't help seeing today in the context of Charlie Chaplin's *Limelight*—I'll talk about Chaplin quite a bit in these lectures, you'll soon know why. In the movie, we see a man slowly taking off his makeup, forcing us to see him as he really is, older, sadder, more ridiculous—in a way turning the mirror back on ourselves. This is the province of photographic fiction: I'm thinking again of Benjamin, his "A Little History of Photography," written in 1931, where he defines the concept of aura by pointing to the work of Eugène Atget, the photographer of Paris. Here's what he says about him: "Atget was an actor who, disgusted with the profession, wiped off the mask then set about removing the makeup from reality too." Farther on he says, "The peeling away of the object's shell, the destruction of the aura," this was Atget's work.

Clowns can be evil, we all know that, we've seen a few. Who? You know perfectly well. I'm not just talking about the contemporary myth of the killer clown, one of those political fictions that first showed up in TV series, comic books, movies, and elsewhere in popular visual culture, then became the stuff of nightmares, of viral rumors, and finally of news stories. And I'm not just talking about the bad clown as a fictional character. I'm talking about, for example, Boris Johnson, Donald Trump, and Silvio Berlusconi, since I'm a historian of the Italian political laboratory who believes that in matters of government Italy often arrived at innovations that only later appeared everywhere else. In all three cases, what we see here is a very careful use of a politics of ugliness and a politics of fakery, the two being closely related. For the moment I'll just draw the connection loosely, but later we'll have the opportunity, I hope, to tighten it up: to show how a politics of ugliness and a politics of fakery can together destabilize our categories of the comic and the tragic, the natural and the artificial, truth and make-believe, laying a groundwork for the indiscriminateness and indifference that disrupt our whole concept of representation—whether in theater, politics, or the visual arts.

The point is to make the mask and the face indistinguishable, because how are you going to unmask reality if it already presents itself in the extravagant paint of fiction? It should be no surprise that this plays out in the capillary realm as well: If a person's hair looks exactly like a wig, if the real starts to resemble the most improbable invention, if it parodies the prosthetic, how are you going to whisk it away? The surest way never to be caricatured is to be one's own best caricature. That's why being ridiculous is not fatal in politics; what's fatal, or potentially so, is being ridiculed. But if you make yourself ridiculous, so extremely ridiculous that no one can do you better, then you're untouchable. We'll come back to this link between the parodic and the prosthetic too, but the important thing here is to recognize the anticipatory power of fiction.

Because we already know what the world will soon see from Trump — who, logically speaking, doesn't yet fully exist today, January 10, 2017. His image is still being fleshed out, it is a fiction only starting to become reality. With Trump we will see reality TV move into government. A novel chapter in the history of the Western powers is about to start, one in which executive authority was playacted before being exercised — and acted on the most vulgar, contemptible, and grotesque stage it is possible to imagine. This is not just an expression of intellectual disdain on my part; the phenomenon has been carefully studied in the case of reality-TV addicts. The addict's attachment to a show comes not from approval but from contempt. This type of power therefore creates a fiction that people love to hate. And this is a potent fiction, immune to the countering force of criticism, indignation, and derision, which it has already forestalled.

And that is what's literally disarming about this type of political obedience — obedience is clearly what it is, and of the most pernicious kind, since it doesn't impose a set of beliefs but of practices, behaviors, gestures, attitudes. It doesn't ask television viewers (or citizens reduced to the ranks of television viewers) for orthodoxy (because you can think what you like) but for orthopraxy (you must behave as you see others behaving on television), and you will like it, and then you'll hate it, but in neither case will it matter since in the end you'll be entirely happy to hate each other.

It's worth going back here to the most penetrating theorists of television's power, those who were writing about it before that power was fully deployed, like Guy Debord in *The Society of the Spectacle* in 1967. They were not so much describing as prophesying, telling us what would happen before it did, maybe because by the time something happens it's already too late. Seen in this light, *The Society of the Spectacle* was a political fiction not so very different from the genre of speculative fiction. When he described the excitement and fervor aroused by commodity fetishism, Debord was painting a collective portrait closer to what we are living today than to what he was living then, at the time of writing.

I won't dwell on this further now, since we'll inevitably come back to it, and for good reason. Because I haven't yet told you what direction I want to take in tunneling a passage from a particular point in an earlier book. What we can sense here, in front of Lorenzetti's "Tyranny," is just what is being masked, what hidden attraction draws us to it. That's why in my 2013 book *The Power of Images* the chapter that deals with this image is called "The Seductions of Tyranny (What the Image Conceals)." We'll look for our passage there, in that parenthesis, our way out. Because as a historian, what interests me now is to pass to the other side of this image, which hides other faces — the smiling, engaging faces of the Italian signors of the trecento, who managed to convince their fellow citizens of the benefits of their good government, who managed to take the drama out of this story painted so solemnly by Lorenzetti, this clash of great principles. It was magnificently painted as well, exhibiting so much intelligence, so many talents, such kindness, such attention to detail, such precision and patience, such attention to the diversity of the real and concern that each should get his due, that all should be represented, with their attitudes, their circumstances, their gestures. And these visible aspects of the world were, in the end, what one holds most dear, and they were fragile, vulnerable, soon to provoke anger, disgust, hostility, and then indifference, disdain, and, finally, nothing.

We need to see the faces of those who did that, who destroyed this world that had been dreamed. We need to understand their power, their seduction, which in the specific context of trecento Italy means understanding the political efficacy of the signorial propaganda that Lorenzetti was

"The Country," detail from *Allegory of Good Government* by Ambrogio Lorenzetti, 1338 (Palazzo Pubblico, Siena)

addressing. This will explain why he had to deploy so much energy to oppose it. His own brother, Pietro Lorenzetti, had gone to Arezzo to work for Guido Tarlati who was both the city's bishop and its signor. You can still see today a Madonna in the church of Santa Maria della Pieve that Pietro Lorenzetti executed for Tarlati. Everything about Tarlati's rule was destabilizing to the political categories of the time. He co-opted the institutions of the commune for the use of the signoria and directly increased his personal power as bishop, although the city had remained staunchly Ghibelline, or allied to the emperor rather than the pope, since Florence defeated Arezzo in 1289. When Tarlati died in 1327, his brothers succeeded him. It was they who commissioned the Sienese sculptors Agostino di Giovanni and Agnolo di Ventura to create the cenotaph of Tarlati that can be seen today in the Arezzo Cathedral. It's characteristic of what Erwin Panofsky called "the elegiacal narrative that dominated tomb sculpture" in trecento Italy. The commemorative monument employed the narrative form of biographical scenes, producing what can properly be called a political fiction. The message is conveyed through a loose succession of episodes, identified by their *tituli* (inscriptions). The same narrative mode was used on the tomb of Azzone Visconti, the signor of Milan, whom I wrote about earlier. Sculpted by Giovanni di Balduccio, of Pisa, between 1342 and 1346, it again testifies to the exchange of motifs and artists in the creation of communal and signorial propaganda.

"Il comune pelato" and "Comune in signoria," two panels from the Guido Tarlati cenotaph (Arezzo Cathedral)

What is referred to today in the debased language of politics as *triangulation* is magnificently illustrated in two allegories on the Tarlati cenotaph. As in Siena, both panels feature a majestic old man with a full beard, seated on a throne and representing the commune. In the first panel, labeled "Il comune pelato" (The commune despoiled), the old man is being stripped of his ornaments by a frenzied crowd; in the second, he is restored to his full dignity and authority, with a group of followers and prisoners kneeling before him — the *titulus* reads "Comune in signoria." The reversibility of allegory in the political realm could not be more strikingly shown. Allegory is a glove that can be turned inside out; or rather, it fits like a glove on anyone who extends a firm hand to grasp power.

This is what is hidden behind the image, this is what lies under the scowl that Lorenzetti painted in Siena: not only the face of a smiling tyranny but the hidden attraction it holds for us. Let us look now at the tombs of the signors of Verona, the della Scalas, who took control of the Veneto in the 1260s and managed to convince its citizens of their intention to provide *buon governo*, notably by supporting artists and men of letters. It was to Cangrande della Scala that Dante dedicated his *Divine Comedy* in 1316, while still composing it. In the letter he addressed to his protector, the Tuscan exile distances himself from the generally skeptical opinion of the signoria ("But the people in their ignorance judge without discrimination"); this allows him to plead his own claim of creative sovereignty, addressing himself to what he recognizes as the similarly sovereign political authority of Cangrande. We'll see that intellectuals are the first to concede to tyranny because it allows them, basically, to set themselves off from the people. I quote Dante's "Letter to Cangrande": "Truly those who draw their strength from intellect and reason, and who have received the divine gift of liberty, are not subject to any custom; nor should this surprise us, for they are not directed by laws but rather the laws are directed by them." Acting along these lines, in 1319, Cangrande reformed Verona's urban statutes, which provided him the legal grounds to undertake a series of municipal planning initiatives. He started with a politics of prestige, embellishing the city square with numerous monuments, but he also oversaw the refurbishment of the city's facilities, restoring aqueducts and water-supply systems, enlarging the warehouses that kept the town provisioned, and maintaining the roadways. The city of Verona thus became, in its material form, a gigantic metaphor for the inscription on Tarlati's cenotaph: "Comune in signoria," the commune realized through the centralized power of the signoria, enhanced by it, largely through overriding the commune's internal conflicts—effectively neutralizing it.

This overriding of the commune is visible in the funerary enclosure between the della Scalas' palace and the church of Santa Maria Antica. There, behind the high railings stamped at every turn with the ladder emblem of the della Scalas, the mounted heroes preside. The bodies of Cangrande I, Mastino II, and Cansignorio lie in raised sarcophagi, elevated onto ceremonial beds. In *The Age of the Cathedrals,* Georges Duby describes it as "the emblem of political triumph. The galloping of jousts and soaring nights of conquest bear away Cangrande della Scala for all eternity." What gallop? What

Scaliger Tombs (Verona)

conquest? It's the gallop of the petrified cavalcade, caught in Verona's dull, perforated, gray stone and outlined against the city's sky. The haughty silhouettes of the equestrian statues call to the mausoleums in the form of miniature cathedrals, of marble canopies or highly elongated reliquaries. This is conquest, the one victory that has meaning: the triumph over death and oblivion. Perched on their pedestals, insolently poised above our heads, the signors have the last word.

Equestrian statue of Cangrande della Scala, c. 1340 (Castelvecchio Museum, Verona)

Take a closer look at the insolence: Cangrande laughs, in the flush of victory. The court poets, who were paid to compose flowery commemorations of his triumph, wrote in Verona that "his face shone with joy." Our own era, more familiar with the sardonic chuckle, sees mostly the jowly, somewhat clownish, and in any case mocking physiognomy of a stocky man who eyes us smugly, as if he'd just pulled a fast one. Which isn't entirely untrue: The della Scala tombs were originally attacks on funerary convention, a kind of triumph of bad taste, so that when we admire them as works of art, we are perhaps allowing ourselves to be impressed by a medieval Trump Tower.

I wrote about this monument in an article called "Un tyran attirant" (An attractive tyrant). What attracted me to him personally was the following hypothesis, which I'll set forth again here on the threshold of this journey into political fictions: The thing that's attractive about tyranny is its fiction-making power, its ability to generate notice for itself but also to generate narrative energy. For all power is the power to create narrative. This doesn't just mean that the tyrant contrives to be seen and understood in the context of fables and plotlines; it also means that he becomes fully effective only when he redirects the life stories of those he dominates. Briefly, the attractive tyrant is fiction itself. And the work of the historian consists in finding a way, if not to counter this fiction, at least to push back against it.

My article was something of a placeholder, the first chapter of a book still to be written — a book that, to be perfectly honest, is taking its sweet time. This book — the one that I'd have liked to get to, since I decided to divulge publicly and perhaps recklessly the difficulty of making a passage — would look at the way that a tyrant, Bernabò Visconti, signor of Milan from 1354 to 1385, made himself into a character in a novel during his lifetime, or more accurately, a character in *novellistica,* or short stories, since what developed in the wake of the narrative revolution started by Giovanni Boccaccio's *Decameron* was the edifying and diverting genre of the *novellistica,* which incorporated topical events into its brief fictions and used real contemporary figures in its plots. In a 2010 article that appeared in an academic Festschrift, I sketched the history of Bernabò's trajectory in fiction as he became a character in the novellas of the mid-fourteenth century.

Bernabò entered the world of fiction and never left it, though he would undergo changes as the literary genre of the short story developed (in the works of Franco Sacchetti, Giovanni Sercambi, and Masuccio Salernitano), with chroniclers often using the anecdotes from these accounts as historical sources. While Tuscan authors, who were generally sympathetic to the values of the commune, portrayed Bernabò as a cruel lord, he appears in the fiction of the times as an eccentric and facetious character, a *beffatore* who plays tricks on others and delivers lessons in political morality to his dupes. We'll return to all this in detail later — exactly when I don't know, but we'll come back to it.

I promised that in this introductory lecture I'd start to lay out the theoretical framework of what we'll call political fictions but without setting it in stone. The definition of fiction has become something of an issue in contemporary literary criticism, a kind of marketplace for theory. The diversity of approaches in defining fiction even among its practitioners is the subject of the sociologist Olivier Caïra's recent investigation, which notably looks at video games. The general context is the postmodern tenet that fiction is everywhere, for the simple reason that "everything is fiction." And everything is fiction because everything is a discursive construction — we know things only through the words that denote them, but they never denote them in a transparent manner. This is what one might call the *artifactual* reading of fiction, which makes no distinction between a documentary film and a feature film, since both are artifacts. This leads to what the researcher Marie-Laure Ryan, who specializes in fictional worlds in the Internet age, calls the "doctrine of panfictionalism."

One of the early and radical forms of panfictionalism, prophetic almost, was the apocalyptic philosophy of Jean Baudrillard. The reign of the simulacrum — which is to say of generalized representation — creates a virtual world that assassinates the real, an event described as having already occurred but gone unnoticed. There's no point in dwelling on the limits of this theoretical radicalism, and it may be enough to remember the quip made by the Czech researcher Lubomir Dolezel: "If you decide to call reality fiction, then you'll need a new word for fiction." Naturally, as Jean Levi has written, "History itself, inasmuch as it represents facts through language, is also fictional and not to be confused with the events it portrays." This doesn't mean that history is indistinguishable from a novel, which is a fiction twice over — not only because "it portrays something that does not exist" but because what it portrays "has being and substance only through its words, which belong to the world of representation."

The doctrine of panfictionalism poses an obvious threat to the historian's ability to establish a system of truth, but the other reason it has failed to make great inroads into theory is that it maintains a classical stance in matters of reference. Literary theory can be a resource here in orienting ourselves in this labyrinth. Gérard Genette, who has devoted a book to this problem, *Métalepse: De la figure à la fiction,* reminds us of the potential confusion of *figure* and *fiction*. The two words have a common etymology: the Latin verb *fingere,* which means to fashion, represent, pretend, and also invent. *Fictio* and *figura,* ancestors of our modern concepts of *fiction* and *figure,* both derive from it, but separately. That is, their denotations must be kept distinct: *fictio* designates action, *figura* the effect of this action. Fiction, in other words, is the operation that creates figures — which is why I speak of political figures and the narrative configurations of these political figures. But at the same time, for Genette "the figure is an embryo or, if you like, a sketch of fiction." Thus, the thaumaturgic or miracle-working power of French kings is more a *figura* than a *fictio*: It derives from a fictionalization of the real and creates a political configuration that reorders the art of storytelling.

Caïra's work, by contrast, aims at offering a deflationist and more minimal definition of fiction, a conceptually parsimonious one that subjects the classic definitions of fiction to Occam's razor. He uncouples fiction from mimesis (fiction need not represent reality), from narrative (fiction is not necessarily a form of storytelling), from language (it is not always presented in words), and even from logic (it needn't be limited to an already formalized universe). The main purport of this work for me is that fiction operates in tension between two poles, the first mimetic (fiction is representation) and the second axiomatic (fiction is a thought experiment—as in Jorge Luis Borges's *Fictions*). Fiction doesn't necessarily pretend, it doesn't always create a possible world. It provides an experiment.

This dual definition (fiction imitates the world but is its own world) allows for a pragmatic description of the variety of fictional practices and strategies. Consequently, and this strikes me as important for what follows, fiction does not stand in opposition to factuality as falsehood does to truth. Furthermore, it frees fiction from the problem of referentiality or non-referentiality. In other words, fiction is a figure of knowledge that is distinct from factual knowledge not because one is false and the other true, but because it puts the question of truth or falsehood off to the side.

That is why, as I say, fiction can be a thought machine. Jean-Marie Schaeffer makes this point in his book *Why Fiction?* We might mention here the current discourse about theoretical fictions (in sociology, for example, but also in the hard sciences). The phenomenon is not new: Frédérique

Aït-Touati has shown the cognitive value of characterizations and fictionalizing tales in seventeenth-century astronomy, for example, which Johannes Kepler called fairy tales. Schaeffer for his part concentrates on what the philosopher David Hume, in *Enquiry Concerning Human Understanding*, calls fictions — and which are actually cognitive illusions. The illusion of perspective, for instance, is an example: We automatically believe in perspectival representations, even when we know them to be illusory, because they conform to conscious perception. Schaeffer continues: "A cognitive illusion is never experienced as a fiction but as a referentially validated representation. By contrast, an artistic fiction needs to be recognized *as a fiction* in order to work properly."

This pragmatic reading of fiction inevitably brings us to the problem of belief and obedience, its political effectiveness. This is the second aspect of our theoretical framing: In what sense can these fictions be called *political*? Let's take the case of a television or film series. We can call it political when it deals with the world of politics, as *The West Wing* or *Borgen* do, but also when it lends itself to a political interpretation, as *Harry Potter* does, according to Jean-Claude Milner. That adjective, "political," refers us to two separate notions, which the philosophy of Claude Lefort, among others, allows us to distinguish: *politics* and *the political*. The latter "doesn't surface in what we call political activity, but in the twin movements of apparition and occultation in the mode in which the society is instituted."

It would be rash, therefore, to decide whether the adjective "political" in political fiction refers back to politics or the political. Historians of the political anthropology of ancient Greece may serve as guides here — I draw on an article by Vincent Azoulay, "Repolitiser la cité, trente ans après." Briefly, the two notions, which derive from the Platonic *politikos*, can be distinguished thus: The community establishes itself, and this self-establishment of the community relies on the regulated access to different institutions, which can be called politics; but the political goes beyond this, as it designates the set of activities whose field of action does not necessarily lie within an institutional framework but draws on highly varied experiences and practices, whose common attribute is that they surface in the context of conflict.

This type of approach, it seems to me, might possibly be in agreement with the kind proposed by some literary critics today, notably those who view history as just another form of the contemporary novel. I'm thinking in particular of Emily Apter and Emmanuel Bouju, whose writings on political fictions have inspired me. They belong to a different tradition of political philosophy, which defines political fiction as "a narrative form of political theory." This informs my understanding of political fiction as being at the intersection of twin tensions: between the axiomatic and mimetic poles on the one hand, and politics and the political on the other. It remains to be seen how effectively this theoretical model will serve to describe medieval history.

Let's start with a few examples. If we restrict political literature to literature about politics, literature that announces itself as political, we are within the corpus studied by Michel Senellart in *Les arts de gouverner,* which mainly covers handbooks for princes. One could look further afield for political fictions in *politique fiction* or speculative fiction. Here I'm certainly thinking of the *Roman de Fauvel,* the collectively written fourteenth-century allegorical poem, whose main text was written in 1314 by Gervais du Bus, the chaplain to Enguerrand de Marigny. A roman à clef, this satirical and allegorical fiction was also a political act; it might open the way for us to revisit the theme of the fable. But we could also turn to more convoluted forms for delivering political messages: Still in the fourteenth century, for instance, we find the political dream. As Christiane Marchello-Nizia has shown, it takes a narrative procedure belonging to literature and transfers it to politics. The *Roman de la rose* starts with a dream of love, described in the prologue. This might seem a strange choice for a fictional frame because of its tenuousness, and we could almost do without it. Yet there must be a reason for it, as there exist many works of this kind: *Songe de pestilence,* also anonymous but attributed to Henri de Ferrières; *Songe du vieil pèlerin,* by Philippe de Mézières; *L'avision de Christine,* by Christine de Pizan . . .

In illuminated manuscripts, the start of a dream sequence is indicated by the setting. We are in an orchard, an enclosed place, an isolated landscape — a utopia, as it were. The author is asleep. The formula prefacing our entry into the dream state is always the same: *It seemed to me that I saw*. At the end the sleeper awakes and draws the lesson from his vision. Between these moments the first-person speaker disappears, and speech itself assumes agency. In the *Songe du vergier*, the "I" disappears to be replaced by the "you" of the dedicatee. The fact that the text is anonymous is not accidental: A mystery surrounds the absent "I," in contrast to the ceremonial "I" of historians: "I, Jean Froissart, treasurer and canon of Chimay"; or "I, Jean Lord of Joinville, seneschal of Champagne."

Why this mystery and remoteness when we know that political literature calls for an author to assume responsibility for his text? The hypothesis proposed by Marchello-Nizia is enticing: The stories' raison d'être is their political lesson. The instruction they offer does not arise from an analysis of events, as in history, but from a vision: We're in the realm of revelation, not experience. Here, unlike in a dream of love, the dreamer is not directly implicated in his vision; it's about the dedicatee, that is, the king. The dreamer provides the locus where the dream unspools, he is its transcriber, but he is not its creator. So why this murkiness surrounding the telling of the dream? It masks a transgression: Someone who is not the king is the source of a royal dream and provisionally the keeper of revealed political wisdom. He has usurped a royal function.

Here we are dealing with explicitly political fictions, deriving from the milieu of politics. But it would obviously make sense to cast a larger net for these "narrative forms of political theory" by remembering that the political, in the Middle Ages, crops up everywhere and particularly where it doesn't announce itself as interceding in politics. This would allow us to bring together all the literary forms of medieval *brevitas*, or short tales, whose stock of exempla has been featured in the seminal work of Jacques Le Goff's team, and it's also here no doubt that we will find the *novellistica* toward which we are patiently inching our way.

IT'S TIME NOW to take stock of this first stage of our journey. To clear away any whiff of conceptual makeshift that my citing such a diverse set of references might bring with it, I'd like to choose as our pathfinder here a privileged guide. In 1977 he wrote: "I've never written anything but fictions." That guide is Michel Foucault. Eleven years earlier, in 1966, he'd described *The Order of Things: An Archaeology of the Human Sciences* this way: "My book is a fiction pure and simple, it's a novel." First it's a fiction, then a novel—the lack of distinction seems surprising. Is it Foucault's way of disarming historicist criticism? The word *fiction* is at once slender and ponderous. To give it a workable consistency, I think you have to understand fiction as falling within the category of experiments: Writing a fiction is subjecting thought to the test of the real.

Fiction is an act of knowledge, and what fiction allows us to know is how our minds work. As Philippe Sollers wrote in a 1963 text called "Logique de la fiction": "Man does not fully know what he is capable of thinking; fiction is there to tell him." Foucault returned to this text many times, all the more readily as Sollers himself was responding to a youthful text by none other than Foucault, the preface he'd written in 1954 to Ludwig Binswanger's *Le rêve et l'existence*. But for both Sollers and Foucault, the crucial experience was reading Borges, for whom fiction's critical power is to provide the experimental test of our own knowledge.

Analytic logic describes how we think and what we think, but it can sometimes lead to the pernicious illusion that the world is logical and rational. The logic of fiction, by contrast, reveals to us the possibilities of thought. This is what an archaeology of conceptual thought attempts to do: open a space in our reality for the possible. It is also the role of philosophy, as Foucault writes in "La philosophie analytique de la politique" (The analytic philosophy of politics): not to discover what is hidden but "to make visible precisely what is visible, that is, to bring into view what is so close, so immediate, so intimately linked to us that we therefore don't see it."

In fact this is exactly how Foucault defined the function of Maurice Blanchot's fiction in a magnificent 1966 essay: It consists "not in showing the invisible, but in showing how invisible is the invisibility of the visible." Showing us how we see, making us more alien to ourselves: This would be Foucault's constant effort, and in doing this, it's true that he never wrote anything but fictions, and these fictions were political fictions. But in describing what he writes, why does he then pretend to hesitate between fiction and the novel? Early on, in a wonderful article on Jules Verne, Foucault laid down the distinction between fable and fiction: The fable is the story that's told; fiction is the system according to which the fable is "recited," "the framework of the relations established, through the discourse itself, between the speaker and what is spoken of."

And it so happens that history, as written by historians, is caught in that framework. Michel de Certeau said as much on the subject of Sigmund Freud's *Moses and Monotheism*: The task of the historian consists in countering the effects of fiction, but there is always a fictional residue in his discourse. Does this weaken it? Yes, if you believe that truth is something observed; no, if you believe it is constructed, fashioned. Foucault is concerned not with the truth of facts but with the historical experiment of truth, and what he calls the history of truth is the history of the force of truth. In "Les rapports de pouvoir passent à l'intérieur des corps" (Power relations pass through the body), he states his intention: "to bring about truth effects by means of a fictional discourse." This allows the translation into fiction of "a politics that doesn't yet exist, starting from a historical truth." Fiction is therefore a system for the production of truth, but also an experiment — the author's experiment, the reader's experiment, for the production of truth.

This is exactly what he said in a 1978 interview about his *Madness and Civilization: A History of Insanity in the Age of Reason*:

It's a book that functions as an experiment, for the person writing it and the person reading it, much more than as a statement of historical truth. For the book to set the stage for this experiment, it of course has to be true in academic terms, historically verifiable. It can't exactly be a novel. Yet the essential doesn't reside in the series of true and historically verifiable statements but in the experiment that the book makes possible. And this experiment is neither true nor false. An experiment is always a fiction; it's something that you set up for yourself, that doesn't exist beforehand, and that will exist afterward. That is the complicated relationship with truth, the way that truth is implicated in an experiment that is not strictly related to it and that, up to a certain point, destroys it.

This question of truth is one we will have to return to soon: how to conduct a history of truth that is in fact a history of the effects of the true. We lack this history today because we doubt the strength of the true, or rather, because many powerful figures doubt the strength of the true. At least I will have understood, after reading Foucault, that what I wrote in *The Power of Images*, a book I have been trying to leave behind, was political fiction, a text that *puts into fiction a politics that doesn't yet exist, starting from a historical truth*. Yes, we have been dreamed by the lovely green-eyed dreamer who, in 1338, loved prospectively those yet to come — in Michelet's words — through "this effort of laborious dreaming by which we raise ourselves from night to day." For the rest, we'll have to see. And if you ask me why I don't just talk directly about Trump if I want to talk about his effect on our present times, why I detour into the political fictions of a bygone era to confront the present, and why I don't just make these political fictions into a novel, I can only say that our archaeology is aimed not at rummaging through the past but at opening up the future. It brings to light a historical truth rendered invisible by its visibility, whose effects bombard the present, but this truth is nothing in itself unless one organizes things in such a way as to effect, within language, an experiment. So let us attempt that experiment.

LECTURE 2, JANUARY 17, 2017

Truth: Before and After

"This course's raison d'être? You only have to look around you" — *Post-factual politics and post-truth era*: three ambiguities — A political lie is "the art of convincing the people of salutary falsehoods," Jonathan Swift — Governance and the demonstration of truth, Foucault's five stages — *Ego sum via, veritas, et vita* (John 14:6) — Thomas Aquinas's transcendental theory of truth — "Probable certainties" and rational procedures for approximating truth — The Church's "orthodoxy of the implausible" versus the layman's robust products of experience — Quentin Skinner: How are historians to deal with beliefs once thought to be true? — Machiavelli's fables: the prince, the lion, and the fox — The "logic of 'as if'" from Derrida to Freud — Claude Lefort, the "effective truth of the thing" and the critique of imagination — Politics as the "effective truth of the matter," as against a politics of things

WE DON'T HAVE A RECORDING of Michel Foucault's opening lecture from the second year that he taught at the Collège de France, only the manuscript page he had in front of him as he spoke. It was November 24, 1971, less than a year after his inaugural lecture. His first year of lectures was published in 2015 as *Penal Theories and Institutions*. It starts: "No introduction" — a sensible preamble. And then: "This course's raison d'être? You have only to look around you — those who might find the subject distasteful will see similarities between their surroundings and what I am talking about." What he saw when he looked around him, at that moment in the fall of 1971, was the political repression that greeted the leftist opposition movement and the strong police presence it elicited in the Latin Quarter — which accounts for his pointing to the concrete circumstances in the lecture hall. What do we see in front of us today? I follow Foucault in seeing our archaeology as intended not to uncover heroically what is invisible to the uninitiated but to show just "how invisible is the invisibility of the visible." Show what we don't see because it's too close, too familiar, too intimately tied to us.

And you'll recall that Foucault used this phrase to describe why Maurice Blanchot's fiction was so effective. You'll also recall that, following a long theoretical journey meant to carry us past the seductions of postmodern *pan-fictionalism* (which suggests that everything is fiction since all reality is apprehended through the artifact of language), I proposed, at least provisionally, a deflationist theory of political fiction, saying that it is held in tension between fiction's mimetic and axiomatic poles. But it wasn't quite enough to cover the journey that I tried to lay out in the first part of my remarks, where I defined power by its capacity to build story and fiction's power as what's attractive about tyranny, its power to impose a narrative.

Because that's what we're discussing here: our weakness when confronted with what is taking shape before our eyes, between the politics of fakery and the politics of ugliness, this sad self-hatred that takes leave of the real in the name of reality. That's what might be urgent about this archaeological project, pursuing not so much the truth of facts as the historical experience of truth, not so much sifting through the past as opening up the future. And that's where Foucault turns up. Looking at Jorge Luis Borges's *Fictions*, he defines fiction as a series of experiments that we make to find the limits of our knowledge, or, conversely, to discover the possibilities of our minds. That's why the author of *Madness and Civilization* could say: "I've only ever written fictions." For if fictions allow us to test our thoughts against the real, their first value is as experiments. How are these fictions political? They emulate the dream Michelet spoke of, the upsurge. Starting from a historical truth they propose a fiction describing a reality that does not yet exist. In this lies the prophetic or anticipatory power of political fiction, and here also what may produce an effect that interested Foucault, the so-called "truth effect." This is the point we've arrived at, on the threshold of a history of truth, that is, a history of the effects of truth, something that we need today all the more because we are having serious doubts about the power of truth in our political lives.

SO I'LL ASK THE QUESTION AGAIN: What do we see when we look around us? At the start of every year, the *Oxford English Dictionary* announces the most significant word of the past twelve months. The word of the year for 2016 was *post-truth*, used thirty times more often in 2016 than in 2015, according to lexicographers at Oxford University. The word has elicited, and continues to elicit today, a vast flood of commentary on the Internet and elsewhere. For a taste of this, I'd recommend a visit to Wikipedia, a site that provides not so much an encyclopedia as a seismograph of the contemporary world. Its entries on the more stable areas of knowledge are fairly mediocre, but on anything that registers tremors, anything in motion, anything taking shape under our eyes, it can be outstanding. The word *post-truth* refers to circumstances, according to the *OED*, "in which objective facts are less influential in shaping public opinion than appeals to emotion and personal belief."

Facts, not truth: a first ambiguity. In English, *post-truth politics* and *post-factual politics* are synonyms. And starting in 2004, people began talking about a post-factual era, a post-truth political environment: This is a second ambiguity or shift, where a mode of political communication — or of propaganda, which is when public opinion is shaped by appeals to emotion rather than facts — comes to characterize an entire era.

Why 2004? Because it was on February 5, 2003, at a meeting of the United Nations Security Council, that the US secretary of state Colin Powell held up a small vial supposedly proving that the Iraqis were manufacturing weapons of mass destruction, thus justifying the war in Iraq. It was a lie, a lie of state, and public opinion started to realize this in 2004, contributing to the spread of conspiracy theories. And yet (and this is the third ambiguity), when a person lies it doesn't do away with the concept of truth. George W. Bush was a liar, Donald Trump is a bullshitter. A liar deliberately departs from the truth, but he knows that the truth is true. Whereas the bullshitter couldn't care less about truth and is just looking to dominate. He has no interest in truth because he is interested only in his own aims. Unlike the liar, the bullshitter doesn't expect what he says to be believed, his only concern is to have others believe in him. Which, it's worth noting, is one of the possible definitions of rhetoric in the Greek *polis*: Rhetoric is the art of governing one's audience by the virtuosic use of a relation to the world that is uncoupled from the real. The rhetor is that effective liar who works his will on others without personal commitment to what he says. And the person who doesn't play this game is what the Greeks call a *parrhesiast,* a man who aims at *parrhesia,* at the courage to speak truth, as Foucault put it — Foucault who became, at the end of his life, the extraordinary historian of *parrhesia,* of the moment when the speaker risks himself and puts on the line his relationship with others by speaking truth.

So two things make for truth-telling: commitment and connection — the speaker's commitment to what he is saying, and the auditors' connection to the truth of the real world through that speech, a truth that rhetoric by contrast alienates the hearer from or masks. In classical terms, it is Demosthenes versus Aeschines, Demosthenes the *parrhesiast* against Aeschines the rhetor, who in fact calls his rival "the monster." Georges Clemenceau devoted an insightful book to Demosthenes, which Pierre Rosanvallon recently exhumed. When Demosthenes speaks, he opens himself up. That, and not his technique of rational argument, is what attracts his audience, buoyed by "the sensation that the whole of his being is engaged in combat." Thus, Clemenceau continues, "speech rises to the level of an active force."

Speaking truth is not only the opposite of the art of political lying, which Jonathan Swift described in "The Art of Political Lying" as "the art of convincing the people of salutary falsehoods." It is also the opposite of all the ways that reality is stripped from political language in our times—through approximation, euphemization, equivocation, and fudging. All these impair the candor, the frankness of language, which the journalist and revolutionary Camille Desmoulins characterized as a specifically republican virtue: "It is in the character of the Republic to hide nothing, to go straight to its goal, openly, to call men and things by their names." To go straight, aim directly at the truth of things, calling them by their names: It's one of the definitions of prose. We'll come back to it.

This is why it's important to distinguish post-truth from political lies. The American philosopher Harry Frankfurt offered a theoretical analysis in his book-length 2005 essay *On Bullshit*. We shouldn't be misled by the title—a professor at Princeton, Frankfurt is a specialist on Descartes's realism. What brought post-truth back into the limelight in 2016 was the campaign for the Brexit referendum in Britain and the presidential race in the United States. While both Boris Johnson and Donald Trump used political lies to win (which is nothing if not commonplace), they also promulgated bullshit that was impervious to refutation (in French we refer to their *bobards*, a slang term from the trenches used by Marc Bloch in 1920). What is most confounding to the media is that post-truth politics and fact-checking should coexist, that journalism is basically incapable of decoding or detoxifying bullshit. An army of fact-checkers couldn't stop a former reality TV host from being elected.

You might think this is simply an internal debate within journalism. In her long article from July 2016, Katharine Viner, the editor in chief of *The Guardian*, showed how social media and, more broadly, the technologies used in alternative medias surround us in what has been called a "filter bubble." Within it we will encounter no opinion, taste, or preference that might conflict with those the algorithm associates with us. This is a perfectly classical (even banal) line of thought about credulity, conspiracy theories, the society of the spectacle, and the breakdown of factual analysis.

And yes, the debate is a bit vague, wordy, confused, weak. And yes, you might have every reason to dismiss it. But you'd be wrong. First, because intellectuals follow the general rule, they are like everyone else: They love to hate television, and that's why they watch it. The analysis of reality TV provided by Bernard Lahire in *La culture des individus* (The culture of individuals) is enlightening on this score. What's happening to us, this ongoing abasement of public debate that could possibly spell the death of democracy, has already happened—we've already seen it on television. It was prophesied by reality TV itself.

The reality TV show has a relaxed connection to reality. It tries to bury the awareness that it is theater by exaggerating its theatricality. We aren't duped when we watch a reality TV show, just as we aren't duped when we look at a post-truth politician. We don't confuse these things with reality, we just watch them, that's all. But that's enough, they don't ask for more, and that's what domination is all about. We should be wary, therefore, of those who advance facts in opposition to post-truth. It isn't factual truth that's the basis for sound political action but our capacity to deliberate and imagine. Hannah Arendt said as much with regard to the US policy in Vietnam in her essay "Lying in Politics": "The deliberate denial of factual truth — the ability to lie — and the capacity to change facts — the ability to act — are interconnected; they owe their existence to the same source, imagination." This brings us back full circle, as you'll have realized, to the definition of political fictions that I proposed earlier.

MORAL INDIGNATION makes no dent in the power of a post-truth government. We need therefore to attempt an archaeology of the use of truth in the exercise of power. In his 1980 lecture course, published in English in 2016 as *On the Government of the Living,* Foucault set aside his investigation of power to look at how governments produce truths. In the first lecture, he outlined five ways of establishing a relation between the art of governing and the demonstration of truth, and I'd like to recap his argument here briefly.

The first way draws on the principle of rationality. The state is based on its own system of reasoning, which can be called — and has since the sixteenth century been called — the reason of state. What the reason of state exposes "is the truth of the state as an object of governmental action." This puts us in the late sixteenth and early seventeenth century, at the time of Giovanni Botero, a Jesuit from the Piedmont and a zealous Counter-Reformationist. His 1589 book *The Reason of State* was the first to define and justify a government's capacity to act according to its own laws, unconstrained by common morality. The idea of a reason of state is often attributed to Niccolò Machiavelli, but in fact it is a product of anti-Machiavellianism. Botero argues against Machiavelli. This moment in the history of the state is the moment when law became an instituting power. From a Foucauldian perspective, it is also the moment when the production of truth became an instituting power. The state generates is own truth, and that is called the reason of state.

Next comes what Foucault calls the principle of evidence, where the government melts away within the empire of truth. In other words, "if men governed according to the rules of evidence, it would no longer be men that governed but things that governed in their place." Foucault attributes the first principle to Botero; the second he attributes to François Quesnay, the author of *Tableau économique* (1758), which contains the first schematic representation of the economy, the foundation of what Alain Supiot has called "governance by numbers."

This physiocratic moment was followed by a third, which was influenced by Henri de Saint-Simon and developed in the nineteenth century—note in passing that Foucault's periods map the successive centuries in a fairly conventional way and lend themselves to formulating a litany of names. It was in the course of this third, Saint-Simonian moment that a category of individuals arose who specialized in the objective knowledge of truth—for example, the *Tableau économique*—mastering areas of knowledge that were not specifically political but nonetheless had a bearing on politics. Today we might call these men "experts." But these experts, for all their claims to expertise, had something to hide—or so it transpired. As Paulin Ismard's work on public slaves in Athens has shown, democracies have distrusted experts for a long time. To put it differently, there exists a structural antagonism between the power of expertise and democracy.

Now, if everyone knew everything there was to know about a society, then all the masks would fall and the government along with it. This is the fourth moment. The name Foucault gives this principle of universal awareness, which is also a principle of governmental overthrow, is the Rosa Luxemburg principle, because he attributes this quote to her: "If everyone knew, the capitalist system wouldn't hold together for twenty-four hours." In fact, this sentence doesn't appear in Luxemburg's oeuvre; it was Cornelius Castoriadis who assigned it to her in *The Imaginary Institution of Society*.

In response, Aleksandr Solzhenitsyn observed that in the socialist system, everyone knows what is going on, and that is what holds it together. The obviousness of what's going on results in complete stasis. This "general, fascinated awareness of the inevitable," is called by Foucault the principle of terror—and this fifth principle is not linked to any individual. "Terror is not an art of governance that hides its goals, its motives, or its mechanisms. Terror, in fact, is governance at its most naked, its most cynical, its most obscene. Its truth paralyzes and, by being so evident, so visible everywhere, becomes intangible and inevitable."

Let's not imagine that we are done with these ancient times. Today we live in the first moment, when the state produces its own reasoning; in the second, when the government melts back into the empire of truth; in the third, when experts take over with a specialized knowledge that power must bend to; in the fourth, when a mounting distrust disrupts that tyranny of experts by crudely revealing the hidden truth of the system; and in the fifth, when the government imposes the terrorizing radiance of an intangible truth. These five Foucauldian moments are not so much successive as superimposed—we can see, listing them, that our present consists of the sedimented past and that each of these layers remains active, even if somewhat surreptitiously. The fourth of Foucault's moments, for example, which he called the Rosa Luxemburg principle, we might rename the "Edward Snowden principle," since the revolutionary hope of setting the world on its ear by revealing hidden truths is one that WikiLeaks has reawakened, though it is as likely to be disappointed as before. For, continuing our translation of Foucault into the present moment, his Solzhenitsyn principle might well be called the Putin principle. Vladimir Putin serenely puts into practice, sometimes with a smile, the very acts that Solzhenitsyn denounced: It is governance "at its most naked, its most cynical, its most obscene," hiding nothing, not even the fact of its cheating, giving a full-frontal view of this paralyzing truth, so patently obvious that it becomes intangible.

WE THEREFORE NEED TO PURSUE this archaeological effort and pierce through the crust of these five sedimented states proposed by Foucault in 1980, since I'm aiming to reach back before this first moment in the history of the systems of truth, which Foucault calls the reasoning of the state itself, and that he also calls the moment of Machiavellian pushback. That's why I'm starting to wonder whether I shouldn't call this lecture "Truth: Before and After." After is where we are now. Will it be the same as before? And what was is like before the reason of state existed? Was there simply a general credulity, imposed by the Church? That, at any rate, is the picture we generally have of the Middle Ages, paralyzed by its naked and obtuse faith. If modernity is the philosophy of disillusionment, then to feel modern we need to project onto the medieval past a hinterland of belief from which we imagine ourselves to be emancipated.

I won't again burden you with problems of periodization (see my book *Ce que peut l'histoire*), but if we accept the time span I proposed in my first lecture — roughly from the twelfth to the sixteenth century—it is clearly from the time of the Gregorian Reform that a new concept of truth emerged. *Ego sum via, veritas, et vita* (I am the way, the truth, and the life): The pope appropriated Christ's words as his own, and Gregory VII declared himself a "doctor of truth." Florian Mazel has made himself the historian of this new pontifical doctrine of authority and truth. What historians have, since the late nineteenth century, agreed to call the Gregorian Reform pertains not just to religious or ecclesiastical history. Beyond the well-known doctrinal and disciplinary aspects, it marks a total rearrangement of power and the shift to a new world order.

Are we sure, though, that it was a *reformatio*? The word comes down to us from the depths of time. Certainly, the authority of the past is what serves to justify profound transformations. And certainly again, a *reformatio* carries with it the obligation of a moral and personal conversion, in the Pauline and Augustinian tradition of reforms that work to interiorize norms. But it could also be read as a *correctio*, a *restauratio*, or a *renovatio*. This last term in particular expresses the new legitimacy that innovation gained in the twelfth century. As with the jurists, the reformers were trying not to bolster tradition but to discover the truth. It was Pope Gregory VII who, in 1073, said to Bishop Wimund: "If perhaps you propose custom as an argument, remember that the Lord did not say 'I am the custom' but 'I am the truth'"—a phrase that was then taken up by monastic reformers, and subsequently by Gratian's *Decretum*.

But what is truth then? It's less than the true faith, and it's more than factual truth. The *vera fides* is the distilled essence of Christ — a revealed truth, absolute and universal. Whereas factual truth occurs in a legal context; it is proposed as one among a number of competing truths. What we are talking about is certainly a political conception of truth, which derives from the norms devised by the reform papacy. But the papacy did not retain cultural hegemony over these norms for long. The history of power in Europe starting in the thirteenth century is the history, as I've said before, of the dispersion of power. Truth, weakened, devolved to the masters of the *studium,* where it was transformed through learned disputation and became a social, political, and rational construct.

For Thomas Aquinas, the status of truth — which is to say the relation between *ens* and *verum,* being and truth — does not rely on the transcendental theory of truth. The true is "principally" to be found in the intellect: Its principle resides there. This does not mean, however, that the human intellect is the source or locus of truth — man is not the measure of all things in medieval Scholasticism — because being has truth only in relation to the mind of God. Hence in Thomist philosophy (and here I take up again Thomas Aquinas's "What is the true?"), "even if the human intellect did not exist, things would still be called true in the accounting of the divine intellect." It's worth noting in passing that this is a most serious question in epistemology. Do mathematical truths exist outside the minds of those who think them? Do they exist elsewhere than in the brains of mathematicians?

Things are substantially true, then, only in the divine intellect. This is transcendental truth. But since the human intellect is where truth operates, it opens the possibility of apprehending a logical truth, as Joël Biard has shown. Here, it is the proposition itself that is the locus of the true. The logico-semantic issues shift to an analysis of human knowledge, in particular in the works of William of Ockham and Jean Buridan. Whence the possibility, for fourteenth-century philosophy, of grasping truth through approximations to the true. Christophe Grellard, a historian of medieval skepticism, has studied this probabilism. In Thomas Aquinas's view, the contingent or accidental can only form the basis for "probable certainties." These can point to the true in some cases and yet be wrong in others. The contingent, particular nature of human events forces us to entertain fragile but still-rational beliefs.

Truth is built by successive approximations, and one arrives at it through ethics. Ethics and politics, for Buridan, therefore require their own logic (that of *subiecta materia*), which is not the logic of the natural sciences. Buridan's evidence through ethics takes up Thomas Aquinas's probable certainty but does not guarantee the infallibility of the truth arrived at, given "the unknowability of certain circumstances." The rational procedures for approximating the true, in ethics, would include deliberation. Here, we've clearly entered a world that thinks truth is arrived at through debate, through argument. This was the case both in the courts and in the universities. There is a movement away from transcendental truth and toward a conception of truth as capable of being molded, I'd even say molded socially.

This opens up the possibility of a social history of systems of truth, which must account for what Catherine König-Pralong calls an orthodoxy of the implausible. For how will the learned react? For the scholarly, a truth is always truer the more unbelievable and unlikely it is, the more contrary to common sense, the more opposed to what clearly seems to be the case. It became a rhetorical device for justifying Scholastic assertions (in the writings of Meister Eckhart, say, and Dietrich of Freiberg), replacing the more classical device of claiming continuity with tradition: I am going to tell you something unbelievable, and it is therefore true. Theological truth often contradicted the evidence of the senses that governs ordinary human activity. Those who controlled this knowledge that ran counter to common sense, this orthodoxy of the implausible, were the doctors. They, for their part, had access to the deep and hidden meaning of the Scriptures. Henry of Ghent compared them to deep-sea divers who harvest pearls from shells on the ocean floor.

While the clerics proposed unlikely truths, some laymen countered them with the sturdy stuff of experience. In the inquisitorial register compiled by Jacques Fournier and later used by Emmanuel Le Roy Ladurie as the basis for his book *Montaillou: The Promised Land of Errors*, we find testimonials of materialistic belief. This was in the first third of the fourteenth century, when Fournier, an inquisitor who would later become pope, was investigating the spread of heresy. Some of his witnesses believed that the soul is composed of blood and wind. One was Guillemette Benet, another Raimond Delaire—both of them peasants. Benet believed in Jesus Christ, the saints, and their miracles, but she did not believe in the immortality of the soul. "Where did you learn this heresy?" the inquisitor asks. "Where did you read this?" "But I didn't read it," she said, "I saw it. One day I saw a child die, and no soul came out of his mouth. I watched like a hawk, but there was nothing. And another day I had a nosebleed, and I realized that the soul is made of blood and wind." The improbability of the Church's dogma conferred authority on doctrine and justified the leadership of the few who were able to grasp its unlikely truth.

WHAT ATTITUDE should the historian take toward the history of truth? In trying to answer this question, I'll take as my starting point "Truth and the Historian," a short text by Quentin Skinner. It was in fact his inaugural lecture at Queen Mary University of London in June 2010 and, in a sense, his farewell to the University of Cambridge. Skinner asks a crucial methodological question: When a historian sets out to interpret the beliefs of the past, should he be concerned with his own estimate of the truth or falsity of these beliefs? No, of course not. All that matters to him is the rationale of the belief system and the historicity of the criteria adduced in its support.

The question of truth per se does not arise for the historian, whose task is to interpret the beliefs that actors in the past thought to be true. But while Skinner accepts this methodological relativism, he rejects the conceptual relativism of Richard Rorty, for whom truth comes down to rational acceptability. The question is not just theoretical; it takes acute form in the history of science. Obviously, you approach the history of science differently when you're recounting the history of something we accept today as true than when you're recounting the history of something we know to be false. In fact, the sciences continue to use theoretical fictions. This difficulty leads Skinner to justify his refusal to interpret texts as expressions of belief, treating them instead as actions. For Skinner, then, we shouldn't ask what an author means but what he's doing by saying what he says, in the way that he says it. Or more precisely, and I quote, "what he is *up to* by saying what he says."

And he gives two examples of this performative conception of interpretation. The first relates to Shakespeare: Since his plays put characters on the stage with different and conflicting points of view, Skinner shows that you would be hard-pressed to define a single moral stance that could be attributed to Shakespeare himself. We'll come back to this when we look at the status of representation in theater and in art, in the context of Ernst Kantorowicz's work—in fact, his book *The King's Two Bodies* starts with an analysis of Shakespeare's plays.

One might argue that plays are fictions and that it would be easier to find statements of belief in a political treatise. For his second example, therefore, Skinner turns to Machiavelli's *The Prince* and its famous chapter 18, where Machiavelli says that those who would maintain their power must learn to imitate sometimes the lion, sometimes the fox. "You should know, then, that there are two ways of contending: one by using laws, the other, force. The first is appropriate for men, the second for animals." A ruler must therefore know how to act like an animal when necessary (*bene usare la bestia*), sometimes imitating the lion, sometimes the fox.

How are we to interpret this passage, which draws on that common form of political fiction known as the fable, where the characters are animals? What's meant by the fable of the lion and the fox in Machiavelli? You might say that Machiavelli is stating his belief that success in politics depends on the ability to recognize the moment when the use of force or fraud becomes inevitable. But Skinner shows that in this text Machiavelli is not so much articulating a belief as intervening in a political debate. He is taking aim at the entirety of humanist culture which sets the manly qualities in fundamental opposition to the bestial; and in so doing, he challenges its very foundation, in this case Cicero's *De Officiis*, whose Book 1 defines force and fraud as the two bestial ways of committing injustice.

What, then, is Machiavelli up to with this fable? I'll refer to a passage from Skinner: "He at the same time quotes Cicero on the nature of *virtus*, reminds his readers of that text, questions one of its cardinal doctrines, satirizes and repudiates it, questions the underlying view of manliness, redefines the relevant notion of virtue, all in one paragraph." Skinner's analysis strikes me as very convincing. It gains further credibility on a closer examination of the text's language. "You should know, then, that there are two ways of contending." The Italian text says *dua generazioni di combattere*. Which is a little strange, unless we compare it, as Jean-Louis Fournel and Jean-Claude Zancarini have suggested, to Cicero's text: *duo genera decertandi*. On a closer examination of Machiavelli's text—philology is the art of reading slowly, of suspending meaning—the Skinnerian hypothesis gains credibility: It is clearly Cicero that Machiavelli is attacking. He is debating not so much with an earlier author as with a character on an imaginary stage, an adversary whose language he shares.

The second way to extend Skinner's analysis is to relate it to contextual facts. For example, the contrast between the lion's strength and fox's cunning also appears, as we've said, in *De Officiis*: "Both are wholly unworthy of man, but fraud is the more contemptible." The image is picked up by Plutarch in his *Life of Lysander*. Lysander was a crafty general who conducted war by trickery and surprise. "For, where the skin of the lion does not reach, he said, it must be patched with the skin of the fox." And it's this animal skin that Machiavelli turns inside out like a glove, if I can put it that way. We know for a fact that while on a diplomatic mission to Cesare Borgia, at an extremely anxious time in his life (his wife, Marietta, was committing "a thousand follies"; Borgia was "very secretive" — *secretissimo* — making his actions impossible to read; the rulers of Florence stood "betwixt two waters"), Machiavelli wrote his secretary, Biagio Buonaccorsi, urging him in a letter dated October 21, 1502, to send him Plutarch's *Parallel Lives* as quickly as possible. Because reading the ancients, as we know, served to guide his actions.

There is also a third way — beyond looking at the language or the facts — to extend Skinner's proposition, and that is to draw on the subsequent appearance in philosophy of these texts that have been imagined as acts. In his 2002 seminar on *The Beast and the Sovereign*, Jacques Derrida (whom Skinner does not cite) discusses Machiavelli's logic of imitation, his logic of "as if," which goes well beyond a run-of-the-mill endorsement of dissimulation to, in fact, destabilize the idea of what is "proper to mankind." "Machiavelli does not say," Derrida writes, "that the prince is both man and beast, or that he has a double nature, but he comes close to saying it." In any case, "the ruler should behave *as if*." Because when it comes to the specific virtues that constitute a practical morality, the ruler needs only to "seem to have them." It's not just a question, says Machiavelli in chapter 18, of justifying a politics of appearances, but of making a radical critique of how political values are judged — that is, ultimately of destabilizing the question of truth in the political realm, of giving it an inherent degree of indeterminacy.

It's worth examining this logic of "as if." In *The Future of an Illusion*, Sigmund Freud disparages what he called "the philosophy of 'As if,'" which consists in the acceptance without belief of "a great number of hypotheses whose groundlessness and even absurdity we fully realize. They are called 'fictions,' but for a variety of practical reasons we have to behave 'as if' we believed in these fictions. This is the case with religious doctrines because of their incomparable importance for the maintenance of human society." For the maintenance of human society, we have to behave "as if": as if we believed. It has a familiar ring—think of all the small children who, "for practical reasons," behave as if they still believed in Santa Claus. Because it's the safe thing to do, because there's a moment of uncertainty when maybe it's better to act "as if." And we know that anthropologists frequently encounter deceptions that are collectively maintained without belief. This lesson is often enough impressed on medievalists, for instance, when studying the cobbled-together sacrality expressed by the rites of royal religion. The practices surrounding coronation offer a good example, when the king, with the complicity of the Church, presents himself as something he is not (he's a layman like anyone else, but he has himself anointed)—"whence the institutionalized practice of an 'as if' that, while safeguarding the interests of the protagonists, is intended to impress civil society," writes Jean-Philippe Genet.

THIS QUESTION OF TRUTH in the political realm is one that I'm going to ask in the context of an extract from chapter 15 of *The Prince,* a very short but well-known extract that contains the expression *verità effetuale della cosa* (translated both as "the real truth of the matter" and "what really happens"). And I'm going to ask myself what Machiavelli is up to when he says what he says (the Skinnerian approach) and also what thought experiment he is inviting the reader to conduct by writing such a political fiction (Foucault's approach). My method will be to examine the language, the context, and the philosophical afterlife of the following passage: "It remains now to consider in what ways a ruler should act with regard to his subjects and allies."

Reading this, we abruptly find ourselves on the threshold of a different book, at a fork in the road that nothing in the convoluted plan of Machiavelli's treatise had announced. "It remains now to consider": It's not the first time that Machiavelli has used a formula that seems to imply continuity while allowing him to go in an unexpected direction. In chapter 11, when preparing to discuss ecclesiastical principalities, which nothing in his plan had prepared the reader for, he seemed to imply that the text would soon reach its conclusion ("It remains now only to discuss . . ."). These abrupt changes in direction serve to put us on alert: Since politics is rife with indeterminacy, one may as well provide the reader with the experience of it. Then, starting at chapter 15, *The Prince* heads in a surprising direction: We are done with examining the variety of forms a state may take, and we are embarking on a discussion of political morality as it applies to a ruler's actions.

A change of direction, but also the reversal of a philosophical tradition: "And since I am well aware that many people have written about this subject I fear that I may be thought presumptuous, for what I have to say differs from the precepts offered by others [*dalle ordine delli altri*], especially on this matter."

Who are these others? That's the whole question, but let's leave it there for a time. I continue:

> But because I want to write what will be useful to anyone who understands, it seems to me better to concentrate on what really happens rather than on theories or speculations. For many have imagined republics and principalities that have never been seen or known to exist. However, how men live is so different from how they should live that a ruler who does not do what is generally done, but persists in doing what ought to be done, will undermine his power rather than maintain it. If a ruler who wants always to act honorably is surrounded by many unscrupulous men his downfall is inevitable. Therefore, a ruler who wishes to maintain his power must be prepared to act immorally when this becomes necessary [*imparare a potere essere non buono, ed usarlo e non usarlo secondo la necessità*].

This is the cardinal maxim of Machiavellianism, the moment when Machiavelli most resembles the Machiavellian mask, on the threshold of the systems of truth that Foucault later inventoried. The next three chapters of *The Prince* articulate this maxim by examining a few princely virtues in the light of this philosophy of necessity: generosity (chapter 16), mercy (chapter 17), and faithfulness to one's word (chapter 18). What interests me here, however, is the relationship between truth and things. The language of diplomacy in Italy has an expression: *le cose d'Italia*. It refers to the unstable system of Italian states, which is always trying to reach a point of equilibrium. We know, with special reference to the work of Riccardo Fubini, that Italy after the Treaty of Lodi was subjected to a complex dynamic of negotiations whose aim was to guarantee *in modo bilanciato* a balance of powers. Italy in the fifteenth century provided the unusual spectacle of a set of fundamentally unstable political entities, bound to the law of necessity, all trending toward absolutism. This was the world in which Machiavelli lived — I mean both this world of political instability and this world on paper that tried to make sense of this instability. He did this in his capacity as secretary of the second chancery of the Republic of Florence, from 1498 until the Medici coup d'état in 1512. And Italy's political language was the language in which he thought and wrote — and acted, I should add — since his exile obliged him to pursue political action by other means, literary means. He needed to find a way to maintain himself. I'll remind you here of the expression Machiavelli uses in our passage: "Therefore a ruler who wishes to maintain his power..." The *arte dello stato* set forth in *The Prince* is entirely bound up with this verb, *mantenere*. It is the art, for a new ruler, of *mantenere lo stato*, which inextricably includes maintaining the state and maintaining himself within his state (*se mantenere nel suo stato*).

But the classificatory language of medieval political theory is no longer operative. "For many have imagined republics and principalities that have never been seen or known to exist." In other words, the Aristotelian idiom has become a dead language — a phenomenon typical of revolutionary situations that, at a stroke, cause a political language to become obsolete. This happens not through the creation of new words but through the political and poetic reactivation of the common language, the vernacular, and of political action. And how is the language to be reactivated? By confronting it with political matters, political things — facts, contingencies, particular situations — which become a testing ground for political truth. This, it strikes me, is how we are to make sense of the expression in Machiavelli's dedication of *The Prince* in which he offers the Medici ruler his "long experience of modern affairs and continual study of ancient history."

That, then, is what Machiavelli intends by *cosa*. But what of *verità*? It does not appear in the usual vocabulary of the Florentine secretary. In *The Prince*, the word appears only twice, the second time in chapter 23, devoted to the *adulatores*, the flatterers "who are found everywhere in courts" but whom the ruler must avoid because they don't speak truth. So what should a wise ruler do? "Choose shrewd men for his service, permitting them alone to speak frankly [*parlargli la verità*], but only when he asks them and not otherwise. But he should ask them about everything, listen carefully to their views, and then make his own decisions." If we examine Machiavelli's *History of Florence,* we will find only a single instance of the word *truth,* but it's significant because it also concerns the question of good advice and a criticism of flattery. It occurs in the letter of dedication where he describes himself to his protector Clement VII as having always held himself "at a distance from adulation" since he has "spoken little about Your Holiness's father" (who was Giuliano de' Medici). He goes on to say: "I scrupulously and invariably avoid violent terms [*vocaboli odiosi*], as being little necessary to the dignity and truth of history."

MACHIAVELLI'S TRUTH, in consequence — the truth of the political realm, of the political thing itself, *la verità della cosa* — is spoken at a considerable remove from the honeyed words of the adulators and the odious words of the hateful. We'll pick up the analysis of our passage here, by following the motion of its swerve — announced as a sharp break with tradition. There's a new *excusatio* ("I fear that I may be thought presumptuous"), a new ambition ("I want to write what will be useful"), and a new boldness ("what I have to say differs from the precepts offered by others"). "Many people have written about this subject": *molti di questo hanno scritto*; and, farther along, *molti si sono immaginati*. Another mention of the others whom Machiavelli wants to distinguish himself from. Who are these others? There are three ways to answer the question. The first is to target the particular adversaries that Machiavelli might have been trying to convince — this would be consistent with Skinner's concept of the text as performance. According to John Najemy, Machiavelli's polemic is particularly directed at his friend Francesco Vettori, whose radical skepticism assigns imagination the role of substituting for words when words fail to provide an account of the thing. For Machiavelli, the imagination is what forms a screen in front of things.

We could enlarge the circle and say that Machiavelli is more broadly targeting the Neoplatonists of late fifteenth-century Florence, chief among them Marsilio Ficino, who developed a theologico-esthetic doctrine of knowledge through imagination. But a more maximalist reading would see Machiavelli as taking on the whole of the Aristotelian and Thomist political tradition, given that while he was not a philosopher, he had a considerable impact on philosophy. It would be reasonable to see this as a challenge to the Thomist position according to which, as I've mentioned in connection with the work of Joël Biard, even if things are substantially true only in God's mind, there is truth in things that take place in the mind of man.

What's at stake here is not simply the reduction of politics to an understanding of government as a means of domination.

The deeper aim is to query the conditions that would make for a knowledge of truth in the political sphere. As Claude Lefort writes in an admirable text entitled "Machiavelli and the *Verità Effetuale*," Machiavelli's boldness is apparent in his concept of the social divide at the base of all political structures and of freedom as the goal of all governments that are not in thrall to tyranny. And this goal is like the goal of an archer who, knowing the arc of his bow, will aim higher than the target he means to hit.

> In taking into consideration the famous statement according to which it seems "better to concentrate on the *verità effetuale* of the matter than on theories or speculations," one concludes too quickly that the concern for what is erases the concern for what ought to be. In critiquing imagination, with its theories and speculations, one neglects a deeper critique of the status of knowledge—not so much the legislator's (who, it is suggested, is guided, however lofty his perspective, by the *verità effetuale*, using force and skillfully exploiting belief), but the philosopher's. For the philosopher is reproached not with being a dreamer, but with yielding to the attraction of the vast power of thought.

Truth in the political sphere is therefore expressed in the form of a dilemma (things are either like this or like that), setting off a disjunctive progression of events (one will either act this way or that way). But contingencies are too variable for the formulation of anything but general rules of political action, and these can never be simply applied if the result is to be true action. Rules exist: *regole, modi,* but generally speaking, *in modo largo,* they are inoperative. One can apprehend them only in the truth of action, *secondo i tempi* or *secondo la necessità*. What Machiavelli brings forth are the conditions for action. But the truth of the thing is something that can't be reached but only approached. Philosophically, therefore, it is a probabilistic truth, an approximation. Lefort states this well in *Le travail de l'oeuvre Machiavel*: "As to truth itself, it is inherent to its essence that it should happen in the hic et nunc of action and that it therefore always, at least in part, escapes representation."

What we perceive is therefore only the effect of the thing — and it's from this phenomenology that political observation is constructed. It is filtered by reading texts, and while the imagination in the theologico-esthetic sense of Ficino has no part in this mental operation — on the contrary, it is imagination that screens off the truth of the matter — it is accessible to sight.

And that's ultimately why, in order to grasp the truth of the thing, one has to *see*. The verb associated with political experience in *The Prince* is *vedere*. Zancarini and Fournel have counted seventy instances of its use, in almost every case referring to the truth of experience. Thus we find the expressions *vedere per esperienza* and *vedere in fatto*. This truth of experience is something that one needs to ascertain (*trovare*) and, consequently, examine (*discorrere*). The link between ascertainment and analysis is bridged by the word *considerare*: Consider carefully things as they are, and you will see, you will agree, etc.

Truth in the political realm, for Machiavelli, is consistent with the truth of painting. It has nothing to do with an overarching image; instead, it is immediate, vibrates with the inner life of things — and that life, crucially, is a social life. It brings with it the indeterminacy of points of view and suggests that the political order lies beyond the threshold of determinacy. Which, by the way, restores the question of Machiavelli's intention. In writing *The Prince*, he didn't express a belief or set forth a truth; he separated himself from the practice of others, and by means of that separation cleared a space where political truth can show itself. "But because I want to write what will be useful to anyone who understands, it seems to me better to concentrate on what really happens rather than on theories or speculations."

Andare drieto alla verità effettuale della cosa, che alla immaginazione di essa. We could have made a purely literary commentary on this sentence, noticing that what goes straight is the prose, and that Machiavelli entrusts all his political hopes to the resources of language, the very movement of his vernacular prose. This prose, in fact, runs fast and straight. In any case, Machiavelli's thinking is often understood as a pushback to the Middle Ages. We talk about a pre-Columbian America; why shouldn't we medievalists describe our field of study as pre-Machiavellian Europe? Yet we could turn the argument around, as Foucault does in his lecture of January 25, 1988 (the third in the course published under the title *Security, Territory, Population*), which poses the problem of the ruler's safety, not the population's security — and in that sense it has links to the old governmentality. But far from believing that Machiavelli opens the modern field of political thought, I'd say that he marks the end of an age, or at any rate that he culminates at a moment when the problem was very much the safety of the ruler and his territory.

What is Machiavelli doing in placing political truth in "the effects of the thing"? What is he up to, as Skinner would say? That's what I have been trying to show here: making political space an open book, visible and available — making it welcoming, undetermined, open to deliberation and the imagination. Politics as the "effective truth of the thing" is basically the exact opposite of the politics of things, as Milner recently defined it to denote our own political wretchedness. Since things govern themselves, the expert on politics is the one who explains what things want — and what they want is what they're silently saying. How many times have we heard, "Things being what they are," or "That's the way things go," or "It's in the order of things to do such and such," which most of the time results in not doing anything. The politics of things is the opposite of the government of speaking beings: It consists in transforming men into things, in the name of what things want. But things don't want anything, and as for us, well, we'll see.

LECTURE 3, JANUARY 24, 2017

An Archaeology of Collective Errors

On the threshold of a history of truth effects — "And giving it back to you, the [American] people": a fiction that prefigures official speech — "The cogs of the grotesque in the mechanism of power" (Michel Foucault) — Alternative facts and truthful hyperbole: medieval reading of a U.S. inauguration ceremony — Origins of the saying *Vox populi vox Dei* — From Marc Bloch's experience of the *bobards* (bullshit) of the Great War to his book on "the deceptive radiance of kings" — Kantorowicz's development from *Frederick the Second* to *The King's Two Bodies*: breaking the enchantment of the theologico-political — The double corporality of kings, a fiction that turns against royals — Shakespeare's *Richard II*, or "the tragedy of the king's two bodies" — Parallel lives in classical times and the plural biography of a Christian individual — The normative revolution of Christianity

WHILE POLITICAL FICTIONS may reasonably be considered a narrative form of political theory, it doesn't preclude the possibility that fiction — in its capacity as a thought experiment that makes visible the invisibility of the visible and thereby tests it against reality — can anticipate future politics through truth effects. From this perspective, the inauguration ceremony of the forty-fifth president of the United States of America on Friday, January 20, 2017, did not disappoint. As Donald Trump declared, the participants had gathered not just to transfer power from one administration to another but for the purpose of transferring power from Washington, DC, "and giving it back to you, the people." The written speech, as posted subsequently in an official Tweet, read: "and giving it back to you, the American people." Now, adepts of Internet culture, by which I mean people familiar with the Batman series, were quick to notice that Trump had departed from the written text to say: "and giving it back to you, the people." These are the exact words delivered (with the same intonation) by the villain Bane after he wreaks havoc and devastation on Gotham City in *The Dark Knight Rises*.

This is incontrovertibly an instance of truth effect: Political power, as exercised or proclaimed, is here conforming to a fiction that endowed it with its grotesque shape ahead of time — thus forestalling any attempt to unmask its imposture since the face we see imitates its own mask and does so in an openly farcical way. On this point also, Michel Foucault provides crucial insight, since he describes in his first lecture in 1974 (published in English under the title *Abnormal*) the paradoxical power of what he calls "the cogs of the grotesque in the mechanism of power," which work openly, strongly, explicitly to disqualify power and base it instead on this "quasi-theatrical disqualification."

I'll quote Foucault more fully: "Ubuesque terror, grotesque sovereignty, or in more sober terms, the maximization of the effects of power based on the disqualification of the person who produces them; this is not, I think, an accident in the history of power, not a misfiring of the mechanism." It's a little vertigo-inducing, but it's just this vertigo of fiction that I'm trying to get to, by evoking Ubu Roi and, in a moment, Emperor Nero. Foucault rightly observed that the history of the Roman Empire offered dazzling examples, from Nero to Elagabalus, of this mechanism "of grotesque power and despicable sovereignty" — up to and including the mean little Italian signors who became *beffatore* in the *novellistica,* as I mentioned earlier. But if we're to look hard at the tyrant, we must at the same time imagine his smiling face, as with the smile splashed across the features of Cangrande della Scala, the mounted hero of Verona.

This business of political fictions brings us to the threshold of the question of truth effects. And that's why I tried earlier to ask (along with Quentin Skinner) what the historian's relation to truth is, insofar as he is dealing with beliefs that people in the past thought to be true. Today, of course, the historian does so in a post-truth context, and I devoted the first part of my last lecture to disentangling this confusing question. Lies, which are counter-truths, had to be distinguished from bullshit, which is an indifference to the very question of truth.

Current events may be dismaying on this score, but they have provided us a generous trove of material. You may know that following Trump's inauguration, there was a press briefing at which the new White House press secretary announced truly extravagant and demonstrably false attendance numbers for the crowd that showed up in person for the ceremony. A day and a half later, on NBC's *Meet the Press,* the show's host, Chuck Todd, pressed President Trump's new counselor Kellyanne Conway on the question. She answered, "Don't be so overly dramatic about it, Chuck. You say it's a falsehood, but our press secretary gave alternative facts." That was on January 22, and the very next day the term "alternative facts" already had an entry on Wikipedia. The site, as I've said, is a seismograph of contemporary life that records each new tremor in the destabilization of our system of truth.

It's interesting to note in passing that the coinage *alternative facts* disturbs the relationship between word and object, introducing a deviation in the prose mode — taking *prosa* in its etymological sense, meaning direct, straight — that republican mode of prose that we defined with Camille Desmoulins as the act of "going straight to its goal, openly, calling men and things by their names." Trump's lexical invention knows no bounds. In *The Art of the Deal,* he coined the term *truthful hyperbole* to mean a kind of innocent exaggeration, a technique for "playing to people's fantasies." As for example when he continued to describe Trump Tower as having sixty-eight floors although it actually has fifty-eight, a fact that is easy enough to ascertain since the fourth floor is labeled the fourteenth, because it makes people feel superior and elevated. When the discrepancy was pointed out to Trump, he said it was a case of truthful hyperbole.

This is the reason why we delved last time into the archaeology of medieval skepticism, prior to the Machiavellian stopblock described by Foucault as the first modern system to develop the relationship between the exercise of power and the display of truth. Even in the context of the Thomist theory of transcendental truth, the medieval Scholastics used the concept of "probable certainties" to approach truth by a rational process of approximation. If only to impose the "orthodoxy of the implausible" that Catherine König-Pralong discussed — the harder it is to believe something, the more it requires obedience. Ordinary people countered this orthodoxy with direct observation from experience. Because the "actual truth of the matter" is plain to see; *vedere* is the key word in Niccolò Machiavelli's political anthropology, and we recognize with Claude Lefort that Machiavellian realism doesn't constitute a criticism of the imagination. Machiavelli's realism also makes use of fictions, and they are fictions that work the imagination. For it is through them that we go straight to "the actual truth of the matter."

Andare drieto alla verità effettuale della cosa, che alla immaginazione di essa. The phrase is picked up by Francesco Guicciardini in his *Dialogue on the Government of Florence,* which claims to *parlare secondo che ricerca la natura delle cose in verità*. Here is Guicciardini: "In judging between different governments, we should consider not so much what type they are, but their effects, calling the government better or less bad which has the better or less bad effects." We could also show how Machiavelli's prose was made to deviate by certain translations into French. One of the first translations, in 1571, by Jacques Gohory, is faithful enough. The one by Nicolas Amelot de la Houssaye in 1683 introduces the idea that erroneous suppositions come from the common people, saying it's better to speak according to the truth of the thing than according to what the common people imagine it to be. And in the Jean Vincent Périès translation of 1823, *immaginazione* is turned into "vain speculations" (see Jean-Louis Fournel and Jean-Claude Zancarini).

That the common people should be introduced as the source of error in the late seventeenth century was clearly not fortuitous. It represents a flagrant betrayal of Machiavelli's thought. In his mind, it was always the learned who erred most grievously on "the actual truth of the matter." This was shown by Sandro Landi, who points out that when Machiavelli in *The Prince* criticizes the *communis opinio* to propose a novel political theory, he is in fact referring to the *communis opinio doctorum,* the general opinion of the Scholastics, the chorus of authorized voices. His attitude toward the opinion of the populace, which appears in chapter 58 of the *Discourses,* is very different: "It is not without reason that the voice of the people has been compared to the voice of God. One sees public opinion making surprising prognostications, so that it seems that the populace, as if by some hidden skill, can foresee their good and bad fortune" (*il suo male e il suo bene*).

This is the central credo of the republican faith, which necessarily believes that the majority are right. Yet Machiavelli's text goes on to seriously undermine this thesis. There are numerous instances in history when the public has been mistaken about the good or evil done to it — more accurately, there have been numerous instances when the public was duped by the most brazen lies. This leads Machiavelli to the main proposition of *The Prince,* chapter 47: "Although men may deceive themselves in general questions, they do not do so in the particulars." His realization that the dominated have a close knowledge of their domination is of great consequence, but sociologists were to take note of it only much later. What interests me now, however, is the first part of Machiavelli's proposition: "It is not without reason that the voice of the people has been compared to the voice of God." What might those reasons be?

We recognize here an adage that informs our concept of the political sphere: *Vox populi vox Dei*. It lies at the foundation of our democratic fiction — I'm using *fiction* here in its legal sense — according to which the sovereignty of the people stands in for divine principle. And it takes the very place of divine principle as a cause that is not engendered but is created by the sole fact of being uttered. That is popular sovereignty: The moment it is declared, it is constituted as a principle. In the book he devoted to this proverb, now some time ago, George Boas shows that the decisive moment for the political effectiveness of this saying was at the time of the American Revolution. The first words of the preamble to the US Constitution, "We, the people of the United States," make sacred the subject designated by the law. The founding fathers gave voice to the American people to found the American nation, and the very act of enunciation constituted the people as a subject (*We*), a subject that did not exist before declaring itself — a declaration that the Trumpian formulation grotesquely upends, *You, the people,* where the dropping of the

We betrays the profound connection between populism and contempt toward the people.

We, the people. Of course, you still need to believe in it. It represents something like a political cogito: not "I think therefore I am" but "We believe therefore we are." This consecration of togetherness is undoubtedly at the origin of political liberalism and modern individualism, whose earliest and most developed example is American civil religion. It is of relatively recent date, at least as far as its sociological description. It was Robert Bellah who, in 1967, first defined it, starting from an analysis of John F. Kennedy's inaugural address of January 20, 1961. As Emilio Gentile has shown, American civil religion has its sacred texts (the Declaration of Independence), its patron saints (George Washington, the American Moses, who led his people out of bondage), its martyrs (Abraham Lincoln, John F. Kennedy), and its icons (the dollar bill, with its motto: In God We Trust).

American civil religion constitutes a "consecration of the political sphere," but this is not to be confused with a "consecration of political power." Nor should it be confused with the "politicization of religion." These distinctions, admittedly, apply mainly to the contemporary world. But we nonetheless have to deal with the embarrassing fact that, according to American civil religion and the more general democratic fiction underlying it, the people's voice is God's voice (and Machiavelli, you'll remember, does not say that one is the other, but that the two can reasonably be compared). We are still within a "philosophy of 'as if,'" and therefore within a legal fiction, where, through a series of transfers, one thing takes the place of the other. This is why it's always so interesting for a medievalist to watch an American inauguration ceremony and to find himself, as it were, at home — particularly when it instances the theologico-political principle of "the king is dead, long live the king," the instantaneous accession to power of the new ruler to replace the old.

Because what founds the modern form of democracy is well and truly an ancient theologico-political maxim, an anaphorical formulation, *Vox populi vox Dei* — its formulation in Latin adding to its luster, imparting timelessness. And where does this maxim come from? Alain Boureau laid out its archaeology some time ago in a dedicated article. The saying does not come from scripture, as one might think. A "voice of the people" does appear in Isaiah, juxtaposed to the "voice of God," but the passage reads: "A voice of the people from the city, a voice from the temple, the voice of the Lord that rendereth recompense to his enemies." Here, the voice of the people is not an articulated expression but a noise, a confused clamor that echoes God's cry of indignation, nothing more. And that's why the first instance of the Latin saying *Vox populi vox Dei* is found in a letter from the poet and theologian Alcuin to Charlemagne in 798: "The people in accordance with divine law are to be led, not followed. And when witnesses are needed, men of position are to be preferred. Nor are those to be listened to who are accustomed to say,

'The voice of the people is the voice of God,' for the clamor of the crowd [*vulgi*] is very close to madness."

The saying was therefore first quoted in a negative context: Those who propose it should be ignored. It demonstrates, at least, that the adage was already in circulation, but as a proverb and therefore outside the control of legitimate culture, which Alcuin believed it was his duty to safeguard. We know of only eight occurrences of the phrase between 798 and 1200, mostly condemning it, and mostly in England. Boureau followed this English thread up to the time of Edward II's forced abdication in 1327, the victim of a conspiracy between his wife, Isabella; her lover, Roger Mortimer; and the English clergy and assorted lords. The archbishop of Canterbury, Walter Reynolds, gave a sermon on January 15, 1327, justifying Edward's removal from the throne as an expression of the popular will. His use of the proverb *Vox populi vox Dei* was only a tactical move, but during the long sequence of royal depositions in England (Richard II in 1399, Henry VI in the 1400s — twice — followed by Edward IV, Richard III, and Henry VII) the saying came to be strongly associated with parties opposed to the monarchy — first the Lollards, then various Protestant splinter groups, after which the saying found its way to America, the chosen land.

The question remains: When did the saying's meaning flip, when was the opprobrium lifted? Boureau puts the date in the late eleventh or early twelfth century, pointing particularly to the Anglo-Norman chronicler William of

Malmesbury, who in 1125 wrote both his *Gesta regum Anglorum* and his *Gesta pontificum Anglorum* — the deeds of the kings of England on the one hand and the deeds of the bishops of England on the other, with his work dividing neatly along the Gregorian break. The saying *Vox populi vox Dei* took on a positive meaning, but it was specifically used to justify the election of bishops. The history of kings, for its part, drew on the notion of *homeland*. In his magnificent 1951 article "*Pro Patria Mori* in Medieval Political Thought," Ernst Kantorowicz shows how the most terrifying injunction in the history of nations (*Dulce et decorum est pro patria mori*) evolved from the extension into religion of the idea of the homeland, with the mystic body of the community fanning the exaltation of the martyr.

In voicing his skepticism about Edward the Confessor's miraculous cures, William of Malmesbury's main concern was to preserve a strict distinction between laymen and clergy: "How false is their notion, who in our times assert, that the cure of this disease does not proceed from personal sanctity, but from hereditary virtue in the royal line." Saintly kings were not a problem for the Church: They performed miracles in their capacity as saints. But for kings to have a miraculous power and transmit it to their descendants by virtue of simply being kings, this was harder to countenance. Yet in France and England, kings were believed to have the ability to cure scrofula, the king's evil, an infection of the lymph nodes, generally caused by tuberculous mycobacteria.

You will no doubt have recognized a reference to one of the founding works on the anthropology of political power in the Middle Ages, Marc Bloch's *The Royal Touch*, originally published in 1924. In the substantial preface he wrote for the French edition of 1983, Jacques Le Goff makes a strong case for the decisive role that the municipal library in the French city of Strasbourg played in the genesis of the work. It was there that Bloch read the German historians, but also there that he met the psychologist Charles Blondel and the sociologist Maurice Halbwachs, both of whom were students of Émile Durkheim. The historiographical innovation of Bloch's book was to leverage Durkheim's sociology of religion to transform the way we look at the past, while preserving history's identity as a discipline.

This explains the history of the work's reception, which has been the subject of a recent analysis by Thomas Hirsch. It stands at a crossroads of the nascent social sciences — Lucien Lévy-Bruhl saw it as an encouragement to study what he then called the "primitive mentality," and only a few of the more blinkered medievalists raised an eyebrow. One of these was Robert Fawtier in the journal *Le Moyen Âge*, who complained that Bloch had "strayed from the area of research this journal is devoted to, strayed even from the field of history." Bloch's study attempted a long-range analysis of a mental phenomenon (the book describes the exhaustion of the ritual by the time of the coronation of Charles X in 1825). But Fawtier also accused Bloch of straying from the field of history when he undertook to go beyond the bounds of what is believable. Bloch would answer the charges the following year in the same journal, saying that while his critic "might know precisely at what point the Middle Ages and 'historical studies' end, I personally am less certain of the limits, and I believe I would be unlikely, in the case of history, to set the boundary — admitting that I dared set the boundary at all — along the same line as my critic."

Bloch thus saw the book as moving beyond methodological empiricism (or what's called positivism, though wrongly), and as Otto Gerhard Oexle has shown, Durkheimian sociology led him to a comparative approach, in order to escape a linear chain of causality. We shouldn't forget that the original subtitle of Bloch's book was "An Essay in Comparative History," and that it offered a close comparison between England and France, really a parallel history — a fact that was universally overlooked in Bloch's time. But if Bloch moved away from methodological determinism, he edged toward a scientific approach, at least as science was then being remade by the upheavals in physics from Alfred Einstein to Werner Heisenberg. Enrico Castelli Gattinara has shown that Bloch, along with Lucien Febvre, understood early and with keen insight the epistemological turmoil caused by relativity and its implications for the robust theories of objectivism. Put differently, what marked them as historians was that they were aware of themselves as contemporaries of the revolution in the physical sciences.

Did this mean that attempts at truth should be discarded? Just the opposite. Because you have to factor in two other experiences of Bloch's, both highly formative: the Dreyfus affair and the war. His father, Gustave Bloch, was a professor of Roman history at the Sorbonne and one of the first to sign the petition by prominent intellectuals asking for a review of Captain Dreyfus's trial. And when Bloch entered the École Normale Supérieure in 1910, the faculty had recently added Lucien Herr, Charles Seignobos, Émile Durkheim, and Charles Andler. As for the war, Bloch served continuously, as a combatant, from his conscription at the start of the war in 1914 to his demobilization on March 13, 1919. It was, he wrote, "a giant laboratory" where he became aware of "the vagaries of memory" and the fragility of human testimony.

For intellectuals who had been drafted, the experience of being under fire provided an often difficult encounter with the people, as Nicolas Mariot has shown, or rather, a test of the conditions under which it might be possible. "It called forth a heroic tenacity that was both terrifying and superb," wrote Pierre-Maurice Masson, and created a social barrier that was for the most part immovable. Jean Norton Cru, who would later play an important role in gathering testimony about the war, noted wrenchingly: "I have a conscience, while they seem to do without." Intellectuals who experienced combat for the most part maintained their social and anthropological boundaries intact. A lone exception, almost, was Robert Hertz, a brilliant student of Durkheim's and a pioneer in the sociology of religion who served as an infantry second lieutenant and died on April 13, 1915, at the age of thirty-three. He left a considerable volume of notes and letters, which were later collected and published by Marcel Mauss. He never stopped working as an ethnologist. Showing what might be called scientific heroism, Hertz continued to make observations and to learn new things — the names of birds, the gestures of everyday life. He understood that the peasants, the rural underclass, wanted to pursue their ordinary lives just as he did. And he wrote absolutely magnificent letters, one of which I can't resist sharing, dated February 14, 1915:

> Yesterday evening, while the fancy city slickers were still wrinkling their noses and registering surprise at being here, the country guys made up a game where they pretended to sell each other the animals that wandered by. One of them would cry his livestock while another would try to bargain him down, quoting prices back and forth in ducats and piastres with much shouting and gesticulating. The seller would lovingly describe the cow's conformation: its udders, its backside, just as he might on the fairground back home. The cow went to the auction block first, followed by a small calf, a pig, and a dog, with the onlookers laughing uproariously. The whole thing probably lasted an hour. They have a surprising instinct and taste for comedy, light, subtle, and good-hearted.

This is not unlike the letter Machiavelli wrote Francesco Vettori from exile, having decided to put his time in exile to use and try to truly understand, to see, what an anthropology of power might look like, there, in his village, on the fly. Not many intellectuals during the Great War understood that they were in the midst of what Bloch recognized as "a giant laboratory," a foundational experiment in the social sciences.

Bloch watched and observed, but what he was trying to understand — as a confirmed rationalist, a Voltairean — was what he himself termed "aberrations," collective illusions, which could only be the product of crude minds. His article "Reflections of a Historian on False News of the War" came out in 1921. He examined the way rumors, stories, exaggerations, and myths originated, developed, intersected, evolved, lost momentum, conflicted with one another, and turned to dust. "False news always starts from a collective representation that preexists it," Bloch wrote, uncovering in the process new ground for the historian. He asked himself about credulity and skepticism as well, writing that doubt is sometimes "as absurd as the blindest faith. At the front, the same man might alternate between slack-jawed acceptance of the most fantastical tales and contemptuous rejection of the most solidly established truths."

We might say that Bloch transfers the concept of the *bobard*, to use a slang term from the trenches best translated as "bullshit," to his analysis of the royal touch in his book of that name. It was his war experience that led to his investigation of political beliefs. That's why Le Goff saw him not only as a pioneer of historical anthropology but also as an inventor limited by his Voltairean rationalism — a rationalism whose origins we understand (the Dreyfus affair, the desire to shore up the system of proof). Most likely Bloch would not have denied this. He dedicated his book to the memory of his father and his doctor brother. At the very end of his book about "the deceptive radiance of kings," he wrote: "It's difficult to read this faith in royal miracles as anything but the result of collective error." He returns to this expression in 1933 in his review of Georges Lefebvre's *The Great Fear of 1789*, describing "the collective error of the 'great fear' as a symptom of the state of the society." He picks out this sentence of Lefebvre's: "The reader will no doubt find it legitimate that, in seeking to explain the great fear, I have tried to put myself in the place of those who experienced it." To which Bloch comments: "In an author whose scientific accuracy, not to say meticulousness, is above all suspicion and who, in his work, is a long way from sacrificing to the gods of Romanticism, it's striking to discover this sentence, echoing as it does what is perhaps best in Michelet."

And that's the question: Must one experience a collective error in order to become its historian? And must one believe the fictions it generates, the better to dismantle them? Let's pursue the investigation through an impossible fiction: For reasons I can't quite explain, I've spent all too much time searching through Bloch's notebooks from the trenches, his correspondence, and the operational reports from the 72nd Infantry Regiment, to which he was posted in June 1915, trying to see if there was ever a moment when he was across the battle lines from Kantorowicz. Kantorowicz, who fought in the 20th Artillery Regiment at Calonne starting in June 1915, was on the same front as Bloch until he was caught up in a gas attack in July 1916 and was transferred to the eastern front in Ukraine.

Why look for traces of this face-off? What could this fiction of Bloch and Kantorowicz in opposing trenches possibly tell us? Obviously, their story could be told more aptly, through the lens of their books, by showing how Bloch read Kantorowicz's *Frederick the Second* in 1927, skeptically at first; how he then came around to it when the second volume was published in 1931 with notes and appendices; and finally, starting in 1940, probably after a third reading, how he labored to shake his fascination with this bewitching and somewhat toxic book.

If you put these two men side by side in the manner of Plutarch's *Parallel Lives*, here's what you'd find. Kantorowicz was the younger of the two; he was born in 1895, and Bloch in 1886. Kantorowicz was Jewish, as was Bloch; a combat veteran, as was Bloch; but after the war he found himself drawn into the circle of Stefan George, a Symbolist poet whose charisma inspired a lyrical patriotism in his admirers, who venerated him as a master. Many brilliant figures were attracted to this strange community, which sought to create an "invisible Reich." The publication in 1927 of Kantorowicz's biography of Frederick II, depicted as the embodiment of the Nietzschean superman, was directly in line with this mystical impulse. On the political front, there's no question that Kantorowicz, as Karl Löwith put it, "opened a path for national-socialism that he himself did not go down." And in fact, while his book was eagerly embraced by the Nazis, Kantorowicz fled to the University of California at Berkeley in 1939, where he ardently defended the modern utopia of the independent university. This led to his other decisive battle: He led the rebellion against the oath of loyalty that Senator Joseph McCarthy was demanding from American academics suspected of Communist sympathies. Kantorowicz himself was not a Communist, but he fought on their behalf.

In 1963, the year of his death, a German admirer congratulated him on the reissue of his biography of Frederick II. He wrote back: "This book, which lay on Himmler's night table, and on whose flyleaf Göring wrote a dedication before giving it to Mussolini, should be left to sink into oblivion" (see Alain Boureau's *Kantorowicz*). During his years in the United States, he never stopped writing against himself, unwriting the recruiting mechanism he himself had set in motion, and deconstructing his fascination with political theology. Whence his submersion in the Middle Ages—with the intent to undeceive our present day (a vain attempt, it goes without saying) and disarm its criminal tendencies.

It wasn't that the Middle Ages offered a peaceable ideal and a return to original purity; clearly, it was just the opposite. The point of the exercise was to search through the archaeology of collective error so as to be wise to it. Kantorowicz's book on royal litanies, *Laudes Regiae,* written from 1934 to 1940, provides a bridge between *Frederick the Second* in 1927, in which the author was still under the spell of the Nietzschean superman, and *The King's Two Bodies* in 1957, in which he methodically dismantled the supernatural legitimation of royal power. In its meticulous analyses of the evolution of liturgical formulae and their musical settings, *Laudes Regiae* examines the capacity of rulers to engineer their acclamation. And as Pierre Legendre observes in his preface to the French edition, it would take a great deal of naivete to believe that this "primitive foundation of the political," which relates to states of trance, occurs only in ancient societies. Accordingly, Kantorowicz pursues his analysis in *Laudes Regiae* up to the acclamations of the Fascists and Nazis. In a passage where his remorse at having been led astray by politics seems to show through, he alludes to the way he himself became ensnared in this trance: "Listening to this song performed by the Italian *balillas,* the hearer will feel himself irresistibly drawn into profound meditation — and if, perchance, that hearer is a historian, he will no doubt meditate on the dangers that attend his profession in the course of exhuming the past." Kantorowicz takes on a horrendous responsibility in *The King's Two Bodies.* I'll conclude with the question that I started with, prompted by another acclamation, this one modern, a contemporary inaugural ceremony, the question of the quasi-theatrical simulacrum.

One often forgets that Kantorowicz's *The King's Two Bodies* begins with a reference to Edmund Plowden's *The Commentaries*. Plowden, an English legal scholar during the reign of Elizabeth I, was very likely the first to explicitly formulate the political theology of the sovereign's double corporality. I'll remind you briefly that *The King's Two Bodies* examines the concept of the king's mortal body being invested with the immortal body of the kingship, which survives and transcends him. This double-bodiedness (or rather, this legal fiction) was constructed gradually, culminating in seventeenth-century England. This was the England of revolutions, and the England too of constitutions. At issue, as Boureau has shown, is a political belief that "crystallized slowly starting in the Middle Ages and dissipated slowly in the eighteenth century." The idea of the king's two bodies was a political fiction that could turn against the monarchy itself (during the English Civil War, Charles I was executed in the king's name) or dispense with a king altogether (hence Kantorowicz's last chapter dealing with "sovereignty centered in man" in the work of Dante). Perishable, fallible man carries the perdurable shape of humanity within him. This lays the groundwork for all the "republican" or parliamentary forms (habeas corpus) of persistence and substitution of corporal duality. Let's not forget that *The King's Two Bodies* was also an archaeological study, as was Bloch's *The Royal Touch*, which starts at a point when the twin-bodies concept was unraveling, and it unraveled at the moment it started to be theorized. It was in Elizabethan England that Plowden formulated the idea as a legal theory and that Shakespeare created a play about the dissolution of the body politic.

This history first and foremost concerns the English monarchy — consider the history of funerary effigies (wax replicas of the king's mortal body), which give visible form to the belief in the king's two-bodiedness. That history was reconstructed by a student of Kantorowicz, Ralph Giesey, in *The Royal Funeral Ceremony in Renaissance France*. Funerary effigies were used in France roughly from 1422 to 1610, a period when the king's mortal remains followed a minutely scripted fictional life. In England, effigies were displayed at royal funerals starting in 1327 with the death of Edward II. The custom was transplanted to France in the wake of the Treaty of Troyes, when Henry VI of England died in Vincennes in 1422 and an effigy was made *ad similitudinem regis* to be placed on his coffin, possibly in Saint-Denis, and certainly in Rouen. When Charles VI of France died a few months later, the responsibility for organizing the funeral ceremonies fell to the Duke of Bedford. He arranged for a funerary effigy of the king to be displayed.

Kantorowicz had already noted the importance of this innovation in the funeral ceremony, saying that it gave royal funerals a new and more triumphal tone: The monarch's mortal remains provided a focus for the funeral proper, while the *persona ficta* of the effigy could be borne abroad in triumph. The glorification of royal bodies reached a high point with the funeral ceremonies for King Francis I in 1547, which lasted almost two months (March 31 to May 22). The theatricality of the funeral rites (and the themes of representation and the masque) bring us back to Shakespeare's *Richard II*. Kantorowicz devoted the second chapter of his book in part to that play, which he calls "the tragedy of the king's two bodies," and in part to a history of deposed English monarchs. He pays special attention to the "horrific" scenes in the play's third act, where the king senses his essential twinness as man and king being torn apart.

The mystic body of the kingdom is taken from him, stripped away piece by piece. King Richard was born twinned with greatness, but he also partakes of human nature, through which he is "the butt of every fool's muttering." In his vulnerability, what Richard loses is the name of king: "Must he lose the name of king? o' God's name let it go," he says, speaking of himself. And in Act 4: "I have no name, no title . . . And I know not now what name to call myself." Also: "You may my glories and my state depose, But not my griefs; still am I king of those." This, in Kantorowicz's view, is the highest and clearest expression of political theology. Jacques Le Brun has taken up the analysis, in *Le pouvoir d'abdiquer*, on the voluntary abdication of a king, who thereby acts treasonously toward himself. In Pierre Corneille's tragedy *Cinna*, it is the emperor Augustus who, at the start of Act 2, meditates on the "unbounded greatness" of a ruler's power, which "No longer pleases once it is to hand / Ambition sated soon turns all to sand." I would direct you to the fine treatment by Myriam Revault d'Allones of what she terms the unmaking of the body and "the interminable ordeal of disembodiment" that Shakespeare presents in *Richard II*.

There is a dizzying play of mirrors at work here. Consider that in 1601, Robert Devereux, 2nd Earl of Essex, was plotting a rebellion against Queen Elizabeth. To give his men courage, he commissioned a performance of Shakespeare's *Richard II*, written in 1595. The famous scene of the king's deposition remained censored from all editions of the work until 1608. The 1601 performance may have been the first in which that scene was acted on the stage. The rebellion plot was uncovered, Devereux was decapitated, and Elizabeth declared: "I am Richard II, know ye not that?"

This play of mirrors reflects the register of fiction under the medieval system, from the Gregorian watershed to the fragmentation of Christendom. How might we describe it? With respect to Christianity on the one hand and law on the other. Taking law first, the work of Yan Thomas is absolutely fundamental. It's clear that once a historian classifies a political belief as a collective error, he quickly finds himself at a dead end. Just as clearly, we can see that the theory of the king's two bodies was above all a fiction, in the legal sense. Roman law, as it happens, gave jurisconsults an extraordinary power: that of transforming things in the world and countering reality with fictional operations. There are two kinds of fictional operations: negative and positive, where negative fictions deny what actually exists. The Cornelia law, for example, validated wills left by citizens who died in captivity. Although captivity theoretically deprived individuals of their right to bequeath property, the Cornelia law created a *fictio legis* according to which everything proceeded as though the individuals had died in a state of freedom. There were also positive fictions, which falsely posited the existence of an action, an event, or a person. The latter directs the course of justice to proceed "as if," the former "as if... not."

Medieval commentators accepted the fictional aspect of law, pointing out that it was no pretense since it announced itself as fiction. Writing in the twelfth century, Azo of Bologna said that "fiction is an interpretation counter to the truth," and it consists "in taking the false for the true" (*falsitas pro veritate accepta*). However, a fiction must be labeled as false. In the fourteenth century, Cino da Pistoia wrote: "Fiction takes as true what is certainly contrary to truth" (*in re certa contrariae veritatis pro veritate assumptio*). This is why fiction cannot be confused with pretense, fraud, or forgery. If medieval jurists accepted the Roman domain of fiction, that is, the power to alter the world within the legal context and adulterate the truth of facts, it was because they marked out its boundaries, defining what were artifices (*artifica*) and forgeries (*figmenta*) in relation to simulacra. Thus, for instance, when they defined the *universitas* as a fictional person (*persona ficta*). It was purely a mental representation, an image, a word: "The *universitas* is but a collection of several bodies, to which a single name applies."

This natural limit — and here it is the human fact of separate bodies — joins up with the Christian dimension of the narrative characteristics of fables, and that's where we come to what is specifically medieval in this fictional register (medieval because it originates in the classical tradition). Here, I would direct you to the work of Glen Bowersock, who describes in his 1994 book *Fiction as History: Nero to Julian* how the Greco-Roman Empire in Nero's time became awash in fiction, confounding the intellectual elite who were products of the classical paideia. Lucian of Samosata had the effrontery to gather his fantastical literary inventions in a book entitled *True History,* with the warning: "My readers must not believe a word I say." He excepted one statement only "and that is that I am a liar."

We must therefore consider the fictional backdrop against which Greco-Roman intellectuals were working, whether pagan or Christian, in order to understand the impact of the Gospels. Bowersock shows, for example, that the theme of resurrection appears frequently in Greek and Roman fictions. Thus it was with the philosopher Peregrinus Proteus, who was burned at the stake but subsequently appeared dressed in white to a witness whose faith was strong; thus it was also with Eumolpus, a major figure in *The Satyricon,* who stipulated in his will that his heirs had to cut his body into small pieces and eat them in public: There was unquestionably a link in the first century of our era between fiction and Christian literature.

Biographical selectivity is not a Christian invention: Plutarch distinguishes between what in a man's past is useful to his readers' edification and what is not. The literary genre of biography had to adhere to normative Jewish requirements: The Gospels must be considered a mythological text from start to finish, and there is no carving out the bits one considers historically significant from the bits one chooses not to believe. One of the characteristics of classical biography is that it is plural, presented in series: famous men, parallel lives, great kings. The Christian exception was to produce a plural biography of a single person. This was the genesis of a distinctive power, the power over narratives — and over the plurality of narratives. This is the great question that has been asked, for instance, by Étienne Nodet, a historian and theologian specializing in the life of Christ: We know that around 180 CE the Christian tradition narrowed the record down to a few different Gospels, four of which were kept. But why stop there? Why four and not just one? Precisely because this plurality of voices created the conditions for what Boureau has called "the event without end," which plays on the disagreements between the different biographies, thereby profoundly altering the status of narration.

An archaeology of this narrative system has been attempted by Emanuele Coccia. Christianity was born of a normative revolution. The Messiah came to bring a new Law, created according to a new model. Its legal code was intended to replace the Jewish legal code, but its novelty was due less to its content than its rhetorical form. What is a norm when it is expressed through narrative rather than specified by a commandment or a precept? How are we to understand the normative when it goes beyond the codification of laws and is embodied in a story that contains no direct formulations applicable to the practical sphere but deals with a whole life? And conversely, what becomes of narration once captured within a normative framework, not to elicit an esthetic response or a cognitive effect but to provide a norm, that is, to fashion a social body?

These are the troubling questions that lie in wait for the historian of political fictions.

LECTURE 4, JANUARY 31, 2017

The Eucharistic Society

Adam speaks the names of the animals — God's trial of mankind, mankind's trial of God — Christian genealogy of the persona and the legal construct of the person as a truthful fiction — Does speculative fiction generate "warnings"? Remarks on the sudden actualization of 1984 — Why four Gospels? A methodological fracture — Divergent narratives with a point of convergence in the Eucharist ritual — The hypothesis of a Eucharistic society — Ambrose of Milan: Don't confuse what you see with what you believe — The cognitive function of the sign, which addresses the mind by way of the senses — The Gregorian break and the insistence on the real presence — The elevation of the host as a substitute for Holy Communion: an "ingestion by sight" — The true novel of the miller Menocchio — Bernard of Angers's conversion, prompted by sensory evidence — Conversion, belief, experience

I'D LIKE TO START with a text by Pierre Michon, a particular favorite of mine called "Trois noms de bêtes pour W.B." (Three animal names for W.B). W.B. is Walter Benjamin, and the animal names are those that Adam, the first man, calls out to God so that all things will have a name. Adam is not so different from Michon as a little boy, who stood in a clearing and, as he remembers it, had to produce the name of a butterfly that landed in front of him, although he'd never seen it before: "Everything says: This is an ally. He's laying his realm at your feet. Say his name. But the little boy doesn't know." Later he'll know, later he'll learn the butterfly's name while paging through a book. And Adam is also at that moment like Benjamin in 1928, in Moscow, abandoned by the woman he'd meant to love, warming himself "at the small brazier of his tears," before realizing that he had to name the things around him: "He is in the clearing of the first language. He straightens up. He is a son of Adam. He can start over, he will start over."

We too can and will start over. Beginning with Adam, because when God created man, as Michon writes, he "changed his technique." God had given names to the day and the night, the mountains and the waters, "the great incorruptibles," even as he created them. But not man; when it came to man, he was silent. "He fashioned him mutely out of earth, then in the twilit aftermath, still unspeaking, he took earth as well to fashion all the other animals." And it fell to man, whom God had not named as he created him, to speak the names of the animals. And he spoke them, he called them out, in a clearing.

God speaks to man, but primarily he prompts man to talk. Idols, on the other hand, which are deaf and dumb, make those who gaze on them deaf and dumb too. Hence the dread that images inspire in clerics, who have always seen them as disquieting blocks of silence. The churchman Bernard of Angers, entering the sanctuary of the Abbey Church of Sainte-Foy in Conques in 1010, asked himself whether or not to believe in the stories of the martyred girl-child Saint Faith, who was said to have worked miracles (in the end, he did believe and even composed *Liber miraculorum sancte fidis,* which is a narrative of the child's deeds and of his own conversion—a conversion to the faith of humble folk, a direct and immediate experience).

For the saint's reliquary statue stood there staring at him mutely, as Michon would write, surrounded by — and here I quote Georges Duby's *The Age of the Cathedrals* — the "golden idols with wasp eyes placed at the doorway to darkness, and no one dared to face their unseeing gaze." Bernard of Angers wrote about the smallness of man when confronted with images, his fear of idols, but also of man's nature, which is to give names to things, give names to living creatures. Such was the power of Adam, the first man, who was already a man without qualities, whose tale of the Fall, which we will now address, was above all a story about averageness. For Adam was not the first to fall: The angels and evil spirits had fallen before him, but theirs was an entirely more sublime story — a large-scale disaster in the heroic style. Adam's fall was not that, yet Adam knew the names of the animals and of all things, while the angels did not. They, according to the Jewish exegesis of the Midrash Rabbah, sang but did not name.

What was the nature of Adam's dominium over living creatures? Was it natural for man to have dominion over nature and the beasts of the field, and what relation did this power have to the act of naming, of categorizing? These questions — which are questions we ask today — were already being asked during the Christian Middle Ages, starting from questions about the Fall of man, that is, the original fault committed by Adam and the moment of his expulsion from the Garden of Eden. Was there politicking in Eden? No, there would have been no need for it. Politics came later, after the

Fall. According to Augustine, it was original sin that introduced a separation between the two states or cities, the city of God and the *civitas terrena,* which he sometimes calls the *civitas diaboli.*

The first inclines toward the love of God (*amor dei*), the second toward the love of self (*amor sei*). But the first preexisted the second, and consequently, according to the commentators (from Peter the Chanter to Hugh of Saint Victor), religious authority existed *ante peccatum* while temporal power was born of man's sinful nature. This is the shameful origin of all power: You have power and exercise it, or you submit to it, tolerate it, accept it, in spite of everything and for lack of anything better, until better comes along. There was a before, and there will be an after: "Then cometh the end," says the first letter to the Corinthians, "when he shall have delivered up the kingdom to God, even the Father; when he shall have put down all rule and all authority and power" (1 Corinthians 15:24). The power of stepping down from office, which so fascinates political philosophy today, is found in the writings of Paul. And medieval commentators have interpreted this, as Philippe Buc has shown in a foundational work that I shall return to: for as long as the world continues in existence, men will govern other men.

The catastrophic event of the first man's disobedience, while it created a rift that man could not repair, called for healing on the part of Christ: "Such was it given us by God; and this being lost by its own fault, can only be restored by Him who was able at first to give it... If the Son shall save you, you shall be saved indeed." And this is what occurred: That is, we live after the Fall, but also after the return of the Christian Messiah. After Christ's sacrifice, the divide between the two cities became blurred, even in Augustine's writings: for the *civitas terreni* is, in spite of everything, a *civitas*, not just the community of unbelievers of the *civitas diaboli*; it can be a political state — and that's why there can be a political Augustinianism, which informs all of the philosophy of power in the Middle Ages and well beyond (at least until the seventeenth century).

This political Augustinianism brings us back to Adam's dominium. What was its nature? To understand it, theologians make use of a fiction — that is, a political and philosophical counterfactual: What would have happened if Adam and Eve had not sinned? Gianluca Briguglia has studied the fictional aspect of this thought experiment, which is closer to a legal fiction (defined in the previous lecture, following Yan Thomas, as one of the operations of law) than to counterfactual history. From Thomas Aquinas to John Locke, philosophers have used this kind of fiction — "an uncertain event, which never happened, will never happen, and is not the object of revelation" — to put to the test the question of the nature of power. Thus Marsilius of Padua: "If he had stayed in that state [if Adam had stayed in the state of innocence], it would not have been necessary to institute and distinguish the various civil professions, either for himself or his descendants, as nature would have provided him all the advantages and pleasures adequate to a human life in earthly paradise, without suffering or weariness." This intellectual challenge, this provocation to thought, raises the question of nature: Did the rupture occasioned by the Fall change Adam's nature, or did man naturally possess virtues, passions, a language, liberty, free will — in short, everything that makes him a political animal? The theological counterfactual (or the political fiction) of an Adam who stayed obedient obliged medieval thinkers to admit that for all that there was a before and an after, man was a political animal before the Fall.

In *The Diary of Adam and Eve,* Mark Twain humorously revisits the unfortunate episode of the apple in the Garden of Eden. He describes Adam as complaining about Eve, "this new creature with the long hair." He didn't choose her, she follows him everywhere, she talks all the time, and he would rather she stayed with the other animals. The serpent tells Eve that "the forbidden fruit was not apples, it was chestnuts" (a chestnut is an old and hoary joke). Commenting on this passage, Emanuele Coccia remarks that while Twain's sketch may depart from the biblical story somewhat, it is faithful in one respect: the Bible's "anti-tragic tendency." It was the first action of the first man at the dawn of the world and it precipitated a catastrophe, yet this biblical origin story offers no memorable scenes of battle, no fury, no superhuman actions. There is nothing savage or impetuous, nothing mythological, only the dull, stupid story of a man without qualities. This man is imprudent and easily influenced, he makes a blunder and realizes it right away, but he doesn't adopt the proud attitude of a great criminal. Instead he is afraid, refuses to admit his fault, accuses Eve, and even accuses God.

What does God do in response? He holds a trial. The transgression is obvious, yet God organizes the first trial in human history. It's a strange one, with God as both prosecutor and judge. But he questions the accused before sentencing him: What Coccia shows is that this reading of the Fall as a trial was not simply a juridical reinterpretation by medieval law, even if the *Decretum Gratiani* uses Adam's trial to prove how natural the procedure is in human law. This interpretation of the Fall is in fact present from the start in the early commentaries of the Church fathers, for it is through Adam's trial, and precisely because he is an average man, that all of mankind is indicted and human nature itself is on trial. And it's all the more important in that if Adam prefigured the mystery of Christ, the trial to which Jesus is subjected mirrors Adam's. When Jesus is tried, mankind judges God in the voice of Pontius Pilate.

I ENDED THE LAST LECTURE with an all too brief mention of Coccia's work on Christianity as a normative revolution in narrative: The Messiah has come to bring the world a new Law, yet the Gospels don't offer a series of commandments or precepts but a dense and poetic outpouring of stories. And these stories disagree: Their divergences constantly call for commentary, giving rise to what Alain Boureau has called "the event without end." One has the sense that an event took place, but the fact of its occurrence recedes toward the horizon of meaning and is constantly in need of commentary to keep from slipping away. The shaky intelligibility of a story that also functions as a legal code raises two diametrically related questions: What is a norm when expressed as a story rather than a commandment, and what is a narrative when it has been subsumed into the normative order?

This is the exact point we'd reached. While Christian literature was part of the proliferation of fiction described by Glen Bowersock as characteristic of the written output of the Greco-Roman Empire starting in the first century (or starting with Nero's reign, which represents an inflection point for our subject, a point I'll return to), the Christian exception consisted in producing multiple biographies of a single person during a period when pagan Roman authors were producing biographical compilations of a gallery of different characters. But this is also why hagiography, the study of the written accounts of saints' lives, shouldn't overlook the fact that the accounts often ended with a set of rules. Narrative had been subsumed by the normative order, and it in turn provided norms for the whole of existence, inextricably mixing life and morality, which is precisely what Giorgio Agamben has called form-of-life.

In the Middle Ages, people believed, or affected to believe, that Gratian and Peter Lombard were twin brothers. Gratian was the semi-mythical figure who had supposedly authored the collectively written *Decretum*, aka "concordance of discordant canons" (1140–1150), and Lombard was the author of *The Four Books of Sentences* (after 1152). Indeed, the former founded canonical law, and the latter Scholastic theology, and the founding of one and the other were twin occurrences. For good measure, a third figure is sometimes added to this legend (a political fiction, by the way), claiming that the founder of ecclesiastical history, Petrus Comestor, was born of the same mother, but from an adulterous union. Of the fable's wisdom, we may at least retain this: that history is always born of adultery. If law and theology are twin disciplines, it is because (as Boureau has shown) they envisage the construction of truth in the same way.

What Gratian's *Decretum* refers to in law as *discordantia*, Lombard's *Four Books of Sentences* refers to in theology as *dissonantia*, but in both cases these discordances or dissonances engender doubt, which leads to investigation; and it's in the clash of testimonies (in the context of inquisitorial law) or in questions (in the context of Scholastic disputes) that truth emerges. "For through doubting we are led to inquire, and by inquiry we perceive the truth," wrote Peter Abelard in his *Sic et Non*. We "perceive the truth" as something that is constructed, collectively, through disagreement, and through the clash of discordances. No one "has" the truth. This cultural and social convergence between the world of judges and the world of scholars created the practical conditions for the cognitive complicity between the investigative procedures and the questions in dispute. Thus occurred the symmetrical creation of the Christian genealogy of the *persona* and the legal construction of the person as a truthful fiction.

This brings us back to the nature of the human species, to Adam's nature before and after the Fall. But we're also back with the double corporality of the sovereign that anchors the *persona ficta* of Ernst Kantorowicz's *The King's Two Bodies*. We approached it in the previous lecture as an attempt to dismantle the spell of the theologico-political, at the point where the fiction becomes reversible and turns like a glove against the person who benefits from it. This is the tragedy of Richard II, the dissolution of his political body, starting when the monarch senses the death of his essential twinness, which had made him an heir both to divine greatness and to human frailty. But for this fiction to operate, it didn't need to be believed, it just needed to be staged. In this it differs from the miracle-working power of monarchs that Marc Bloch, noting a likeness to the *bobards* or falsehoods of World War I, described as the "deceptive radiance of kings." That's why we spent a long time in the previous lecture digging into what I've called the archaeology of collective error — essentially taking the French translations of Niccolò Machiavelli that I started the lecture with in a contrary sense, translations that, in the seventeenth century, changed "imagination" into "erroneous suppositions of the populace." In using the term *communis opinio*, or general opinion, Machiavelli referred not to the opinion of the common folk but to the conceits of the learned, the chorus of authorized voices. He believed that these were more likely to mislead than the universal opinion, whose assessments were generally accurate, for (and I quote): "It is not without reason that the voice of the people has been compared to the voice of God."

And while I'm reviewing things I said earlier, I'd like to respond to a comment from an audience member, who has criticized me for being a hardwired anti-Trumpist, fixated on current events. Just to be clear: I intend my analysis of unfolding events to be an element in the diagnosis of the present time, but I am not claiming a privileged vantage point or, worse, expressing mockery or contempt. We are all obviously in the thick of it, we are all in the same boat, there's no extracting ourselves from the story in progress, which is truly global in import. The thing worth noting is our own confusion. And the moral indignation that the situation provokes is probably as useful morally as it is ineffective politically.

We hear of a renewed fascination in the United States with George Orwell's *1984*, which has to be seen more as a symptom of this confusion than a response to it — a symptom of great interest to a person studying political fictions and literature's capacity for anticipation. Why are we rereading *1984*, which appeared in 1949? Literature neither predicts the future nor wards off its dangers. It does anticipate, in the sense that it sounds the alarm about a catastrophe that generally doesn't occur, or not in the imagined way. This is what Pierre Bayard, exploring literature's capacity for premonition, calls “warnings” in his recent book *Le Titanic fera naufrage* (The *Titanic* will sink) — so with Franz Kafka’s *The Trial*, for instance, we might note in passing that it is oddly consonant with both Adam’s trial by God and God’s trial by man, both of which cases show a disproportion between the crime and the punishment.

One thing is certain at any rate: Ever since it became clear that the year 1984 would not play out as Orwell described it in his dystopian tale, we no longer read his novel as an anticipation or prefiguration of a totalitarian regime. We now know that totalitarianism is not a category intended to describe a political reality but one intended to make political reality conform to a predefined pattern, and specifically in the period following World War II, when liberal democracies were intent on showing that Communism was the pursuit of Nazism by other means.

In a sense, totalitarianism is a political fiction, an experiment first proposed in a fable (by Orwell, in 1949), then modeled in political theory (by Hannah Arendt, in 1951). And we know that what subsequently occurred, what is occurring today, stands in for it and has no name. If we are political animals, it’s incumbent on us to give it a name. Orwell imagined the tyranny of a “Ministry of Truth” — that’s not what came into being, and we don’t know if what did come into being is any better or worse. “The Party told you to reject the evidence of your eyes and ears,” says Winston Smith, the protagonist of *1984*. And: “Not merely the validity of experience, but the very existence of external reality, was tacitly denied by their philosophy." That is what I'm going to talk about here: the way that a certain orthodoxy of the implausible caused the testimony of one's eyes and ears to be rejected during the Middle Ages. What the novel described was how propaganda could hollow out a space in people, a receptive emptiness, once the real was obliterated and physical experience denied. The "evidence of your eyes and ears" that Orwell mentions — it could refer to common sense, but it could also refer to that sixth sense, that glancing knowledge Machiavelli ascribes to the populace, by which they know who or what is dominating them.

It's not exactly the Party, the entity feared by antitotalitarian thinkers, that is speaking when the White House press officer Sean Spicer says, "Our intention is never to lie to you," before adding, "I think sometimes we can disagree with the facts." But if it isn't the Party, it's something else that we aren't quite sure what to call, a fiction that is taking corporeal form under our eyes. And what we need to understand is, just what is the assumption of corporeal form, and what is capable of using us to fashion a form that is monstrous? That's the question that Thomas Hobbes's *Leviathan* asks. Antonio Gramsci read Niccolò Machiavelli's *The Prince* replacing "Prince" in every instance with "Party." We could just as well read Orwell replacing "Party" with "Prince." But at all events, we must adopt Bloch's questioning with regard to collective beliefs and the denial of direct observation.

MOVING ON. What we know about the public life of Jesus comes to us from comparing the four Gospels, written either by those of his disciples who became apostles (Matthew and John) or by the others who collected testimony from his disciples (Mark and Luke, who presented the testimony, respectively, of Peter and Paul). Common wisdom has it that the Church established the authority of these four Gospels by eliminating all the other Gospels in the second century. But what exactly was the Church in the second century? Certainly not a central authority capable of exercising censorship. Irenaeus of Lugdunum is said to have been the first to recognize the canonical nature of the four Gospels, writing in his treatise *Against Heresies* (AD 170): "Furthermore, there cannot be a greater nor a smaller number of Gospels." Why four? "Because the earth on which we live has four regions, served by four chief winds." But why these four, why exclude the Gospels of Peter and Thomas, why these four accounts that do not particularly agree and whose details are in many instances discordant?

We have every reason to wonder. Doubt, inquiry, truth: these are the elements of the method used by a historian such as Étienne Nodet. But he doesn't deploy them to cast doubt on faith. Nodet is a Dominican friar, teaching at a biblical studies school in Jerusalem, and his work is intended to show that faith has nothing to fear from reason. It's the basic outline of the Scholastic plan, as you'll have noticed: Doubt leads to inquiry, and inquiry to truth. But what truth? For

Nodet, it's the truth of faith, the truth that, in some sense, is impervious to attack from history. In his book *Historical Jesus?: Necessity and Limits of an Inquiry*, he helps define the point at which history is incapable of furthering our understanding of Jesus. There were in fact attempts, largely in the Orthodox Church, to use the four canonical accounts to create a "harmonized Gospel." But this attempt fizzled and never came to fruition, for the good reason that the narratives needed to be kept in contradiction. Because these narratives are not simply a recital of the facts and actions relating to Jesus, they are articles of faith. They serve to prove that Christ accomplished what was foretold in the Scriptures, that he said and did all that was prefigured in the ancient books of law.

He accomplished this by getting himself talked about, and the divergent narratives find their point of convergence in the performance of a ritual, which is one of commemoration. That ritual is the Holy Eucharist. It traditionally consists of two parts: The Liturgy of the Word, followed by the sacrament proper, the Eucharistic mystery, where bread and wine are transubstantiated in the priest's hands and before the congregation into the body and blood of Christ. Presence through the Word, presence through bread and wine: the actualization of God's presence is proclaimed, then manifested in the signs received during Communion.

For one's relation to God comes through song and sacrament. The relationship is not mediated by the mind, it engages the body, literally, through the absorption of the host. The Liturgy of the Eucharist ends with the dismissal, which is far more than an order to disperse and return to one's own hearth. Christ sends forth the faithful on a mission, bearers of a word that is greater than themselves. God bestows language, the power to speak; it is he who gives the ability to use language. We're back now with this task that is peculiar to man, Adam's task before the Fall, when he was already a political animal, having the power to name the things of the world and the living creatures that approached him, whether fearsome or familiar, savage or gentle, and whether he wanted to or not.

Here's what I wanted to talk about: medieval society imagined as — I'm proposing a slightly bold title — a "Eucharistic society." I'll start from the hypothesis that the mystery of the Eucharist is truly, as Nodet proposed, at the heart of the narrative revolution of Christianity and therefore of its capacity for fiction — completely different, clearly, from the mythological thinking of ancient Greece and Rome. Being just the sketch of a narrative, it is more *figura* than *fictio,* to return to Gérard Genette's nomenclature. And this narrative revolution, as we've seen, is also a normative revolution, a way of bringing all narrative within the realm of dogma. That's why the figure of the Eucharistic mystery configures society as a whole; it is the "sketch of a fiction" that simultaneously shapes, invents, represents, and counterfeits (all equivalents of the Latin *fingere*) society.

But it does so in an obscure way, one that's hard to believe and is even highly improbable. This is why I now propose to call the Eucharist in medieval society a metaphor rather than a figure — we can think of it as a guiding metaphor. I draw here on the philosopher Hans Blumenberg and what he has proposed calling "metaphorology." I'm interested in it because it leads to a theory of prefiguration, something we'll need later on. For Blumenberg (I offer this brief and provisional account by way of a placeholder), legitimacy in modern times constructs a world that is not reliable but that is legible. Metaphor outpaces our ability to conceptualize, it rides ahead of the world's legibility. It allows us, in short, to be bearers of a word that is beyond us.

In the early days of Christianity, the celebration of the Eucharist was an act of memory for the community of believers, in keeping with Christ's injunction: "This do in remembrance of me." What is it they did? They drank the wine and ate the bread (it would have been ordinary, leavened bread) to commemorate Christ's sacrifice, with the bread being a symbol of his body and the wine of his blood. It was a symbol and no more. Christ was present in the sacrament as a figure, and there was the same distance between the host and the body of Jesus as there is between the sign and the thing it signifies. And here we'll reintroduce an old friend, Ambrose of Milan, whose fourth-century congregation asked him a ticklish question: What proof do we have that we're receiving the body of Christ and not ordinary bread? What Ambrose answered in his treatise *De sacramentis* was: Don't confuse what you see with what you believe. The eye of the body sees the appearance of bread, but it's the eye of the heart that leads toward Christ.

We therefore have to look beyond appearances to see the invisible, and, if I may commit the sacrilege of quoting the White House press secretary in January 2017 as a gloss on Ambrose, accept to "disagree with the facts." Might this theory of the Eucharist be something like an alternative fact, requiring the faithful to develop a knack for seeing the invisible through the screen of appearances? This analogy is highly inappropriate, and I already regret suggesting it. Let's go with Augustine instead, who puts it magnificently in one of his sermons: "The reason these things, brothers and sisters, are called sacraments is that in them one thing is seen, another is to be understood. What can be seen has a bodily appearance [*speciem corporalem*], what is to be understood provides spiritual fruit [*fructum spiritualem*]." Such, according to Augustine, is the nature of the sign, whose first function is cognitive (as Irène Rosier-Catach has shown): It "makes something come into consciousness" (*in cognitionem venire*). And it does so by "offering itself to the senses"; this is its visible form, with "visible" perhaps extended to include all the physical senses. Thus the sign has a tangible nature, and its function is to be intelligible. It establishes a passage from the visible to the invisible. This idea, which Augustine formulated in his *On Christian Teaching*, rests on the conviction that tangible realities can give access to a knowledge of hidden realities.

Coinciding with this conception of the sacrament as symbol was a certain closeness between the congregation and the altar where the sacrifice was commemorated; both the congregants and the clergy ate the kind of bread that was commonly eaten. But starting in the ninth century, the distance between the sacred and the secular world increased. Christ's sacrifice was celebrated with unleavened and unfermented bread (creating a split with Eastern Christianity), and the elevation was practiced. This tended to create a greater separation from the mystery. Theologians nonetheless continued to defend the Augustinian theory of the sign, though its relation to liturgical practices grew increasingly precarious. Disputes about the Eucharist developed. As Aurélien Robert has shown, when Berengar of Tours defended the notion of *conversio intelligibilis,* he hewed strictly to the Augustinian tradition. What does the mystery of the Eucharist change? Not the nature of bread. On the sensory level, the bread is still bread. But it isn't seen as such, because its consecration makes it into a sign of Christ's body. In consequence, if a conversion occurs it is not on the physical plane but on the plane of understanding — a *conversio intelligibilis.*

But Berengar of Tours was roundly attacked by theologians, with the backing of Leo IX and Gregory VII, and by the main proponents of Church reform as well. Summoned by the councils of Rome and Vercelli, he was forced to recant his doctrine, which was specifically condemned in a papal bull of 1059. The bull asserted that "the bread and wine are the true body and true blood of Christ: they are physically received and truly eaten by the faithful." This was the Church's new doctrine, and it struck like a lightning bolt. The sacrament of the Eucharist brought about a metamorphosis that, by 1140, began to be called "transubstantiation." The host no longer symbolized an act of memory, it was materially the body of Christ. One ate him, physically experiencing the actual presence of Christ in the bread, whose substance had altered. His presence was not spiritual in nature but material.

This concept of real presence, which became settled in Church doctrine and practice definitively after the Fourth Council of the Lateran in 1215, was a theoretical power play: It imposed a doctrine of Eucharistic realism that has no basis in Scripture. Here we move away from Nodet's apologizing approach, which attempts a convergence between his semantic analysis of the Gospels and the celebration of the Eucharist as Catholics practice and understand it today—that is, as history transformed it. All of this is the result of a complete reversal, which turned the old orthodoxy (Berengar of Tours was a true follower of Augustine) into the new heresy. Any person who continued to say what used to be believed would be struck down. The Gregorian rift became a conceptual revolution, not to say a revolution pure and simple, imposing a second Christianity that reorganized the world from end to end, widening the divide between clergy and laymen.

The full consequences of the Gregorian revolution positing the real presence of Christ in the Eucharist have been worked out most thoroughly by Jérôme Baschet. The extraordinary nature of transubstantiation meant that congregants worshipped the actual presence of Christ. The elevation of the host therefore took its place at the heart of the liturgy. Congregants were kept at a distance from the mystery: They no longer drank from the chalice, Holy Communion became infrequent, and the faithful were enjoined to watch from a distance. The elevation of the host came to be perceived as a substitute for Communion and was characterized by theologians as a *manducatio per visum*, an "ingestion by sight." In other words: Look, and it will enter your body. The ritual of the elevation of the host, a practice that became widespread in Europe in the thirteenth century, has been shown by Roland Recht to organize Gothic architecture into a system "that makes visible, at a given point in space, the real presence of Christ." And that given point is the vanishing point at the altar toward which all gazes converge. The rhythmic succession of the arched spans, the alignment of the walls, the perspectival effect of a world ordered from bottom to top all take their departure from that point. The increasingly vertical church architecture that, starting in the twelfth century, reached ever higher into the heavens was not driven by an urge to show prowess but reflected a world organized around the elevation.

*Seven Sacraments Altarpiec*e by Rogier van der Weyden, 1445–1450 (Royal Museum of Fine Arts, Antwerp)

This spatial system that organized belief through the sense of sight is visible in the Flemish painter Rogier van der Weyden's *Seven Sacraments Altarpiece*. The central panel shows Christ's crucifixion in the church, and the great height of the cross increases the verticality of the building. It is truly Christ, and it is truly now: The women grieving at the foot of the cross are contemporaries of the congregation that would have been milling around in the church. The past and the present stand on an equal footing — and if there is no before and after, it's because time has been abolished. Behind the cross, a priest, visible from the back, celebrates Mass. It is the mystery of the Eucharist; he is elevating the bread, transformed into the body of Christ. For the Eucharist has become what Miri Rubin calls a "super-sacrament": The whole constellation of sacraments is ordered around the mystery of the Eucharist. The left panel depicts baptism, confirmation, and penitence; on the right panel are the ordination of a priest, marriage, and extreme unction — seven sacraments, then, within a single faith, all in the shadow of the cross.

Making Christ's actual presence visible at "a given point in space," writes Recht. Yes, but what space? The ecclesiastic space, understood as an imbricated system of metonymies, where the institution of the Church is embodied in the building, the house of God. Dominique Iogna-Prat has demonstrated that the ecclesia's building came to be seen as containing the whole of the ecclesia as an institution, whereas the Church that Christ instituted was originally meant to be built on the "living stones" of the faithful, thus separating itself from Judaism by the twin process of spiritualizing and interiorizing. The monumentalizing of the Christian community effected a "personalization" of the ecclesiastical building, giving it "the visibility of an instance of power," that of the Church triumphant.

For the Church didn't stop at polarizing its religious buildings as sacred spaces but extended their sacredness into the social space around them. We might describe here the invention of a new feast day dedicated to the Holy Eucharist, again in the thirteenth century, the Feast of Corpus Christi, during which the consecrated host, displayed in a transparent monstrance, is carried through the town under a canopy, following a service whose liturgy and office were devised by Thomas Aquinas. This procession, where the sacred object ventures outside its usual surroundings, represents a taking possession of the urban space — we know today that the ceremony of royal entry into a city was modeled, starting in the fourteenth century, on the Corpus Christi ritual. The king, also carried under a canopy, thus became a living host.

We can now understand that the doctrine of the real presence of Christ in the Eucharist does not simply exalt the sacred precinct where the mystery occurs and the power of those who conjure it. In fact, it contributes to the spatial organization of what Baschet continues to call the "feudal system," based on the polarization of consecrated places. For this imbricated system of metonymy (where the part is assimilated with the whole) ritually manifests the unity of the whole of Christianity, since partaking in the Lord's Supper induces communion with the universal Church. In other words, "by ingesting the body of Christ (the host), the communicant is incorporated into the body of Christ (the Church)."

On this point, Baschet draws on the overall theory of the ecclesia advanced by Alain Guerreau in 1980, in a sharp and scathing book called *Le féodalisme: Un horizon théorique*

(Feudalism: A theoretical horizon). Already, Guerreau was proposing that the doctrine of real presence made the Eucharistic sacrifice a ritual of "non-symmetric reciprocity," in which three pairs of oppositions were superposed: profane/sacred, lay/clerical, and dominated/dominating. This is very much what Guerreau means by "feudalism," this total — not to say totalitarian — system of dominium in which the Church and society are two coextensive realities that meld together in the ecclesia. That is why, and here I quote Guerreau, "suppressing transubstantiation was practically a direct attack on feudal relations." And it was on this very point, as we will soon see, that the Protestant challenge focused, at least in its Calvinist version.

It's clear why describing medieval society as what I propose to call a "Eucharistic society" may be seductive. Other than that it offers an overarching theory that allows us to discard the old paradigm of the feudal totality, it aligns that theory with a chronology of the European powers from the thirteenth to the sixteenth century that has currency today. But I've already mentioned that there is a risk in taking the Gregorian goals and desires for social realities, confusing an ideological project with its implementation, and ignoring the fact that the history of the European powers from the thirteenth to the sixteenth century was also the history of the failure of the Gregorian project to encompass political society. In a word, and to refer again to Orwell, it's a question of understanding that there was no medieval Big Brother.

It may still be appropriate to speak of a Eucharistic society, but we need to identify all that this guiding metaphor fails to address, all that it leaves in doubt or open to question, recognizing the fractures in political blocks, the looseness in systems of belief, the patching and cobbling, the compromises in meaning — in a word, to speak like Michel Foucault, all that the idea authorizes in the way of counterarguments. These cracks in the theory are what we will immerse ourselves in during the next lecture. But we can already start to shed some light on them with the well-known and unusual case of Menocchio. A miller from the Friuli whose real name was Domenico Scandella, Menocchio was interrogated by an inquisitor from the Holy Office about his highly idiosyncratic cosmogony on two separate occasions, first in 1583–1584, then in 1599. He was tried and finally condemned and executed for brazenly maintaining before the judges his belief that God had not created the universe but had been created by it, that the universe had come together the way a mass of cheese coagulates out of milk, that we are "products of nature" just as the worms that he'd seen appear on the surface of cheeses are, and that we are quite a bit like those worms, like the angels, like all creatures born out of chaos. I quote him: "Everything that we see is God, and we are gods. The sky, earth, sea, air, abyss, and hell, all is God." I quote him, that is to say, I quote *The Cheese and the Worms,* Carlo Ginzburg's great book. Ginzburg, by the way, has often said how crucial his reading of Bloch's *The Royal Touch* was to his decision to become a historian.

But come to think of it, did Menocchio believe in the Eucharist? He did believe in it, and it's the only sacrament in which he did believe. His belief, though, was a little idiosyncratic, and the judges took exception to it: A priest, Andrea Bionima, reported that the miller, looking at a wafer, said, "I do not see anything there but a piece of dough, how can this be our Lord God?" It's always the same issue: There's what I see, and there's what I am asked to believe. Menocchio admitted to having said those words, but he refused to say that he didn't believe in the Eucharist. Why? "I like this about the sacrament, that after one has confessed, one goes to take Communion, and receives the Holy Spirit, and one's spirit is joyful; as for the sacrament of the Eucharist, its function is to control men, made up by men through the Holy Spirit; and the celebration of the Mass is a device of the Holy Spirit, and similarly the adoration of the host, so that men will not be like beasts."

"So that men will not be like beasts": Menocchio's highly personal vision of the Eucharist is not solely instrumental—"its function is to control men," how better to describe this Eucharistic society that, in the 1580s, was slowly unraveling before his eyes. His vision is not solely instrumental, because it brings human anthropology into the mix, just as the Scholastics' inquiry into Adam's nature probed the limits of the human, and just as political fictions put the possibilities of thought to the test of reality. The Eucharistic metaphor doesn't sweep everything before it—it leaves an unassimilable, nonconvertible remainder, perhaps the very thing that Michel de Certeau calls the weakness of believing.

For we must return to the signal occurrence of unbelief as the impossibility of believing, and all the more so as the learned had imposed what we have called, following Catherine König-Pralong, the "orthodoxy of the implausible." I mentioned her analyses of the testimony recorded in Jacques Fournier's *Registre*. Some confessed their disbelief in the immortality of the soul, explaining that, like Guillemette Benet, they had noticed that when a child died, its soul did not exit its mouth. Then there was the case of Aude Fauré, another peasant woman who appeared in court before Fournier. The date was July 1318, and it was the first case of deviation from orthodoxy to come before the judge. Fauré was denounced by her neighbors for having professed her inability to believe in the real presence of Christ in the host. Her husband had reproached her for it, and she was disappointed at her own inability to believe. She didn't broadcast her disbelief to others, perhaps because she would have preferred to share in the general belief, but there was nothing for it, she couldn't make herself believe. "When I'm in church," she told the inquisitor, "and they raise the Body of Christ for all to see, I can neither look at it nor pray to it, and when I try to look at it, a kind of *anbegament* [hindrance] comes before my eyes."

Fauré appeared in court eight times from July 15 to August 7, 1318, at which point she was sentenced to a series of fasts and pilgrimages but was spared the disgrace of having to wear the yellow cross. The judge ruled that Fauré understood her error as stemming from an inability to believe. She had even explained the "hindrance" before her eyes as caused by trauma. In her youth, she saw a woman give birth in the street, saw "the disgusting thing that women expel when they give birth, and seeing the body of the Lord raised at the altar, considered that He had been soiled with the same filth." The case is clear enough from a psychoanalytic perspective: Fauré's faith had been polluted by sexuality.

The historian and anthropologist Jean-Pierre Albert has analyzed this case, along with many others, in an important article called "Qui croit à la transsubstantiation?" (Who believes in transubstantiation?). The inability to believe in the Eucharist was not, contrary to what Emmanuel Le Roy Ladurie suggests in *Montaillou,* imposed by "the most radical Cathar faction of the local population." It was not a heresy, though heresy would enter into the question. The difficulty of believing was inherent to the metaphor of the Eucharist, residing at its very heart. And this difficulty of believing is what I'd like to look into.

A word in conclusion, returning to Bernard of Angers, the schoolman who entered an obscure church in the Auvergne, sure of his learning and the social superiority it conferred on him, convinced he was slumming among savages. He'd been told that in those parts, they worshipped idols. He'd been told that the idols worked miracles, and that the belief in them (he used a Latin word, "superstition," to disqualify it from the outset) traveled like a spark along a trail of gunpowder, through rumors and word of mouth—he called it *fama vulgarium*.

And so it started all over again. What exactly? This bothersome business of images, which had already disrupted the West in the time of Charlemagne. In Byzantium, iconoclasm was a heresy practiced by the state. There, imperial Christianity endured, making the Christian East a continuation of classical antiquity, an extenuation of it, I might say. But there remained a latent iconoclasm in the anxious recesses of people's minds. Images were distrusted, making it necessary to shut them away (in books and cloisters). So you had to go out there for yourself, go there so as not to believe in them, travel far from home to revisit memories, meet those living ancestors we know as savages, and perhaps God would grant us the mercy of becoming Romans once again, early Christians, the kind that burst into temples to knock over idols and destroy statues.

In fact, these reliquary statues look like small Roman gods. They are known as *majestas*: Their wooden cores contain relics, conductive bodies that allow the flesh to effect miracles. The statues are memorials to what Peter Brown called the exceptional dead. The first statue that Bernard saw belonged to Saint Geraud: Geraud of Aurillac, a knight who became a monk. The text continues: "I turned to my companion Bernier and addressed him in Latin: 'What think you, brother, of this idol? Would not Jupiter or Mars have approved of such a statue?' Bernier, taking guidance from my words, answered with considerable spirit, hiding his criticism behind his praise." It's hard to imagine a more bald-faced connivance between intellectuals . . . At any rate, we watch them try not to believe, not fall into a commonly held belief, not be caught up in what we have come to know as a "collective delusion."

But things would play out differently. Bernard would succumb, fall prey to a belief he thought himself strong enough to withstand, be turned around — but let's just call it for what it was: be converted. This *conversio,* however, would be the reverse of what we spoke of earlier, the *conversio intelligibilis* that goes from the intelligence of experience to the intelligence of the heart. Here it would be the opposite: He would let himself be overwhelmed, turned inside out by sensory experience.

We know this even as we open his book, since Bernard of Angers's tome, written between 1013 and 1020, is called *Liber miraculorum sancte Fidis.* So how did it happen? The text signals it from the start, betrays it, or in Ginzburg's expression, leaks it. "Given that learned men had good reasons for viewing the practice as superstitious, I too, in my ignorance, believed that the custom was entirely contrary to the Christian religion." We have to understand these two things together: being ignorant with good reason. But what's wonderful and quite touching here is that this is not the learned ignorance of Nicholas of Cusa but the ignorance of learned schoolmen.

So there he was, acting cocky in front of the statue of Saint Faith. He'd traveled on past Aurillac to Conques. In the ninth century, the monks of that pilgrimage center had stolen from the town of Agen the relics of Fides (Faith), a young female Christian martyr whose historical status is unclear. She was a little girl, and she performed little-girl miracles. This is the *novitas,* which renders the miracles *inauditi.* "So many miracles concerning such minor things," wrote Bernard of Angers. A saint who died at the age of eleven, she restored the eyesight of mules, brought chickens back to life, multiplied bracelets, stole jewels from noble ladies, and made fun of knights — miracles that show a degree of social mockery (looked at in historical context, as Dominique Barthélemy has done, they align with a critical view of knightly violence). But it might also be noted, from an anthropological perspective, that she embodied the role of the trickster: "The inhabitants of Conques, with the perspective of country folk, call them the *jocas* of Saint Faith." They understood perfectly: The miracles were the pranks of a saint who was not a *puer senex* but a child having fun.

Was that what overcame Bernard of Angers's defenses? Was that what allowed him to lock eyes with the wasp-eyed idol? In any case, he describes himself in front of the statue. First, he'd been impressed by the many people crowding around him. The ambulatory, a feature of church architecture designed to help disperse crowds, had not yet been invented. He felt that the statue was looking at him. He composed a prayer: "Saint Faith, whose relic lies within this likeness, save me on Judgment Day." Ever the same dialectic of the wheat and the chaff: reviving faith, bringing it back to its core, ridding it of its useless husk. "At that point I smiled at my student Bernier beside me."

But this time, he wouldn't get off so easily. The statue looked at him, looked through him. He was caught. All his defenses crumbled, all his intellectual arrogance melted away. Of course, it's a conversion story, we shouldn't fall for it — the *Liber* is dedicated to Bernard of Angers's master, Fulbert of Chartres, and we know that the cult of Saint Faith was already a belief shared by the legitimate disciplines of scholarly culture. Should we understand this as a defeat of the rational mind, which capitulated to a belief in miracles? Perhaps, but for good reasons, reasons related to experience, in which we might hear echoes of Bloch, Ginzburg, and Kantorowicz, echoes of all who've tried to grasp the weakness of belief. And it doesn't stop us from appreciating today the justification for a kind of knowledge through experience that unsettles many certainties. I quote Bernard of Angers, writing in 1010: "If the extraordinary novelty of these miracles concerns you, I ask one thing of you above all, my brothers: when I return from Conques, go there yourselves, not so much to pray as to observe, that you may not judge wrongly and categorically something that you do not know. In fact, you will yourselves proclaim its truth once you have actually experienced it."

LECTURE 5, FEBRUARY 7, 2017

Cannibalistic Power

Louis VII dreams that the prince offers a goblet of human blood to his lords — The royal supper as metaphor and prefiguration — The medallion of the king as a "sacramental host of state power" — The subversion of a ceremony: King Louis XVI's Flight to Varennes and his ignominious return — When Christian belief is weak, violence against Jews mounts — The legends of the desecration of the host and the murder of Simon of Trent — Cannibalism as the monstrous inversion of the metaphor of the Eucharist — Why must kings hunt? Louis XI's passion for hunting as a pathology of power — "They say that we partake of human flesh": the anti-Christian polemic and the first accusations of anthropophagy — How the word "cannibal" came to Christopher Columbus's ears — Exocannibalism as an anthropological taboo — Montaigne: we are the barbarians

THE STORY IS ABOUT A KING who dreamed. His name was Louis VII, a very pious king, one of the chief founders of the royal religion, to whom a son was born on August 21, 1165. It was a miraculous birth, said the chroniclers, for the sovereign was very old (just think, he was forty-five), and his successive wives (Eleanor of Aquitaine, Constance of Castile, and now Adela of Champagne) had given him only daughters, so that he despaired of producing an heir. He'd thrown himself on the mercy of God, implored him, started to lose hope, organized great assemblies of the people where the clergy and the faithful joined in collective prayer: "Grant me a son who will inherit the kingdom of the Franks and govern it with strength, that its enemies may not say: *Your hope and your offerings have been in vain, and your prayers have come to nought.*"

His prayer was rewarded, and a son was born to Louis VII. This was Philip II, first nicknamed "Dieudonné" (God-given), until his military victories (notably at Bouvines, on Sunday, July 27, 1214) earned him the epithet "Augustus," from *augere*, for augmenting the kingdom. Philip Augustus's reign, from 1180 to 1223, has long been characterized by historians as the coldly rational tenure of a king mainly interested in his government's efficiency. This ignores the aura of wonder and eschatological expectation that enveloped Philip's person and reign, which we understand better today. Eucharistic symbols were an important part of this aura. Christ often appeared to Philip in the shape of a host (in 1184, for instance); the Anonymous of Béthune described him alone in his tent on the eve of the Battle of Bouvines eating bread and drinking wine from a golden cup; Rigord, in *The Deeds of Philip Augustus*, described this act of blessing as taking place in the company of his knights.

The long patience of the Capetian kings in waiting for their royal line to produce a saint was almost rewarded by the advent of Philip Augustus, as Jacques Le Goff has shown. But it was his son, Louis IX, who would claim the prize of sainthood. Yet Philip was already a credible candidate for canonization, and his chronicler Rigord, a monk at the abbey of Saint-Denis, composed *The Deeds of Philip Augustus* during the lifetime of his subject, apparently to compile a record.

This would explain why the narrative model of the *Deeds* (a genre that relates the facts and deeds surrounding a king) is contaminated here, at least in the book's early portions, by the narrative model of the *Vita* (a genre that extols the virtues of a saint). Rigord places the account of a vision at the very beginning of his text, Louis VII's vision prior to his son's birth. Here is the passage: "In his sleep, the king saw his son in a dream, even before his birth. It seemed to him that Philip, his son, held a golden goblet full of human blood, and from it he was toasting his leading men, *and they all drank of it.*" The Latin text reads "*et omnes in eo biberant,*" echoing the Gospel of Mark 14:33, "*et biberunt ex illo omnes,*" in the context of the Last Supper, which is commemorated in the Eucharistic celebration. "At the end of his life he reported this vision to Henry, bishop of Albano, legate of the Apostolic See in France, making him swear *in God's name* that he would not reveal this to anyone before the king's death. When King Louis died, Bishop Henry made the vision widely known among the clergy."

What did this vision mean? Was it a premonition? Why does it have the form of a royal Last Supper, as the allusion to Mark suggests, and why did it have to stay secret? It was a fiction, one that announced future political developments, but also one that was clearly informed by the Eucharistic metaphor. A metaphor, using our definition from the last lecture and borrowing from Hans Blumenberg, is a figure that anticipates the legibility of the world, appears in advance of its becoming intelligible. What Rigord described was a royal Last Supper, and when his account was included in the *Grandes Chroniques de France,* the illustration made this explicit. Problematically, this episode appears in only one of the two extant manuscripts of *The Deeds of Philip Augustus,* and some historians believe it's a late addition by Rigord's anonymous continuer.

What then is the source of this story? It surfaced in a work by the Welsh historian Gerald of Wales, *De principis instructione,* written between 1190 and 1217—hence after what John Baldwin calls "the decisive decade" of Philip Augustus's reign, in which his policy of modernizing the administration and conquering territory declared itself. This perhaps explains why Gerald gives a more explanatory, rationalist, and historical version of the prophetic vision, writing that the king offered the chalice to the assembled nobles according to the order of their claims on the crown, as announced by King Philip Augustus when he took power in 1180: first to his relatives from Champagne, then to the count of Flanders, and finally to Henry II Plantagenet. Thus, he announced in advance the order of his political conquests—the mystic body of the kingdom was taking shape through an act of Communion, while the shadow of danger loomed overhead.

If the vision was a later addition based on the episode of Philip's accession, why did it not incorporate an explanation? What is most likely is that Rigord inserted an event into his narrative that he had knowledge of, while failing to understand all its implications. But the important thing here is to grasp all the implications of this spectacular royal Last Supper. The implications are obviously political, which is why Éric Bournazel and Jean-Pierre Poly are right in interpreting Louis VII's dream as an allusion to the myth of the Holy Grail and the Round Table: Philip is the new Perceval, keeper of the Holy Chalice, and we know how often Philip Augustus's followers evoked Arthurian legends, sometimes filtered through the prophecies of Merlin.

But this royal vision also clearly suggests the "Eucharistic society" described in the preceding lecture as the governing metaphor of a medieval society that submitted to the theology of the real presence of Christ's body in the host and his blood in the wine. I tried to describe all the implications of this Eucharistic realism, which the Gregorian power play imposed, and which affected the architecture of churches and the architecture of the Church, as well as the architecture of society as a whole. It permeated the imagination of the people, who were forced to fall in line with this new orthodoxy of the implausible, and it did violence to the Augustinian tradition of the sign. We know that in the second half of the twelfth century, accounts of seeing stigmata, bloody hosts, and visions of the suffering Christ at the moment of the Eucharistic sacrifice all increased, bloodying the Christian imagination. This speaks to the difficulty of seeing, of believing—you remember Aude Fauré, the peasant woman, who saw the host behind a veil of blood, a veil of her own blood. And Philip Augustus also had a number of these mystical visions. His father too, prior even to his birth, dreamed of him as a Christ-king awaited by his people.

What we have here with this royal dream, this prophetic and possibly self-realizing fiction, which is the political form of the dream described in the first lecture in Micheletian terms (that is, in a literary, revolutionary light), this fiction that reveals and overthrows, that unsettles the past and opens up the future, disembowels it and offers it to view — what we have here is an example of the extension into politics of the domain of the Eucharistic metaphor. The royal religion was a calculated borrowing from this form of sacrality — when, for instance, the king's ritual entry into a city was modeled on the Corpus Christi procession, making the Feast of the Most Holy Body and Blood of Christ into a Feast of the King. Society thus became politically eucharistic by fits and starts, obliquely, through borrowings and transferences (this is how theologico-political takeovers are usually described).

For the term *sacred monarchy* is necessarily ambiguous. Does it refer primarily to the coronation, an essential moment in the royal liturgy? If so, we are ignoring something that unquestionably became part of the definition of the monarchy from the fourteenth century on: the principle of instantaneous succession. As to the term *sacrum,* it doesn't necessarily refer to communication with invisible powers. As Ernst Kantorowicz has shown, there is a *sacrum imperium* that is not a borrowing from the vocabulary of the Church. The expression "royal religion," used in the late fourteenth century by Jean Golein in his *Traité du sacre,* draws on the specific meaning of the *religiosus* as a man who has left the profane world behind without necessarily having joined the Church. The king therefore takes his place in a sacral hierarchy, and the sacral character of the royal person simply reflects a partial borrowing from the theological model.

If secular power holds any sway in the Eucharistic society, it does so by inserting itself into a hierarchical system. This was shown by Alain de Libera in his course on *L'invention du sujet moderne* (The invention of the modern subject), where he defines the medieval world as a hierarchy parasitized by conversion. Early on, the hierarchical vision of Dionysius the Aeropagite was based on levels, where one spoke to the Supreme Being by addressing one's direct superior; the medievals injected an element of Augustine into the mix, making conversion — which is the invention of the subject without mediation — a disruptor of the hierarchy; from which it was a short step to mysticism. That's why I was saying that there was no Big Brother in medieval times, because there was simultaneously this power that asserted itself through something that was hard to believe, asserted itself *from the very fact* that it was hard to believe — the theology of the implausible — creating the conditions for this political friction.

I won't dwell on this well-known point of theologico-political history regarding the joint construction of the subject and royal authority beyond suggesting that more attention be given to the metaphoric force of Eucharistic realism in the instruments of power. What comes to mind, for instance, are the passages that Louis Marin devotes in *Portrait of the King* to the medallion he calls a "royal host" and a "sacramental host of state power." Because it is displayed, touched, exchanged, the medallion is (as are coins) "a sign of and a monument to absolute political power, in its infinite representation." I'd also mention Paul Ricoeur's observations on the relation between the visibility of a face and the legibility of a name set in the hardness and resplendence of metal. It picks up on Marin's concept of representation since "to relate the story of a king in a narrative is to make it seen. To show the story of a king in an icon is to relate it." The crime of counterfeiting coins was thus assimilated with lèse-majesté, or treason against the king, since it was the king's portrait that was damaged.

To understand the medieval ritual of the monarch's ceremonial entry into a city, to demonstrate its kinship with the Feast of Corpus Christi, we need only consider its inversion during the French Revolution. The Flight to Varennes, King Louis XVI's attempt to escape from Paris on the night of June 20, 1791, and especially his pitiable return, offer a political instance of a subversion of ceremony. For it was Louis XVI himself who perpetrated regicide, symbolically, by disguising himself as a valet to escape. "Demeaning metamorphosis," wrote Jules Michelet in *History of the French Revolution*, wondering what might have happened if the king had not hidden his regalia and coronation robe in the trunk of his coach.

"Who would have dared arrest him if, opening his clothes, he had shown his raiment?" A valid question. Instead, Louis XVI stripped himself of his majesty, exactly as Shakespeare's Richard II had done: "I give this heavy weight from off my head, / And this unwieldy scepter from my hand, / The pride of kingly sway from out my heart." This undoing of the kingly body produced a fatal desacralization. And how did Louis's adventure end? Concerned at not seeing the Duc de Choiseul, Louis stuck his head out the coach window in Sainte-Menehould, and the townspeople recognized him. Why? Because his portrait was printed on *assignats*, on pay slips, during the French Revolution. He was asked for his passport, and his carriage, as in a fairy tale, was turned into a "suspicious berline."

Mona Ozouf has described this incident as the death blow to the French monarchy, and also to the belief in the benevolent and Christian paternalism embodied in Louis XVI's kingship. The king's return to Paris on June 21, 1791, was in fact the last royal entry, an inverted ritual that resembled a funeral procession for monarchy or, in Michelet's words, "an excommunication by silence." The spell had been broken. The *Cahiers de doléances*, or lists of grievances, had previously expressed universal and unalloyed obedience to the king, but his flight shattered it. At the trial of those implicated in the Flight to Varennes, the testimony of one of the king's bodyguards is significant. Accused of having been more loyal to the king than to his country, he answered that he didn't understand the distinction: "I declare my belief that king and

Miracle of the Desecrated Host by Paolo Uccello, 1467–1469 (Urbino)

country are indivisible, and nothing can make me separate one from the other." King and country are, in fact, the obverse and reverse of the same medal.

Yet, as we discussed earlier, the idea of transubstantiation is hard to swallow. What we need to understand is that the unseating of belief doesn't happen all at once, in a flash of heretical insight—and if I attempt to describe the Eucharistic society as a political fiction, it's not to construct a medieval Big Brother but to understand its internal fault lines. Transubstantiation was hard to believe in. This was true from the start, right from the twelfth century, and the first to pay the price were the Jews. Antisemitic violence in a Christian context has always been the horrific marker of a weakness in belief, of difficulty believing, due to the choice the Church invariably makes when it's confronted with alternatives and heresies, which is to opt for the one that's hardest to believe in. This would be the moment to bring in the theme of the

desecrated host, and the antisemitic fantasy of Jews committing ritual crimes. Let's take the infamous case related by the Florentine chronicler Giovanni Villani, which is supposed to have occurred in Paris in 1290. A Christian woman, needing to redeem a coat that her husband pawned after losing at cards, sells a consecrated wafer to a Jewish merchant. The merchant returns home, where he tries to fry the wafer, but blood miraculously spurts from it, attracting the local men-at-arms. Subsequently, the host is solemnly reconsecrated. The woman is sentenced to hang, and an angel descends from the heavens. The scene was depicted by Paolo Uccello in a tempera-on-panel predella commissioned by the Confraternity of the Corpus Domini for their church in Urbino. This image chimes with another, nearly contemporary event. On Maundy Thursday of 1475, in the town of Trent, a two-and-a-half-year-old boy named Simon disappeared. Three days later, his body was found at the bottom of a well near the house of

a Jew, Samuel of Nuremberg. The murder was immediately attributed to the Jewish household. The podesta Giovanni de Salis, seconded by Bishop Johannes Hinderbach, prosecuted the Jews in court. The suspects were tortured and finally confessed their guilt, giving a detailed description of the infanticide they had committed, which followed a specific ritual. They'd planned to collect the child's blood to make unleavened bread, which would then be mixed with wine to bless their seder meal. A quick trial followed, and the defendants were condemned to death.

A sprinkling of such accusations first cropped up at the time of the first Crusades (in 1144 in Norwich, 1171 in Blois, and 1182 in Zaragoza), but it was in the fifteenth century that large numbers of these accusations started being made: in Innsbruck in 1462, Trent in 1475, and La Guardia in 1490. Texts and images alike stress the twin facets of Simon's murder. A close analogy is drawn between the child's martyrdom

and Christ's, making the story a powerful tool for antisemitic propaganda. As Andrea Martignoni has shown, the images of Simon establish the attributes of his martyrdom, creating a sort of parallel with the *Arma Christi,* the Instruments of the Passion: the scarf, the pincers, the knife, the needles, the bowl. The original crime of the Jews is thus repeated in the violent murder of a young Christian child, a symbol of innocence. The images further elevate Simon, by the "grace of the brush," to the status of blessedness, enveloping his head in the sun's rays, a sign of God's special favor.

We could continue with the description of this "Easter Rising" of antisemitic prejudices, and the paroxysms of violence against the Jews in Christian contexts generally, as markers of the difficulty of believing, a difficulty provoked by the Church's doctrinal choices. But I'd like to go in a different direction, the difficult and disagreeable direction suggested by the antisemitic fantasy of ritual crime. I'm talking about devouring, the act of devouring—starting from Louis VII's dream, as recounted by Rigord in *The Deeds of Philip Augustus,* which is retold by Gerald of Wales in *De principis instructione* and also appears in works by Benoît de Sainte-Maure and Gautier Map.

Let's look at a different royal dream, one by William II of England. One day, the king was out hunting and got lost in the woods. Hungry, he spotted a chapel in a clearing. He entered and found the body of a deer laid out on the altar. He would have known that the deer was a symbol of Christ (its flesh is supposedly impervious to rot) and that hunting deer therefore has the religious meaning of a spiritual quest. He was also aware that the meat was raw, but being very hungry, he ate the deer. All of a sudden, the deer turned into a blood-drenched man. Terrified, the king remembered his dream, the one he'd had the night before: He'd been hungry and found himself eating human flesh. In the morning, he'd gone to the bishop of Winchester to ask for an explanation. The man on the altar was Christ, the bishop answered, and being a tyrant you devoured him whole.

This dream is a monstrous inversion of the Eucharist, and contrasting it with Philip Augustus's dream of the royal Last Supper, chronicled by Rigord, in which Philip offers his barons a goblet of blood to drink, is enlightening, as Jerzy Pysiak pointed out in a 2002 essay. The Christ-king Philip Augustus does not devour the body of his kingdom, instead "he injects revivifying blood into his country's limbs." These two examples, then, show us a good king who, Christlike, offers himself to be eaten and drunk, and a bad king who devours his people. Perhaps, but at the time Pysiak wrote, we hadn't yet seen the episode of *Game of Thrones* where Walder Frey devours a pie containing the flesh of his dead sons before being killed. And we hadn't seen the strange dream sequence at the beginning of Pierre Schoeller's film *L'Exercice de l'État*, in which a naked woman is devoured by a crocodile in the office of the Minister of Transportation. We hadn't seen it, but once we have, we also see the threatening shadow that looms over Philip Augustus's royal Last Supper. Exactly as in that painted room in the Palazzo Pubblico in Siena, that room I'm trying to leave behind, where Pietro Lorenzetti painted his frescoes in 1338. Let's start there, with these two political dreams, separate but face-to-face, one across from the other. That's what I'd like to talk about, this cannibalistic power.

So let's pick up the story, if I may, by looking at biblical glosses. Philippe Buc has analyzed the way commentaries of the Bible produce a theory of power that agrees with our definition of political fiction. I draw here on his important work, *L'ambiguïté du livre*. Why are books ambiguous? Christianity is a religion of the Book, and *Lectio Divina* ("divine reading") is at the center of monastic life, university study, and all intellectual activity generally. But the problem of any religion anchored in history is to create and maintain a balance between the letter and the human spirit. As Jacques Le Goff writes in his preface to Buc's book, what is necessary is "for the Book not to block progress, and for progress not to make the Book obsolete." That's what prophets are for: prophecy is a radical means for updating norms. This is why, in times of spiritual expectation, prophecies thrive and multiply. But strictly speaking, from a theological perspective, Jesus was the last prophet. The Book is closed, but it remains infinite, a polysemic body subject to interpretation. "An ever-growing river of exegesis flows through the Middle Ages; the flood is that of a tradition inventing and transforming itself behind a mask of continuity."

The gloss has formal rules (marginal or interlinear) and intellectual rules (anagogy, allegory, tropology), which Buc sets out in detail. The technique of the biblical gloss first developed in the second half of the twelfth century, especially in the grande école of the town of Laon (studied by Guy Lobrichon). With respect to power, glosses addressed the episodes and maxims of the book of Kings and the book of Samuel, but also the New Testament and the epistles of Paul. At the end of the twelfth century, the glosses were for the most part allegorical: When the commentator read *rex*, he understood "apostle," "upright man," or "saint," but rarely "king." This mechanism of sublimation was already a means of taking a position: It was a way of suggesting that in the final analysis the real kingdom was internal. It was a way of rejecting secular power as something accidental, something arising from sin, accepted for want of anything better, despite oneself, and only while waiting for better to come along. A first change occurred over the course of the thirteenth century: Glosses became more and more literal. When the commentators read *rex*, they understood "king." Which was a way of accommodating royal power, once more in an Augustinian sense, to the Eucharistic society.

According to Buc, the Bible commentators saw the affirmation of the monarchy as a "race toward wisdom," to which they opposed their own monopoly over true knowledge. Whence the gloss on Isaiah 11:7: "And the lion shall eat straw like the ox." Meaning that the lion (the king) is no more worthy than the ox (the peasant) to eat the ear of wheat (the spirit); he must make do with the straw (the outer envelope of the letter). For only the cleric knows how to separate the wheat from the chaff. However learned he may be, the king is on a par with the peasant in dealing with a text. He doesn't know what to do. He takes it all, he devours it. This means he can't be trusted with exegesis. And that's why when the king has a vision, in both of the cases I mentioned, he seeks out a high-ranking cleric to discover its meaning. What have I done? What am I being told? What's in my head? If he gets an answer, it's one that makes him feel guilty (you're a tyrant), or else he'll only find out after he's dead. The sovereign therefore has to be denied access to knowledge. This fact is confirmed by Peter the Chanter and by Stephen Langton, and the *Bible moralisée*, or Moralized Bible, given to Louis IX says it loud and clear: A king cannot be an exegete. From this follows a highly effective political metaphor, which contrasts the manducation of ecclesiastics with the devouring of sovereigns. The first is positive, the incorporation of subjects into the *corpus mysticum*: Saint Peter eats the faithful because the Lord of Heaven offers himself to be eaten in return. But the lords of this world, by contrast, do not offer themselves up. They take. They do not build, they devour. This cannibalism is the monstrous reverse of the Eucharist. That is why monarchical ideology has to abandon this terrifying metaphor and appropriate the metaphor of priesthood instead. But it can only be done in small stages, in bits and pieces.

Thus the Eucharistic metaphor is a political fiction that, like all political fictions, is reversible. Its flip side is the image of a predatory power whose main distinguishing mark is venery, hunting. Predation and Communion are the obverse and reverse of power. If the lay aristocracy devotes so much energy to hunting, it is neither to feed itself nor to train for war but to perform what Alain Guerreau has called a rite of marking and domination. Large-animal hunting (bear, and then lion, when that animal replaced the former as king of the beasts) and falconry (the hawk is emblematic of nobleness) became the two fundamental hunting activities of the aristocracy.

Hunting remained, at all events, one of the few social activities that unequivocally separated the lay aristocracy from the clerical aristocracy. This no doubt explains why, ever since the Gregorian Reforms, the Church has taken a stand against hunting, finding arguments in the Bible to denounce "the heads of nations, dominators over the beasts of the field, men who disdain the birds of the air." And that is also why the theme of the hunter king holds such a large place in medieval literature and art. Emperor Frederick II wrote a famous treatise on falconry, which his son Manfred, according to a chronicler, read and reread "like a treatise on politics." Hunting was political in the sense that it expressed the ability of the sovereign to domesticate untamed nature, triumph over chance, and prevail over the animal kingdom.

While the king hunts, the prelate commands obedience through words alone. From this perspective, as Jacques Dalarun has shown, the Franciscan tradition of the *poverello* was less ineffectual than ordinarily recognized: The *poverello* cut a powerful figure, precisely the opposite of the predatory hunter king, reflecting a dispossession from power, but clearly in favor of a yet greater authority. The *poverello* renounces strength for something stronger even than strength. And that's why Louis IX, aka Saint Louis, did not hunt and also why Louis XI hunted so frenetically that his contemporaries grew concerned about it, and that's why an author such as Thomas Basin points to Louis XI's passion for the chase as the cause of the War of the Public Weal. He presided over a tyranny where, to quote Claude de Seyssel, "a man's murder was sooner pardoned than the killing of a stag or a boar." The question of hunting rights in the *Cahiers de doléances* should not be taken as primarily of folkloric interest, because what's at issue here with the hunter king is the very figure of tyranny.

The hunter king acts the beast. As Niccolò Machiavelli described, he is sometimes a fox and sometimes a lion. And if he's both one and the other, it's because he has to forget that he was once a bear. If we agree with Michel Pastoureau, the question of the animality and savagery of secular power is reflected in the figure of the bear, as the king of the beasts. But are bears beasts? Medieval bestiaries put them halfway between animality and humanity. The bear is man's Other: He has man's height and build, man's standing posture, and the same arrangement of the organs. A man only has to cloak himself in a bearskin to "play the bear" — and there are numerous instances of such pagan bear festivals.

But this simulacrum hides a deeper connection. In the Middle Ages, knowledgeable authorities affirmed that the cross between a bear and a woman (or a man and a she-bear) produced viable offspring. Hence the many legends of "bear children," born of the amours of a woman held prisoner in a cave and the brown, hairy animal goaded by unbridled sexuality. The kings of Denmark, it's worth noting, took pride in being descended from bears, and by vaunting their bear ancestors they made the rulers of Sweden and Norway envious. It's worth noting too that the very name of the mythical King Arthur has an ursine origin: *art*, which derives from the Latin *ursus*, means "bear" in Old Irish. There was in fact a taboo against mentioning bears, which led to various paraphrases: "honey eater" in the Slavic languages, and "brown one" in the Germanic, whence *bear* in English, *Bär* in

German, *björn* in Swedish, qualifiers that contributed to an abundant suite of names.

Feared for its strength, the bear was possibly worshipped as a tutelary power in ancient societies. Pastoureau, venturing into the minefield of controversy over the interpretation of Paleolithic cave art, and focusing on Le Regourdou in the Dordogne where a double grave was found with a brown bear in one and a Neanderthal in the other, asserts that there was indeed a bear-worshipping religion, and that traces of it can be found in Greek myths (Artemis is the goddess of bears) and Celtic legends. If so, the historian can trot out his implacable scenario, showing that the medieval Church, conscious of the paganism implicit in the symbolic elevation of the bear, went to great lengths to dethrone the putative king of the beasts and replace him with a successor who would be more amenable to Christ's laws: the lion.

Having started with a history of heraldry and moved on to a history of bestiaries and colors, Pastoureau is above all a historian of symbol systems in the medieval West, where the main concern is to determine how the qualities that stand in opposition to each other (blue/red, lion/bear) form a system. One could go further and say Pastoureau is primarily a historian of symbolic devaluation. A question we might ask is, what is the exact nature of the intentionality he attributes to such collective actors as the Church, which "decided to replace the bear with the lion," hatching "strategies" to bring about its project ("fighting the bear, taming him, branding him as the devil"), all of it carried out over several centuries ("a long-term action")? It's nonetheless true that his framing of the issues has made Pastoureau's books powerfully persuasive.

For how can we resist the power and poignance of the demonstration? First we see the bear persecuted: The great hunts in the time of Charlemagne are likened by Pastoureau to campaigns to eradicate this troubling pagan divinity. But more effective even than physical harassment is the symbolic taming and tempering of the bear. We have many hagiographies of Western hermits and saints in which a bear casts off its savage spirit to become the saint's humble and servile companion (from Saint Gall to Saint Martin), helping him carry his belongings, collect his strayed sheep, and found an abbey. The easy-tempered, oafish bear thus came into being: first, in the symbolic order, then in actuality at fairs and markets. To make the bear fall entirely from his pedestal, it was only necessary to demonize him. His brown color, hairy pelt, rages, and lustfulness all tended to identify him with the forces of evil. Thus was the bear's place vacated and another animal installed on his throne: the lion.

This leaves the stuffed toy so often found in children's cradles in the West, the teddy bear, which also derives from a story of power—the famous one of President Theodore Roosevelt refusing to kill a shackled bear during a hunt. Clinging to the teddy bear's plush and protective form, today's children are perhaps restoring to the bear its preeminent role at the dawn of mankind: that of first god.

LET'S HYPOTHETICALLY PROPOSE a fundamental tension between Communion and predation. It will help us understand why men who wield power play the beast—we'll drop a placeholder here and return to it later. But we have to go beyond this opposition between ecclesiastical manducation and political devouring, we need to look at the more troubling question of the symbolic relation between the Eucharist and devouring by savages. We know that the Eucharist was at the heart of the religious controversy in the sixteenth century. A decisive moment, as Thierry Wanegffelen has noted, was the first dispute in the summer of 1534 between the bishop of Avranches, Robert Céneau, and the Protestant reformer from Strasbourg Martin Bucer. The latter was urging Catholics to return to the early Scholastic doctrine of Thomas Aquinas, which conciliated to some extent between the new theology of the real presence of Christ in the Eucharist and the Augustinian tradition of the sign. But conciliation had become impossible, and the Affair of the Placards of October 17, 1534, in which seditious placards were posted even on the door of King Francis I's bedchamber in his castle at Amboise, specifically denounced the doctrine of transubstantiation—and we know that the transubstantiation question is what led to the extremes of religious conflict.

What would be needed is an emotional history of what Frank Lestringant has called the "sacred horror" inspired in Calvinists by the bloody and barbaric rite of the Eucharist. These weren't clashes of opinions but of strong emotional responses — one camp experienced Communion as a delicious feast, the other reacted with disgust, to the point of vomiting. If Christ was the son of man and the son of God, Communion was anthropophagy. The execrated mystery of the Eucharistic sacrifice, which transformed bread into the body of Christ, was a perversion that ran counter to the progress of civilization, the progress from raw to cooked. This revulsion at the devouring of human flesh runs through such works as *Les tragiques* by Agrippa d'Aubigné and Shakespeare's *Hamlet,* especially the death of Polonius.

What was being reenacted in the sixteenth century was the accusation first leveled at Christians by pagans in the middle of the second century: "They say that we partake of human flesh," Justin Martyr recorded. The charge of anthropophagy was addressed by Athenagoras and again by Theophilus of Antioch. Pliny the Younger wrote about the Christian supper euphemistically as "an unreasonable and baseless superstition." Greek and Roman authors referred to Communion allusively, speaking of "the feast of Thyestes." This was a reference to Seneca's tragedy by that name, in which Atreus takes vengeance on his brother Thyestes for seducing his wife by getting him to eat his own children, a fact that he gradually reveals to Thyestes by showing him the remains of their butchered bodies, thus causing him unbearable pain. *Thyestes* is the great tragedy of paroxysmal violence. And starting in the second century, Christians were accused of communing at the feast of Thyestes.

Later, during the Wars of Religion, these paroxysms actually took place. I won't dwell on it, but in his great book *Les guerriers de Dieu* (God's warriors), Denis Crouzet has described scenes of trance in which anthropophagy was invested with sacredness and a group of communicants pretended through a feast of violence to re-create the mystical alliance between God and his people, an alliance broken by heretical rebellion. The liver was eaten, a symbolic site of the Passions, and also the heart, held to be rotten in heretics. Eating a spoiled heart was "a sacrifice or an offering of oneself, in imitation of the Sacrifice of He who took upon Himself all the sins of the world."

Why not give these anthropophagi the name "cannibals"? The history of this term, which has been reconstructed in the works of Lestringant, poses the Adamic problem of the limits of the human — and it was in fact the discovery of the New World that directly challenged all earlier Christian anthropology based on the nature of the first man. On Sunday, November 4, 1492, Christopher Columbus, admiral of the oceans, landed on an island we know to have been Cuba. The Arawaks came out to meet him. And beyond that? *Hombres de un ojo*, "men with but one eye, and others with the muzzles of dogs who ate human flesh." What we are reading is a complex document: The text known as *The Journal of Christopher Columbus* is a reconstruction based on Bartolomé de Las Casas's *History of the Indies*.

Columbus heard what he wanted to hear, that he had

arrived at the far edge of the world where the fantastic people conjured up by Pliny the Elder, Solinus, and Isidore of Seville lived. Cyclopes and dogheaded men. And what else? What other fabulous creatures beyond those listed in Pierre d'Ailly's *Imago mundi*, which Columbus brought with him: the Blemmyes (men without heads whose eyes and mouths were on their torsos), the Panoti (who wrap themselves in their long ears to sleep), the Artabatites, the Satyrs and fauns with cleft feet, the sciapods, the antipodes, the hippopods who run like the wind, and the pygmies who ride goats into battle. Columbus relied on what he had read in Pliny's *Natural History*. Then on Monday, November 26, 1492, he queried the Arawak again: What people lived farther away? Their enemies, the Cariba. These were in fact the Carib of the Lesser Antilles (the word has given us "Caribbean"). The word *cariba* most likely meant "bold." But Columbus heard *caniba*, giving rise to a portmanteau word. He heard in it the Latin root *canis*, so these were men with the heads of dogs. But in the syllable *can* he also heard the Great Khan of Tartary. This meant he had arrived at the place he'd hoped to reach. Later, on December 24, sailing along the coast of Civao (the Indigenous name for Haiti), he would hear "Cipango."

Here is what he wrote in his journal: "And so I repeat what I have said on other occasions: the Caniba are nothing else than the people of the Grand Khan, who must be very near to these people and possess ships, and they must come to take them captive, and as the prisoners do not return, they believe that they have been eaten." Columbus had seen Caribs, eaters of the Arawak, but he didn't want to believe that they were anthropophagic. Thus the word that would give us *cannibals* is a product of denial. For a long time, the descriptions and illustrations of cannibals presented them as cynocephalic, or dogheaded. Cannibals entered literature in 1533 with Rabelais, and Lestringant has detailed the cannibal's progress through the great travel accounts: André Thevet's *Les singularitez de la France antarctique, autrement nommée Amérique* (1557); Hans Staden's *True History and Description of a Country in America, Whose Inhabitants Are Savage, Naked, Very Godless, and Cruel Man-Eaters* (1557); Jean de Léry's *Histoire d'un voyage faict en la terre du Brésil* (1578).

All attested to anthropophagy. And all interpreted it as a ritual. Thevet, followed by Léry, who borrowed much from him, thought it was motivated by vengeance. Although pleasure was clearly taken in eating human flesh, Thevet preferred to believe that pleasure was of secondary importance.

In fact, this anthropological taboo—the ritual reading of cannibalism—would persist for a long time, both with regard to necrophagic endocannibalism, associated with funerary rituals, and with regard to predatory exocannibalism, at least when survival was not at stake. Anthropologists today accept the fact that established, predatory cannibalism is gastronomic cannibalism, driven by gluttony, whose only justification is "because it's good." Why is that so difficult to accept? We provide no other justification for our carnivorous diet. And as Claude Lévi-Strauss has noted, a carnivorous diet is an "expanded cannibalism." In his 2001 essay "A Lesson in Wisdom from Mad Cows," he writes: "A day will come when the thought that, to feed themselves, men of the past raised and massacred living beings and complacently exposed their shredded flesh in shopwindows will no doubt inspire the same revulsion that the travelers of the sixteenth and seventeenth century felt toward the cannibalistic meals of the Indigenous peoples of America, Oceania, and Africa."

Sixteenth-century Europe had already seen its certainties destabilized. The discovery of cannibals in the New World coincided with the discovery of barbarism in antiquity. We are the barbarians of the world: this was the great discovery of the Age of Discovery. And it's why Las Casas's *A Short Account of the Destruction of the Indies* has to be read in the future tense. The "destruction of the Indies" was the destruction of the West and not just the damage that the West had perpetrated in the Americas. That's why, as Roger Chartier has shown, the engravings made by the de Bry family in its edition of Las Casas's *A Short Account* (1598) were used as the iconographic basis for the anti-Spanish pamphlets of the rebels in Holland and served as models to denounce the atrocities of the Wars of Religion. That's also why the priest Jean de Léry, who witnessed the anthropophagic practices of the residents of Guanabara Bay in Brazil in 1557, laid the greater weight of barbarism on the heads of Europeans, not

Indigenous Americans. Cases of anthropophagy among the besieged Protestants in the town of Sancerre shocked him more than those he described in the context of the Tupi warrior ethic.

This is definitely what's at issue in "On Cannibals," the crucial chapter in Michel de Montaigne's *Essays*. The author directly engages with the scandalous heart of savagery: the anthropophagy of the Indians of the New World, based on firsthand accounts from Brazil. His text comes close to reflecting what we might call an ethnographic view, with Montaigne avoiding any value judgment for as long as possible.

Michel de Certeau has written a superb essay on "On Cannibals" entitled "Le lieu de l'autre" (The other's place). What was most important, according to Certeau, was for Montaigne to write, thereby inventing his own space. Thus, and I quote: "A discourse on the other is the way to construct a discourse authorized by the other." This space is my space, inasmuch as it's a space where the other speaks. This is what Certeau calls *heterology*, which is "a Western ethics of writing." The other is an inaccessible presence in the text, and the author is a reappearing passerby in his fragmented work. "Not being a cannibal, there remains the possibility of writing, reckless writing." For in this art of acting in two spaces, a person can determine what exists in one place that is absent in the other. And between here and there, one always runs the risk of the boomerang effect: Criticism inevitably bounces back on the criticizer. That's why the sentence "Nothing human is alien to me" cannot be a maxim of common morality, it's the watchword of writing itself.

And this creates the conditions for a welter of conflicting resemblances and differences: By making cannibals out to be men like us, we set ourselves at a distance from ourselves, make ourselves alien, exile ourselves from our most robust certainties, starting with the certainty that we are not alien to anyone. Thus will our ordinary lives, and here I quote from Book II of the *Essays*, offer "effects as admirable as those one ventures forth to collect from alien countries, alien centuries."

This recognition is what makes for the beauty of Montaigne's description of the cannibals' way of life, beyond the humanist goodwill it so clearly manifests. And it's why we have to make the effort to be wary of ourselves, to achieve a certain detachment: Just because we like an idea doesn't mean it's true. Montaigne's general argument is familiar enough. He describes the natives' simple ethics, their friendliness, nobility, valor. And when he gets to the ritual anthropophagy, he describes the practice patiently, avoiding euphemisms, in a neutral way. For an Indian warrior to put his adversary to death and consume him is imagined as a ritual practice, thus lifting it into the symbolic sphere. "This is not, as people think, for nourishment, as of old the Scythians used to do; it is to betoken an extreme revenge."

This is a magnificent job of ethnographic description — foundational not only in the field of literature, as Certeau has shown, but also in the human sciences, which today openly reflect their kinship to literary narrative. Philippe Descola has argued, in *Beyond Nature and Culture,* that Montaigne provides an exceptional, almost heroic, instance of questioning the certainties of Western naturalism, specifically its conviction that man's internal faculties set him apart completely from all other beings. In his *Apology for Raymond Sebond,* for example, Montaigne proposes that animals may have a certain capacity for language — a claim that Descartes scathingly refuted.

The important lesson here is what we might call, following Gérard Lenclud, a principle of parity, which is at the base of any attempt to understand others. It is also a requirement for historians, who must, as Paul Veyne has written, describe strange and foreign situations, far from the here and now, events "from alien countries, alien centuries," as Montaigne would say, and rather than label them as not being believable, or criticize other peoples for their credulity, to give the reader "the means to say that in their place he would have believed as they do." But the principle of parity (equal-time history, we could call it) does not necessarily result in the vulgar relativism denounced by the high-minded and quick to judgment who infest the public sphere. In fact, the book by Lenclud that I'm specifically drawing on is called *L'universalisme ou le pari de la raison* (Universalism, or the wager of reason). Montaigne may well use the category of barbarity as a way of relativizing the category of savagery. But in no way does he deny the savagery of cannibalism.

Pervading cannibalism, Montaigne writes at the end of his description, is a "barbaric horror." But we too are barbarians — and it's at this point that Montaigne starts in on the famous passages about the cruelty of the conquistadors and the violence practiced in the West. Here he is:

> I am not sorry that we notice the barbarous horror of such acts, but I am heartily sorry that, judging their faults rightly, we should be so blind to our own. I think there is more barbarity in eating a man alive than in eating him dead; and in tearing by tortures and the rack a body still full of feeling, in roasting a man bit by bit, in having him bitten and mangled by dogs and swine (as we have not only read but seen within fresh memory, not among ancient enemies, but among neighbors and fellow citizens, and what is worse, on the pretext of piety and religion), than in roasting and eating him after he is dead.

This is a literature of the real, one of uncommon violence: It's not about something read but something seen, here at home. What then can we still say about the anthropophagi of Brazil? This: "So we may well call these people barbarians, in respect to the rules of reason, but not in respect to ourselves, who surpass them in every kind of barbarity."

It's clear how vital these words are today. Our violence neither excuses nor explains the violence of others — but as the violence of others is not foreign to us, it may at least help us to acknowledge our own. This is also the principle of symmetry, which in no way undermines the claims of reason contained in the idea of universality. For here is the high-water mark of this chapter of the *Essays*: Yes, cannibals are barbarians, but barbarians with regard to the rules of reason, not "in respect to ourselves, who surpass them in every kind of barbarity." This is the point that triggers what I have called the text's second effect. Ever since Montaigne, European consciousness has accused itself of barbarity, and this self-accusation, which Annemarie Schwarzenbach has called the "European malady," is perhaps Montaigne's most precious legacy—hence the serious resentment one can feel toward those who worship national identity and ignore what constitutes the heart, though perhaps the toxic heart, of Europe's collective consciousness: the anxiety of now being the world's barbarians.

Ever since, we have been born already fissured, disturbed, uneasy. The fissure is very intimate, but it is also very ancient: It's the scar that history has given us, and this history in particular—the history of the world's expansion. All of Rousseau's philosophy, for instance, bears witness to it. Thus, for instance, in his *Discourse on the Origin of Inequality*, where he makes the cannibal that Montaigne meets the spokesman for a universal wisdom from which we are now estranged. Montaigne relates that the Indians were extraordinary orators—he had met one in Rouen who told him three things, "three things of which the third is lost to me, grieving me deeply."

LECTURE 6, FEBRUARY 21, 2017

Confronting the Leviathan, I: The Visual Event

Why do we give things visual form? — The reversibility of all political fiction: the king's two bodies and habeas corpus — The *Miracle of the Desecrated Host* by Paolo Uccello — "Eucharistic theater, in which medieval Jews are used to illustrate a doctrine" — The savages of the New World and the savageness of the Old — Again face-to-face with the monster: Will it devour or incorporate us? — "A democracy, in fact, is nothing more than an aristocracy of orators, sometimes interrupted by the temporary monarchy of a single orator" (Thomas Hobbes) — Understanding Hobbes by identifying the positions he is arguing against (Quentin Skinner) — The three fields of *De Cive*'s frontispiece (1642): the heavens, the empire, and freedom — The state of nature and of freedom, "where any man may rob and kill another": man hunting man and the return of cannibals

THE ADVENT OF AN IMAGE is always an event, and that's what I'd like to address here, the image event, the image act as the advent of meaning. Why is it that at times (but not always) we give things visual form? Why are ideas sometimes condensed into a figure, stopped dead, rather than allowed to keep flowing in fictions? Why do we use images and not just narratives, and, more specifically, at what moments? Walter Benjamin, in the seventeenth of his "Theses on the Philosophy of History," calls these moments when the dialectic is brought to a halt "cessations of happening": "Where thinking suddenly stops in a configuration pregnant with tensions, it gives that configuration a shock, by which it crystallizes into a monad."

I'm proposing to retrace our steps and summarize the earlier lectures in pictures, the way you might ford a river, seeing what we've already seen, especially what I've discussed earlier without the accompaniment of a visual illustration, and we'll try to understand what thought events crystallize with the advent of an image. The point of departure, then, was a familiar image, an ever-familiar image, a tyrant's mug. (See image on page 9.) He's back, there he is. How do you stare down a tyrant, wipe the makeup from a reality that so closely resembles the fictions intended to ape it? (See image on page 10.) Then on to more appealing faces, those of the Italian lords of the trecento (see image below), who simultaneously dominated the discourse, captured attention, and drew mockery. It's not about staring down the tyrant at this point but giving a face to tyranny, coming to terms with the tyrant's power of seduction. We then hypothesized that what is attractive about a tyrant is the very power of fiction.

Close-up of face of Cangrande della Scala on equestrian statue, c. 1340 (Castelvecchio Museum, Verona)

But what is fiction? If all power is the power to animate a narrative, fiction allows us to test thoughts against reality. Fiction sets in motion truth effects that inspire counter-behavior, possibly even future politics — and no fiction is ever anything but political.

Which is why it's important to take seriously fiction's capacity to anticipate. Power, let's remember, can assume the likeness of a fiction that has previously given tentative form to that power, including in its more grotesque aspects. The forty-fifth president of the United States, at his inauguration on January 20, 2017, used words that immediately reminded some listeners of the populist speech by the Batman villain Bane, who promised to restore power to the common folk ("and giving it back to you, the people"). An image of Trump as Bane has appeared on the walls of American cities — and once again we have a mask (or muzzle) glued to the skin.

Whence the necessity of addressing the question of truth, that is, the history of truth effects — and truth-speaking. This is not just a history of eloquence, which is the art of binding others to the words one speaks. Thus, in one of Lucian's fables, the chains attached to Hercules's tongue are threaded through the ears of those who hear, follow, and obey him. Those chains are given visible form in this page from a 1550 edition of Andrea Alciato's *Emblemata*. The humanist Alciato was born in Milan in 1492, taught at Avignon and Bourges, and authored the first book of emblems, published in Augsburg in 1531. What is an emblem? "A particular kind of epigram," says

144 SCIENTIA.

Eloquentia Fortitudine præſtantior.

Arcum læua tenet.rigidam fert dextera clauam,
Contegit & Nemees corpora nuda leo.
Herculis hæc igitur facies?non conuenit illud
Quòd uetus & ſenio tempora cana gerit.
Quid quòd lingua illi leuibus traiecta cathenis,
Quēis fiſſa facileis allicit aure uiros?
An'ne quòd Alciden lingua non robore Galli
Præſtantem,populis iura dediſſe ferunt?
Cedunt arma togæ,& quamuis duriſsima corda
Eloquio pollens ad ſua uota trahit.

"Eloquentia fortitudine praestantior,"
from Andrea Alciato's *Emblemata*

Alciato, which is to say an object that is "taken from history or nature, and capable of assuming an ingenious meaning." So an ingenious meaning is not the meaning that meets the eye but the meaning that becomes apparent when you stop and consider. It is not the meaning of the thing itself: *Verba signifiant, res significantur* (Words signify, things are signified). But with emblems, things *can* signify. And what allows them to say something beyond their sole existence is their accompanying text or commentary.

Which leads us to the invention of political iconology, whose most famous, terrible, and powerful illustration we will begin discussing today: the frontispiece of Thomas Hobbes's *Leviathan*. But have patience, because to understand it we will need to round up all that we tried to grasp in the second and third lectures, which were devoted to truth effects and the effect of belief, centered on the counterintuitive idea that the learned elite can impose their power through an orthodoxy of the implausible, lectures that were basically permeated with the general idea of reversibility. Every political fiction is reversible, it can be turned inside out like a glove, as I've often said, not only when a political belief gradually loses intensity (as, for instance, the belief in the miracle-working power of kings) but when its polarity is reversed. This is the case with the juridical operations we call legal fictions, and also with the organicist metaphor of the king's two bodies, in which the immortal and mystical body of the kingship takes up residence in the mortal body of the king, an instance of "immutability within time."

This bodily duality on which the king's *persona ficta* is based is not specific to the theory of monarchy, which is just one of its detours. It made it possible to avoid two other options on which the transcendence of kingly power might have been based, both of which had been rejected by history: a Christic kingship, and a sovereignty embodied in law (Frederick II). The Church always managed to do in these claims to kingly transcendence. The notion of the king's two bodies, then, is very much a fiction, one that could be turned against the king (as it was during the English Civil War, when King Charles I was decapitated on January 30, 1649, in the name of the monarchy), or one that could do without him altogether: hence the last chapter of Ernst Kantorowicz's book, devoted to "a human-based kingship" in the works of Dante. Perishable, fallible man carries within him humanity's eternal form. And this lays the groundwork for all the "republican" or simply parliamentarian (habeas corpus) forms of persistence and substitution of corporeal doubleness.

But what also jars with this idea of the quiddity, the thisness of the human body, which had been developing since 1350, is, as Alain Boureau has shown, the concrete perception of the body's singleness. When you get close to a king, you see only a king. You don't see kingship. It was in these terms that Philippe de Commines, in the prologue he addressed to the archbishop of Vienna, spoke of his familiarity with King Louis XI: "I saw in him, as in all the other princes I have known or served, both good and evil, for they are men like us." In a sense, when Pierre Grégoire, a French jurist from the late sixteenth century, wrote that "the Majesty of God appears in the Prince *on the exterior,* for the benefit of his subjects; but *on the interior* there remains what is human," he was letting the cat out of the bag: The theologico-political mystique was reduced to an external display of royal insignia. You don't even need a Shakespearean tragedy on the unmaking of the royal body for everything to become pitifully disjointed.

Thackeray caricature of Louis XIV, dressed and undressed

This caricature by William Makepeace Thackeray, for instance, disassembles Hyacinthe Rigaud's famous portrait of Louis XIV, juxtaposing the pomp of royal dignity and the king's small body. As much as to say, if that's all there is, it's easy enough to disassemble. It's just regalia.

Think back to Jules Michelet's comment about Louis XVI on his Flight to Varennes in June 1791: "Who would have dared arrest him if, opening his clothes, he had shown his raiment?" The grandeur of royal dignity and the frailty of the king's nature could be considered the heads and tails of the royal medal, which Louis Marin has called the "ceremonial host." And then there was the brutal inversion of the royal *entrée*, or entry ceremony, when Louis XVI returned to Paris, the archetype of a subverted ritual. Think too of the many instances of iconoclasm. Think of the description in Louis-Sébastien Mercier's *Tableau de Paris* of the insurgents' disappointment after they toppled Louis XV's equestrian statue. It fell, and there was nothing inside. "All was hollow, statue and power." Similar accounts exist of the fall of the Vendôme column in May 1871, which raised a cloud of dust that settled on the heads and shoulders of the onlookers and blanketed the square. It left the insurgents disappointed, troubled, realizing that for far too long they'd been obeying *that*. This is iconoclasm's political lesson: It exposes the vacuity of the fetish. Which is why political iconology brings with it the possibility of iconoclasm, what Bruno Latour calls "iconoclash," which is the ability to form an image of the destruction of images.

We need only open our eyes, said Michel Foucault. Open our eyes to what is eyeing us, the "wasp-eyed golden idols," such as the reliquary statue in the Abbey Church of Sainte-Foy in Conques, because the laity are invited to a *manducatio per visum* of the mysteries, an ingestion by sight. The raising of the sacramental host makes visible the real presence of Christ, according to the Eucharistic realism that the Gregorian power play imposed, insisting on that interpretation of the Eucharist precisely because it was hard to believe. Which is why, in the fourth lecture, I proposed giving the name "Eucharistic society" to the social form for which transubstantiation was a metaphor. This social system was a spatial system, structured according to a hierarchy of visibility, and the image that best catches this structure, arrests it visually, is the *Seven Sacraments Altarpiece* by the Flemish painter Rogier van der Weyden (see image on page 122). The central panel presents Christ crucified in the church, and the height of the cross raises the building's verticality. It is really Him, and it is really now: The women crying at the foot of the cross are contemporaries of the churchgoers, the very same people who would have been milling around inside the church.

The past and the present are on an equal footing. And if there's no before and no after, it's because time has been abolished, brought to a standstill: images immobilize. Behind the cross, a priest, seen from behind, celebrates Mass. This is the mystery of the Eucharist: He holds up bread that has been transformed into the body of Christ. On the left-hand panel are depictions of baptism, confirmation, and penitence; on the right-hand panel the ordination of a priest, marriage, and extreme unction – seven sacraments relating to a single faith, in the shadow of the cross. But this doesn't reflect a totalitarian takeover, a kind of medieval Big Brother. What's being depicted instead is the weakness of belief, which tests the soundness of the Christian community. And once again, fiction provides the test.

Communion of the Apostles by Justus of Ghent, 1472–1474 (Gallerie nazionale delle Marche)

In Urbino, this fiction was made visible, especially in the altarpiece for the Church of the Corpus Domini. The congregation was a lay confraternity whose statutes date back to 1351. It was sponsored by Pius II in the context of his projects for a crusade against the Turks after the capture of Constantinople, projects that ritually reactivated the cult of the Blessed Sacrament, calling for numerous Corpus Christi processions. In the 1460s and 1470s, the fever of the crusade myth expressed itself through a kind of Eucharistic panic, a transubstantiative fervor.

The scene of the altarpiece is unusual. Jesus is offering communion to the apostles. Duke Federico da Montefeltro (who supported the confraternity financially) is shown wearing a red cap, in conversation with the Jewish physician Isaac, unless he's talking to Caterino Zeno, the shah of Persia's ambassador to Urbino. The point is that the crusade was imminent, and that everyone would be brought into the Eucharistic society. The painting is attributed to the Flemish painter Justus of Ghent, whose real name was Joos van Wassenhove and whom Giorgio Vasari singles out in the prefix to his *Lives of the Most Excellent Painters, Sculptors, and Architects* as one of the pioneers of oil painting, pointing out that he "painted the panel of the communion of the Duke of Urbino." We get a good look at Montefeltro, but he seems more a bystander than a participant in the scene. The attribution to Justus of Ghent is undisputed, as we have the fraternity's records of payment to the painter between February 1473 and October 1474. These registers also tell us that Piero della Francesca turned down the commission after seeing the already completed predella—he was given compensation for his travel expenses on April 8, 1469.

What was the predella that so impressed Piero della Francesca that he refused the commission? It was the Urbino predella, painted in tempera on panel between 1467 and 1468, depicting the *Miracle of the Desecrated Host*. (See images on pages 146–9.) This work was also commissioned by the Corpus Domini confraternity. It has been heavily damaged, since masons in the Urbino palace apparently used it for years as a scaffold plank. The story unfolds over six panels, cinematically. A Christian woman, oppressed by poverty, offers her coat as collateral to a pawnbroker, who is clearly Jewish. When the loan comes due, the woman is unable to repay her debt. The lender offers to return her coat in exchange for a consecrated wafer. The poor woman accepts. That's what we see in the first scene, with the host clearly visible against the background of a dark book at the end of the counter. The Jew stabs the host, which starts to bleed. Guardsmen see a rivulet of blood issuing from the Jew's house, and they arrest the moneylender and his family. We see them in this second scene battering down the door while one of the children cries and the other presses into his mother's skirt. That's the second panel, which reduces the narrative to a single moment of suspended time.

In the third panel, a procession led by the pope, who wears a tiara, returns the host to the altar in a monstrance so that it may be reconsecrated after the sacrilege. The sinful woman is about to be hanged: The tree's branches have been cut, and a ladder has been placed against its trunk, but at the very moment when she is to die, an angel stays the executioner's hand. This is the fourth panel. No doubt it is concurrent with the fifth, where the Jewish moneylender and his family are burned on the public square, in front of soldiers carrying banners with the letters SPQR. In the last and final scene, two angels and two demons argue over the body of a woman, who is dressed in red and laid out on a catafalque. Presumably it is the sinful woman facing divine judgment. The angels stand by her head and seem about to carry her off, while the devils look ready to retire. The repentant sinner, it would seem, has had her prayers answered.

It was Pierre Francastel, in an article published in *Revue archéologique* in 1952, who first recognized the source for the Urbino predella in the Parisian Miracle des Billettes, which occurred in 1290 and was first recounted by Giovanni Villani: Jonathas, a Jewish pawnbroker, obtains a consecrated host in return for canceling a debt and tries to torture it in imitation of Christ's Passion: He stabs, lacerates, burns, and boils the host, which bleeds but proves indestructible. Such scenes have often been depicted, as in this sixteenth-century stained-glass window from the Church of Saint-Éloi in Rouen. But what happened in the Parisian tale? The opposite of the story Paolo Uccello depicts: the Christian woman in his story runs away and disappears; the Jewish woman in the Paris story converts to Christianity, baptizes her children and saves them; only the Jewish pawnbroker is burned at the stake. In the version from the Papal States, however, there

Miracle des Billettes stained-glass window
(Church of Saint-Éloi, Rouen)

was no forgiveness. All the Jews died, though the Christian woman was saved. But the Christian community emerged from the ordeal whole.

Francastel has also analyzed different formal properties of the Urbino predella: the partitioning of its sequences by columns; the pairing of opposite scenes, organized according to their differing vanishing points; the choreography of the golds, grays, and blues, dominated by the vivid reds; the melodic line of the hilltops against the sky, rising and falling as though each panel were in movement past the spectator, the whole punctuated and interrupted by vertical elements, giving the impression that the figures themselves are passing from one panel to another. This astonishing traveling-shot effect recalls the no less astonishing effects Uccello achieves in his *The Hunt in the Forest*. It perhaps mimics an actual movement, that of the decorated carts in the processions commemorating the miracle during the Feast of Corpus Christi. Francastel even saw it as "the transposition of mimed scenes." In any case, the miracle and the scenes from ordinary life are bathed in the same chromatic balance, dominated by scarlet, and partake of the same elegant choreography. Everything occurs as though the sacred had been reabsorbed into the ritual, making reality and miracle indistinguishable. This is very much the meaning of this work, which Francastel has described as "corporative."

Starting from the Parisian prototype of the Miracle des Billettes in 1290, it's possible to trace the invention of

Hunt in the Forest by Paolo Uccello, 1470 (Ashmolean Museum, Oxford)

a complete scenario that is amplified from one telling to another, and from one place to another: from Brussels in 1369 to Passau in 1477. In a book that is both profound and profuse, Jean-Louis Schefer analyzes this "Eucharistic theater, in which medieval Jews are used to illustrate a doctrine." Tales of their obstinate and repeated assaults on the sacrament caused Jews to be identified with deicide. Images were the end point, or point of resurgence, for a Christian antisemitism that had a long ancestry and a subterranean presence in the social imagination, one that occasionally manages to resurface. At the

end of the eighteenth century, in his *Tableau parisien,* Mercier again mentions the Billettes chapel (it is today the Protestant church on the rue des Archives), and we can trace antisemitism's course through literature from Shakespeare and the character of Shylock in *The Merchant of Venice,* to Honoré de Balzac's "The Atheist's Mass" and Anatole France's *At the Sign of the Reine Pédauque,* by way of *Dracula* by the Irishman Bram Stoker.

In fact the blood-drinking Carpathian monster derives from a line of fictional characters that extends from Gilles de

Rais (the model for Bluebeard) to the ogres in the fairy tales of Charles Perrault, who invariably express the pathology of power through killing and devouring children. Dracula is based on the legend of Vlad the Impaler, the ruler of Wallachia, a historical figure whom the king of Hungary enlisted in his struggle against the Ottoman Empire and who was beheaded in 1476—his head then being sent to the Turkish sultan. Stoker had access to this legend and others, starting from the overview by Augustin Calmet, *Treatise on Vampires and Revenants: The Phantom World: Dissertation on Those Persons Who Return to Earth Bodily*, published in 1751, at a time when the relationship between the House of Habsburg and the Ottoman Empire was once again a topic of concern, as were debates over the Eucharist. For the issue underlying the vampire legends, read as political fictions, is the powerful nexus between the imagination of contagion and the pathology of power as a disequilibrium in the substances of the soul and the body.

The general trend was toward a paroxysmal heightening of the theological fiction of the desecrated host. Still in the 1470s, we need only look at the images arising from the accusations of the ritual murder of Simon of Trent on Maundy Thursday in 1475. I'll summarize the story: The body of two-and-a-half-year-old Simon was found at the bottom of a well near the house of a Jew, Samuel of Nuremberg. Almost immediately, Jews were accused of the murder. The podestat Giovanni de Salis and Bishop Johannes Hinderbach brought a lawsuit against them. Under torture, the accused confessed their guilt and gave a detailed description of how they had committed infanticide, following a specific ritual. They needed to collect the child's blood for the unleavened bread that they would mix with wine to bless their seder feast. The trial was brief, the defendants were sentenced to death, and Simon was beatified.

We see him here, in this woodcut, published in Augsburg two years later, in 1477. Simon's image, as Andrea Martignoni has shown, includes all the attributes of the martyrdom of the Passion of Christ: the garrote, the pincers, the nails, the bowl to collect the blood. And Simon already wears the halo of the saint he will become. Suspended from a rack are a doll

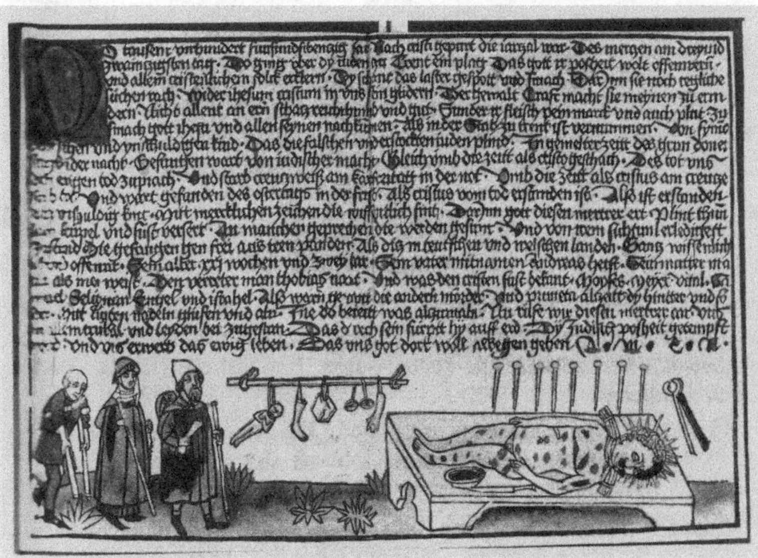

Simon of Trent and the Three Pilgrims
by Johannes Matthias Tuberinus, 1470

used for enchantments, a book (no doubt a collection of prescriptions for Jewish rituals), and a severed limb. We're back among the cannibals.

This heightening of the symbolic code also appears in another representation of the murder of Simon of Trent, engraved in Hartmann Schedel's *The Nuremberg Chronicle*, published in 1493. These images are excruciating, but you have to realize that they were flooding Europe at this time. Jews were exaggeratedly depicted: Their traits are an antisemitic caricature, they wear the yellow badge, and some wear a cornered or pointed cap, their names indicated by a label.

Simon of Trent, in Hartmann Schedel, *The Nuremberg Chronicle* (Nuremberg, 1493)

If we look back to the Jewish merchant depicted by Uccello, by contrast, there is nothing to crudely signal his identity according to the usual iconography of antisemitism. He wears Florentine dress, his headgear is in the current style, and he has no distinguishing characteristics — especially not the yellow badge, mandated in 1215 by the Fourth Council of the Lateran as a mark of shame at a time when society as a whole was going through a period of marking identities (a general time of badges, seals, and signatures). What identifies him as a Jew appears discreetly on the chimneypiece, where there are three coats of arms: a scorpion, clearly a mark of infamy; the head of a Moor on a shield, an allusion to the Crusades; and a seven-branched star.

These discreet heraldic devices in the Uccello predella create what Schefer calls "a kind of 'motion blurring' of likenesses, a flux of similitudes," that allows us to see the sacrilege. Note how the host is brandished like a badge, or like a seal on the book behind it. The Christian woman's gesture turns the pawnbroker's counter into a satanic inversion of a church altar, and her betrayal becomes an inverted elevation of the Host. But note also how the scene in which the Jewish family is put to death echoes the Passion of Christ, with each person wearing bloodred clothing that blurs their individual identities and bloodies them. The ritual profanation turns the Jew into a second Judas, since he subjects the host to torture and, according to the doctrine of the real presence, Christ's body as well. The deicidal Jew, having killed Christ in effigy and replayed the Passion in the Eucharistic key, is now in turn subjected to the agonies of the Passion.

The Eucharistic society cannot be described, therefore, as having been an all-encompassing and soothing fiction. It generated violence, and its first victims were Jews, but it would soon extend beyond the bounds of Christian antisemitism. In the last lecture, we tried to understand it by describing cannibal power as the devouring temptation to dominate. King Louis VII dreamed that he would have a son, Philip, who would offer his nobles a chalice from which to drink the blood of Christ. This episode of *The Deeds of Philip Augustus* by Rigord appears in a fourteenth-century manuscript of the *Grandes Chroniques de France* that clearly illustrates the incident as a royal Last Supper—I mentioned it without showing it, but here it is, from folio 223r of manuscript Fr 2813 in the Bibliothèque nationale de France. I cannot, on the other hand, show you the dream that contrasts with this one, in which, as Gerald

"The Dream of Louis VII" in *Grandes Chroniques de France* (Bibliothèque nationale de France, Département des Manuscrits, Français 2813, folio 223r)

of Wales described it, King William II devours a bloody stag. In this instance — to revisit the analysis made by Jacques Derrida in his seminar *The Beast and the Sovereign* on the passage in Niccolò Machiavelli's *The Prince* where the prince chooses to act like a beast, either a lion or a fox — the ruler acts like a "Last Supper beast," because what's at issue is a contrast between political devouring and ecclesiastical manducation.

But here again the symmetry doesn't hold up, and cannibalism as a monstrous inversion of the Eucharistic metaphor spills out beyond political theory to haunt every conception of power. At the time there was a perceived symmetry

Engraving depicting cannibalism, by Theodore de Bry, *Collected Travels in the East Indies and West Indies*, Hans Staden, 1594 (British Library)

between our ancient ancestors and savages, between the discovery of an anthropophagous New World and an undeniably savage Old World, which was witnessing the atrocities of that European civil war known as the Wars of Religion. Less than twenty years after Michel de Montaigne wrote "On Cannibals," the engravings produced by the de Bry family for its edition of *A Short Account of the Destruction of the Indies* by Bartolomé de Las Casas were used as an iconographic basis for the anti-Spain pamphlets of the Dutch rebels and served as models for denouncing the atrocities committed during the Wars of Religion.

Tracing the influential trajectory of Las Casas's work, which gave resounding expression to Europe's bad conscience, Roger Chartier has described the genealogy of the modern sense of unease, which consists in flattering oneself that one feels properly ashamed. I remind you that when Las Casas's book was originally published in Seville in 1552, it was intended to bear witness to the twin crises arising from Spanish colonialization: a crisis of legitimacy with respect to the Iberian government of the New World, and a crisis of conscience stemming from the conquerors' atrocities. Las Casas had gone to Chiapas as a bishop in 1543 and observed firsthand the destruction wrought by the encomienda system, which characterized Spanish colonization in the Americas after the Laws of Burgos were promulgated in 1512. It was a human and pastoral disaster, which would bring about the abandonment, depopulation, and desolation of the Indies.

Las Casas intended to provide a *relaçion* of this threat. His text would command authority because of its firsthand testimony and directly observed facts. But because it participated in an ongoing political debate and time was short, the relation was necessarily brief, even *brevissima*, as the original text termed it. Its purpose was to inform the crown that the encomenderos were "dishonoring God and stealing from the king" — these were the last words in the book. Las Casas unquestionably wrote in order to defend the massacred natives (he'd opposed Juan Ginés de Sepulveda at Valladolid on this score), but he also wanted to defend Spain — and here his text takes on a prophetic and apocalyptic tone: The destruction of the Indies would also be the destruction of Spain.

In the years 1578 to 1583, a translation of the *Short Account* into Dutch by the Flemish Protestant Jacques de Miggrode appeared, which was then translated into French and English. This brought the work into the context of the rebellions in the Protestant provinces of the Spanish Netherlands. The text hadn't changed, but its impact was entirely different. The purpose of the translation was stated on the title page: "To serve as an example and a warning to the XVII provinces of the Netherlands," followed by the couplet "Happy is he who develops wisdom / After seeing harm come to others."

The book's adaptation to its new purpose was fairly perfunctory, but the depth of the European crisis of conscience (which Jean-Frédéric Schaub has called "a high point in the consciousness of human abasement") can be measured from the Frankfurt edition of 1598, the first to be illustrated with the seventeen engravings produced by the dark talents of Theodore de Bry. Developed for another series entitled *Théâtre des cruautés des hérétiques de notre temps* (Theater of the cruelty of the heretics in our time), it presents the afflictions of the Indigenous people — who were flogged, humiliated, and tortured — in the iconography of the Massacre of the Innocents. The engravings would have a wide distribution independent of the book, and in the context of the increasing violence during the Wars of Religion would later serve to illustrate the French, English, and Dutch editions of Las Casas that I previously mentioned. They became the iconographic matrix for the ubiquity of barbarism.

We now come face-to-face with the monster in *Leviathan*, by Thomas Hobbes (see frontispiece on page iv). He looks at us, we look at him. We look at him today knowing that it's all bound up in this image and that it has been for a long time, everything, all our modernity. The Leviathan represents something like a triple change: in our political state, our moral state, and our legal state — a change of era, and a new social organization. Luc Foisneau has written about this in a wonderfully lively book, *Hobbes: La vie inquiète* (Hobbes: Anxious life). The anxiety referred to is not anguished, and the book's epigraph is this fine sentence from *Leviathan*: "We are to consider that the felicity of this life consisteth not in the repose of a mind satisfied." As Foisneau puts it, Hobbes "locates our happiness in the very anxiety of our desiring lives." Note that our anxiety is not such as to dissuade us from acting but, on the contrary, prompts us to find rules and motivations for action.

Yet how are we to act? There's no agreement on what constitutes a good life — no shared sense of what happiness is, or even of how life should be lived. Which is why we can no longer base political bonds on a natural inclination that would make us seek out the company of others. Men don't have a natural instinct leading them to assemble. Just the opposite, their passions divide and separate them one from another. Why, then, should we live in society, since we don't love each other? Politics can no longer be anchored in a Platonic idea of the good, nor can we reject the idea that morality enters into political action, as Machiavelli proposed. So what is one to do? Hobbes says: Agree on sovereignty and justice, obey the state and stand with it. For this great beast that watches over us is not, as in the pastoral version, a familiar animal that herds the flock while remaining outside it. It envelops us, aggregates us, organizes us, "For the reason of our Obedience, is not drawn from the will and command of our Pastors, but from our own benefit, as being the Salvation of our Souls they watch for."

This great beast is thus a monster, but is it a benign or an evil monster? Does it incorporate by devouring or by manducation? Is it the fulfillment of the Eucharistic society or a manifestation of cannibal power? We don't yet know, because we are face-to-face with the image — and confronted by the image, we have to ask ourselves the only question that matters, the question that Horst Bredekamp asks in his fundamental book *Leviathan: Body Politic as Visual Strategy in the Work of Thomas Hobbes*: Why does Hobbes need a visual image in order to think about the state? Why, after the Wars of Religion, is he unable to reimagine the state without a pictorial representation? The frontispiece provides a screen against which we read Hobbes's complex text. Gottfried Wilhelm Leibniz would characterize *Leviathan* as "a book as monstrous as its title indicates." The image is not just an illustration but inserts itself between reader and book, stopping us in our tracks; we are arrested by a visual event.

Its title is one thing, but its frontispiece? I'll get back to the authorship of the drawing on which the engraving is based, but one thing is certain: The specialists all agree that Hobbes was behind the frontispiece, that he inspired it, imagined it. And he is the only political theorist among his contemporaries who commissioned a frontispiece for his book. So what exactly is a frontispiece? The term comes from architecture: *frontispicium,* meaning *frontis hominis inspectio,* and referring to the main, or front, aspect of a building, illustrating its proportions and principal effects. Furetière, at the end of the seventeenth century, described it thus: "The face and main entry of a large building, presented frontally to the viewer." The frontispiece is therefore a book's facade, marking its access architecturally — as we see here in a 1531 edition of Galen's *On Anatomical Procedures.*

Frontispiece to Galen's *On Anatomical Procedures*, 1531

In passing from architecture to the book, the frontispiece (which, properly speaking, is a metaphor) assumes the meaning of a preface for Furetière, who describes it thus: "A notice placed at the head of a book to instruct the reader on the order and arrangement that has been followed, and what he must know to use and understand it readily." Louis Marin has observed that in the nineteenth century, *Le Littré*, the standard French dictionary, no longer defined "preface" as an advance notice of a book's composition (it is just "a preliminary discussion, placed at the start of a book") but those characteristics were in fact transferred to the frontispiece: "An engraving facing the title of a book, whose subject is analogous to the work's purpose and spirit."

Marin explored this analogy in his celebrated analysis of the frontispiece to the prose tales that Perrault dedicated to Mademoiselle, the niece of Louis XIV, in 1695. We find no imposing architecture here, just a chimneypiece, a nameless and ageless woman telling a story, a candle, and a cat that looks at us with baleful eyes. On the door, two plaques have been nailed. The larger names the anonymous storyteller as "Ma mère Loye," or Mother Goose; the smaller hides a cryptic name (the engraver's? the author's?), an inscribed name that remains illegible. This erasure is the work's signature, drawing our eye toward the keyhole, as in Perrault's *Donkeyskin*. It's the point of this frontispiece, according to Marin, which is to strip the tales of their author's name so that they become "fairy tales." Over time, the name "Charles Perrault" would itself become anonymized:

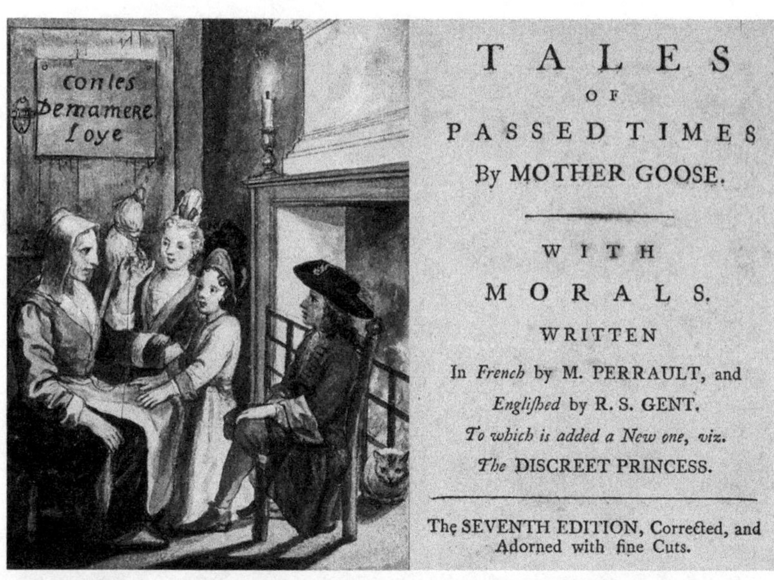

TALES
OF
PASSED TIMES
By MOTHER GOOSE.

WITH
MORALS.
WRITTEN
In *French* by M. PERRAULT, and
Englished by R. S. GENT.
To which is added a New one, viz.
The DISCREET PRINCESS.

The SEVENTH EDITION, Corrected, and
Adorned with fine Cuts.

Frontispiece to Charles Perrault's *The Tales of Mother Goose*, 1695

The tales would bear the vague predicate "Contes de Perrault," in which the proper name would no longer register.

But for our part, let's make the name Thomas Hobbes resonate a bit. He was born a twin to fear, he would later write, for his mother went into labor at the shock of hearing, in 1588, that the Spanish Armada was approaching, and he died at the age of ninety-one in 1679. He was first a humanist, attending a school in Malmesbury, Wiltshire, in southwest England, before arriving at Oxford in 1603. There he discovered geometry and developed an interest in physics, optics in particular. But his training was in literature and the classics, the *studia humanitatis*, and his first published work was a complete translation of Thucydides's *Eight Bookes of the Peloponnesian Warre.*

Frontispiece to Thucydides's *Eight Bookes of the Peloponnesian Warre*, translated by Thomas Hobbes, London, 1629

The edition included maps, one of them a large-scale foldout map of Greece, which Hobbes had drawn himself and labeled with all the place-names mentioned by Thucydides. He worked at the Hardwick library, where he found the resources he needed to develop the visual eloquence of his frontispieces: emblem books, as we've said, but also the first works to have complex emblematic frontispieces, like Francis Bacon's *The Advancement of Learning* and Robert Burton's *The Anatomy of Melancholy*. These truly have visual eloquence, in Quintilian's humanist sense: They have a hidden power to move and engage our minds.

Looking at the frontispiece of the Thucydides translation, we can see that it encourages both a vertical and a horizontal reading — but it's the confrontation between the two axes, embodied on the left by Archidamos, the king of Sparta, and on the right by Pericles, the leader of the Athenian democracy, with the two generals pictured as caryatids, facing off at the start of the book about their war, that gives structure to the whole. Sparta versus Athens: two urban landscapes, above, but also two ways of deliberating, below. Under the figure of Archidamos, the aristoi engage in active debate with their king; under the figure of Pericles, the citizens listen to a speech — or, in some cases, don't really listen. On the democratic side, we see passivity, and Quentin Skinner comments on the image using this quote from *The Elements of Law, Natural and Politic*, a subsequent work by Hobbes: "A democracy, in fact, is nothing more than an aristocracy of orators,

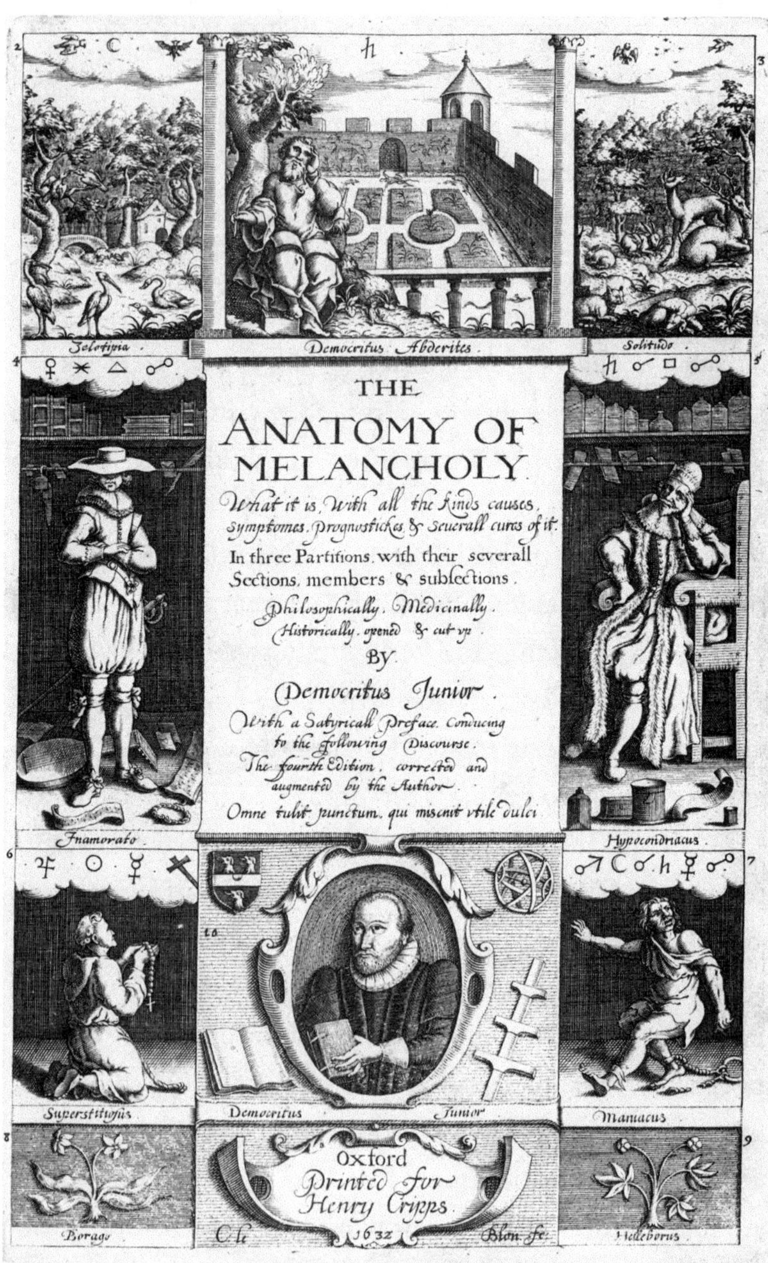

Frontispiece to Robert Burton's
The Anatomy of Melancholy, third edition, 1628

sometimes interrupted by the temporary monarchy of a single orator." Pericles's rule was just such a temporary monarchy. And we know how Hobbes, using a selective reading of Thucydides, makes Pericles's funeral oration into a defense of the "government of the principal man," the man who dominates in a democracy.

Here, the orator is a dictator, a dictator in the fullest sense of the word: Someone who allows himself to be dictated to by the crowd that he in turn subjugates, excites, and flatters. This implies a criticism of eloquence, a criticism of the voluntary bond. (See image on page 176.) Which brings us back to the *Emblemata*, because if there are chains linking the tongue of the eloquent speaker to the ears of the obedient hearers, who is holding whom? Which is the slave and which the master in a dictatorship? To understand Hobbes, we have to place him in the context of the arguments he is opposing—this is Skinner's method of conducting a history of ideas, which doesn't look at general theories but reconstructs problems, polemics, and conflicts. We need to historicize Hobbes's thought by noting that after England erupted into civil war in 1642, he attempted to rehabilitate absolute monarchy. But we also need to understand the adversary he took on: the republicanism of the Romans, as it had been reactivated by the Italian city-states in the humanist era, and as it was depicted in Ambrogio Lorenzetti's *Allegory of Good Government*. This voluntary bond, this cord linking free citizens to a virtuous government, defined what freedom meant to the Romans—and subsequently to

Detail from *Allegory of Good Government* by Ambrogio Lorenzetti, 1338 (Palazzo Pubblico, Siena)

the Italian city-states. In Roman law, what strips a man of his freedom is his subjection to an arbitrary power. When a master is introduced, a free man becomes a slave. But what Hobbes made a point of showing is that freedom can be lost or taken away even in the absence of arbitrariness if we don't desire our freedom and don't practice it. If, however, we pursue our own desires — which is why it's all a question of desiring bodies — then we may remain free even while obeying the state.

This is the idea that the frontispiece of Hobbes's *On the Citizen* makes visible. Hobbes had left London in 1640 for Paris, where he would remain in exile for eleven years. His treatise *On the Citizen* sets out to make ecclesiastical government a bulwark against civil war. There exists a manuscript on parchment dated 1641 that includes a drawing of the frontispiece, shown here as it appeared in the 1642 edition — there were others as well, and Bredekamp has studied their iconographic variability. This one has the name of the engraver, *Math*[*eus*] *f*[*ecit*], referring to the Parisian artist Jean Matheus. Yet the author's name appears only as a set of initials: T.H.

The three fields of the frontispiece illustrate the three sections of the book: heaven and hell as the realm of *Religio,* peace as the prerogative of *Imperium,* and war as the state of *Libertas.* The upper register is partitioned off by a transverse beam, and Christ himself, above, separates the chosen from the damned. Note that material bodies are resuscitated, not souls. In the lower section *Imperium,* or government, has all the attributes of sovereignty — the scale and the sword, which is pointed upward and draws its authority from God, promising us paradise. *Libertas,* however, is embodied by an American Indian, scowling, whose arrow points downward, to hell on earth. Liberty promises us hell on earth. Because liberty is the state of nature in which man is a wolf to man, where "any person may rob and kill another." There are Indians hunting, but what is their prey? It's a manhunt. And on the edge of the image, a gruesome meal is underway: Two cannibals are cooking the remains of a butchered human.

We're back with the anthropophagi. And the reversibility of political fictions. Hobbes has adopted the visual formulae

Frontispiece of Hobbes's *On the Citizen*, Paris, 1642

Algonquin chiefs by Theodore de Bry, in Thomas Hariot's
A Briefe and True Report of the New Found Land of Virginia, 1590

used by de Bry for his idyllic images of the Algonquin chiefs in *A Briefe and True Report of the New Found Land of Virginia* by Thomas Hariot. The bodies are beautiful, powerful, peaceful; their nature may be savage, but they are pacific and free. Hobbes writes counter to this European dream, a dream that was the inverse of the nightmare Europeans were living, having becoming the barbarians of the world. See how, in this magnificent book by Hariot—wherein the noble savage is invented—the Indians choreograph a magnificent scene, the very inverse of what the Europeans were inflicting on them at the same moment.

The frontispiece of *On the Citizen* is a threshold, but it opens through a curtain that is attached to the transverse

Native men and women dancing around a circle, by Theodore de Bry, 1590

Europeans at war with native men, by Theodore de Bry, 1590

beam and bears the name of the work, explicated by a verse from Proverbs 8:15: "By me kings reign, and princes decree justice." Note how the words are curved, because the curtain is filled out by the wind. But what's behind it? There's something hidden. It's an arcanum, a profound secret.

What the frontispiece shows, this monument providing an entry to the book—and this is even more true of the frontispiece to *Leviathan,* compartmentalized and architectural in structure with its wooden frames, but whose center remains thoroughly veiled—is an arcanum. The image is a hidden door. It veils or screens off as much as it reveals. The reader has only to enter in order to see what there is to see. In *Leviathan,* the curtain shows that there's something hidden, the curtain makes visible the fact that not everything is in view. It's a theater, but a Baroque theater, where the curtain drops from above when the performance starts. It hasn't yet dropped, and the performance is set for the next lecture.

LECTURE 7, FEBRUARY 28, 2017

Confronting the Leviathan, II: None Knows What a Body Politic May Do

Writing *sub rosa*: Spinoza's wax seal — In praise of readings that draw blood, that "remove the petals and prune away the leaves, so as to expose the thorns" (Jean-Claude Millner) — *Leviathan*'s frontispiece as an image of sovereign power that "visibly absorbs more than it challenges the recent revolutionary changes" (Quentin Skinner) — The *mortal god* of the image, the republic's head, not its soul — The Leviathan as a sea monster and the commonwealth's maritime empire — The dizzying effect of detail, the headiness of sharp definition — The hand-drawn prototype of the engraving — Politics as the art of bringing things near or removing them to a distance — Decapitation of the body politic: When the general loses his head, "the group vanishes into dust, like a Bologna flask with its top broken off" (Sigmund Freud)

AN OPEN, FIVE-PETALED ROSE, a stem with long spines, the initials B.D.S., and at the bottom the motto *caute*. This is the wax seal Spinoza closed his letters with. The art of the emblem, like the art of the motto, intends to pose an enigma. It does so through concision and ellipsis. The enigma's interpretation is only seemingly simple. The philosopher has a spiny name, with the initials B.D.S.: Benedictus de Spinoza. He writes sub rosa, "under the rose," that is, in strict confidence — a meaning that has had currency since the Middle Ages. Hence the Latin motto *caute*, an adverb meaning "cautiously," modifying an implied action verb. We could take it as "I write cautiously" or "I act with caution." *Caute* has given us the pejorative French word *cauteleux*. To be *cauteleux* is to act with a mixture of caution and cunning. But cunning can take different forms — nothing says a wise man can't be cunning too.

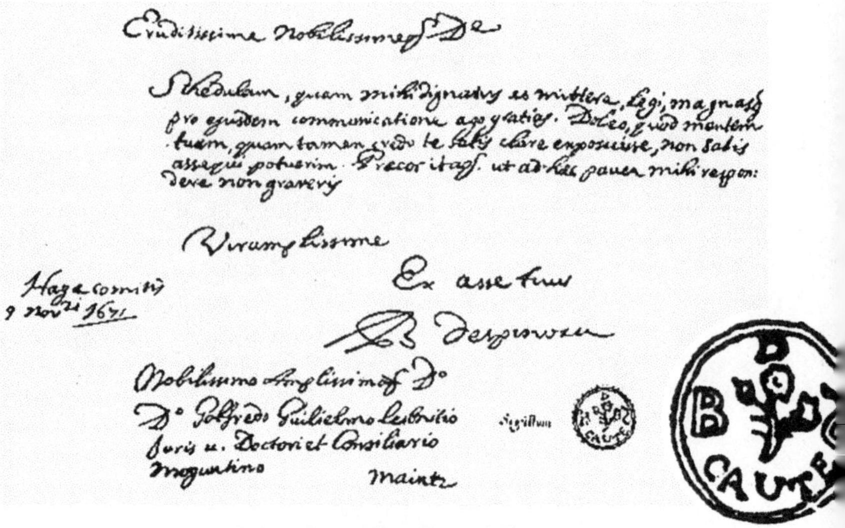

Eruditissime Nobilissimeque De

Schedulam, quam mihi dignatus es mittere, legi, magnasque pro ejusdem communicatione ago gratias. Doleo, quod mentem tuam, quam tamen credo te satis clare exposuisse, non satis assequi potuerim. Precor itaque ut ad haec pauca mihi respondere non graveris

Vir amplissime

Ex asse tuus

B. despinoza

Hagae comitis
9 nov.is 1671

Nobilissimo Amplissimoque Do
Do Gotfredo Guilielmo Leibnitio
Juris u. Doctori et Consiliario
Moguntino

Maintz

Spinoza's seal [inset] on a letter

Jean-Claude Milner, however, is not cautious. In his book *Le sage trompeur: Libres raisonnements sur Spinoza et les Juifs,* he proposes a difficult interpretation of the emblem, starting from the principle that mottos are not elliptic but brachylogic. A grammarian, Milner distinguishes simple ellipsis from brachylogy, where the motto seems concise because it has been truncated. A word is missing. It has to be restored for the motto to be understood.

Let's take, for example, the motto of the United States as it has appeared on its seal since 1782: *E pluribus unum.* Literally: "From many, one." The verb is missing, but the syntactic relation can supply it. In context, it becomes something along the lines of: "Out of plurality, unity arises." Let's note in passing that a similar embodiment occurs in the image that interests us, the Leviathan, and let's also note that the populist phrase "and giving it back to you, the people" triggers the dissolution of this embodiment: From many into one, and I'm going to give this *one* back to you, the people. But who is this people? Is it the multitude or is it the body politic? An act of dissolution, at the very moment of an inauguration, which is just a little dizzying. Hence the Spinozistic title of this lecture. Milner writes as a grammarian, but he also writes as a philosopher: His interpretive method supports what he calls an "ethics of impropriety," which is to say that he defends and illustrates readings that are difficult, thorny, wounding.

And so we need to relate *caute* to an actual quotation that it truncates. The most common comes from Baldassare Castiglione's *Book of the Courtier*, where it appears in the form of a proverb: *Si non caste, tamen caute* — "If not chastely, then cautiously." Initially, it may have alluded to priestly celibacy: "If you be not chaste, at least be cautious." Spinoza's correspondents would have been able to extrapolate the intended meaning. He invites them, seemingly, to take part in a form of indecency. In other words, the motto functions as a warning, but it doesn't so much advise one to be cautious as to cautiously hide one's impropriety. And this within a chosen circle of the learned and like-minded. Spinoza had no qualms about infringing on ordinary propriety, that is, "undermining what the generality of men hold worthy of respect."

In interpreting the rose emblem, one therefore has to distinguish between the petals and the thorns. One must read

Spinoza the spiny in just the way one would pick a rose, carefully, without pricking one's fingers on the thorns. That's if you believe a rose's thorns are there to protect the petals. But what if it's the opposite? What if the truth is in the thorns, not in the petals? In that case, contrary to general opinion, it's the flower whose delicate beauty protects the spiny stem. This is how to make sense of sub rosa: Read me under the rose, and you expose yourself to being scratched, to participating in the *non caute* or incaution that is the final goal of all reading. What protects the thorns is thus the softness of the petals, and like a transgressive gardener Milner sets about "plucking the petals and pruning away the leaves to expose the thorns."

We will try to do the same to arrive at the truth that wounds — the truth promised to us by the monster (see frontispiece on page iv), which we have to imagine. How shall we do this? By starting from the principle that when you can't bring yourself to speak a hurtful truth yet don't want to remain silent, the only solution (as Leo Strauss said) is to make the truth pass for a lie. Is that what political fiction is? Yes, it is doubtless also that. The Leviathan is monstrous, indecent, incomprehensible, incoherent, contradictory, whatever. It's like the state in Nietzsche's eyes, "the coldest of all cold monsters." But it has the impassive face of a truth that wounds and, in order not to appear too improper, presents itself as a falsehood. That is exactly what political fiction does.

In his autobiography, which he wrote in Latin couplets in 1672, Thomas Hobbes describes his encounter with the French polymath Marin Mersenne and his discovery of the natural sciences as a tipping point in his intellectual career. Following that, he wrote, *Nam philosophandi / Corpus Homo Civis continet omne genus* (All philosophy consists of three elements: the body, man, and the citizen). Hobbes wrote *Leviathan* in 1641, and its frontispiece is very much an act of imaging, meant to institute the political philosophy he wants to set forth. This is what we tried to understand in the last lecture: what a visual event can be, and why thought must come to a standstill in a figural, spectral, and perhaps theatrical way — and that's the point we had reached, staring at the curtain before the start of a Baroque performance, waiting for the curtain to drop.

We'd come to that point, face-to-face with the Leviathan, with a visual event that is also an agglomeration of many pairs of eyes: power, offering itself to view. And that's why we have an appointment today with all those who've looked at this image, many with imposing names: Horst Bredekamp, Giorgio Agamben, Carlo Ginzburg, Quentin Skinner. We particularly followed in Skinner's footsteps, trying to understand Hobbes by reconstructing what he was arguing against, namely the Roman and neo-Roman concept of freedom. It was neo-Roman insofar as it expressed itself in the visual eloquence of the Italian communes — we think of the *Allegory of Good Government* in Siena, of course, but also of all the things that Niccolò Machiavelli saw and made visible.

Countering this, Hobbes asserts that we are not free simply because we live in a free state; we're free when we exercise our freedom. Conversely, the subjects of an absolute ruler are just as entitled as those living in a democracy to believe that they possess freedom, again provided they make use of it. As he writes in *Leviathan*: "There is written on the turrets of the city of Lucca in great characters at this day the word LIBERTAS, yet no man can thence infer that a particular man has more liberty or immunity from the service of the commonwealth there than in Constantinople." For an Englishman in the seventeenth century, the contrast couldn't be greater between the very model of the obstinately resistant republican form of government — that model was by then no longer Venice or Siena, but Lucca — and the temptation of Oriental despotism, frighteningly and seductively embodied in the Ottoman sultan, the great other — frightening because seductive, or possibly vice versa.

Is he terrifying or protective, this big animal who, unlike the watchdogs of a pastoral society, does not gather us together but incorporates us? Will he just herd us together or will he devour us? We don't know. Hobbes says about his treatise that he wrote it "without other design than to set before men's eyes the mutual relation between protection and obedience." He also writes in his dedication that he does not take an interest in men but in the seat of power. He doesn't write to console or to prevent. He writes to provoke. To understand him, again by contrast, let us look at another image.

The frontispiece of the *Eikon Basilike* is the best known of the images depicting King Charles I as a royal martyr.

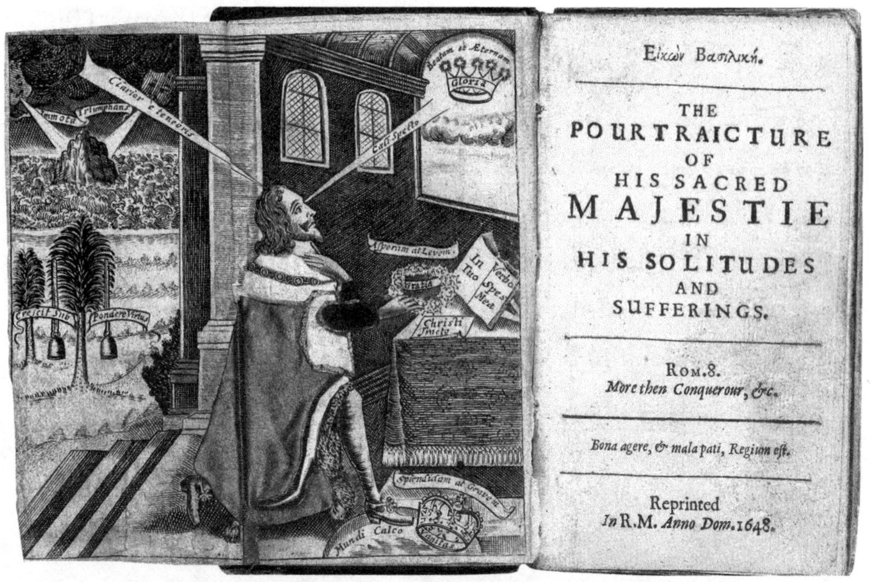

Εἰκὼν Βασιλική.

THE
POURTRAICTURE
OF
HIS SACRED
MAJESTIE
IN
HIS SOLITUDES
AND
SUFFERINGS.

ROM.8.
More then Conquerour, &c.

Bona agere, & mala pati, Regium est.

Reprinted
In R.M. *Anno Dom.*1648.

Frontispiece of *Eikon Basilike*, engraved by William Marshall, 1649

When Hobbes moved from England to France in 1640, this was the eventuality he was fleeing, specifically the attacks on absolute monarchy that would result in Charles's beheading. The first edition of the *Eikon Basilike,* published in February 1649 — whose composition must therefore predate the tragedy, from the royalists' perspective, as the king was beheaded in January 1649 — purports to be a work by the king himself. In fact it was composed by the chaplain John Gauden, the future chaplain of Charles II. Its frontispiece, engraved by William Marshall, shows the king kneeling before an open book that reads: "In your word, I place my hope." Charles has removed his crown of kingship, which bears the word "vanity," and grasps the crown of thorns. He holds it in his hands, allowing him to gaze on the crown of celestial glory. Which is why he still wears all the insignia of royalty. He is dead, but he triumphs — he is Christ. He hasn't stripped himself, as dramatized in the scene by Shakespeare. His kingship derives from the unfailing solidity of his moral virtues. He resembles a storm-battered rock, facing the rage of the people, *immota triumphans,* imperturbable triumph. His strength comes from God, the power to shine forth in the darkness that he's been cast into. All this he owes to his moral qualities.

By contrast with this image, we can characterize the frontispiece of *Leviathan,* in Quentin Skinner's words, as "a representation of sovereign power that visibly adopts far more than it rejects the recent revolutionary changes." By becoming subjects of the state, by submitting their many individual wills to its one will, the citizens have made obedience the glue that binds a fictional person called the body politic. Hobbes calls this artificial man the "commonwealth," or "state," in which the "sovereignty is an artificial soul." We are part of it, but not in the same way that we are present in the world. For there are in fact two different worlds in which we live simultaneously: the natural and the artificial. The first is made up of bodies in motion, governed by the laws of nature; the second of a single unmoving body that we have ourselves created to regulate our relations with others. It is the sum of our pacts and covenants.

But how does the incorporation occur? In chapters 16 and 17 of *Leviathan*, Hobbes describes the agreement that the individuals in a multitude make to authorize one person to act in their name. This representative of the words and actions of others is termed an artificial person. I myself won't be present, but my artificial representative will. The act of authorizing a sovereign representative, however, brings about a transformation: "A multitude of men are made *one* person when they are by one man or one person represented." This brings us back to the Scholastics' question about the Eucharistic society: Even if you believe in it, you have to understand how it comes about, how it's possible to think it. The unity created by a political covenant is not a real person but an artificial one. Hobbes calls it the commonwealth, relating it to the Latin *civitas*, which he equates with the state. Fictive or not, Hobbes gives it a name: "This is the generation of that great LEVIATHAN (or rather, to speak more reverently, of that *mortal god*) to which we owe, under the *immortal God*, our peace and defense." It's very rare for him to name this entity—he does so only a few times in the whole work. But we are very much before a stage curtain that says "Leviathan," referring to a biblical monster, the title of a book, and the artificial person of the state. For the sovereign is the soul of the commonwealth, its anima. He inhabits it, unifies it, animates it.

We can see that as rich and powerful as the image of the frontispiece is, it doesn't make all of Hobbes's philosophy visible: The sovereign doesn't figure as the soul of the state but as its head, in keeping with the common medieval trope. The head of the sovereign grows out of the body of the people, out of the covenants his subjects have made between themselves. This head is not in contact with heaven, nor does it reflect unusual virtues; this crowned head diverges in every way from the one in the *Eikon Basilike*, which belonged to a sovereign in defeat. The Leviathan is nothing but his own triumph and the apparition of his triumph, that is, a power unlike any other and toward which all eyes are directed. But a head is fragile, as we'll see, and can topple. And heads have already fallen in England more than once. What happens then to the body politic?

And why is this power beyond all common measure, as Job 41:33 proclaims: "Upon earth there is not his like"? It's because this unifying, pacifying power brings together civil and ecclesiastic authority, holding the sword in its right hand and the crozier in its left — reversing the usual medieval depiction, by the way. The Leviathan is the judge of all matters that its sword can slice through, in both the spiritual and the temporal realms of law. He towers over all the forces of destruction pictured in the two sets of five emblematic vignettes, which need to be read horizontally to compare their effects and vertically to measure the accumulation of their destructive powers.

In interpreting the emblems, the easy part is working our way down, comparing the fortress to the church, the crown to the miter, the cannon to lightning. This last is the *fulmen excommunicationis,* the papacy's weapon of mass destruction. And on what are these conceits based? On armaments (crossed swords, muskets, pikes, flags, drums), pictured on the lower left of the frontispiece as trophies, expressing not just military might but also the ability to mobilize; and on an arsenal of words, pictured on the lower right as forked arguments (on the three-pronged fork at left is written *Syl/logis/me,* on the two-pronged fork in the middle *Spiritual/Temporal,* on the leaning fork *Direct/Indirect,* on the two-pronged fork on the right *Real/Intentional,* and on the horns below them *Di/lem/ma*). As to the two vignettes at the bottom, they show scenes of fighting: a battlefield on the left, and on the right a session of Scholastic *disputatio*. It takes place in the closed environment of the university *quaestio*. As the learned doctors look on, the champions of the two camps face off, one offering his open palms indicative of rhetoric, the other opening a book.

Leviathan argues on two levels, as did *On the Citizen,* which was discussed in the previous lecture. But it does so architecturally, and after looking at Hobbes's translation of Thucydides we came to understand that the frontispiece was the book's facade.

The lower half of the *Leviathan* frontispiece is set off by a wooden rod and subdivided into two lateral columns. Everything is organized and hierarchic, like the spaces of a wall cabinet; this one is divided into a triptych with the central panel veiled. What we have here is not just the Baroque-era theater game of dissimulation, of withholding the hidden part, but an instance of the arcane, in the sacred sense of the term — an arcanum game, not an arcade game. There is the suggestion, as with a triptych altarpiece, that the panels are opened on special days. Here, the word "Leviathan" is at once the book's title, the monster's name, and the name of the image.

The upper register is something akin to an apparition. While everything on the bottom register is structured, even complexly structured, the upper portion is a borderless, painted panel. Again, like an altarpiece panel, it refers back to the emblems in the lower register (there is, in fact, a military sector on the lower left of the top portion, and a civil sector in its center). This colossus is so terrifying that, as we read in the Book of Job: "Terror danceth before him."

The colossus seems to rise like the sun above the horizon line, or he's an automaton hoisted by some theater mechanism. Either way, an apparition. What appears is just his torso and the upper part of his body. If we try to reconstruct his full body according to the proportions of Leonardo da Vinci's *Vitruvian Man*, as Reinhard Brandt has done, his feet would rest on Hobbes's name in the lower section. But he doesn't rest, he floats — no doubt because the biblical Leviathan is a marine animal and we should imagine the sea lying beyond the hilly landscape. What we have then is a sort of whale or gigantic fish whose scales are made of his obedient subjects. If that's true, Behemoth and Leviathan stand in opposition to each other as do earth and sea — and the commonwealth in question is none other than England, a maritime power, something that Carl Schmitt, a formidable commentator of Hobbes, has discussed at length.

The engraving itself, when one has a chance to examine it up close, to scrutinize it in the original edition, induces a dizzying sense of detail, a heady sharpness of definition that no reproduction can approach. To give some idea of the scale, consider that the beast's right hand is twelve millimeters across, and that two separate faces are visible at the base of the thumb. The majority of the figures are less than a millimeter in height. Bredekamp, in his capacity as an art historian, has described the line of descent of the "brothers of the Leviathan," the different versions of the frontispiece that have appeared since 1652, owing to translations (into Dutch in 1672) and new editions (a second English edition in 1670). What is visible is the gradual erasure of the figures as the plates become more and more used, until a new engraving of the frontispiece was undertaken in 1750, resulting in a new lineage of posthumous descendants, made fresher but more metallic.

I will pass entirely on discussing attribution. Ever since the late nineteenth century, the designer and engraver Wenceslaus Hollar has been considered the author of the frontispiece on the basis of biographical convergences and stylistic traits. Originally from Bohemia, he moved to Paris and traveled in the same circles as Hobbes. Bredekamp has questioned the traditional attribution on stylistic and

Frontispiece to the 1750 edition of Thomas Hobbes's *Leviathan*

Ink drawing by Abraham Bosse in manuscript of *Leviathan* presented by Hobbes to King Charles II

technical grounds, having tracked down the sources of the pictorial motifs and examined the drawing on parchment. There is a unique first version of the Leviathan in the Egerton manuscript at the British Library, which is on parchment and intended for King Charles II — Hobbes having offered the king a presentation copy of his book in manuscript. The frontispiece was drawn in ink. It appears to be the prototype for the engraved image, give or take a few details.

Bredekamp offers a different hypothesis. He points to an artist who, like Hollar, could have collaborated with Hobbes given his biographical details but whose name is much better known: Abraham Bosse. A student of Jacques Callot's,

Bosse was one of the foremost engravers of his day. Says Bredekamp: "Given the Leviathan's detail and delicacy, an alternative attribution to the Parisian artist Abraham Bosse assumes particular importance."

The attribution of an anonymous artwork is an act of social magic that requires a certain patronymic logic: the name of a great artist, and the name of a great art historian. I won't take sides on the subject, beyond expressing a polite skepticism at the speed with which the academic community has accepted this reattribution. (None of the arguments Bredekamp advances strike me as justifying the "certainty" he speaks of a few pages after proposing Bosse's name.) But the reattribution does have the virtue of dramatizing the image: Bosse was a Calvinist, engaged in the intellectual, artistic, and political project of geometrizing the world, a project that ran afoul of the principles of the Académie Royale de Peinture et de Sculpture in Paris. Imagining the encounter of this domestic exile with the English exile Hobbes casts the episode in heightened relief. The major interest I can see in this possible reattribution is in suggesting a relation between the frontispiece of *Leviathan* and the engraving Bosse made in 1650 called *Melancholia*.

In the engraving, we see a man aping a monkey. He is plunged in his dark thoughts and holds the same pose, ironically, as the lecherous animal seated on the table where he rests his elbow to support his crowned head. Is this Charles II, who faced accusations of licentiousness? It's at any rate a

Melancholia, etching by Abraham Bosse, c. 1650

capricious king, whose mantle features images of women's heads, all of them looking curiously outward — this "flip side of the coin" helps us notice what's missing in the body of the Leviathan: There are no women or children, only men.

Let's go back, then, to comparing the engraved Leviathan with its sketched prototype. Two crucial differences: The first is that the face of the sovereign in the ink drawing is more clearly a portrait of Charles II, whereas in the published version it is more nearly an emblem; the second, which is more significant still, is that the myriad men in the drawing who make up the king's body face in the same direction as the king. In point of fact, they look out at the reader. But who is the reader? A very particular person: King Charles II, as he looks at the book. In both the drawing and the engraving, therefore, the subjects direct their gaze toward the sovereign: either toward his actual body, when he is physically present and looking at the book, or toward his mystical body, his pictorial representation.

This body politic, then, is nothing more than that: the aggregated obedience of individual men, the agglutination of their frightened loneliness, the gathering together of the fear that the colossus inspires. What is the consistency of the fear this cold monster inspires? Ginzburg has studied this political emotion in a recent analysis of the frontispiece of Hobbes's *Leviathan,* which depicts the nightmare of the devouring of individuals by the cold monster of the state. "I was born a twin to fear," Hobbes wrote in his verse autobiography — for, you'll remember, his mother gave birth to him just as the Spanish fleet was threatening to land on the coast of England. It was the fear of persecution that drove Hobbes to flee in November 1640, after the manuscript of his *Elements of Law* began to circulate clandestinely in an incomplete version. Written in May 1640, it glorified monarchical power. Hobbes, adopting Euclid's approach, tried to set forth the rules of political action, at a time when the most pressing need was to maintain civil peace. Everything else had to be subordinated to that effort, since Europe was in the throes of the Wars of Religion, and the question of the legitimacy of a state based on a covenant of mutual fear was under intense debate. The question was anything but theoretical: What is the value of a covenant arrived at under constraint—for instance, the fear of religious persecution? What mutual fear allows us to join together?

Ginzburg's interpretation fleshes out the expression "to fill with fear." What we're being shown in the famous frontispiece is an instance of filling: "Leviathan, an artificial creation, stands against those who, through their covenant, *created* it, as an awesome and threatening object."

Thucydides's description of the plague that struck Athens in 429 is justly famous. It paints a picture of customs disrupted and the normal world upended: "People looked for quick profits and pleasures, as life and riches were equally ephemeral." This passage has colored our understanding of the Black Plague, particularly as Giovanni Boccaccio returned to it in his *Decameron,* offering us a picture of what he'd read rather than seen. In fact, the plague of 1347 did not provoke the anomia that Thucydides described, the suspension of the regulating power of norms. Recent archaeological findings, notably in London's cemeteries, have shown that populations almost never give in to panic when it comes to observing funerary customs.

Francesca Falk has noted that the two figures standing nearest the cathedral in the *Leviathan* frontispiece wear the beaked mask characteristic of doctors specializing in the plague. This town has been struck by the plague. The question arises, has it fallen into a state of lawlessness? The multitude is like a diseased population in need of care — and susceptible to what Michel Foucault called biopower. But for the very reason that it's a population and not a people.

Translating Thucydides's description of the anomia that arrived in Athens with the plague in 429, Hobbes uses the verb "to awe": "Neither the fear of the gods, nor laws of men, awed any man." The word is used to designate what is terrible (awful) and what inspires respect (awesome). Thus it expresses the essentially political nature of fear, different from the theologians' *timor Dei.* It corresponds to the Latin *vereor,* which can be translated sometimes by "terror," sometimes by "reverence."

The dissolution of the body politic, the political void we call anomie, was believed by Thucydides to occur when *phobos,* or the fear of the gods, stopped being felt: "Neither the fear of the gods, nor laws of men, awed any man." But what is at play here is not the fear of the gods, it is political fear, *vereor*, meaning both a sacred terror and reverence. Ginzburg begins his 2009 essay "Fear Reverence Terror: Reading Hobbes Today" with these words: "I will speak about terror, not about terror*ism*. I am convinced that a word like 'terrorism' does not help us understand the murderous deeds it usually refers to." Yet he comes back to it at the very end of the article, citing the bombing of Baghdad in 2003, pointing out that the US military operation was code-named Shock and Awe. The stupor created by shock is undoubtedly a sacred terror — the same as that inspired by the monstrous animals in the Book of Job: Behemoth and Leviathan. This is the *emati* of the Hebrews, as it appears in Exodus 23:27: "I will send my fear before thee, and will destroy all the people to whom thou shalt come, and I will make all thy enemies turn their backs unto thee."

Mutual fear being the glue that binds the state together, the sovereign has the obligation to name the danger that threatens. For fear on its own creates no commonality: Men may agree that they feel fear and disagree as to the danger facing them. Hence Hobbes writes in *Leviathan*: "For being distracted in opinions concerning the best use and application of their strength, they do not help but hinder one another, and reduce their strength by mutual opposition to nothing."

What does the sovereign do? He rallies the strength of all by designating an enemy. And that enemy is not necessarily tangible. In an empire, the whole world is a danger to those who live in the capital — they do not feel threatened precisely because they live in opulence. The work of politics consists in making distant danger visible, bringing it close at hand. Hobbes uses an optical metaphor: "For all men are by nature provided of notable multiplying glasses — that is, their passions and self-love — through which every little payment appears a great grievance, but are destitute of those prospective glasses — namely moral and civil science — to see afar off the miseries that hang over them and cannot without such payments be avoided."

Politics is the art of bringing things near or pushing them away. Its business is with optics and point of view, and everything depends on whether one is looking through a magnifying glass or a telescope. (Do we not talk about seeing through the wrong end of the telescope?) This politicization of optical instruments, imposing the viewpoint of an armed gaze, has been highlighted by the foundational works of Noel Malcolm. He stresses Hobbes's interest in perspectival distortion. The "prospective glasses" that Hobbes mentions in *Leviathan* allude to the then recent optical inventions in anamorphosis published by Jean-François Niceron in *La perspective curieuse.* The experiment uses an optical device with a multifaceted lens, cut in a complex way. If the device is directed toward a specific point in an image, diffracting several figures on rhomboidal or trapezoidal surfaces, another image is formed at the center from the curved or straight fragments of the deformed

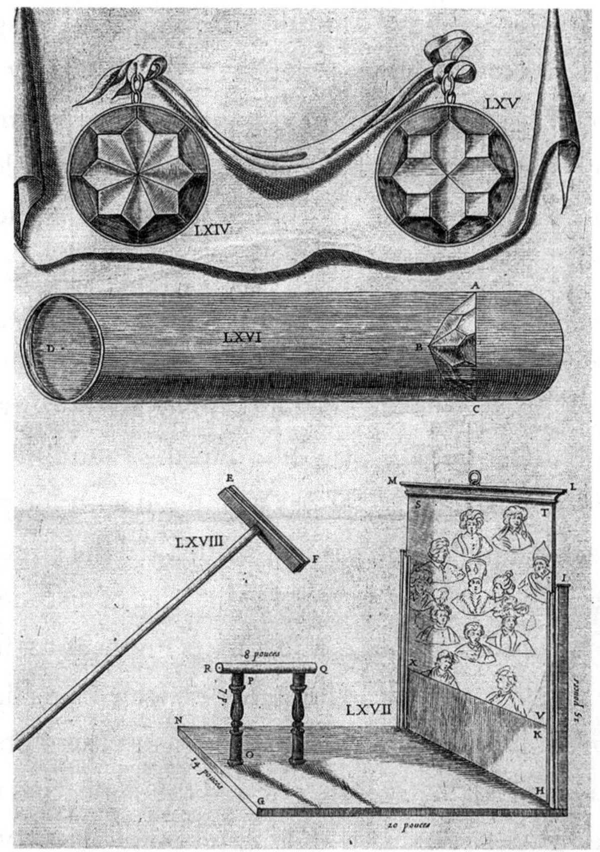

Diagram of optical experiment by Jean-François Niceron
in *La perspective curieuse*, 1638

surface. The amusement, politically, is that all these characters are more or less wearing turbans and therefore more or less Turks, yet with the fragments of their figures one creates the illusion of an idealized Western sovereign. The ideality of the ruler being perhaps nothing more than an optical illusion.

The interest in optical distortion was primarily of scientific import. In a foundational book on the rebirth of scientific studies, Steven Shapin and Simon Schaffer put a spotlight on the social history of the emergence of the laboratory in the 1650s. Serving as a place for the recognition and legitimation of experimental science, this social institution paralleled the spread of coffeehouses in the public sphere. The scientific controversy between Robert Boyle — who was using an air pump to conduct experiments on the effect of atmospheric pressure — and Hobbes was about the history of truth as a product of the forms of social life. Boyle was a convinced experimentalist (which would lead to the founding of the Royal Society in 1660); Hobbes countered with the principles of natural philosophy. Boyle challenged the concept of the vacuum, while Hobbes rejected the idea of disorder. The dispute was political, but not just in its implication for the relationship to royal power. For Hobbes, who overestimated the importance of his physical discoveries, natural philosophy and political theory were one and the same: that which has no body does not exist, and to prevent civil war one has to eliminate the vacuum.

This is very much what the frontispiece of *Leviathan* shows: an instance of political infilling against the pitfall of civil war, of a monstrous nature that dominates with its abhorrence of a vacuum. But the fact that this idea is expressed visually is also significant for the Hobbes-Boyle controversy, as Boyle saw graphic expression as one of the most powerful rhetorical means of establishing the superiority of reasoning from experience. The experimentalist faith was propagated via images, which explains why it was crucially important for Hobbes to use his frontispiece to create a vision. And all the more so as a political reading could be made from the anamorphoses: The sovereign's face could be diffracted into a turbaned figure, closer to a Turkish sultan than a most Christian king.

Was the figure of the ideal king an optical illusion created by anamorphosis? The crucial passage in Malcolm's discussion brings the image of the Leviathan together with a text that Richard Fanshawe addressed to Charles II in 1647 on the subject of sovereignty. It reads:

> His Highness may have seen in Paris a marvelously composed painting that, while showing the ordinary observer a multitude of small figures, presents to the viewer who looks at it from a particular perspective a portrait of the Chancellor. It's as if the painter intended to show, by a most ingenious philosophy [...] that the body politic is composed of a great number of material bodies, each of them whole and composed of a head, eyes, hands, etc., which also form the head, the eye, or the hand of the other body, and furthermore that private men cannot survive if the body politic is destroyed.

The question at issue, then, is this: Of what is the body politic made, and what can unmake it? The body of the monster is like a swarm of frightened figures, or perhaps it is a beehive. The kingdom of the bees has been the model of absolute power since antiquity (the swarm surrounds the king to protect him) but without violence (the bee king is clement, his stinger is sterile). As we'll see later, a feminine principle and a masculine principle are no doubt in contention here. But we should also understand this body politic as an unstable swarm, a state of equilibrium that threatens to fall apart at any moment. This is the subject of chapter 29 of *Leviathan*, which treats of the dissolvent force of "the liberty of disputing against absolute power," that is, the power of slander—for what would happen if all these little people opened their mouths instead of opening wide their eyes? If they started to talk? If they argued, discussed, contested, or even reviewed critically what was told them? Then one would realize that this method of composing a body politic was highly problematic. Then one would see, as Hobbes says, "the little worms which physicians call *ascarides*." Hobbes's mortal god is monstrous if only for that.

And what would happen if the body were decapitated? What would happen to the coalescence of the aggregated individuals? When you look at the Leviathan you immediately see the possibility of dissolution. In *Group Psychology and the Analysis of the Ego*, Sigmund Freud analyzes how a military unit disbands when an army loses its leader or when a rumor that "the general has lost his mind" gains ground. Then, says Freud, "the group vanishes into dust, like a Bologna flask when its top is broken off." It's embarrassing that we haven't come up with a better image for the soul of the body politic than the cork on a flask. The flask, without its cork, can no longer contain the perfume.

Hobbes's mortal god is monstrous only for his size. He's a colossus — Hobbes compares him to an automaton — and he's a composite body. The question of the compositeness of the body politic raises the issue of its potential decomposition, and the question of what can make or unmake it. Then there's the realization that none can know what a body politic is capable of. And if the uncertainty of this image brings one's thinking to a standstill, it also provokes the anxiety that the whole thing may come to an end at any moment. What was presented as the majestic apparition of the sovereign body carries within it the risk of decomposition, of dissolution, given that the crowd can always melt away, that it can return to its amorphous state as an idle and fearful population. These are the questions that we'll look at in the next lecture.

LECTURE 8, MARCH 7, 2017

Confronting the Leviathan, III: Morphology and History

Saint Francis of Assisi dreamed he was a mother hen — The feminine principle: the Virgin Mary spreads her cloak to incorporate the faithful — The bosom of Abraham: religion as "the need for the father's protection" (Freud) — Gender uncertainty: remarks on the sexual indecision of Christian anthropology — The Leviathan, out of the instituting multitude, makes the instituted people — An image exerts pressure "either through familiarity or shock" (Horst Bredekamp) — A history of composite forms: Arcimboldo's *Vertumnus* as a political panegyric — Uncle Sam's face reflects the melting pot — Chairman Mao: one face standing in for the anonymous crowd — The Leviathan in France (1652): "heroic, regal, sunlike, and just" — Imagining the face of the state: Hyacinthe Rigaud — The Leviathan as a prophecy of the automation of power relationships — Tacitus: "They invent and then believe in their inventions."

ONE DAY, Francis of Assisi had a dream — or, more accurately, he had a vision in his sleep. Thomas of Celano reported it in 1247 in what has long been called the *Vita secunda*, the second Life of Saint Francis, whose eighth centenary Jacques Dalarun has recently marked with a new translation. I quote: "He saw a small black hen, almost like a tame dove, her legs and her feet tufted with feathers. Many chicks milled insistently around the hen, trying to find a place under her wings." *When the man of God arose from his sleep* (Matthew 1:24), he interpreted his vision thus: "'I am the hen,' he said, 'small in size and dark in color.' Living innocently, she has all the innocence of a dove, who, being a rare bird in that century, flies freely up to the heavens. The chicks are the friars who have grown in number and in grace, and whom Francis's virtue is unable to defend *against the agitation of men and the contention* *of languages.*" He sees a hen, a little black hen that is trying to gather its young, and he says, That's me, clearly that's me, at the head of a religious order that's starting to expand.

How does one institutionalize charisma, how does one govern multitudes, how does one prevent the agitation of men and the scattering caused by Babel ("the contention of languages")? And how at the same time understand that there's no moment more political than the moment of dispersion and that joining together only becomes politically effective at the point when the process is reversed?

After all, there is another interpretation of the myth of Babel. If the hubris of man, who wanted to ascend to the heavens, caused mankind to enter, as Dante says, "into the region of dissemblance," it was also because men did not build the tower only from pride but also as a haven. The crowd that was reorganizing itself after the Flood was a frightened crowd, one that longed for a place that would never be submerged under the waves, and high enough to forge an alliance with the heavens. A crowd, as Hobbes might have said, that came together in "mutual fear." Yet God ordered his people to scatter not to punish but to save them. The human species dispersed over the surface of the earth — and here Dante joins with the Jewish commentary on Babel: "As man's languages multiplied, so too did his horizons. No place on earth would be unmarked by humankind and its attempts to establish a residence," writes Erri De Luca in *Noyau d'olive*. Mankind thus became in a sense ineradicable — men would always persist somewhere.

But let's return to Francis's dream. It's a political dream, a vision, since it makes a question of government visible. Dalarun has consistently shown how Francis of Assisi used divestiture from office, his renunciation of domination, as the active principle of his exercise of power. That's why Francis haunts radical political philosophy, which even today, especially today, is enraptured by divestiture from office, the sublime gesture of giving up power — ignoring, or pretending to ignore, that this evokes the very powerful figure (powerful because stronger than strength) of charisma in politics, which again only comes into its own at the moment when power and office are stripped away. Thus the figure of Francis of Assisi speaking to animals embodies the opposite of the hunter king, who dominates animals. Also Francis, alter Christus, is not one who eats but who is eaten, who governs while rejecting any semblance of devouring.

Francis of Assisi wants to be a "mother hen" to the friars — not a devouring or intrusive mother, not a cruel mother or a mollycoddling one. No, a little black hen, as innocent as a dove. Dalarun has shown how this "feminine principle" played into the construction of Francis of Assisi's political persona, heading an order that he did not dominate — he was at its head but not its leader. How was he to convey this? In his famous note to Brother Leo, he addresses him *sicut mater*, "like a mother." Does that mean that he intends to protect him or lecture to him, to smother him with affection? No, says Dalarun, who corrects the translation after a detailed philological analysis to "as mother" — because in hermeneutics, even small changes can have a big effect. Francis writes "as mother," *da madre,* as the Italians would say — and it has nothing to do with expressing affection. Francis adopts the female principle, he makes himself a woman as God made himself a man, he acts as a woman to give himself entirely to his brothers.

Dreaming of himself as a mother hen who gathers her chicks under her wing, Francis creates a political fiction that provides a vision of the government to come, the vision of a governess — and what we mean by a governess is a benevolent serving woman. To govern is to serve, it is not to crush, but to govern in the way a mother governs her children, as "Sister Mother Earth . . . sustains and governs us," Francis would write in his "Canticle of the Sun." And if Francis insists on the fact that the hen is small and black, and that she has trouble gathering her young, it's precisely to mark himself off from the ample, majestic, shimmering cloak of the Virgin that fans out like a pair of superb, generous, golden-brown wings. One thinks here of the iconography of the Virgin of Mercy.

There are many examples we might show. Here is a superb painting from the fifteenth century by Pietro di Domenico da Montepulciano, now in the Musée du Petit Palais in Avignon. In a classic but still foundational text, Paul Perdrizet has shown that the figure of the Virgin with her cloak was Cistercian in origin, giving visible form to the particular devotion of Bernard of Clairvaux. It marks above all the divine election of a social group, a religious order, and this Cistercian matrix

Virgin of the Misericordia by Pietro di Domenico da Montepulciano (Musée du Petit Palais, Avignon)

was reused by the mendicant orders, then in the thirteenth century again by the brotherhoods — the Italian *misericordie* and the Venetian *scuole* in particular, on whose banners the motif appeared. That's what's happening here, as there are penitents in the foreground. By extension, it would soon be the faithful as a whole who would assemble under the protection of the Virgin's cloak.

But this maternal principle is complemented by that other paradisaical place, the bosom of Abraham. Here the elect are

The Bosom of Abraham, 1321–1322
(Gracanica Monastery, Kosovo)

gathered in like-seeming groups to nestle in the patriarch's lap. The bosom of Abraham is the place where the righteous wait for Judgment Day and it is also "the possible name of different places in the hereafter," writes Jérôme Baschet. But Abraham is paradoxical as the originator of a lineage, being both a patriarch and a parricide. The figure of Abraham as progenitor allows Christians to claim both their descendance from Judaism and the break in their descendance from Judaism, whose patriarch confirms the religion's ethnic nature. But in John 8:38–39, when Jesus is asked whether he has the same father as the Jews, that is, whether he is descended from Abraham — since descent is imagined as a family tree — he answers that he has a far more eminent father who is in heaven. A father, then, whose roots are in heaven, not on earth.

Abraham's paternity thus expresses the superiority of a spiritual over a fleshly paternity. It does so by playing on sexual ambivalence, by oscillating between a paternal figure and a maternal role, between God the father and the Church as the Virgin mother, between the desire to protect and the urge to incorporate, as Baschet has shown in *Le sein du père* (The father's bosom), basing his argument on a very ample corpus of images. He shows that these figures give visible form to the complexity of meaning of the word *sinus* in Latin — since the elect find repose in Abraham's bosom, *in sinu Abrahae*, paradise being nothing more than a reunion with the father. And what did Freud say about religious feeling in general if not that it was "the need for the father's protection"? And this protection takes, at least in part, the form of corporal inclusion.

The image makes visible the strange complexity of the Latin meanings of the word *sinus*. It could be described as being in tension between two main meanings: interiority on the one hand ("in the bosom of"), and sinuosity on the other (*sinus*, in the mathematical sense, is a concavity, a curve, a fold, a crease). Hence there are four large configurations of meaning. The first is geographical: The *sinus* can be a chasm, a meander, a bay, or any curve in the shoreline. The second is related to clothing: as a fold in a garment, and in classical Latin the fold in one's toga serves as a pocket for carrying objects. The bodily meaning is more complicated. The *sinus* is an interiority that can refer to the female genital organs, but it euphemizes them. When we talk of Christ taking form in his mother's womb, we certainly use the term in utero, but *sinus* can also be used here to replace *utero*. This is why, from the bodily perspective, *sinus* can refer modestly to the breast and the space between a person's open arms. If one is *in sinu*, one is in a person's arms, on their lap, against their breast, taken up, taken in, included; one is enfolded in another's body without being literally inside the body. Whence the fourth meaning, which is metaphorical and abstract. When Augustine talks about memory, he says that it comes to reside, to nestle, in receptacles located *in sinum mentis*. *Sinus* here comes to mean a spiritual interiority, which one might call the heart or soul; *sinus meus* is the secret of the soul that hides and shelters in the folds of intimacy. See how extraordinarily complex are the concepts surrounding this term. A last remark: All these meanings are positive ones — there are no bad recesses in Abraham's bosom.

The methodological proposition of Baschet's book might be called serial iconography, where figures anonymously play out the possibilities of a word until all possibilities are exhausted. It's worth noting that the political iconography to which the frontispiece of *Leviathan* invites us is the opposite; there it's a question of understanding the explosive power of a particular image act (as I have called it), which gives visible form to a conceptual novelty, yet without containing it entirely. For the image, complex as it is, does not convey the fact that in Hobbes's text, the sovereign is the soul that animates the commonwealth's body, not its head. For the moment, let us simply say in regard to the Virgin of Mercy that "the fantasy of sharing the womb is attenuated and displaced: It is redirected outside the body and expressed through the mediation of a textile." This woven body represents the spiritual parent — illustrating a church tenet, namely the superiority of spiritual over carnal parenthood.

We can see that these two images, which I would call the stock of available images of Christian incorporation in a Eucharistic society, bring some confusion to the genre. In his *Historia Scholastica,* Petrus Comestor writes: "This place is called the bosom of Abraham in reason of its tranquility, as one would speak of a mother's bosom." *Ut sinum matris dicimus*: We come once again to the *sicut mater* of Francis of Assisi, which is to say the metaphoric power for Christian anthropology in the passage from masculine to feminine. The father plays the woman, Jesus is the son and mother of the Church, while the Virgin Mary is his mother and also his daughter, hence his bride in God, and the Church fathers are in consequence the fathers of their mother. Indistinctness of sex is basic to the anti-genealogical discourse of Christian incorporation through spiritual parenthood.

If Christian anthropology establishes both a hierarchy between the two sexes and a substantial unity between them, it follows from the fact, as Baschet has shown, that it melds together the two dualities that constitute a human being (soul and body, masculine and feminine). For the moment, let's hold on to the fact that it's from these two iconographic models of incorporation — the Virgin of Mercy and the bosom of Abraham — that we must understand the frontispiece of Hobbes's *Leviathan*.

Not that the image proceeds from them directly. What I'm looking for instead is the eruptive force of this image act, what I have proposed calling its visual event — a term that may not do justice to it, as we'll see. To grasp the combustive flash of this image, one might attempt other genealogies of the notion of incorporation. Here, for instance, is the seal of the commune of Meulan, appended to a document dated 1195 and representing the commune's assemblymen. The twelve faces of the town magistrates, arrayed in three rows, look out at us communally, and it's clearly their closeness that forms the moral person that authenticated the document. The number of magistrates is certainly an allusion to the apostles, though the motif is secular — as was true for 80 percent of the municipal seals in France in the Middle Ages, according to the census made by Christian de Mérindol in *Corpus des sceaux* (Corpus of municipal seals), comprising 739 seals, belonging to 434 towns.

Seal of the council of the Commune of Meulan, 1195
(Centre Historique des Archives Nationales, Paris)

In a book on the organicist metaphor of the state as a living body, *Il corpovivente dello Stato: Una metafora politica,* Gianluca Briguglia has traced the notion's genealogy from John of Salisbury to Hobbes, by way of Marsilius of Padua and Niccolò Machiavelli. The first use of the metaphor of the body politic was by John of Salisbury in *Policraticus* (1159), in which each limb and organ was associated with a particular function, sometimes even a specific government post, except the soul (which was identified more broadly with the clergy) and the feet (the peasants).

The body metaphor prompts arguments about preeminence. Who governs the body? Is it the soul? Is it the heart? Is it the head? The political possibilities these questions raise are interesting, especially when expanded to related concepts, and especially in the sixteenth century when the idea of the circulation of the blood was gaining currency. If the king is at the heart of the kingdom, it might suggest a heliocentric model of the kingship. The sovereign as heart challenges the power of the priesthood. The most radical line of thought was to follow Machiavelli in imagining a headless body politic, in which the circulation of the humors required the cooperation of all the organs, with each able to challenge the head for preeminence. That is what Jacques-Louis David shows in his famous painting *Tennis Court Oath, June 20, 1789*. What we

Oil sketch for *Tennis Court Oath* by Jacques-Louis David, 1790–1794 (Musée Carnavalet, Paris)

see is the constitution of a new body politic, one that is in competition with the king's body, which on this particular day was absent, allowing the new body of the revolution to be formed. The underlying metaphor of the state as body is what has caused medical terms to infiltrate political language: regime, constitution, etc.

In 1651, *Leviathan* was, quoting Quentin Skinner, "a representation of sovereign power that ... visibly absorbed more than it countered the revolutionary changes that had recently occurred." What did we see in the last lecture? We saw a colossus appear, a sea monster before whom "terror dances," floating above the horizon line, looming over the bottom half of the frontispiece — the emblematic, hierarchical, and compartmentalized half that is readily decipherable. For the enigmatic aspect, you have to look upward. It's to the upper portion of the frontispiece that you have to raise your eyes to access the "reading that wounds," the reading promised us, if you'll remember, by the thorns of Spinoza's rose. The king looks at us; he fixes his eyes on ours. But he himself is nothing more than the agglutination of the eyes fixed on him. In the original drawing of the frontispiece, the prototype for the printed version, all eyes were directed toward the actual body of the king, since the person holding that copy of the book, its sole reader, would have been the king himself, Charles II. But the engraving — by definition — allows not just the king but all men to see, and a reversal therefore occurs. In the engraving, the three hundred or so men who constitute the king's body have turned around. They still look at the king's body, but his represented body.

This mortal God is an artificial creation since he consists of the "Pacts and Covenants, by which the parts of this Body Politique were first made." Made by whom? This we saw too, made by a sort of optical illusion, by anamorphoses and transformations. That's why the question of the visible is important. What this artificial creation transforms is the political iconography of the royal body as a mirror. As, for instance in this 1534 portrait of Duke Alessandro de' Medici by Giorgio Vasari, which was analyzed by Diane Bodart as an optical metaphor for the body politic. The armor, whose polished metal creates a reflective surface, turns the prince into his own mirror. In the field of governance, there's a literary genre called the "mirror of princes." But princes aren't the only ones who read these mirrors, because the characteristics of royals are reflected there for anyone to see, in the corpus of works on the art of good governance. Here it's the opposite, since the prince turns into his own mirror, and in seeing him we see ourselves. Vasari offers the aptest comments on his own painting, writing: "The arms that he bears, white and gleaming, are such as the mirror of princes should be, that his peoples might be reflected in the actions of his life."

Studying Hobbes's visual strategies, then, allows an understanding not just of what the state represents but of what brings it into being. That's what this image shows, what it reveals about the text for which it provides a facade. But

Portrait of Alessandro de' Medici by Giorgio Vasari, 1534 (Uffizi Gallery, Florence)

there is also what the image hides, what it is incapable of showing. The king is the soul of the body politic, its anima, the principle that animates and unifies it—whereas here he is only its crowned head, its leader, raising concerns about its dissolution. What would happen if this body were decapitated, or eaten away from inside by these men, should they decide to open their mouths instead of just their eyes? What the image does not show is what Hobbes says in *Leviathan,* that this cold-blooded animal is a machine, or rather that it engages the "artificial life" of its mechanisms in the manner of automata.

Its engine is the "mutual fear" of the subjects, who need the sovereign to designate their enemy. This fear, which is the glue that holds the state together, is not terror but reverence, which is why Hobbes uses the term "awe" to translate the anomia that Thucydides describes as having paralyzed plague-stricken Athens, because the word contains elements of both fear and obedience. That is the point we'd arrived at, at the edge of this completely deserted city. Look: There are two plague doctors visible on the edge of the image. The beast rises up between sea and land, looming above the city it does not inhabit. The streets are empty, the town is uninhabited except for a few soldiers and plague doctors. The city seems to have lost its population — unless the population was transported in its entirety, beamed upward, deported into the body of the Leviathan. That sounds a little scary. If the city is empty, it's perhaps because everyone is inside the king's body.

What may help us here is Lucien Jaume's analysis of the "fictive person" in *Leviathan*. If the sovereign is an "artificial man," it doesn't just mean that he is the reflection of his subjects, as in the reverse representation of the mirror prince. In other words, the state may be a fictive person, but this doesn't mean its power is metaphorical or its consistency unreal. Or else, we have to take the poetics of the metaphor seriously:

Hobbes replaces the organicist metaphor with an artificialist one, so that the Leviathan ends up living, truly living, an actual life, in its body—whence the importance of saying that the Leviathan moves as automata do.

What is this displacement, this metaphor? It's the aspiration to unity. The Leviathan creates the people: From a scattered, atomized multitude (*multitudo dissoluta*), from a disparate collection of individuals, on the basis of the covenants they pass among themselves, it makes a single body—and this body is the people. In other words, out of the instituting multitude, the Leviathan makes the instituted people. But within this people, the individuals instituting it are still recognizable. The particularities have not been erased in the mass that constitutes the one. That's why this political body is not a mystical body, why it isn't endowed with theologico-political eternity. That's over and done with, and it ends with Hobbes. Multiplicity, therefore, is not entirely dissolved in the singleness of a name, as in Pauline conversion. What is it that Paul says in Galatians 3:28? "Ye are all one in Christ Jesus." The Church announces itself as Catholic and universal, but in doing so creates a hiatus between itself and the *katholou* of the Greeks (which designated the whole, tending toward the one) and between itself and the *universus* of the Romans (which designates the one into which the all is converted). This hiatus brings the theologico-political to a full stop, but we've gone on beyond that, since particularities have in some sense not been erased here.

Taking up this analysis in his book *Stasis: Civil War as a Political Paradigm*, Giorgio Agamben observes that the disunited multitude is always capable of returning to the state of a multitude dissolved—politics offers the possibility of new groupings, but also of dispersal. The people really exist only at the moment of choosing their sovereign, making the body politic an impossible concept, "always already in the process of dissolving, even in the constitution of its sovereign"—the key word here being "constitution" which is both a medical and a political term—and we understand better why the unity of the artificial person is nothing more than an optical device. Here's what the image shows: The image shows the people to be missing. The people appear even at the moment they disappear, at the moment they submit so as to dissolve. I quote Agamben: "The people are therefore an absolutely present entity, which, as such, can never be present and can therefore only be represented." This is why Agamben calls *Leviathan* a text that is "so densely and perhaps so ironically eschatological"—it announces its own loss, its own defeat.

We now understand the phantom character of the state better, haunting the frontispiece like a specter—for Hobbes the state was literally a ghost. But we also understand why this apparition can only be made visible in all its singularity by an image, or an image act, as Horst Bredekamp puts it. The state forms and manifests itself as a representation—not just an act of delegation but the forming of a figure. The state

Seated Giant by Francisco Goya, by 1818

is an apparition that is always next to its shadow; it finds its strength in it, or rather its greatness — and when Hobbes talks about the state, he always mentions its great size. It's a colossus. We could show other images to demonstrate how art has historically imagined giants made from the agglomeration of those who obey them, a tradition that arrives at the melancholy of Francisco Goya's colossus. It is instituted into the figural corpus, or, in psychoanalytic terms, into fantasy — an acknowledgment of the colossus's power to excite imagination. The fictive person is, then, an exposed body — exposed to destruction — but we have to say with Philippe Crignon,

Colossus, attributed to Francisco Goya, after 1808

who has analyzed the Hobbesian relationship between representation and community: "This institution of representation allows for being united, on condition that the 'political body' no longer be thought of as the 'mystical body' of the republic, whose a priori condition was incarnation."

Much more than the visual event we discussed in an earlier lecture, what we have here is an image act, in the sense of Bredekamp's *Image Acts: A Systematic Approach to Visual Agency*. Although images have no life of their own and are only artifacts, they develop more than mere presence, they develop a power that they exercise over the viewer and that symbolically conditions the rules of action. Thus, the image of the Leviathan is not just the mark or emblem of the state but its sign — that is, and I quote Bredekamp, "it comes to be an engine for action, either through familiarity or shock, which are the two possible ways that an image exerts pressure on those who look at it." And this pressure is not mediated by language. The image acts directly, for as Hobbes writes in *Leviathan*, pacts and covenants are always in danger of being broken by the signatories "during the time men live without a common Power to keep them all in awe." So that's what the image is: a visible power that commands awe and respect.

We can describe how this political fiction of the composite body, placed so as to command respect, became iconographically familiar. We'd then be hard put to draw the line between morphology and history. Because that, in the end, is what I'm looking for, to explore this question, following Carlo Ginzburg, of the relations between morphology and history. Hobbes's mortal god is monstrous only because of his size. He's a colossus that Hobbes compares to an automaton, and his body is composite. Can we sketch out the history of this form here? It picks up on an earlier iconographic tradition, represented by Giuseppe Arcimboldo.

The "composite heads" of Arcimboldo fascinated the surrealists, who saw these agglomerations of fruits and flowers metamorphosed into human faces as a joyous rendition of the self, whose presence is scattered in the savors of many things. In a famous text, Roland Barthes recognized the

Vertumnus by Arcimboldo, 1591
(Skokloster Castle, Sweden)

rhetorical force in this "energy from displacement," which played as much on metaphors as on visual resemblances (for instance, when a small prune became the pupil of an eye).

But Arcimboldo in fact composed political panegyrics. In 1563, the Milanese painter, who was strongly influenced by Leonardo da Vinci's style, became "the learned painter and portraitist of His Majesty the emperor of the Holy Empire" at the Habsburg court, according to the words of an official document. Arcimboldo was certainly learned, notably in the natural sciences, which then enjoyed great favor at the Viennese court. But his position as a court painter also made him one of the great organizers of royal celebrations.

We have difficulty understanding today why Rudolf II found it flattering to be represented in the painting *Vertumnus* (delivered to him in Prague c. 1590), with a pear for a nose. In fact, these court portraits are inseparable from the poems that accompanied them. In the case of *Vertumnus,* the humanist Gregorio Comanini took on the task of fixing (and perhaps forcing) the painting's meaning so as to make it politically compatible with royal propaganda. Vertumnus is the Roman god who presides over the change of seasons. By representing Rudolf II in the god's likeness using a mix of summer fruits and winter vegetables, Arcimboldo in a sense crowned his *Four Seasons* series with an imperial likeness that triumphs over time. The image is sovereign, for it announces a golden age in which abundance does away with nature's constraints.

Arcimboldo's art is certainly rhetorical, as Barthes well understood, but his rhetoric is also political. The playful aspects of this court art still need to be distinguished from the ironic. As Philippe Morel has justly noted, "The question that arises is to know whether Arcimboldo's compositions 'are' a panegyric of the emperor or whether they 'become' a panegyric through the exegetical filter of the poem composed for the emperor as an accompaniment to the paintings."

In an essay entitled "Composing the Body Politic," Dario Gamboni has studied the visual evolution of the composite

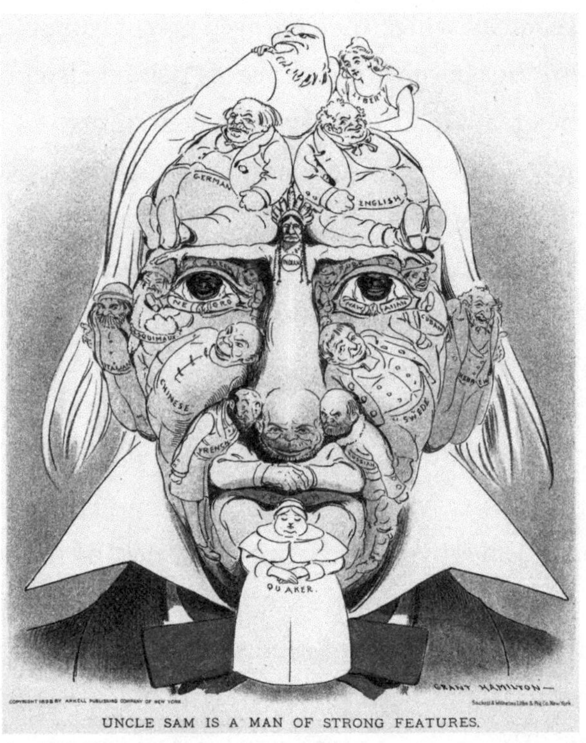

"Uncle Sam Is a Man of Strong Features"
by Grant Hamilton, *Judge*, 1898

portrait in political illustration. In 1898, the political cartoonist Grant Hamilton created a humorous cover for *Judge* magazine that we could describe as the depiction of a great man — in this case, Uncle Sam — in the age of representative democracy. Very much a melting pot, the America portrayed here is composed of nineteen figures representing a variety of ethnic groups, symmetrically arrayed: Germans, Englishmen, Greeks, and Turks, with Italians at one ear and Jews at the other, and an Indigenous man as the nose, but crucified,

Caricature of Napoleon with naked corpses composing his face, 1810

while a Quaker at the bottom counterbalances the nation's Puritan origins—and note the Black pupils. This political fiction, as with others we examined earlier, can be turned inside out like a glove. In an English caricature from 1810, Napoleon's face is depicted as a mass grave: It is composed of the naked bodies of the victims of his wars. A photomontage called *War President*, posted anonymously to the Internet in 2004 and now attributable to Joe Wezorek, presents a portrait of George W. Bush made from a mosaic of the victims of the Iraq War—but using only American victims, proving yet again that an image speaks loudest by what it fails to say.

Thus Hans Belting, the anthropologist of images, in his 2013 book *Faces*, analyzes another political face, from a body that is not composite (though perfectly composed), that of Chairman Mao Zedong. Starting in 1949, Mao was the public face of a body representing the multitude, a face that was equivalent to all other faces, the head of a "Great Leader" and a placeholder for the anonymous crowd. We might look now at another frontispiece, the one belonging to Mao's

Portrait of Mao, frontispiece from *Quotations of Chairman Mao Tse-Tung*

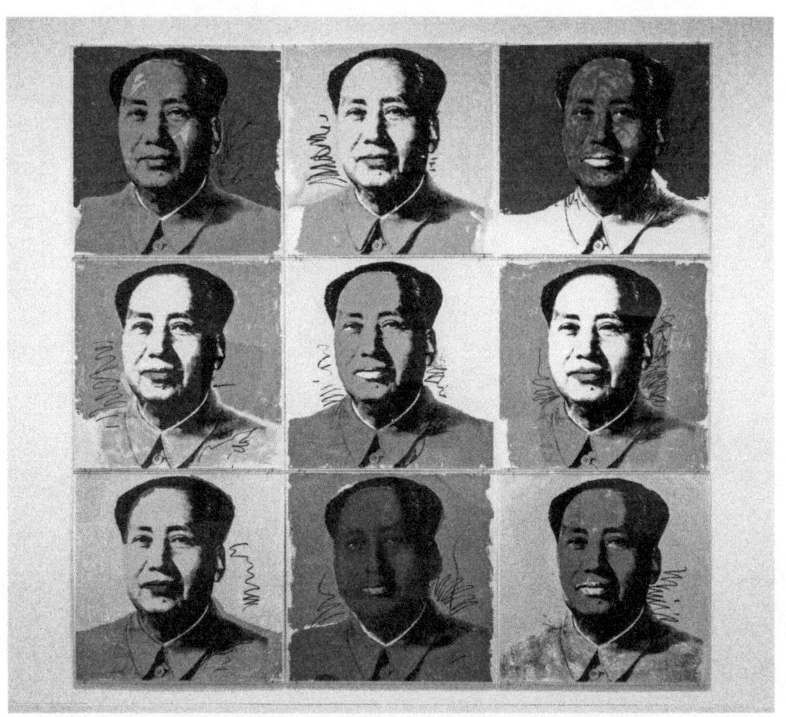

Mao by Andy Warhol, 1972 (Art Institute of Chicago)

Little Red Book (aka *Quotations from Chairman Mao Tse-Tung*). This Chinese state icon was used by Andy Warhol for his silk screens of Mao as a pop idol, showing the "facial consumerism of a market society dominated by advertising." But in wanting to rival Communist propaganda by engaging the technology of mechanical reproduction, Warhol missed the fact that this icon was only seemingly immutable: Every year, the monumental oil portrait displayed on Tiananmen Square was retouched, repainted, revised, and aged. It too experienced the passage of time.

Poster of Chairman Mao, aged

In confronting the Leviathan, basically, we confront Ginzburg's dilemma between morphology and history. Will the image produce shock or habituation? What we need to grasp is the political imagination that this image does violence to—and what changes it therefore prophesies. In that sense, the analysis fits well with what I've called political fiction. The history of the visual adaptations of *Leviathan*'s frontispiece shows that it wasn't yet acceptable in all places or times. Hobbes published a book in France in 1652 entitled *Le corps politique ou les éléments de la loi morale et civile* (The body politic, or the elements of moral and civil law), which was recently examined by Yann Lignereux. It's a translation

Frontispiece, *Le corps politique ou les éléments de la loi morale et civile* by Thomas Hobbes, 1652

of *Elements of Law,* but its frontispiece is an adaptation of the frontispiece of *Leviathan,* which had appeared a year earlier. Because the image needed to be adapted to the book's physical format, the lower section was removed entirely and the upper portion elongated. The architecture of the church was altered: With only one steeple it was now in the Gothic style — we are therefore in France. But if we turn to the figure of the king, we notice two major differences: First, the face is rounder and the crown more simply drawn. The colossus looks down on us benevolently. It's hard not to see him as a rising celestial orb, in the French tradition of the iconography of the sun king. Secondly, he is no longer standing squarely facing us but slightly in contrapposto, like the Gaulish Hercules. And as he has also swapped his crozier for a scale, we can say that this Leviathan is "heroic, royal, sunlike, and just."

But let's continue to look for differences. The king's body no longer contains an anonymous, internal crowd, their differences negated by indistinctness. Instead we find men and women cheek by jowl, not all of them absorbed in contemplation. Some kneel, some turn away, some seem to be arguing — one mother is protecting her child. And if we look more closely, we see that they are clustered by kind: clerks and magistrates in the left arm, soldiers in the right. Is it because the hierarchical and unequal society of the Kingdom of France was not compatible with the original figure? In Lignereux's view, the alterations have to be understood as a change in the political iconography toward what he calls a "reflected king." During the reign of Louis XIII, the handsome figure of the Renaissance prince — a motif reenchanted for a time by Henry IV — was replaced by a likeness of the state, and the task at hand was very much to visualize the face of the state, which was conceivable only through the traditional iconography of the French monarchy as being heroic, sunlike, and just.

This visual history of the sovereign's body reached its vanishing point, its point of indistinction, in the famous monumental *Portrait of Louis XIV in Ceremonial Robes* by Hyacinthe Rigaud, painted in 1701. This official portrait, subsequently reproduced ad infinitum, was the culmination of the trend

Portrait of Louis XIV in Ceremonial Robes
by Hyacinthe Rigaud, 1701 (Musée du Louvre, Paris)

to personalize royal power entirely within a body, prior to its being contained entirely within the hand that holds the rod of command. As a result of acting the king, of making a show of his desire to act the king, through which he becomes totally embodied in the glory of the monarchy, Louis XIV cannot show anything but himself. He no longer provokes fear but admiration, a major political passion that calls for an honorable kind of submission, one that acknowledges one's own smallness and requires bodily engagement.

In an essay called "Un morceau de roi" (A piece of king), Gérard Sabatier observes that exposing one's leg becomes a signature of sovereignty—it foregrounds a majestic body, behind which the symbolic dimly appears. The whole is impressive and fragile, and the sovereign's bearing elicits astonishment. The king himself, in the flesh, provokes the image act, as Henri de Saint-Simon tells us in an extraordinary story that occurred at the great theater in Compiègne in 1698. A military reenactment was in progress, some simulated battles, and a certain Canillac, a regimental colonel in the Rouergue infantry, was ordered to seek out the king and obtain orders directly from his lips. Louis was seated on a platform near the Marquise de Maintenon watching the reenactment unfold below. He was probably holding a spyglass. Saint-Simon describes the soldier arriving at the royal platform through the low door of a staircase. He writes: "As Canillac came up, he saw the monarch all at once and at a glance, and his astonishment was such that his physical mechanism fell in step with the impressions of his soul, and he was dumbstruck, speechless and unable to hear; it took him some time to recover. He mumbled his message, heard very little, and climbed back down the stairs so full of the vision he had just seen that he was unable to regain his composure."

A political vision that leaves one speechless ("he was dumbstruck"); the effect of astonishment ("so full of the vision he had just seen"); the emotional "mechanism" that matches stride with the soul's impressions. What better definition of power can we hope for than this? Power casts a spell over us for quite a while without our being able to recover our composure. Quite a while, but that means only for a time, especially if you're counting on the majesty of a mortal body. Louis XIV was so old and gout-ridden, he was putting the kingship at considerable risk by conjoining within him the king's two bodies — the risk would in fact be fatal. But what he interposed in the path of a civil war was the fragile life of a man's body.

This is perhaps what I was looking for in considering *Leviathan*, in gazing fixedly at the monster — a mortal god who prophesies the automatization of relations of power, a politics of things that proceeds from a government by numbers. At the turn of the seventeenth century, as the Galilean revolution began to describe the world in mathematical language, that moment in history when the West's understanding of itself as a Eucharistic society met with pushback. A certain idea of the human individual, of the body politic, came to an end there. Which doesn't mean that it didn't remain active. We still feel the power of the aura, this appearance of distance however near the thing producing it may be, this power to make us raise our eyes toward what's looking at us, this swarm that buzzes with our own fears, against which the politics of the trace must take up arms.

MUST WE END with the most unpleasant of all readings of *Leviathan*? In 1938, Carl Schmitt published *The Leviathan in the State Theory of Thomas Hobbes*. It's an insidiously antisemitic work, if only (as Yves Charles Zarka has pointed out) for the systematic assigning to authors of a kind of literary yellow star: "Leo Strauss, a Jewish academic," "Spinoza, the first liberal Jew," "the Jew Moses Mendelssohn." In a speech he gave in 1936, "The German Science of Law in the Fight Against the Jewish Spirit," the author recommends that "all writings by Jewish authors should be jointly shelved, as a matter of library practice, in the Judaica section."

As far as Schmitt was concerned, Hobbes had the wrong monster. I quote:

> An oft-cited English prophecy from the twelfth century said, "The lion's cubs will turn into the fishes of the sea." But Hobbes's Leviathan took the opposite course: a large fish has been erected as a symbol of state formation, following a process typically used by the land powers of continental Europe. The Island of England and its fleet, having set out to conquer the world, needed neither an absolute

> monarchy, nor a standing land army, nor a state bureaucracy, nor the legal system of a law-driven state, as would be the case for the states on the European continent.

What Hobbes should have depicted was the Behemoth, as it's from the *nomos* of the earth that his horrific program of government and destruction would come into being—in place of which, his sea monster has failed. For Schmitt, the Leviathan was a failure as a great man, as a machine, and as a symbol.

We are before the Leviathan, writes Ginzburg, as we are before what Aby Warburg called *Pathosformeln,* formulas of pathos. Not face-to-face with pathos but with its reduction to immobility, with an idea that has pathos as its object: This is the truly disarming power of images, this is what Ginzburg means by a political iconography that allows us to examine the procession of images. The frontispiece of *Leviathan* makes visible, with a new image, some very ancient words, which it puts back into circulation, reactivates, reanimates, and gives new movement to. For the men who constitute this mortal god are driven, Ginzburg writes, to "stand in awe of their own imaginations." We find an echo here of words spoken long ago by Cornelius Tacitus in *The Annals,* book 5, chapter 10: *Fingunt simul creduntque*—"They make up fictions and then believe them."

LECTURE 9, MARCH 14, 2017

Fiction's Stowaways

The composite face, a sign of the state — Return to the "secularization debate" — The body politic as "the symbol for the absolute and superhuman character of sovereignty" (Giorgio Agamben) — Kings, beasts, and the "the power of life and death" — Carl Schmitt and Erik Peterson: secularized theological concepts and theologized political concepts — Did *Leviathan* pick the wrong monster? Behemoth and the *nomos* of the earth — The coup d'état: "To show nakedly what they try to obscure every day by means of a thousand artifices" (Gabriel Naudé) — The intellectual's job is to "put names to things, give the mind a housecleaning, and throw out the words that are dead" (Jean-Richard Bloch) — The appearance of the Fool in *Leviathan*, chapter 15 — The free rider, a stowaway in the political system — Confronting violent reasoning head-on

IN THE PREVIOUS LECTURE, the curtain fell for good on the frontispiece of *Leviathan*, after we attempted for the third time to penetrate its visual event, one that imagines the face of the state. It is a composite face, and not just the mark or emblem of the state but its sign. It institutes the state in the figurative world as an image, that is, as the immobilization of a thought that precipitates as a figure rather than continuing to flow in fictions that spin out ever further narrative configurations. Because no one has lost sight, I hope, of the general aim of these lectures, which is to give if not a theory of political fictions, at least a historical method for grasping them. And we're approaching the end and, therefore, the moment to take stock, at least provisionally.

And Thomas Hobbes's sea monster, a mortal god who is at once an artificial person, whose body is constituted of the fear it inspires, literally filled with fear, but a fear that oscillates between terror and reverence, a body in which cluster together those whose mutual fear cements a desire for obedience, this fictive person of a Leviathan, then, renders visible what a fiction is. Or rather what makes a fiction, which Cornelius Tacitus expressed in three words: *Fingunt simul creduntque* — "They make up fictions and then believe them." Words on which we ended the previous lecture.

That lecture's title, "Confronting the Leviathan, III: Morphology and History," articulates the dilemma facing us — with a nod to Carlo Ginzburg, who made the tension between morphology and history the living spine of his work as a historian. Is fiction fundamentally impervious to history? If so, we would need only a limited number of fictions, a set repertoire more or less, and the very fact of this limited set would make history relatively predictable. To remain alert to political danger, for instance, it would be necessary in every era to attend Shakespeare's plays. Or on the contrary does time deform fictions, gradually making them unrecognizable, therefore not predictive and insidiously dangerous?

Tracing the long lineage of composite faces from Giuseppe Arcimboldo to contemporary protest art, one might be tempted to believe in a ghostly history of images, their persistence, their survival. Yet what we sought in looking at Hobbes was an image act, a drastic shift in political imagery. And we found it in a sense, as the lecture was wholly devoted to taking leave of what you could call the medieval organicist metaphor, or at least the metaphor of a Eucharistic society threatened by cannibalism, since that was the hypothesis we proposed, one in which incorporation makes use of an indeterminate feminine principle (the mother hen, the Virgin's cloak) and an equally indeterminate masculine one (the father's bosom).

Leaving the organicist metaphor behind, we turned to the artificialist metaphor — and Hobbes's automaton is very much a political fiction in Michel Foucault's sense, as discussed in earlier lectures, since it offers a fictional representation of "a politics that does not yet exist, based on a historical truth." This artificialist metaphor prophesies the automation of power relations, it is a politics of things (as Jean-Claude Milner would say) legislated by a government of numbers (as Alain Supiot would say). That's why the body politic, which we now see as a modern configuration, is no longer consistent with the "mystical body" of the monarchical state, whose a priori condition was incarnation.

From this perspective, Hobbes represents — to a greater extent even than Niccolò Machiavelli — a threshold, an inflection point in the chronology I propose to establish for this history of the Western powers, a chronology that more or less coincides with what political historians have called the "second Middle Ages," heralded at one end by the Gregorian Reforms, yet without any fixed point at which they could be said to stop or encounter pushback. A credible date would be the Galilean years of the 1640s. This is why the inflection point represented by Hobbes is so important.

Might this partitioning of political eras restart the secularization debate, or more accurately superimpose itself on it? We could follow Jean-Claude Monod in characterizing in those terms the political crisis of the twentieth century, which was intimately linked to the historical experience of the war and the struggle against countries where the religious worldview had dissolved into national fanaticism. Seeing two periods become superimposed, or one period resurface in another, is of interest to us. And for that moment in the secularization debate to have been understood in terms of the Middle Ages is doubly interesting to us. Hence it is often historians of Fascism (like Emilio Gentile) or of Nazism (like George Mosse) who have examined the question of secular religion. Medieval historiography did not emerge unscathed from this conceptual upheaval. We spoke earlier of Ernst Kantorowicz, who in 1927 wrote panegyrics to Frederick II's "secular mystique of absolute power," in which he discerned a form of secular sacrality. This was clearly conceived as a "weapon against the Weimar Republic," in Otto Gerhard Oexle's phrase. Once cured of the political mysticism that dizzied his youth, Kantorowicz strove tirelessly to dismantle the metaphor that undergirded it conceptually. And we know that *The King's Two Bodies* constitutes a methodical and scathing criticism of the idea of secularization.

Kantorowicz was still explaining himself just two years before his death, in an important article from 1961. "We are too often drawn to speak of the 'secularization' of ecclesiastical thought and institutions in relation to the modern state," yet starting in the twelfth century, he continued, "what happened was not the secularization of the spiritual realm but rather the spiritualization of the secular realm." This chiasmus, this rhetorical figure juxtaposing inverted terms, was in fact the Gregorian chiasmus. At this point, we could make a Kantorowiczian critique of Kantorowicz (and his theologico-political theory of the king's two bodies) based on the blind spots in his thinking—which most often were not voids but points of support, resources for making the point of view itself visible. The process involved deliberately ignoring certain texts in a way that's still fascinating, touching even. At the time when Kantorowicz was writing, in 1929, a young classical scholar named Elias Bickerman had described the imperial Roman apotheosis: After the emperor's death, his attendants pretended to continue caring for his effigy, which was laid out on his bed and treated as a patient. Only after seven days was the ruler declared dead. This ritual of a double death existed among the Roman emperors even in the absence of any political theology, a pagan ceremony that Bickerman likened to the funerary rites of French and English sovereigns in the Middle Ages. Kantorowicz and his students were aware of this research but never acknowledged it. Admitting the pagan origin of the medieval ceremony would have compromised their central thesis about Christian political theology. So Bickerman's theory was not refuted but simply set aside.

In *Homo Sacer,* Giorgio Agamben takes up the subject and puts forward the idea that the emperor doesn't have two bodies but two lives within a single body, one natural and the other sacred, the product of a "strange symmetry." As with *homo sacer,* the sovereign's body cannot be sacrificed, and its murder is not a homicide (the murder of a *homo sacer* being less than homicide, and the murder of a sovereign more). This is what makes Louis XVI's beheading scandalous — not so much his death itself as his being condemned to death. Historians of power need to take seriously Agamben's proposed rethinking of the interpretation of royal funerals, which he places "in a new and less anodyne light." They not only manifest the continuity of sovereign power but the sovereign's surplus of sacred life. "From a symbol of everlasting *dignitas,* the metaphor of the body politic becomes the symbol for the absolute and superhuman character of the sovereignty. Expressions such as *The king is dead, long live the king* should be understood much more literally than we ordinarily do. When the sovereign dies, it is the sacred life on which that sovereign's power was founded that is invested in the person of his or her successor."

This cipher for the absolute character of sovereignty, which is both superhuman and subhuman (which is why, in Machiavelli, the king plays at being a beast, and why the specter of cannibalism, of monstrous animality, surrounds the sovereign's power), explains why that person is sovereign for whom all men are potentially *homines sacri,* that is, killable — though not needing to be sacrificed. We should remember here the work of Yan Thomas on the phrase from Roman law *vitae necisque potestas,* which derives the "power of life and death" from the father's unconditional power over his male offspring. This, of course, has sinister implications for the paternalistic formulae used to describe kingly power, since "the little father of the people" is the person who has the power to kill his entire people. And that is why bringing into play both the male and female principles of power, as was done in the Middle Ages, was a prudent approach.

We must therefore extend our genealogical understanding, dive into the poisonous heart of this phantasm of the total state, which takes the Leviathan image as its icon and elixir. Aided by the research of Alain Boureau, we know that Kantorowicz, while fighting with the right-wing nationalists against the Spartacist uprising in Berlin, took his precepts in political theology from the works of Carl Schmitt — I warned you of an unpleasant reading, of a stripping away of the rose's petals so as to be scratched by its thorns, and here it is.

In answer to Schmitt's abrupt claim in 1922, in his book *Political Theology,* that "all significant concepts of the modern theory of the state are secularized theological concepts," Erik Peterson, a brilliant historian of the Church fathers and a Protestant who had converted to Catholicism, wrote in his magnificent essay "Monotheism as a Political Problem" that these significant concepts of the modern theory of state claimed by Schmitt to be secularized theological concepts were in fact Roman political concepts that had been theologized. Exactly like the era of imperial funerals that Bickerman described and Kantorowicz chose to ignore.

And why does Peterson do this? He wants to set up in opposition to Schmitt's subversive political theology a kind of indivisible core of Trinitarianism that would be fundamentally resistant to any idea of sacred power. Basically, he wants to save Christianity, restore its irreducibility to politics, and therefore its sacredness, preserve its purity. We can understand why he would do that, yet he offered so powerful a refutation that Schmitt felt bound to respond and, in 1937, wrote his *Political Theology*.

In *The Kingdom and the Glory*, Agamben takes the history of this controversy as the guiding thread of his demonstration, extending it with his use of the concept of signature, which he defined explicitly elsewhere: "Secularization acts within the conceptual system of modernity as a *signature*, which refers it back to theology. Just as, according to canon law, the priest who returns to secular life must wear a sign indicating the order he belonged to, so a 'secularized' concept exhibits as its signature the fact that it formerly belonged to the theological sphere."

This allows us to resolve the dilemma between morphology and history: History is truly spectral, it derives from the return of the things we dread. "What is a specter made of?" Agamben asks in a fine and troubling text, reprinted in the collection *Nudities*, called "On the Uses and Disadvantages of Living Among Specters." What is a specter made of? "Of signs, or more precisely, of signatures, that is to say, those signs, ciphers, or monograms that are etched onto things by time. A specter always carries with it a date wherever it goes; it is, in other words, an intimately historical entity." This is what allows us to consider a history of images as a ghostly rethinking of returning haunts; they are phantoms, yes, but stamped with a date — which thus gives free rein to the form (images must be allowed to do as they please) and also to history (we mustn't let images have their way with us).

The Leviathan is a ghost that appears between earth and sea, and throughout his life Schmitt fought against this phantom. It served as his ally against idealism, as a way of conceiving the mechanization of power relations, reinvigorating the dream of a "total state" founded on anthropological pessimism. The idea that "man is a wolf to man" sat well with him. His point of view in 1922 was that of a radical Catholic whose bête noire was Max Weber and the Weberian idea of the state as anonymous machinery: Schmitt was a "decisionist." He refuted Weber's model, calling for theologico-political realities to have a real and weighty presence, to which in 1933 he gave the name "political leadership," *Führung*. He joined the Nazi Party on May 1, 1933, and adopted the concept of racial identity, which he described as basic to political leadership. In *State, Movement, People,* his most openly and brutally Nazi text (that is, aligned with the Nazi Party), Schmitt declared that the concept of political leadership "does not derive from allegories or Baroque-era representations . . . It is a concept that is immediate and contemporaneous, with real-world presence." He therefore holds it to be necessary for the Führer and his partisans to share an unconditional racial identity.

Historians of the Third Reich have amply documented Schmitt's failed attempt to serve the Nazi movement. He was suspected of political Catholicism, of wanting to attribute divinity to the state, of developing a non-Völkish ideation. In late 1936, the SS journal *Das Schwarze Korps* launched a campaign against him. He was ousted and would never become the official jurist of Nazism he had hoped to become. He was disappointed in Nazism but never repented belonging to the party. It simply didn't go far enough, or at least never went as far as he did. His 1937 article "Der Staat als Mechanismus bei Hobbes und Descartes" has to be understood in this context, as does the book that followed in 1938, *The Leviathan in the State Theory of Thomas Hobbes: Meaning and Failure of a Political Symbol*. The translation and republication of this book in France in 2002 set off a firestorm of intellectual debate. Its preface by Étienne Balibar, which hit an exposed nerve, portrayed the book as a useful criticism of the radical left in representative democracies. The work is openly antisemitic, if only (as Yves Charles Zarka has shown, and as I've mentioned before) for its systematic assignment of a kind of literary yellow star to certain authors. Schmitt also asserted in a speech he delivered in 1936, "The German Science of Law in the Battle Against the Jewish Spirit," that it should be a principle of library science to shelve all works by Jewish authors in the Judaica section.

Schmitt listed the ways that the Leviathan fails as a political symbol. The first death it causes is the death of the Great Man: The Leviathan destroys him from the inside, by "technological neutralization," since the machine can function without anyone to run it. But in separating state and society, the Jews — for it is they who are responsible, from Spinoza to Meyerbeer — contributed to the breakup of the "big machine" and therefore to the second death from the Leviathan. The death of the king always has these two moments: He dies first because he is no longer inhabited, then the machine auto-destructs. We should take this line of thinking seriously, starting from Bruno Karsenti's *La question juive des modernes: Philosophie de l'émancipation*, a major contribution to understanding the interrelation between modernity, assimilation, and antisemitism, based on the thinking of Heinrich Heine, Émile Durkheim, Marc Bloch, Leo Strauss, and Émile Benveniste. Because, in point of fact, faced with the problem of emancipation, these authors have focused on the dissociation of society and state.

But that's not where we are with Schmitt — we're on the opponent's side. Schmitt's thinking about Hobbes transitions into a theory of political mythology. To Schmitt's way of thinking, Hobbes chose the wrong monster. I quote:

> An old and oft-quoted English prophecy from the twelfth century states: "The lion's cubs will be turned into the

> fishes of the sea." But Hobbes's Leviathan has taken the opposite path: a big fish has been proposed as a symbol of the typically continental process of state formation among Europe's land powers. Having set out to conquer the world, the British island and its fleet needed neither an absolute monarchy, nor a permanent land army, nor a state bureaucracy, nor the legal system of a law-based state, as would be the case for the nations on Europe's continent.

What Hobbes should have depicted is the Behemoth, a terrestrial monster, for it's with the *nomos* of the earth that his horrific program of government and destruction would be realized—the program that Schmitt hoped for and that we must fear. Instead, Hobbes's sea monster failed. Hobbes chose the wrong monster, which is to say that the Leviathan would occur but not, as is often the case with political fictions, in the place where it was conceived. Political fictions do undergo displacement, and this displacement is called metaphor. The sea monster foundered, in the sense of a shipwreck, but this failure can *return.* This is the question of prefiguration, which Hans Blumenberg has examined as part of his study of metaphor.

Wolfgang Palaver has shown, in the afterword to the controversial 2002 reissue of Schmitt's book in French translation, that the text itself is at fault for the subsequent debate over its interpretation, with some reading it as an apology for Nazism and others as a coded critique. After the war, Schmitt would send out his book with a kind of handwritten errata sheet that began with these words: "Attention! Perhaps you have heard of the great 'Leviathan' and feel the urge to read it? Beware, dear reader! It is a highly esoteric book, whose intrinsic esoterism increases the further you penetrate into it. Best not to touch it! Put it back on the shelf! Do not pick it up again, whether your hands are clean and cared for or whether they are red with blood, in keeping with the times." The warning, for that's what it was, was dated July 11, 1938, and confirmed in June 1945, with the notation that "seven years have elapsed." The word "confirmed" tells us not to expect the slightest remorse on the author's part, and whether one's hands are washed or red with blood it's better to put *Leviathan* back where one found it, because it's an entirely coded book—as announced by the book's frontispiece, its facade, threshold, and ford, with the veiled section which is always an invitation to the dangerous hermeneutics of esoterism. And Schmitt signs his note: "Benito Cereno."

Who is Benito Cereno? He's a character from a work of fiction and a shipwreck survivor, the eponymous protagonist of a novella by Herman Melville. The story tells of a ship's captain, a sealer, who anchors near a small island off southern Chile in 1799. There he discovers another captain, Benito Cereno, who claims to have run aground with his slave ship and to be in need of food. In fact, Benito Cereno is lying. The slaves have mutinied and he is their puppet. By signing "Benito Cereno," Schmitt is protecting himself behind a fiction, suggesting that Europe's power brokers pretend to control their own destiny when in fact they've surrendered to a slave rebellion. Their story is a trap, and Schmitt suggests that *Leviathan* is an esoteric text that hides what it pretends to show.

To hide what one cannot say, that is the seventeenth-century definition of a coup d'état. A coup d'état, wrote Gabriel Naudé in 1639 in his book *Considérations politiques sur les coups d'État*, is like a storm: "One sees the thunder hit before one hears it rumbling in the clouds." That's obviously the most troubling political situation: You're awaiting an event, you fear its occurrence, and you fail to understand that at the very moment it happens it will already have happened. In other words, the lightning of political action slices through "night and fog," and the noise that accompanies it is only heard afterward. A coup d'état is prepared in secret, but what is revealed when it occurs is the secret of the state, with the abruptness characteristic of political action. "An epiphany of violence accompanies action," writes Louis Marin in his sparkling preface to the reissue of this text. "Its flash dazzles and blinds in the moment of execution."

Naudé, who was Cardinal Mazarin's librarian, composed his text in Rome, during the time leading up to Galileo's trial. His conversations with Cardinal Guidi di Bagno and his friends led him to always assume that violence had a role in the founding of any authority. And Italian political practices, which he described overall as Machiavellian, prompted him to overhaul French political theory, subvert it by introducing a radical principle of realism, and defetishize the history of France, for instance taking the baptism of Clovis I as the model for all subsequent coup d'états. He also denounced the "hoax" of the Maid of Orleans as politically motivated.

Naudé's book was a dangerous one. He published his *Considérations politiques* in an edition of only twelve copies. The point was to "show nakedly what they try to obscure every day by means of a thousand artifices." It exposed the esoteric thinking that is used as protection and that makes the author a stowaway in his own text. When the hidden secrets of a state are abruptly revealed, they must be held within a close, like-minded circle. By disseminating his *Coup d'État: The Technique of Revolution* far and wide, in 1931, Curzio Malaparte failed to follow this rule and was thrown in jail. The socialists accused him of Fascism, and Mussolini painted him as seditious. His book was dangerous, since it could be used equally by those wanting to overthrow the state and those wanting to defend its legality. This, of course, is the dilemma posed by Machiavelli's *The Prince*. Commentators have debated endlessly over how it is meant to be read, while Machiavelli simply puts his reader in a position to see the indeterminacy of politics straight on and to give what happens a name.

These are the same words that Jean-Richard Bloch used to defend his friend Malaparte in a letter dated November 20, 1931: When danger threatens, the intellectual's job is to "put names to things, give the mind a housecleaning, and throw out the words that are dead, the concepts that are outworn, and the ways of thinking that are out of date." And to do that, you need to see the adversary unwaveringly — look at him, unmask him, and in any case see him straight on. And what allows us to see him straight on is fiction.

The curtain, it now seems, has not quite fallen. Someone is moving behind it. Is this a theatrical effect? A coup d'état? A grand gesture? There is a stowaway inside the big beast, a fictional character. He appears in chapter 15 of *Leviathan*, and Hobbes calls him "the Fool." He speaks in praise of injustice, arguing that modern man wants only to satisfy his own happiness. If others want to make covenants, follow reason, and obey the laws they've made, why not? says the Fool. But as for me — since I'm unafraid of God — what do I gain by it? Wouldn't I do better to exempt myself from this political loyalty? What would be most advantageous, says the Fool, is for everyone to obey except me. And it goes without saying that each person can make the same calculation.

This is a serious matter, for the Fool appears at a key moment in Hobbes's narrative. Men are on the verge of an agreement to emerge from the state of nature, they have made a pact, but the mortal god has not yet gained their respect — the image of the monster has not yet appeared on the horizon. What would happen if a grain of sand clogged the machinery of this artificial person, the state, before the automaton ever got underway? We are (we are always) in the uncertain, suspended, and eminently dangerous situation where the multitude can return to its state of dissolution — the state of civil war.

Because, as we saw in the two preceding lectures, the Leviathan is structurally unstable. It takes a scattered and atomized multitude and turns them into a people, instituting them into a body politic; but this body politic is always threatening to unmake itself and return to its initial state. The dissolved multitude would then go back to the state of nature, a state of disunity, and it is this return to savagery that we call civil war. We saw it as we followed the trajectory of an image, a haunt, a ghost stamped with a date, those images of cannibalism that crossed over from the New World peopled by savages to the Old World made savage by the Wars of Religion — think back to those engravings by Theodore de Bry that illustrated accounts of travel to the land of the cannibals and also denounced the miseries of civil war in Europe. The same images can be used to show the barbarity of others and the fact that we ourselves are the world's barbarians. And there is nothing to decry or despair about in this movement, this metaphor, through which the barbarity of others sharpens our awareness that barbarity is everywhere. Because we understand, as Michel de Montaigne does, that this is the very movement of what he calls civilization.

This is why the people are always undergoing dissolution while the sovereign is constituting himself. Ever absolutely present, the people can never be entirely represented. Would you say this dread applies only to England during its seventeenth-century revolutions? Yet these are the very terms that, for example, Jacques Rancière uses to describe our democratic exhaustion today. To say the people are represented is to believe that the entity preexists the political process. But that's not the case, the opposite is true, since it's the political process that institutes the people. And the representative system then produces a demonic double: It creates the fiction of a people that is ill-used, a people that is suffering, a people that lacks representation. This is a scene that plays out at every election. Every election creates a monster, one that is ever more threatening, of a people that is not adequately represented, and every election revives the ever more bitter disappointment of not finding embodiment — but embodiment is exactly what calls forth the theologico-political ghost of the mystical body, when what is needed is a body politic.

Let's pick up the thread of the Hobbesian story. Here's the man, the Fool, who brings on disgrace. His arguments are the ones that need to be seriously addressed. The scene is quite clearly theatrical: An actor is advancing, perhaps even playing a role, with a mask over his face, but in any case he provokes a dramatic turn of events, or at least a new development in the plot. Here, and I quote from *Leviathan,* is his provocation: "[H]e questions whether injustice, taking away the fear of God — for the same fool has said in his heart there is no God — may not sometimes stand with that reason which dictates to every man his own good, and particularly then when it conduces to such a benefit as shall put a man in a condition to neglect not only the dispraise and revilings, but also the power of other men."

The Fool is therefore a modern Epicurean, or a hedonist, the Leviathan's cynical oath breaker. He doesn't hold it against others that they make vows, but since he doesn't believe in God he exempts himself from having to keep promises. He seems to say: Make covenants, but don't count on me, because I'll respect them only as long as they're in my interest but no further. The most rational course, after all, is to avoid paying the price of establishing justice, even if it exposes one to public reviling. Hobbes will therefore confront the Fool, and it's in fact crucial for Hobbes to refute him, correct him, reeducate him, by showing him where he's wrong in his calculations — because the argument clearly has to engage the Fool on the grounds of his own pragmatism. There is no point in telling him that his stance is immoral — he seems to understand the fact and even enjoy it. He has to be proven wrong. He has to be shown that his strategy can backfire, that it's in his interest to be just, while adopting his instrumentalist vision of the social world. This is a fundamental issue, it's what Luc Foisneau discusses in *Hobbes: La vie inquiète* (Hobbes: Anxious life): How can you salvage a theory of justice in a society based on contracts and the calculations of the contracting parties?

Hobbes's intruder is a skeptical objector who has to be answered seriously. No doubt he is playing a role, he's what Gilles Deleuze called a "conceptual character," an intermediary that philosophy puts forth to sharpen its concepts. And it's not enough just to provide an answer, that's not how it works in a Socratic dialogue. Look at Callicles in Plato's *Gorgias,* who holds that might makes right. He is not a foil, a sparring partner, but a tough adversary, because it's hard to give good reasons for following the rule of reason. And that is why fiction organizes confrontations with tough adversaries. It's also why the conceptual characters in the history of philosophy are unpleasant, insistent, and often brutal. From Plato to Diderot, by way of many others, they assume the role of violent reasoners.

Céline Spector has offered a fascinating group portrait of these adversaries in *Éloges de l'injustice: La philosophie face à la déraison* (Elegies to injustice: philosophy confronts unreason). The point is to show that political philosophy must respond to this question of egotistic resistance realistically, that this stance is its primary challenger. The confrontation of philosophy and its double is therefore a powerful political fiction which calls into question principles of justice and rationality. The challenge today lies with the figure of the free rider, a hidden passenger in the political system who does not call the rules into question but exempts himself from following them, arguing ingenuously that it's perfectly reasonable not to contribute to social conventions despite benefiting from them.

Hobbes's Fool has caused great quantities of ink to be spilled by proponents of rational choice. Is he not the modern hero of individualism, since the Leviathan is not very likable? If he is the one who derails the machine and sabotages the automaton, is he not the figure of a liberator? What is going to bring about emancipation if not this individualistic, sovereign, atheistic, and disillusioned criticism? He is not just an opportunistic freeloader. The Fool is first and foremost, as the text makes clear, an atheist: "[F]or the same fool hath said in his heart there is no God." He says it in his heart, so it's not just something he says out loud: He believes it. Starting in 1640, Hobbes was often accused of atheism, but by giving the statement to a fictional adversary, he can avoid the charge. The Fool is really Hobbes's Other. But at the same time, the Fool adopts a Hobbesian stance, saying that he wants above all to promote his own happiness. He is simply pointing out the vulnerability of covenants in a society where, in fact, the fear of God and the aristocratic honor code are shaky. As Foisneau has shown, the Fool poses a challenge.

The duel is all the more crucial in that the conceptual person is the philosopher's double and bases his argument on the philosopher's utilitarian doctrine. He must therefore be persuaded that he hasn't worked out all the consequences of his position, and for starters that he may not be alone in adopting it. The argument is crucial because what hangs on it is whether or not the Leviathan will come into being, whether we will see "the fragility of the colossus with feet of clay, or the solidity of the well-founded state, that mortal god." The specter that Hobbes invokes and puts before the

Fool is none other than civil war. It's possible that there's a Machiavellian ghost behind the Fool, since this modern-day prince would have all communal morality bow down to necessity. For "murderous Machiavel," as Richard III calls him in Shakespeare's *Henry VI*, had become the big bad wolf of the Elizabethan stage.

The Fool must renounce power, absolute power — the kind of power that consists in surrendering to the tyranny of one's desires. It might also be possible to show, in the historic context of *Leviathan*'s composition, that the Fool also assumes the role of the regicide who has come to power. Behind him there is likely another phantom, namely Oliver Cromwell, the iconoclastic, fanatical, and puritanical usurper. For Hobbes's response to the Fool takes two different paths: He addresses both the atheist and the believer who is convinced that tyrannicide will lead him to his heavenly reward. Hence this conceptual character superimposes the hedonist and the believer into the dramatically powerful figure of the cynical dissembler — think, for instance, of Molière's *Tartuffe*.

Political fiction serves in this instance to give a characteristic figure to what is thinkable. This figure can be terrifying — Spector includes the Marquis de Sade in her analysis, along with other violent thinkers who refuse to sacrifice their desires for the sake of justice. But without justice, without confronting what fiction allows us to grasp, philosophy and history are made helpless, particularly given the new figures of evil in politics. And it is they whom we need to confront head on.

During the third lecture, I quoted a passage from the course Michel Foucault gave in 1974. It concerned the "abnormals" who exemplify the paradoxical force of what he calls "the cogs of the grotesque in the mechanism of power," the grotesque terror that engenders "the maximalization of the effects of power arising from the disqualification of the person producing them," and he cited Nero as a shining instance of this "despicable sovereignty." During his lifetime, Nero was the hideous, grimacing mask of an extreme power that was immune to caricature because he was himself so excessive and despicable; strangely, this did not disqualify him from holding sovereign power but actually qualified him for it. If I may, we'll start and end the next lecture with Nero.

LECTURE 10, MARCH 21, 2017 (1)

What Is "Prefiguration"? Reverse Genealogies

Maupassant channels Proust — Precursors as the joint product of an author and his readers — Reverse genealogies, counter to the literary belief in predestination — "Making use of prefiguration was a way of conferring certainty of decision on an action" (Hans Blumenberg) — Alexander the Great, Frederick II, and Napoleon followed in the footsteps of illustrious predecessors — Three Lives of Sultan Baybars — The parodic double — Solomonic kings in France, Castille, and Ethiopia — When fiction anticipates (Marc Bloch) — Nero: "What an artist dies with me" — Tyranny in the Middle Ages, patterned on Nero's cruelty — "Like Nero when he burned Rome, I'd like to hold a harp in my hand, on a balcony, from where I could look down on the flames that will devastate my country" (Marquis de Sade)

“**HOW OFTEN** had a woman’s dress not thrown at him in passing, with its evaporating breath of scent, a host of forgotten events.” The author of this quotation? Marcel Proust, of course. And yet it’s not: The sentence comes from an 1889 novel by Guy de Maupassant, *Strong as Death*. It appeared there, yes, but in the meantime we’ve read Proust, or we know about him anyway — let’s just say this is ground that Proust covered. Once we’ve ascertained that the author of this text (Maupassant) was not an influence on Proust, we have to acknowledge that the text we’re reading is not a text by Maupassant but a text by Maupassant read by contemporary readers who read in the wake of Proust, and *in light of* Proust. In consequence, a new text arises from the first, in anticipation of the second. And that text would not exist without the subsequent one — so we can say that the first plagiarizes the second, in anticipation. This is what the critic Pierre Bayard has called, in a 2009 book of that title, *Le plagiat par anticipation* (Anticipatory plagiarism).

Saying that Maupassant plagiarized Proust in anticipation is a way for Bayard to spin out a theoretical fiction in the Oulipean vein. That's his modus operandi: He *improves failed books,* he describes how *the* Titanic *will sink,* he asks what would happen *if works of literature had different authors* — I am quoting a few of the titles of his more recent books. In short, he fictionalizes fiction. Putting the syllogism aside, and the comic effect of demonstrating an absurdity, the plagiarist is simply a precursor, but — and this already appears in Jorge Luis Borges's famous essay "Kafka and His Precursors" — his creation is a kind of coproduction between himself and his reader.

We are well aware that confidence in literature's premonitory capacity is one of the effects of literary belief. Yet literature no more predicts the future than it staves off its dangers, which is why a literary criticism of anticipation can only address anticipation in hindsight. If we believe that the political fictions of Kafka or Orwell prefigure a future political reality — and are therefore political fictions in the sense we've tried to understand in this set of lectures — it's because we are living that political situation today and recognize that what we are living has already been experienced, prospectively, in political fictions, another hypothesis I have wanted to test in these lectures.

The theoretical fiction put forth by Bayard is therefore less subversive than it might seem. It reestablishes the glory of an author's literary posterity, restores the concept of greatness, and sits well with an ordered history of lineages and celebrities. It implies the simultaneous presence of texts in a contemporaneous time that Judith Olszowy-Schlanger calls "the memory of works of literature," which, I believe, more radically attacks the chronology of literary history. Because basically the question we've also tried to understand is how reverse genealogies might be constructed. Already for André Malraux — as we learn from an article by Joël Loehr called "Pour une histoire littéraire au rebours" (For a literary history in reverse) that appeared in *Poétique* in 2010 — it's not the ancestors who beget their heirs but the latter who resuscitate their precursors. Whence the need to establish backward or reverse genealogies. Whence the need in essence to ask ourselves: What is it to prefigure?

This is what Hans Blumenberg does in *Präfiguration: Arbeit am politischen Mythos* (Prefiguration: When myth makes history). We've already mentioned Blumenberg as a theoretician of metaphor. When the world is unreliable yet still legible, metaphor outstrips our ability to conceptualize by going out ahead of the world's legibility. It's in this sense that we spoke of a Eucharistic metaphor, and it's also in this sense that Blumenberg's philosophy of history (which is a philosophy of modernity) leads to a theory of prefiguration.

In his short, gripping text, Blumenberg runs through a series of portraits of historical figures — conquerors for the most part, such as Alexander the Great, Frederick II, Frederick the Great, Napoleon Bonaparte, and Adolf Hitler — who acted "in such a way as to bring about what had been written." These great men believed — and it's a belief widely shared among men of power — that they could avoid missteps by walking in the footsteps of a prestigious predecessor: "Making use of prefiguration was a way of conferring certainty of decision on an action, of removing the possibility of its being interrupted, and also of giving a definite character to its outcome, since it would not get lost in the byways of personal arbitrariness." Thus it's the uncertainty of a historical action, the fact that any decision generates a fog of blindness — not because of ineptness on the part of the ruler but because of the very nature of force — which makes the reinvention of the past necessary, that is to say, the work of myth.

That, in fact, is what interests Blumenberg: the persistence of mythical thinking in the rationality of modern man. The short text mentioned above is an abandoned chapter of his monumental 1979 opus *Arbeit am Mythos* (published in English in 1985 as *Work on Myth*). It's a chapter that was dropped, because of the discouragement of "having to remember Hitler again and again." I'd like to quote from a letter that Blumenberg wrote to one of his book's reviewers, Götz Müller, a letter published with the documents accompanying the French edition. He says that he withdrew this chapter, which was originally entitled "Stalingrad as Deriving from Myth," and which describes the way Hitler basically made all his strategic decisions convinced that he'd been prefigured by Frederick the Great and Alexander the Great, and that he'd been foreshadowed as well by Frederick II and Napoleon Bonaparte. His hesitations, furthermore, were not questions of command but of prefiguration. This chapter, which Blumenberg eventually abandoned, had "totally ruined [his] taste for the book." What is in this text that is so unpleasant? We gather that Frederick II of Hohenstaufen "was not just a figure who was mythicized a posteriori, though the circle around Stefan George certainly did mythicize him, but what came first were Frederick's own efforts to mythify himself, which he pursued tenaciously." Ernst Kantorowicz has, in fact, noted the many actions that Frederick II took from a desire to replay the epic of Alexander the Great, as handed down and altered in the medieval traditions of the *Alexander Romance* — especially having himself crowned the king of Jerusalem during the Crusade of 1229. Thus it was in fiction, in romance narratives, that Frederick II's actions were prefigured, giving rise to political fictions whose consequences were anything but fictional. In the end, it always comes down to the same thing: an obsession with strengthening the legitimacy of Western kingdoms by using fictional Eastern monarchies.

Prefiguration of this kind clearly guided Napoleon Bonaparte — no other political rationale is imaginable. His expedition to Egypt in 1799 can only be explained by the belief he once expressed as follows: "We must go to the Orient. All great glory comes from there." So Napoleon was also a new Alexander, and not just for his ephemeral conquest of Egypt but because he rummaged in the Alexandrian storehouse of political imagination for the springboard that would magnify his conquests within the mythical meaning of history.

I wouldn't have the temerity to speak in this hall, where Pierre Briant taught for a number of years, about how European political culture remembered Alexander the Great. I'll simply direct you to the summation Briant gave in *Alexandre: Exégèse des lieux communs* (Alexander: An exegesis of the truisms). Alexander is quite clearly the historical figure who has fed prefigurational mythmaking more than any other. I'll limit myself to a single example, perhaps a somewhat unexpected one, to examine how the dynamic of prefiguration engages with the fictional power of literary invention.

I'll start with the figure of Baybars, the fifth sultan of the Turkish Mamluk dynasty of Egypt, which was founded in 1250 and stayed in power until the Circassians took over in 1382. Baybars's reign lasted seventeen years, from 1260 to 1277, and was characterized by an intense attention to image. The question is always the same: How does a ruler reach mythical status, how does he become a figure of legend in his own lifetime? To provide an account of Baybars's reign, Jacqueline Sublet has translated three Lives, and it's on this collection of biographies in translation that, lacking the requisite languages, I'll base my remarks.

The first is a eulogistic account, written by Abd al-Zahir, the secretary to the sultan's chancery, who was born in Cairo in 1223 and started composing his book during the ruler's lifetime. Its title, literally, is: *The Resplendent Garden: History of the Magnificent Sovereign*. The second is by the great Egyptian historian al-Maqrizi, who was born in Cairo in 1364, where he studied law, then became an inspector of markets and an administrator. He wrote what was both a description of Egypt and a chronicle of the Ayyubid and Mamluk dynasties. It appears to be a reconstruction of the fate of sultans in imperial terms. This second biography is important for understanding Baybars's posthumous life. The third biography is the *Sirat Baybars* (The romance of Baybars), in the Syrian version dating from the Ottoman period. A collection of popular legends, it relates the picaresque adventures of a character whose noble origins would seem to promise him a brilliant destiny but who constantly needs the help of his companions to get out of trouble. Here are some of the section titles: "The Childhood of Baybars," "The Flower of Truancy," "Cairo's Lower Depths," "The Emirs' Betrayal," "Murder in the Hammam." The universe of this romance is narrow but crowded: Everything happens in Cairo, within the space of a few days.

From that perspective, the Baybars romances have a certain kinship with *One Thousand and One Nights*. The 160 tales that make up the anonymous collection of the *Nights* — or 190 tales, if you add in the main stories that appear in other narratives — have filtered out into the global imagination to such an extent that few people other than specialists think to assign them a very precise geographic or historical origin. Yet, in the convoluted maze of their transmission, they tell of the romance of Islam. Not the fantastical romance of the wonders of the Orient but the very real one of a narrative tradition that has its roots in the oral tradition of Persian and Indian storytellers and in the written culture of the collection's compilers from Baghdad to Cairo. It makes this inexhaustible reservoir of the imagination part of a continuous tradition. And we shouldn't be surprised to see historians make use of the Baybars romances, if not as a historical source, at least as a resource for generating images — and not just for want of anything better, as the documentation on Baybars was extensive.

In the *Sirat Baybars,* the hero always has at his side a cunning, crafty person, the *ayyar*. He's therefore a figure of derision, the parodic double of the adventurer: "You by courage, I by trickery," Baybars is constantly saying to his ironic double. They are friends from the trenches, having met by chance, and the *ayyar* often comes from the underworld. He is the occasion for discussions of the sovereign's duties and for flights of social satire. And this obviously leads to the question of the political domestication of derision, which interests us because one of our concerns at the beginning of these lectures was to know whether political derision could have a dissolving effect on nasty governments. And what we see is that rulers can become fictional heroes in their own lifetimes, but they generally achieve that status accompanied by an ironic double — in some sense the best possible bodyguard for their posthumous life. And reversals, in any case, are a standard feature of the story: We read, for instance, that the great qadi of Cairo, Saladin, was in fact a Christian priest; and the patriarch of the Church of Genoa was Gunit, a Muslim. They have not converted but have each usurped their identity and their religion — proof that faith is easy to counterfeit. One of them knows that he is the other, and the other knows that he is the one; in a sense, then, that's how they govern the world. This is followed by subtle play of false conversions, which is one of the drivers of the plot.

In an important essay, Anne-Marie Eddé has identified the biblical and mythological figures that Baybars appropriated to fashion his image of an ideal sovereign. Prominent among them is Alexander the Great, although his name takes an altered form in the list of Baybars's honorifics: He is *Iskander al-zaman* (Alexander of Time), to which is added *sahib al-qiran* (Master of Constellations), alluding to his birth under an auspicious star. This astrological forecast of the coming reign appears in the Iranian versions of the *Alexander Romance*, and Baybars's identification with the Macedonian conqueror was strengthened by the fact that Baybars had driven back the Mongols — whence his legitimacy and popularity in Mamluk Egypt — just as Alexander had kept at bay the nations of Gog and Magog.

These titles of Baybars's appear in inscriptions in Damascus, in a church converted into a mosque dating from 1266–

1267. Of even greater interest is the mausoleum Baybars built over the supposed tomb of Moses, which Islamic tradition locates to the southeast of Jericho. Baybars crowned it with a *qubba* and tacked on a prayer room, whose foundation dates from 1269. The inscription emphasizes his war against the infidels and Mongols. This is where to look for the link between Moses, Alexander, and Baybars, for the Syrian versions of the *Alexander Romance* often assign Alexander a companion, his cook Andrew, known in Islamic tradition as al-Hadir. Once again, we find a ruler shadowed by his double, an ironic double.

Baybars also had his al-Hadir. During the years 1266 to 1268, the sultan dedicated himself to attacking Christians, especially in the Armenian principality of Cilicia, where he destroyed monasteries and enslaved the population. According to Eddé, he was at that time under the influence of a spiritual director, Sheikh al-Hadir al-Mihrani, a hermit from Galilee who lived near the tomb of a companion of the prophet. His influence derived from his gift for divination. A contemporary Coptic historian saw him as a shady character, "a highway robber, a protector of disreputable people, an abuser of women and children." The Christian hostility toward him is easily explained: It was al-Hadir who had the Church of the Crucifixion in the Holy Sepulchre in Jerusalem demolished, killing the officiant in the process; and he destroyed the great synagogue of Damascus during Ramadan in 1271 by holding a feast there that ended in an orgy.

The honorifics were dropped after 1273, the date when al-Hadir fell into disgrace and Baybars cast him out. But while Baybars's entourage wanted to see al-Hadir killed, the sultan was attentive to his spiritual director's prediction: "Little time will separate the end of my life and yours." In 1277, back from an expedition to the land of the Rum, Baybars gave the order to free al-Hadir — but the vizir had him strangled in his cell instead. As predicted, Baybars himself died twenty days later.

And Alexander wasn't alone. Among the biblical and mythological figures Baybars appropriated to fashion his image as an ideal sovereign, Eddé has also identified Abraham, Moses, and Solomon — the latter heavily "Islamized." In Christian countries the biblical model of a Solomonic kingship was probably in greater political use than any other: We could cite the Castilian example, and notably Alfonso X of Castile, who reigned from 1252 to 1284. But we should also mention Ethiopia, whose sovereign was a model of the sacred king. The Ethiopian negus, or "king of kings," was thought to be descended from Menilek, the son of King Solomon and the Queen of Sheba. God tasked him with making Ethiopia into a new Israel.

The figure of Solomon, however, was somewhat problematic, as Marc Bloch showed in an unusual essay published in 1925 under the title "La vie d'outre-tombe du roi Salomon" (The afterlife of King Solomon). Solomon was the embodiment of a wise and fair king, but he was also, in the Latin Bible, a depraved sovereign with seven hundred wives and three hundred concubines. Furthermore, several spurious Greek treatises of the early centuries of the Christian era, as well as the Jewish tradition reported by Flavius Josephus and abundantly drawn on in medieval literature from the twelfth century, show him as a king who was also a magician and an exorcist, able to compel evil spirits to obey his will. There needed to be some tailoring of his legacy, as the whole of it couldn't be used in the prefiguration of his spiritual heirs. Jean-Patrice Boudet, for example, has shown that in defining Alfonso X as a Solomonic monarch — thus bringing prefiguration to bear — the emphasis was on Solomon's jurisprudential and cultural policies. Alfonso was called El Sabio, which means both "wise" and "learned." This covered both his elaboration of the great legal code of the *Siete partidas* and his esoteric knowledge of magic, which led to the development of an Alfonsine astrological science based on the Latin translation of the *Sefer Raziel HaMalakh* (The book of Raziel the angel), a treatise on Jewish magic, under the title *Liber Razielis*. Similarly, we find the same Solomonic dimension ascribed to Robert, King of Naples in the fourteenth century and to King Charles V of France. Finally, Maribel Fierro has carried the investigation even further by asking whether Alfonso X might not actually have been the last Almohad caliph. She is pushing back here against the unwillingness of historians to recognize the debt that Alfonso's politico-cultural project owed to Arab thought and writings, as well as their general ignorance about the Almohad era and its conception of knowledge.

So mythic prefiguration is the writing down of a sovereign's actions ahead of time—which is why political fiction can be anticipatory. This was the case for King Louis IX (Saint Louis) of France, a contemporary of Baybars; for Alfonso the Wise; and for Frederick II, as Jacques Le Goff has shown. The figures of David and Solomon were obviously used to burnish a royal legend. The novelty, though, was Louis IX's assimilation of the myth of Josiah, King of Judah. It was likely a discovery made by Louis's first biographer, Geoffrey of Beaulieu. The comparison was picked up a second time by Vincent of Beauvais, and it appears most particularly in the ordines, the liturgical services for the canonized Saint Louis.

What justifies the comparison? Both kings had two-part lives. The first part was an innocent, righteous childhood. When Josiah was a child, "he did that which was right in the sight of the Lord, and walked in all the way of David his father, and turned not aside to the right hand or to the left" (2 Kings 22:2). So here was a child who wore the royal crown (Josiah was eight years old) and who was wise, a *puer senex* in the hagiographic mold. He did not deviate from the path laid out by his ancestors. This is the definition of "governing right": *rex a rexte regendo*. He is called a king who governs right, who proceeds without deviating. This kingly rectitude consists in striving toward a previously determined plan, one that is fully accepted without reserve or wavering. So Josiah was a child king, innocent and righteous. Louis IX wanted to be such a child and assumed the role fully. And the son of Blanche of

Castile was that good child, but at a certain point Louis's life took a different turn. The fact is well known, it happened at the time of the Crusade and of his capture, when he returned haloed by his defeat and adopted another mode of life that was more directly Christlike. This brought him on the path of what has been called his reformist prescriptions, though they were actually purgative prescriptions, or reforms in the sense that reformation is primarily a spiritual ideal, before becoming an administrative requirement. All this is well established, and all of it happened in the eighteenth year of his reign, as the Bible tells us about Josiah.

What the Bible says in 2 Kings 22–23 is that Josiah had the Temple restored in the eighteenth year of his reign, and there he found the book of the law. Josiah and his people went up to the house of the Lord, where he renewed his covenant and led the religious reform by driving out the prostitutes and obliterating the last traces of paganism. Hence Louis IX knew what he had to do, his program was already laid out. He would act as had been written. He set off to wage war against the pharaoh, was killed, and his body was brought back to Jerusalem. All this was a prefiguration of the Passion of Louis. But the memory of Josiah, known as the "Ecclesiast," was a "mixture of incense" as sweet as honey. And Geoffrey of Beaulieu starts his *libellus* with an evocation of Josiah, then relates the life of Saint Louis, and ends with these words: "What else is left to us, unless it is the perpetual memory, so perfumed, so honey sweet, so melodious in the Church of

God of our Josiah." Louis IX is more than a second Josiah, a further Josiah, he is *our* Josiah. He is of our time, he is ours, and he allows us to relive a saintly story.

Le Goff maintains that in the thirteenth century abstract and purely ideological comparisons—for example calling someone the "new Constantine"—were no longer enough. Regnal history had now become individualized, and a historic resemblance was needed to found a politically coherent narrative. Let's take another example, an extreme example: the figure of Attila the Hun, who was reworked by Hungarian historiography to become a patron figure. The identification of the Huns and the Hungarians first surfaced in the West during the Hungarian incursions of the ninth century, and Hungarian chroniclers endorsed this identification, identifying Buda Castle as having belonged to Attila. But it was toward the end of the thirteenth century that a Hungarian historian by the name of Simon of Kéza, a clerk at the court of King Ladislas IV, wrote the *Gesta Hungarorum*, which established an origin legend for the Huns and Hungarians that glorified their common past. Reexamining the classic sources for the history of Attila, notably Jordanes, Simon first refuted the demonic origin of the Huns, though it was the dominant account in the historiography, and presented them instead as a human race with noble origins; then he linked the history of the Huns to the Bible. The original Hun society was egalitarian and resembled both the ideal society of the Church fathers and the Round Table of the Arthurian knights. It was a horizontal society. And Attila became an ideal king: bold but measured, cunning but vigilant, with the power of a conqueror — and gave himself the titles "king of the Huns, terror of the world, scourge of God."

Are we once more seeing "the cogs of the grotesque in the mechanism of power," to requote Michel Foucault, and "the maximization of the effects of power arising from the disqualification of the person producing them" of which he spoke in *Abnormal,* citing Elagabalus and Nero as shining examples of "despicable sovereignty"?

Nero was an extreme figure who embodied the dysfunction of power, and Donatien Grau has devoted a book to him entitled *Néron en Occident* (Nero in the West) — a work that its author has called "historiopoetic." It details the history of this emperor's ability to create fictions and arouse fiction-fueled energy. Nero, the last blood descendant of Augustus, who was adopted by Emperor Claudius, assumed the full mantle of the Augustinian legacy as the coinage he issued amply demonstrates — the series of numismatic images forms a great text, a narration of power. An often overlooked feature of Roman history is that its text, its major text, is the series of coins Rome issued. Nero wanted to be the *optimus princeps,* and Seneca (see his *De Clementia*) makes him out to be the very image of a sun king, notably in his revival of Apollonian imagery. As the New Apollo, and therefore as a poet, Nero would usher in a new golden age of bucolic verse — this may remind some of you of the way the seasons were abolished in

Giuseppe Arcimboldo's composite faces. Contained within bucolic poetry is the idea of the return to the golden age, which cancels time by accelerating it — and there was the idea specifically that the first five years of Nero's reign, which were always singled out in Roman literature, were idyllic years, a golden age.

This theme is expressed so emphatically in the prologue of Lucan's *Pharsalia* that some historians (notably Pierre Grimal) have wondered whether the praise wasn't ironic — and nothing is trickier than gauging the degree to which an ancient text is or is not parody. Nero coincided with an extraordinary flowering of literature, known as the Neronian revival, which included Horace, Virgil, Ovid, Tibullus, Propertius, and Livy. The fourteen years of his reign are documented in major works such as those of Seneca, Lucan, and Petronius. Most important, as Glen Bowersock has observed, the eruption of fiction into classical literature had the effect of disrupting the intellectual framework based on the ancient Greek paideia.

Nero's suicide in AD 68 marks a caesura in Roman history. It's the moment when fictional literature made its entry onto the stage — we discussed this when we spoke of the writing of the Gospels. And AD 70 is also the moment when the first accounts of the life of Jesus were set down, within this same literary context. In *The Annals*, Tacitus wrote that he was exposing "the empire's secret." In what sense? His history spelled the end of Rome's domination by aristocrats from the great republican families. Nero was essentially called cruel (*saeuitia*). His *furor* turned him into a tragic figure, particularly in Seneca's dramatic writings. But it's in the works of Tacitus and Suetonius that the "biographemes" or discrete biographical elements woven through the life of Nero assumed definitive form: the deaths of Britannicus, Agrippina, and Seneca; the burning of Rome and Nero playing the lyre while the city was in flames; Christian persecution; and Nero's suicide in Phaon's villa. These were the elements that formed the reservoir from which all subsequent rememberings of Nero would be drawn. These scenes, especially in Tacitus, are always described as if they were part of a play, as if they had already been dramatized, with Nero making his life story into a tragedy. Most often, he himself is absent — which is clearly what theatricalized his role. He is present as a ghost. At her death Agrippina bared her midriff to her killer, pointing at the womb from which the emperor was born, and said, "Strike here." Tacitus relates this in *The Annals*, while Suetonius adds a scene in which Nero visits the body of his mother and orders an autopsy.

This theatricalization becomes even more pronounced during the great fire of Rome. Tacitus reported: "A rumor had gone forth everywhere that, at the very time when the city was in flames, the emperor appeared on a private stage and sang of the destruction of Troy, comparing present misfortunes with the calamities of antiquity." When one event occurred, Nero acted out another, staged its prefiguration.

Which is why he exclaimed on his deathbed, "*Qualis artifex pereo*" (What an artist the world is losing by my death!). Tacitus depicts him in poetic terms as a tragic character, at the same time as he depicts him in political terms as a tyrant. And both facets needed to be understood at once, that was the empire's secret. The same theatrical processes constituted the tragic character, in poetic terms, and the tyrant, in political ones. The scenes of fratricide and matricide are the tragic foundation of Nero's reign.

The Jewish and Christian exegetes of the Middle Ages gave Nero's story a millenarian reading: Nero was one of the incarnations of the Antichrist. Silvère Menegaldo has recently told the history of the transformations of the Nero myth, starting from an unusual text called *Les faiz Néron le cruel homme* (The deeds of Nero, cruel man), which presents the emperor as an avatar of the Devil. This literature culminates in the fourteenth century with an anonymous work called *Noiron li Arabis*, which presents an extraordinary mash-up of hateful figures that includes Nero, Satan, and Mohammad, providing the reader a useful summary of all that should be hated. The fantastical vein that made Nero into an Antichrist continued into the sixteenth century with such works as Agrippa d'Aubigné's *Les Tragiques*.

But we shouldn't take these fantastical imaginings about grotesque cruelty too lightly since this was the way that thinking about tyranny was conducted in medieval times. Fiction, and especially fiction about Nero, provided thought experiments on the subject. All the more so since, until books 11 to 16 of Tacitus's *Annals* were discovered by Giovanni Boccaccio in 1362 (these were the sections dealing with Nero's depravity), medieval political thinkers had drifted away from Tacitus. The reappearance and wide availability of these texts made the fifteenth century a notably Tacitean century. Nero was present in the minds of Leonardo Bruni and Niccolò Machiavelli as a ghostly but seldom mentioned presence. He was an explicit presence in Étienne de La Boétie's *Discourse on Voluntary Servitude* as a "rabble rouser, executioner, wild animal" and a "nasty monster." But at the same time, the figure of Nero was available for exploration by poets, painters, and dramatists, especially in the seventeenth century. Again it served to mark the outer limits. In *Hamlet,* for example, in the soliloquy that starts "'Tis now the very witching time of night," when the prince of Denmark gives in to the temptation of an extreme exercise of power — extreme but not unnatural — we find: "O heart, lose not thy nature; let not ever / The soul of Nero enter this firm bosom. Let me be cruel, not unnatural." This is force taken to its limits, an extreme use of power, but not an unnatural one.

No sooner is a figure made available to fiction, however, than it becomes truly uncontrollable. Even Tacitus's name circulated in the fifteenth and especially the sixteenth century in a disordered way. From the moment that Machiavelli was put on the Index of Forbidden Books, Machiavellianism was identified with Tacitus's name. All that was "Machiavellian" and couldn't be said was heaped on Tacitus. It became the mask that replaces the face. In 1562, Girolamo Cardano published his *Encomium Neronis* (In praise of Nero), which would subsequently be republished by the libertine Gabriel Naudé. And there again, no one knew how to read the panegyric to Nero, no one understood what it meant, or else they understood it all too well — it was the kind of political indeterminacy that libertines strove for. Critics have not reached a consensus on the status of this text, which Alexander Roose has recently called a "treatise of suspicion." Should it be read as belonging in the rhetorical tradition of the paradoxical eulogy? Gorgias wrote a eulogy to a housefly. However one reads Cardano's text, it opens up an avenue for thought, raises the possibility of a counter-history. For Cardano's way of going about his task is clear — and on reflection terrible: He criticizes Tacitus and denounces the Christian order that accepted the Roman author; in short, he casts doubt on the witness. And once you have cast doubt on the witness, you can overturn the image the witness has supplied. Here is Cardano: "Thus it was by these judges and these witnesses that Nero was condemned." He no longer needs to praise Nero, only to criticize those who testified against him. He can muddy the waters just by suggesting that Nero might have had a reason to exercise power as he did, a reason that escapes us.

After that, other possibilities surface, ones that are truly uncontrollable and in no way limited by the general ideas to be found in Tacitus. Among the freethinkers of the seventeenth century, and later in the writings of Fénelon, Voltaire, Diderot, and the Marquis de Sade, Nero assumed a positive image as a ruler. In de Sade's *Juliette,* Nero and Machiavelli meld their traits to become the quintessential de Sade heroine. And so the libertine Olympe Borghèse says to Juliette: "Like Nero when he burned Rome, I'd like to hold a harp in my hand, on a balcony, from where I could look down on the flames that will devastate my country."

But we need to ask the hard question: Is there a tacit attraction, an elective affinity, between tyranny and philosophy?

LECTURE 11, MARCH 21, 2017 (2)

Pastiche, Postiche, and the Power of Parody

Intellectuals believe in magic — "What was Aragorn's tax policy?" (George R. R. Martin) — The ruler as the living law and as good shepherd — "You can't imagine how great a monster the empire is" (Tiberius) — Albertino Mussato's *Ecerinis*: a foul beast and a fecund womb — Lucidity and betrayal in Dante — Parody, satire, and speculative fiction in *The Death of King Arthur* — Reversal, displacement, and parodic projection in the *Roman de Fauvel* — "The first, daily, and inexorable duty befalling Hitler on awaking was to recreate his physical resemblance to himself" (Jean Genet) — Hitler's "ontological theft" of Charlie Chaplin's moustache (André Bazin) — "A real war of annihilation, where the continued existence of one protagonist is possible only at the cost of eliminating the other" (Jean Narboni) — Laughter without comedy — "It's as if people have a physical repugnance for the truth" (Klauss Mann)

INTELLECTUALS BELIEVE IN MAGIC. They believe in the sorcery of words, they believe that you can change the world with them. As in *Harry Potter*. In *Harry Potter: À l'école des sciences morales et politiques* (Harry Potter: Lessons in moral and political science), Jean-Claude Milner invites us to read the books, or see the films, as a way of thinking about managing the "knowledge-power" of enchanters. Dante was accused of being a magician, for the very reason (which we'll come back to) that he believed in the bewitching power of words. And what does Voldemort's experience tell us? "When the philosophers, the historians, the specialists in literature, and the literate generally decide to work on behalf of a tyrannical power, that power becomes practically impossible to overcome and its crimes almost impossible to denounce." There's no need, I think, to develop more fully the idea that the big popular television series or movie franchises are the political fictions of our time, and that what they always show is the crushing power of intellectuals to bestow legitimacy on tyranny or to withhold it.

Think, for instance, of *Game of Thrones,* as it has been analyzed by the philosopher Mathieu Potte-Bonneville. He demonstrates the ways in which the series is Machiavellian from start to finish. First because it breaks with the classic timeline of the heroic fantasy, which—as is evident in *The Lord of the Rings*—unfolds according to the tripartite rhythm of Christian salvation (J. R. R. Tolkien was a practicing Catholic). The hobbits leave their shire, meet powerful forces from the past (the ancient kings buried in barrows), and clamber joyfully through the mountains with nature spirits; they then enter the second age, which is the age of war; afterward, they emerge from the war and return to their beautiful shire, land of sovereignty and salvation. Three ages, each of them distinct, whereas in *Game of Thrones* time is driven onward by the onset of winter and entirely governed by the element of war.

Here, it's not enough for a good king to come to the throne for everything to return to order. Potte-Bonneville quotes a very telling interview with *Game of Thrones* author George R. R. Martin in *Rolling Stone*: "Tolkien can say that Aragorn became king and reigned for a hundred years, and he was wise and good. But Tolkien doesn't ask the question: What was Aragorn's tax policy? Did he maintain a standing army? [. . .] And what about all these orcs?" Thus *Game of

Thrones adopts the Machiavellian position of judging a government on its results and not on its principles, assessing its capacity to maintain power rather than acquire it, and tracking the ability of the rulers to resist the tyranny of their own emotions. This is what's always striking in *Game of Thrones*, that the rulers never stop, that they always go too far. They never desist after a necessary act of cruelty, they go on to their destruction. Those who should normally keep them from doing so are their advisers. So I'll ask the question again before we part ways: What are we to make of this unspoken attraction between tyranny and philosophy?

In an article entitled "Comment les philosophes ont légitimé la tyrannie" (How philosophers have legitimized tyranny), Pierre Vesperini describes how the philosophers of the Roman Empire created the framing text for the imperial system under the Flavians and Antonines by elaborating two major principles of legitimacy. And these two principles of legitimacy retained their robustness in medieval and modern political culture. The first relied on the theological and cosmic foundations of the emperor's power, whose legitimacy came from being inscribed in the order of the universe. Two different figures of the ruler derived from this principle: The first conceives the emperor as the "living law"—the term first appeared in the works of Diogenes, a neo-Pythagorean who wrote an obscure treatise called *On Royalty*. To say that the ruler is the living law comes down to legitimizing arbitrary behavior, but once the expression was coined it passed into Augustinian propaganda, and from there into Justinian's *Novellae,* after which it was used to found the principle of medieval law known as *lex animata.* Its invention coincided with the need to stabilize imperial Roman power. The second figure deriving from this principle of legitimacy presents the ruler as shepherd. It was Suetonius who first gave currency to this image, reporting that Emperor Tiberius refused his governors' request to raise taxes by saying: "A good shepherd must shear his sheep, not flay them." The pastoral model of the ruler therefore developed in the imperial context and came to Christianity later.

This first justification of a ruler's authoritarian power (as the living law and as good shepherd) comes from Plato's *Republic,* as does the second argument for legitimacy, which is that imperial power conforms to the divine order of the world, and the divine order chooses wise men to govern. The emperor is wise because he masters himself and can shake off the tyranny of his own passions. From this, we come to the idea of the government of the emotions — especially of *ira,* anger, which Augustus had learned to master by reciting the Latin alphabet, whereas Claudius never learned to master it, and the descriptions in Suetonius of Claudius's facial contortions are truly repugnant. The ruler is wise also because he accepts divine providence and the company of philosophers.

And it was philosophers who taught tyrants how to make their tyranny bearable. Because tyranny is a slippery slope, practically irresistible. So said Emperor Tiberius, according to *The Annals* of Tacitus: "He declared that everything mortal was uncertain, that the more power he obtained, the more he found himself on slippery ground [*in lubrico dictitans*]." To his friends, when they congratulated him, he said: "You can't imagine how great a monster the empire is." This comes from Suetonius's account, as does the speech Tiberius gave on acceding to power (he ruled from AD 14 to 37): "I shall always be consistent and will never change my ways as long as I am in my sense; but for the sake of precedent the senate should beware of binding itself to support the acts of any man, since he might through some mischance suffer a change." The emperor warned the senators, as a preventive measure, against a possible change in his mental health (*sanae mentis*).

Tyranny is an engine of pleasure, its motion is perpetual (in the classic sense, because the effect is greater than the cause), fed by a cruelty that is necessarily excessive, and a brutality that is necessarily monstrous. It is a huge monster, to which one loses one's mind, and when Tiberius speaks to the senate, that's what he tells them: I can only promise you what I'm in a position to promise, up to the moment I go crazy. But tyranny is also an engine that, because of the very excesses of its practitioners, works toward its own destruction—as Xenophon knew, as did also Matteo Villani, who continued the *Cronica*. "Even as tyrannies rise up, increase, and consolidate, at their very heart sprouts the fateful seed that will bring them discord and ruin."

Once again we are confronted with the tyrant's face—confronting the man who smiled at us from the top of his pedestal: Cangrande della Scala. He is perched, a mounted hero, above the imposing Scaliger tomb in Verona, smiling at us as if to say: Come, tyranny has grown soft and supple in the hands of philosophers, I am supported on all sides, and you philosophers come too, continue your work of appeasing tyranny. Dante accepted the invitation. Dante dedicated his *Commedia* to Cangrande, in 1316, when it was still unfinished. When the Holy Roman Emperor Henry VII died unexpectedly in August 1313, the imperial dream had already faded away, and the minor lords whom he had named imperial vicars (and to whom he had delegated his sovereign power) found themselves with a free hand. That whole generation, the generation of Dante and Marsilius of Padua, who sought in the emperor a defender of the peace, all who believed that the empire was the embodiment of a vision of harmony, found themselves saddled after the emperor's death with the lords who'd reigned in the emperor's name and now continued to dominate with an entirely free hand. Among them was the lord of Verona, Cangrande, trying to attract artists and men of letters to his court by making a show of his interest in "good government." And what if seigneury—which is to say the power of a single man extending over a whole territory—was the future of the commune, or at least the only way out of the tangle of conflicting claims? This is the choice that Dante made, contrary to the republican civic culture of communal Italy — a scandalous choice, and a betrayal of his Florentine political heritage. He expressed this choice and justified it in a long letter. In 1316, Dante published the *Inferno*, revised the *Purgatorio*, and started the *Paradiso*. In his letter of dedication to Cangrande, he commented on his own unfinished work, putting freedom of action at its heart, the most precious freedom that God has given man and a gift that men all too rarely make use of: "If one takes the work allegorically, the subject is man insofar as, by the merits and demerits of his life, given his freedom of will, he must answer to justice, which rewards and punishes." In distinguishing the allegorical from the literal, Dante applies the methods of biblical exegesis to his own text. This is typical of him: Had he not already in his *Vita Nuova* presented a compendium of his early poems along with a commentary? He makes a case in his commentary on the *Commedia* for his sovereignty as an artist — I'll bypass the question of whether the first part of the letter to Cangrande is authentic, which Carlo Ginzburg has questioned, although I think his doubts are mostly unfounded. It's either by Dante or a Dante follower who, in some sense, has Dantean materials to hand; and in any case no one doubts the authenticity of the second part, where Dante justifies his support for seigneury.

> The chorus of praise for Your Magnificence uttered by the public has produced different effects on different men: some are elated, hoping for prosperity; others dejected,

> fearing ruin. In truth, I once believed that the plaudits addressed to you were highly exaggerated, given what one might expect from the actions of a modern man. But so as not to remain too long in uncertainty and to see with my own eyes the things that I had heard of, I visited Verona — as the queen of Sheba travelled to Jerusalem and Pallas to Mount Helicon. And I was then able to see your great exploits, see your beneficial deeds and benefit from them; thus, while I had once thought that the statements regarding you were exaggerated, I was obliged to recognize just how exceptional your actions were.

Dante rationalizes his betrayal, his choice, by distancing himself from the general opinion, by making an effort to be supremely indifferent to what opinion might say.

> But the people in its ignorance judges without discernment, and just as they think that the sun measures a foot in diameter, in the realm of morals they allow themselves to be led astray by their silly credulity. But we, to whom it is given to know what is best in us, must not follow in the footsteps of the herd but must rather correct the errors that they make. Truly, those who draw their strength from reason and the intellect and have received the divine gift of freedom are not constrained by any custom; and this should not surprise us because they are not inspired by the law, but the law is inspired by them.

The framing text that I spoke of, the accompanying text to the *Commedia* that constructs an argument for the acceptability of tyranny, is found here in Dante's self-justification.

The date is 1316, and Dante has chosen to support Cangrande. But others, contemporaries of his, had made the opposite choice, and they produced political fictions based on a different set of prefigurations — other reverse genealogies. Such a one was Albertino Mussato, a notary from Padua, himself a victim of the political storms that darkened the commune's future. Accused of treason and forced to flee while a mob ransacked his house, he took up arms against Verona. When he composed his tragedy *Ecerinis,* Padua had fallen to the conquering Veronese army but not yet been subdued politically. The da Carrara family became signors of Padua, yet Cangrande besieged the city all the same, in 1319. Meanwhile, Dante had entered into the service of the "tyrant," who finally took Padua in 1329, the year Mussato died while still in exile.

Ecerinis, then, was written as part of the fight, a combat play. It was read publicly on Christmas Day three years in a row: 1315, 1316, 1317. Contemporaneously, Giotto painted the frescoes of Padua's Palazzo della Ragione: With words and pictures, the friends of liberty tried to defend the spirit of resistance. The impact of these civic ceremonies can be measured by the commentaries they elicited.

The works of Mussato belong to a particular social context (the notarial class) and to a particular intellectual context

(Paduan pre-humanism). Giuseppe Billanovich has argued for the cultural importance of the city of Padua. At the center of its small circle of literary figures was Lovato Lovati, the son of a notary. All were avid students of classical antiquity, looking to establish the legitimacy of the communal government, which was then undergoing a period of instability. They excavated the earth around towns and searched libraries. It was in this way that Lovati found what he believed to be the tomb of Antenor, Padua's mythical founder. What he really discovered was the Etruscus manuscript of Seneca's tragedies. Others in his circle include Pietro Albano (philosopher, physician, alchemist) and Marsilius of Padua. All supported the use of Latin, which is why Mussato's literary project turned its back on Dante, failing to grasp the modernity of poetry in the vulgar tongue.

As for its political composition, Padua was a classic Italian commune in its popular phase. Since the fall of Ezzelino III da Romano in 1254, the political regime had widened its social base (the *Consilium majus* comprised a thousand citizens) and eliminated the Magnats and clerks from positions of power.

The originality of *Ecerinis* lies in the fact that it draws on history. Mussato led off with a depiction of the immediate past (northern Italy from 1313 to 1315), then addressed his own time by taking a detour not into mythology but history, and specifically the fall of the Ghibelline signor Ezzelino, Emperor Frederick II's man in Italy. This was recent history, as Ezzelino had died just two years before Mussato's birth, but it was a history permeated with myth. Mussato's pen had already given Emperor Henry VII the fate of a Senecan hero: a fortunate, promising start, followed by the *fortuna volubilis* that led the errant hero to his destruction. At the moment when Mussato was making the opposite choice from Dante, when he was gathering his city's classical culture, its immediate past, and its recent history to form a barrier against encroaching tyranny, he piled together his three histories. He piled together Seneca, Ezzelino, and the da Carraras. He targeted a contemporary figure (Cangrande), likening him to a character from sixty years earlier. His relationship to Ezzelino's terrorist power is comparable to our own relationship to the 1930s.

Ecerinis fits into the genre of tragedy not because of its unhappy outcome (the story ends happily) but because of the "sublime style" that Dante, in *De vulgari eloquentia,* calls *tragicus.* In that sense, we're not far from epic writing: The play is in fact composed of a long narrative, interspersed with songs from the chorus, and the dialogue is intended solely to push the narrative forward. In a letter to Cangrande, Dante relies on a nonce etymology of "tragedy," saying it derives from "the song of the billy goat," *tragos oda.* The play would begin, therefore, with the rank smell of the male goat and end in gaiety, the smell of sanctity, like an inverted hagiography. We shouldn't forget that at the time Seneca was considered a Christian. In consequence, *Ecerinis* owes as much to Boethius as to Seneca, and the political monstrousness belongs as much to Theodoric as to Nero.

The opening scene is in every sense dramatic and presents the unnaturalness of tyranny. The references are mythological and derived from Seneca — from *Medea,* the birth of the Atreides, etc. Ezzelino becomes the archetype of the tyrant. The play opens with the rumor of the signor of Verona's satanic birth. The model here is the coupling of Pasiphae with the monster and the birth of the Minotaur, related in Seneca's *Phaedra*.

In this first scene, Ezzelino's mother tells her son the secret of his birth: He was not conceived by his father but by a monstrous beast that emerged from the smoking bowels of the earth to possess his mother. The tragedy depicted here seems entirely in keeping with Dante's definition of tragedy and his false etymology from "song of the male goat." Ezzelino learns of his birth with delight ("Speak, Mother, / For all that is grand and savage is grateful to my ears"), because this supernatural ancestry offers him the promise of being evil to an extreme degree. "We will be judges worthy of our paternal court, if we perform acts that conform to our father's kingdom: war, death, ruin, perfidy, cunning, and the perdition of the whole human race, that is what our father wants." Logically enough, the chorus addresses the last words to the audience: "To the extent that you are able, be forewarned and learn this inexorable law."

A foul beast and a fertile womb: It's impossible today not to hear Mussato's warning as an echo of the universal struggle against barbarism, the "inexorable law." The poet — Mussato was in fact the first to be publicly crowned as a poet, before Petrarch even, in the year 1315—played repeatedly on this similarity between different times, even to the ritual of holding annual public readings of *Ecerinis* in Padua, which harked back to the political origins of Greek tragedy, a song of freedom that was sung only when freedom was threatened.

We might raise the question of Mussato's political lucidity. I've contrasted the two portraits of Cangrande, and I have to say that it escapes me: traitor, betrayal, resistance. But what does Mussato say about seigneury? In fact seigneury, as a political process, is not born of a monstrous coupling. It just isn't true, a seigneury doesn't start that way: It's a slow, silent trend, prompted by the dysfunction of communal institutions. To identify it with a political monster doesn't seem the right way to conceptualize it. Dante, who plays the villain in this story, proposed a different view—perhaps influenced by political opportunism, as he certainly found refuge in the court of Cangrande—but also in keeping with his ideological commitment. Dante's intention was to demythologize Ezzelino's demonic origins, though he clearly situated him in Hell. He refused to interpret Ezzelino's citadel, which towered in the sky, as a defiance pointed at God. He described it as "a hill, not very high, from which came a torch that laid waste this countryside. We are both of us born from the same root."

Aside from comedy and tragedy, there's a third form of political fiction that can be used to strip villainous rulers of their veils: satire, parody, pastiche. We've discussed, in the case of a panegyric to Nero, why it can be difficult to distinguish genuine acclamation from its parodic double. And we've seen that all these figures, from Alexander to Baybars, were shadowed by their parodic doubles. When this element is present from the start, we might expect that any attack on an authoritarian ruler based on parody or skepticism would have a lessened effect, a diminished intensity. So let's look at a political fiction that belongs to the genre of speculative fiction: I'm thinking here of the *Roman de Fauvel,* a collective allegorical poem of the fourteenth century, whose main text was written in 1314 by Gervais du Bus, the chaplain of Enguerrand de Marigny. And note that it is strictly contemporary: Dante and Mussato were active in Italy while the *Roman de Fauvel* was being composed in France. It is a roman à clef, a satirical and allegorical fiction that is also a political act. We might consider taking another look at the theme of the *fable,* and at the relation between parody and satire. Roger Bellon has recently shown, for instance, that branch XVI of the *Roman de Renart,* called "Renart empereur," was a parodic rewriting of the Arthurian romance *The Death of Arthur,* part of the Lancelot-Grail Cycle.

The plot goes as follows: King Noble must fight a lightning war against the Pagans, who have invaded his kingdom. Meanwhile, Reynard, whom King Noble has put in charge of safeguarding the kingdom and the queen, has managed, thanks to a forged letter, to take Noble's place: He becomes emperor and weds Queen Fière! When Noble returns from the war against the Pagans, he is obliged to lay siege to his own castle. Reynard, despairing of breaking through the troops encircling him, attempts a night sortie, planning to kill the king in his sleep. The operation fails, and Reynard is captured and sentenced to torture, but the king pardons him in the end and the tale comes to a close with a return to the harmony that reigned at the outset: Noble rejoins his wife at the palace, and Reynard returns to Maupertuis, ready for a new round of adventures. Note that the parodic trio (Noble, Fière, and Reynard) is analogous to the trio in *The Death of Arthur*.

All Reynardian writing is rewriting. The teller and his audience already know the whole Reynard saga, and the task at hand is to derail the narrative using farce. But here, everything is topsy-turvy: Reynard is allied with Ysengrim and isn't hungry, though Reynard the Fox is famine fiction. Yet in this telling everything is at the high-water mark. In short, it is carnival time. The Reynardian text seems to parody itself here, bending the familiar structures—this is the kind of writing, once again, that we associate with a series. The aim of the Reynardian parody is clear: to draw on literary models and use characters from earlier branches to present a principal female character, the queen herself, as degraded. Fière is the reverse image of Guinevere in *The Death of Arthur*. The author of "Renart empereur" continues the project of undermining the saga that the earlier authors of "Jugement de Renart" and "Siège de Maupertuis" had started; he belongs among the authors of romance who specialized in "the destruction of courtly myths."

"Renart empereur" might then be called the parody of a parodic reversal, of a fiction that had reached its endpoint. *The Death of Arthur,* written circa 1230, abruptly ends the cycle of the continuators of Chrétien de Troyes and kills everyone off, including the romance itself. It is a romance full of tournaments, as if knightly adventure had dwindled to a simulacrum of itself; it is a romance invaded by feudalism, and a disordered feudalism at that; the tracery of personal connections can't protect the Arthurian characters from the private wars that bring about the final downfall; it is a romance that inverts the figure of Arthur, who had until then been the personification of a king who is obedient to custom, who takes counsel but does not govern, who has no individual will but is simply the guarantor of a code. In short, by parodying *The Death of Arthur,* "Renart empereur" constructs a satirical reversal of the death of courtly literature itself.

The parodic reversal of medieval literature is aimed less at individual works than at whole genres, hence knightly practice is its primary target. If Arthurian political fiction fades into parodic reversal, the secular theater also appears to have acted as the "laboratory" for a mocking intertextuality. Drawing on the corpus of fabliaux, the theater depicted the courtly tradition in a poor light and instituted a desacralized vision of the world, all the while establishing a network of correspondences between the plays themselves, as evidenced by *Courtois d'Arras* and *Le Jeu de la feuillée.* Parody, especially theatrical parody, is characterized by a "space of performativity" and practiced within the topsy-turvydom of the festive sphere, employing a subtle mix of gravity and irony.

This is what puts the very concept of romans à clef and other keyed works at peril. The writings of Jean-Claude Mühlethaler probe this playful intentionality of medieval parodic literature, following the play of parodic inversions, displacements, and irradiations — see his "Le dévoilement satirique: Texte et image dans le *Roman de Fauvel*" (Satirical unveiling: Text and image in the *Roman de Fauvel*), in a 2009 issue of *Poétique*. Satire as an expressive register has affinities with animal fables and allegorical tales. The *Roman de Fauvel* is about a horse (Fauvel) whose rise in the papal and royal courts brings all of society crashing down. The satiric finger-pointing borrows literary tropes from the *Roman de la rose*, reconfiguring the political events that marked the end of the reign of King Philip IV of France into allegory — criticism hides behind the veil of fiction.

The so-called interpolated version of the *Roman de Fauvel* exists in a single exemplar, manuscript 146 in the Bibliothèque nationale de France. Its narrative, its 78 miniatures, and its 130 musical pieces make it an extraordinary instance of a successful collaboration between the arts. Text and images join to denounce the moral decline that afflicts the nobility, the clergy, and even the common people after they have declared their allegiance to the horse Fauvel. The prologue, written in 1310 by Gervais du Bus, a notary in the royal chancellery, opens with ten lines announcing its program, accompanied by an illustration of Fauvel the horse holding court with all the attributes of sovereignty and the pope and several kings gathered to curry him: "Because of Fauvel, whom I see being gently curried — and not harmed at all, I have sunk into melancholy, for this animal is highly pampered. Fauvel is often represented in paintings, but many don't know whether to take it as mockery, or wisdom, or madness. And that's why I'll say whatever comes into my mind about this animal without equivocating."

Fauvel on his throne, detail from manuscript by Gervais du Bus and Raoul Chaillou de Pesstain, c. 1318–1320

Why this melancholy? It's the sadness of Adam after the Fall — the sadness due to uncertainty of interpretation. Dante makes a point of detailing the allegorical meanings of his work, but du Bus does not. He no longer knows whether he should interpret the story as mockery, wisdom, or madness. And the reason he doesn't know is because he's looking at the image. The relationship between the figurative and the allegorical destabilizes the text. It's also what sent these lectures off the rails, when we paused for three successive lectures over the visual event of the *Leviathan* frontispiece.

The narrator wavers between the fear of being the butt of a joke and the conviction, which was dominant in the Middle Ages, that images are meant to instruct and commemorate — which is why the *Roman de Fauvel* incorporates music. The narrator's words appear to be the authorized personal commentary of a "painting." The reader, who holds the manuscript in his hands, identifies the painting with the miniature he sees at the bottom of the page. What resists in the image, which represents Fauvel holding court, is the impossibility of turning it around carnival-style. In medieval culture, the horse cannot be considered ridiculous: It isn't as if a donkey were holding court. In chivalry the horse is the knight's companion par excellence. An aristocratic readership, well-versed in the feats of Tristan and Lancelot, would have felt disconcerted looking at the image of Fauvel surrounded by his fawning admirers.

In the *Roman de Fauvel*, the topsy-turvy world of the carnival, which is normally relegated to the margins of Gothic manuscripts, is in the center of the page and at the center of attention. But this representation undergoes transformations, on the model of Ovidian metamorphoses. Through allegory, the *Roman de Fauvel* attains a degree of generality that allows it to transcend the actual events that prompted it and be adapted to a variety of references, as is usual with satirical writing. The transcoding of historical reality allows the work to remain readable for decades, even centuries. By giving Fauvel a horse's traits and especially those of a hybrid being, the illustrations of manuscript 146 manage to keep the romance from being only a criticism of the government at the time of Philip IV and his sons. They make it a manifesto denouncing all abuses of power and any government that ignores the common good.

The prophetic violence of satire comes about through unveiling: Satire lifts all veils and strips away all masks. But here we return to one of our first thoughts, the anxiety expressed at the beginning of the lectures: How are we to unmask the appealing face of a tyranny wreathed in smiles? And conversely, how are we to unmask the faces that proactively protect themselves from satire and caricature by presenting themselves as parodies of parodies, like a fiction that manages in some way to fictionalize our attempts to undercut it? In the first lecture, I used a photograph of Charlie Chaplin from *Limelight*, saying "I'm going to talk about Chaplin, you'll soon know why." Well, you've had to wait. The photo showed a man who is slowly removing his makeup and who lets us see him as he is — older and more ridiculous — which is a way of turning the mirror on ourselves. It's time to conclude with him.

In *Prisoner of Love*, Jean Genet describes the political fiction that, for a man of power, is tied to the attributes he has chosen for himself: Winston Churchill's cigar, Yasser Arafat's kaffiyeh, Adolf Hitler's mustache.

> The first, daily, and inexorable duty befalling Hitler on awaking was to recreate his physical resemblance to himself—the dustbroom of his clipped, nearly horizontal mustache, each of its browns seeming to emerge from his nostrils, and the part in his glossy black locks, whose strands were as strictly forbidden to stray to the wrong side of his frozen forehead as the swastika was forbidden to point left, though whether his eyes smoldered with anger or cajolery might vary.

We have a description of the first, the inexorable duty of the person who wants to *resemble himself*.

Today, these identifiers function as logos—you only need to stylize one on the cover of a book to suggest something you're not stating explicitly. Take, for instance, the cover of *Look Who's Back* by Timur Vermes, where you will find what historians of hirsuteness call a toothbrush mustache. This form of mustache was popular in Germany in the 1920s, where it had a variety of names including *Zweifinger* (two fingers) but also *Chaplinbart*, because it suggested Chaplin's Tramp. This character's troubling resemblance to Hitler was often remarked on in the 1920s, to the point where Chaplin himself discussed it. He even claimed at one point to have filmed *The Great Dictator* as an act of revenge for what the film critic André Bazin, writing in *Esprit* in 1945, called Hitler's "ontological theft." But the essay of Bazin's on which I intend to draw going forward, "Pastiche or Postiche, or Nothingness over a Mustache," goes far beyond this anecdote. It's a profound meditation on one of the most daring moves that Chaplin makes, which is to juggle paradoxically with déjà vu and resemblance.

We might start with the film's epigraph, which parodies the disclaimer that often accompanies fiction: "Any resemblance between the dictator Hynkel and the Jewish barber is purely coincidental." Chaplin of course plays both the barber from the Jewish ghetto and the dictator, the one who resembles the dictator he so strikingly resembles. The film opens with the despot's harangue — a scene that is about far more than just his barking, bellowing tones and turns out to be a scathing take on the relation between totalitarian rule and technology — and it ends with the barber's long, humanist monologue ("A Call to Mankind"), which also plays with reproducing the human voice through technology and diffusing it out into the landscape. This ending acquires impact from its being Chaplin's own entrance into the world of talkies. It's the first time he speaks. He is responding to the entreaties of the ghetto dwellers, who tell the barber: You have to speak, it's our only chance.

The disclaimer at the start of the film is ironic, considering that the film was shot despite the diplomatic pressure that

Germany exerted on American studios to dissuade them from the project, starting in 1938. When the film was released in the United States in 1940, the context had changed — and it's said (though the fact is contested) that Hitler, who'd obviously forbidden the film's release in Germany, acquired a copy for himself and watched it twice. So it was not impossible that the studios, who had cravenly resisted making the film for three years, had insisted on the inclusion of the traditional disclaimer. But no: This was a statement about a *fictional* character's resemblance to another fictional character, which was said to be unintentional. The film is anachronistic from the start. It begins with a long prologue that picks up on Chaplin's earlier film *Shoulder Arms*, about a Jewish soldier who emerges from World War I in a state of amnesia. Memory occupies a prominent place in the film, but it's a forgetful memory.

The disclaimer might then be seen as justified, given the difficulties that Chaplin faced in getting the film made. But in fact it is subverted, because the resemblance between the barber and the dictator, which could have driven the plot, is ignored from start to finish, even in the final scene where there's a substitution. The residents of the ghetto never notice, any more than the high functionaries in the chancellery — despite the fact that Commander Schultz and others travel back and forth between the two worlds, not one of them notices the resemblance.

Jean Narboni wrote a book called *Pourquoi les coiffeurs? Notes actuelles sur* Le Dictateur. Briefly to explain the title,

"Why the barbers?" is a Jewish joke that exists in a million variants, but the gist of it is that one guy says to another, "You know, they're going to kill all the Jews and barbers." And the other guy says, "Why the barbers?" It's what Theodor Adorno calls "failed humor." Normally it doesn't make you laugh; it's Jewish humor. So Narboni's book returns to this fascinating failure in the realm of fiction. What is Chaplin's film about then, if the resemblance is completely ignored? "Perhaps something much more serious than attributes of similar pilosity […] but about a real war of annihilation, where the continued existence of one protagonist is possible only at the cost of eliminating the other." The story is not driven by the familiarity of mimetic qualities but by "the canceling power of the unknown double."

That's why the film is from the start anachronistic, prophetic in its awareness of Nazism's mass extermination and courageous, but unavailing — reopening the dizzying discussion as to the utility or inutility of parody. What is striking here is how the assignation is resisted, most particularly when the barber makes his statement.

In this we may recognize what Adorno said about Samuel Beckett, that there was laughter without comedy, which is the opposite of low mockery, of the Fall — there's no Fall here. In this crisis of resemblance where there's no Fall, one can only think of what Klaus Mann wrote in *Contre la barbarie*: "It's as if people are afflicted with a kind of physical repugnance for the truth."

BIBLIOGRAPHY

Abelard, Peter. *Sic et Non: A Critical Edition*. Edited by Blanche B. Boyer and Richard McKeon. University of Chicago Press, 1977.

Agamben, Giorgio. *The Omnibus Homo Sacer*. Stanford University Press, 2017.

———. "On the Uses and Disadvantages of Living among Specters." In *Nudities*. Translated by David Kishik and Stefan Pedatella. Stanford University Press, 2010.

———. *Stasis: Civil War as a Political Paradigm*. Translated by Nicholas Heron. Stanford University Press, 2015.

Aït-Touati, Frédérique. *Fictions of the Cosmos: Science and Literature in the Seventeenth Century*. University of Chicago Press, 2011.

Albert, Jean-Pierre. "Qui croit à la transsubstantiation?" *L'Homme* 175–176 (2005): 369–96.

Allott, Stephen. *Alcuin of York, c. A.D. 732 to 804: His Life and Letters*. William Sessions, 1974.

Ambrose. *De sacramentis*. Herder, 1990.

Aquinas, *see* Thomas Aquinas.

Arendt, Hannah. "Lying in Politics." In *Crises of the Republic*. New York: Harcourt Brace Jovanovich, 1972.

———. *The Origins of Totalitarianism*. Harcourt, Brace, 1951.

Augustine. *The City of God*. Translated by Marcus Dods. Modern Library, 1983.

———. "Sermon 272." In *Sermons*. Edited by John E. Rotelle. Translated by Edmund Hill. New City Press, 1993.

Baldwin, John W. *The Government of Philip Augustus: Foundations of French Royal Power in the Middle Ages*. University of California Press, 1986.

Barthélemy, Dominique. *Chevaliers et miracles: La violence et le sacré dans la société féodale*. Armand Colin, 2004.

Baschet, Jérôme. *La civilisation féodale: De l'an mille à la colonisation de l'Amérique*. Aubier, 2004.

———. *Corps et âmes: Une histoire de la personne au Moyen Âge*. Flammarion, 2016.

———. *Le sein du père: Abraham et la paternité dans l'Occident médiéval*. Gallimard, 2000.

Baudrillard, Jean. *Perfect Crime*. Translated by Chris Turner. Verso, 1996.

———. *Simulacra and Simulation*. Translated by Sheila Faria Glaser. University of Michigan Press, 1994.

Bayard, Pierre. *Comment améliorer les oeuvres ratées*. Les Éditions de Minuit, 2000.

———. *Le plagiat par anticipation*. Les Éditions de Minuit, 2009.

———. *Et si les oeuvres changeaient d'auteur?* Les Éditions de Minuit, 2010.

———. *Le* Titanic *fera naufrage*. Les Éditions de Minuit, 2016.

Bazin, André. "Pastiche or Postiche, or Nothingness over a Mustache."

In *Essays on Chaplin*. Edited and translated by Jean Bodon. University of New Haven Press, 1985.

———. "Sur *Le Dictateur*: pastiche et postiche ou le néant pour une moustache." *Esprit* (1945).

Bellah, Robert N. "Civil Religion in America." *Daedalus* 96, no. 1 (Winter 1967): 1–21.

Bellon, Roger. "'Renart empereur': *Le Roman de Renart*, ms. H, branche XVI: une réécriture renardienne de *La Mort le roi Artu*?" *Cahiers de recherches médiévales* 15 (2008): 3–17.

Belting, Hans. *Face and Mask: A Double History*. Translated by Thomas S. Hansen and Abby J. Hansen. Princeton University Press, 2017.

Benjamin, Walter. *The Arcades Project*. Translated by Howard Eiland and Kevin McLaughlin. The Belknap Press of Harvard University Press, 1999.

———. "Karl Krauss." In *Selected Writings: Volume 2, Part 2: 1931–1934*. Edited by Michael W. Jennings, Howard Eiland, and Gary Smith. The Belknap Press of Harvard University Press, 1999.

———. "A Little History of Photography." In *Selected Writings: Volume 2, Part 2: 1931–1934*. Edited by Michael W. Jennings, Howard Eiland, and Gary Smith. The Belknap Press of Harvard University Press, 1999.

———. "Paris, the Capital of the Nineteenth Century: Exposé of 1935." In *The Arcades Project*. Translated by Howard Eiland and Kevin McLaughlin. The Belknap Press of Harvard University Press, 1999.

———. "Theses on the Philosophy of History." In *Illuminations*. Translated by Harry Zohn. Edited by Hannah Arendt. Mariner Books, Houghton Mifflin Harcourt, 2019.

Biard, Joël. "Vérité logique et vérité métaphysique dans le nominalisme tardif." In Jean-Philippe Genet, ed. *La vérité: Vérité et crédibilité:*

Construire la vérité dans le système de communication de l'Occident (XIIIe–XVIIe siècle). Éditions de la Sorbonne, 2015.

Bloch, Jean-Richard. Letter to Curzio Malaparte, Nov. 20, 1931. Cited in Curzio Malaparte, *Coup d'État, the Technique of Revolution*. E. P. Dutton & Co., 1932.

Bloch, Marc. "L'erreur collective de la 'Grande Peur' comme symptome d'un état social." *Annales* 5, no. 21 (May 1933).

———. "La popularité du toucher des écrouelles." *Le Moyen Âge* (January–April 1927): 34–41.

———. "Réflexions d'un historien sur les fausses nouvelles de la guerre." *Revue de synthèse historique* (1921).

———. *Les rois thaumaturges: Étude sur le caractère surnaturel attribué à la puissance royale particulièrement en France et en Angleterre*. Gallimard, 1983.

———. *The Royal Touch: Sacred Monarchy and Scrofula in England and France*. Translated by J. E. Anderson. Routledge and Keegan Paul, 1973.

———. "La vie d'outre-tombe du roi Salomon." *Revue belge de philologie et d'histoire*, t. 4, fasc. 2–3 (1925): 349–77.

Blumenberg, Hans. *Paradigms for a Metaphorology*. Translated by Robert Savage. Cornell University Press, 2010.

———. *Präfiguration: Arbeit am politischen Mythos*. Suhrkamp, 2014.

———. *Work on Myth*. Translated by Robert M. Wallace. MIT Press, 1985.

Boas, George. *Vox Populi: Studies in the History of an Idea*. Johns Hopkins Press, 1969.

Bodart, Diane. "Le prince miroir: métaphore optique du corps politique." In Philippe Morel, ed. *Le miroir et l'espace du prince dans l'art italien de la Renaissance*. Presses universitaires François-Rabelais, 2012.

Book of Baruch. Edited, reconstructed, and translated by Emanuel Tov. Published by Scholars Press for the Society of Biblical Literature, 1975.

Borges, Jorge Luis. *Collected Fictions*. Translated by Andrew Hurley. Penguin Books, 1998.

———. "Kafka and His Precursors." In *Selected Non-Fictions*. Edited by Eliot Weinberger. Translated by Esther Allen, Suzanne Jill Levine, and Eliot Weinberger. Penguin, 1999.

Botero, Giovanni. *The Reason of State*. Cambridge University Press, 2017.

Boucheron, Patrick. "Bien qu'il fût cruel, il y avait dans ses cruautés une grande part de justice; l'étrange popularité litéraire d'un justicier sans pitié, Bernabò Visconti." In Olivier Mattéoni and Nicolas Offenstadt, eds. *Un Moyen Âge pour aujourd'hui:* Mélanges offerts à Claude Gauvard. PUF, 2010: 63–71.

———. *Ce que peut l'histoire*. Collège de France, 2016.

———. *Faire profession d'historien*. Éditions de la Sorbonne, 2010.

———. *The Power of Images: Siena, 1338*. Translated by Andrew Brown. Polity Press, 2018.

———. "Tout est monument. Le mausolée d'Azzone Visconti à San Gottardo in Corta de Milan (1342–1346)." In Dominique Barthélémy and Jean-Marie Martin, eds. "Liber largitorius." Études d'*histoire médiévale offertes à Pierre Toubert par ses élèves*. Droz, 2003.

———. *Trace and Aura: The Recurring Lives of Ambrose of Milan*. Translated by Lara Vergnaud and Willard Wood. Other Press, 2022.

———. "Un tyran attirant." *Critique* 823 (December 2015): 933–47.

Boureau, Alain. "L'adage *Vox populi, vox Dei* et l'invention de la nation anglaise." *Annales ESC*, no. 4–5 (1992): 1071–1089.

———. "Droit et théologie au XIIIe siècle." *Annales ESC* 47, no. 6 (1992): 113–25.

———. *Kantorowicz: Stories of a Historian*. Translated by Stephen G. Nichols and Gabrielle M. Spiegel. Johns Hopkins University Press, 2001.

Bournazel, Éric, and Jean-Pierre Poly. "Couronne et mouvance dans la France de Philippe Auguste." In Robert-Henri Bautier, ed. *La France de Philippe Auguste: Le temps des mutations*. CNRS Éditions, 1982.

Bowersock, Glen. *Fiction as History: Nero to Julian*. University of California Press, 1994.

Bozoky, Edina. "La représentation idéale d'Attila et de son royaume dans l'historiographie médiévale de Hongrie." In Anne-Hélène Allirot, Gilles Lecuppre, and Lydwine Scordia, eds. *Royautés imaginaires (XIIe–XVIe siècles)*. Brepols, 2005.

Bredekamp, Horst. *Image Acts: A Systematic Approach to Visual Agency*. Translated by Elizabeth Clegg. De Gruyter, 2018.

———. *Leviathan: Body Politic as Visual Strategy in the Work of Thomas Hobbes*. Translated, edited, and adapted by Elizabeth Clegg. De Gruyter, 2020.

Briant, Pierre. *Alexandre: Exégèse des lieux communs*. Gallimard, 2016.

Briguglia, Gianluca, and Irène Rosier-Catach, eds. *Adam, la nature humaine, avant et après. Épistémologie de la chute*. Éditions de la Sorbonne, 2016.

Brown, Wendy. *Walled States, Waning Sovereignty*. Zone Books, 2017.

Buc, Philippe. *L'ambiguité du livre: Prince, pouvoir et peuple dans les commentaires de la Bible au Moyen Âge*. Beauchesne, 1994.

Caïra, Olivier. *Définir la fiction: Du roman au jeu d'*échecs. Éditions de l'EHESS, 2011.

Calmet, Augustin. *Treatise on Vampires and Revenants: The Phantom World: Dissertation on Those Persons Who Return to Earth Bodily, the*

Excommunicated, the Oupires or Vampires, Vroucolacas, &c. Edited by Clive Leatherdale. Translated by Henry Christmas. Desert Island Books, 1993.

Castelli-Gattinara, Enrico. *Les inquiétudes de la raison: Épistémologie et histoire en France dans l'entre-deux-guerres.* EHESS, J. Vrin, 1998.

Castoriadis, Cornelius. *The Imaginary Institution of Society.* Translated by Kathleen Blamey. MIT Press, 1987.

Certeau, Michel de. *L'écriture de l'histoire.* Gallimard, 1975.

Cicero. *De officiis.* Translated by Walter Miller. Heineman, 1913.

Coccia, Emanuele. "La comédie du droit: Adam et le premier procès de l'histoire humaine." In Briguglia and Rosier-Catach, eds. *Adam, la nature humaine, avant et après. Épistémologie de la chute.* Éditions de la Sorbonne, 2016.

Comestor, Petrus. *The Historye of the Patriarks.* Edited from Cambridge, St. John's College, MS G. 31 by Mayumi Taguchi; with parallel texts of *The Historia Scholastica* and the *Bible Historiale.* Winter 2010.

Commines, Philippe de. *Mémoires.* Edited by Joël Blanchard. Hachette, Le Livre de Poche, 2001.

Crignon, Philippe. *De l'incarnation à la représentation: L'ontologie politique de Thomas Hobbes.* Classiques Garnier, 2012.

Crouzet, Denis. *Les guerriers de Dieu: La violence au temps des troubles de religion (vers 1525–vers 1610).* Champ Vallon, 1990.

Dalarun, Jacques. *To Govern Is to Serve: An Essay on Medieval Democracy.* Translated by Sean L. Field. Cornell University Press, 2023.

Dante Alighieri. "Epistle to Cangrande della Scala." Available at https://faculty.georgetown.edu/jod/cangrande.english.html

Debord, Guy. *The Society of the Spectacle.* Zone Books, 1994.

De Luca, Erri. *Noyau d'olive*. Translated by Danièle Valin. Gallimard, 2013.

Derrida, Jacques. *The Beast and the Sovereign*, vol. 1. Edited by Michel Lisse, Marie-Louise Mallet, and Ginette Michaud. Translated by Geoffrey Bennington. University of Chicago Press, 2009.

Dolezel, Lubomir. *Possible Worlds of Fiction and History: The Postmodern Stage*. Johns Hopkins University Press, 2010.

Duby, Georges. *The Age of the Cathedrals: Art and Society, 980–1420*. Translated by Eleanor Levieux and Barbara Thompson. University of Chicago Press, 1981.

Eddé, Anne-Marie. "Baybars et son double: De l'ambiguïté du souverain idéal." In Denise Aigle, ed. *Le Bilad al-Sam face aux mondes extérieurs: La perception de l'Autre et la représentation du souverain*. Damascus, 2012.

Falk, Francesca. *Eine gestische Geschichte der Grenze*. Fink, 2011.

Fawtier, Robert. "Marc Bloch: *Les rois thaumaturges*." *Le Moyen Âge* (1926): 238–44.

Fierro, Maribel. "Alfonso X 'The Wise': The Last Almohad Calif?" In Ivy A. Corfis, ed. *Al-Andalus, Sepharad and Medieval Iberia: Cultural Contact and Diffusion*. Brill, 2010.

Foisneau, Luc. *Hobbes: La vie inquiète*. Gallimard, 2016.

Foucault, Michel. *Abnormal: Lectures at the Collège de France, 1974–1975*. Edited by Valerio Marchetti and Antonella Salomoni. Translated by Graham Burchell. Picador, 2003.

———. "The Analytic Philosophy of Politics." Translated by Giovanni Mascaretti. *Foucault Studies* 24 (June 2018).

———. *History of Madness*. Edited by Jean Khalfa. Translated by Johnathan Murphy and Jean Khalfa. Routledge, 2006.

———. *On the Government of the Living: Lectures at the Collège de France, 1979–1980*. Translated by Graham Burchell. Picador, 2016.

———. *The Order of Things: An Archaeology of the Human Sciences*. Vintage Books, 1973.

———. *Penal Theories and Institutions: Lectures at the Collège de France, 1971–1972*. Macmillan Publishers Ltd, 2019.

Francastel, Pierre. "Un mystère parisien illustré par Uccello: Le miracle de l'hostie d'Urbino." *Revue archéologique*, 6th series, 39 (1952): 180–91.

Frankfurt, Harry G. *On Bullshit*. Princeton University Press, 2005.

Freud, Sigmund. *The Future of an Illusion*. Revised and edited by James Strachey. Translated by W. D. Robson-Scott. Doubleday, 1964 [1953].

———. *Group Psychology and the Analysis of the Ego*. Edited and translated by James Strachey. Norton, [1975] 1959.

Fubini, Riccardo. *Italia quattrocentesca: Politica e diplomazia nell'età di Lorenzo il Magnifico*. FrancoAngeli, 1994.

Gamboni, Dario. "Composing the Body Politic." In Bruno Latour and Peter Weibel, eds. *Making Things Public: Atmospheres of Democracy*. MIT Press, 2005.

Genet, Jean. *Prisoner of Love*. Translated by Barbara Bray. New York Review Books, 2003.

Genette, Gérard. *Métalepse: De la figure à la fiction*. Seuil, 2004.

Gentile, Emilio. *Politics as Religion*. Translated by George Stanton. Princeton University Press, 2006.

Gerald of Wales. See Giraldus Cambrensis.

Giesey, Ralph. *The Royal Funeral Ceremony in Renaissance France*. E. Droz, 1960.

Gilmore, Mikal. "George R. R. Martin: The Rolling Stone Interview." *Rolling Stone*, April 23, 2014.

Ginzburg, Carlo. *The Cheese and the Worms*. Translated by John and Anne C. Tedeschi. Johns Hopkins University Press, 1980.

———. "Reading Hobbes Today." In *Fear Reverence Terror: Five Essays in Political Iconography*. Seagull Books, 2017.

Giraldus Cambrensis. *Concerning the Instruction of Princes*. Translated by Joseph Stevenson. J.M.F. Books, 1991.

Grau, Donatien. *Néron en Occident: Une figure de l'histoire*. Gallimard, 2015.

Grellard, Christophe. *De la certitude volontaire: Débats nominalistes sur la foi à la fin du Moyen Âge*. Éditions de la Sorbonne, 2014.

———. *Jean de Salisbury et la renaissance médiévale du scepticisme*. Les Belles Lettres, 2013.

Guerreau, Alain. *Le féodalisme: Un horizon théorique*. Sycomore, 1980.

Guicciardini, Francesco. *Dialogue on the Government of Florence*. Cambridge University Press, 1994.

Hertz, Robert. *Sociologie religieuse et anthropologie: Deux enquêtes de terrain, 1912–1915*. Edited by Stéphane Baciocchi and Nicolas Mariot. PUF, 2015.

Hirsch, Thomas. *Le temps des sociétés: D'Émile Durkheim à Marc Bloch*. Éditions EHESS, 2016.

Hobbes, Thomas. *Leviathan*. Penguin Books, 1968.

Iogna-Prat, Dominique. *La Maison Dieu: Une histoire monumentale de l'Église au Moyen Âge*. Seuil, 2012.

Irenaeus, Saint, Bishop of Lyon. *Treatise of Irenaeus of Lugdunum Against the Heresies*. Society for Promoting Christian Knowledge, 1916.

Ismard, Paulin. *La démocratie contre les experts: Les esclaves publics en Grèce ancienne*. Seuil, 2015.

Jaume, Lucien. *Hobbes et l'État représentatif moderne*. Presses universitaires de France, 1986.

Kantorowicz, Ernst. *Frederick the Second: 1194–1250*. Constable, 1931.

———. *The King's Two Bodies: A Study in Medieval Political Theology*. Princeton University Press, 1957.

———. *Laudes regiae: A Study in Liturgical Acclamations and Mediaeval Ruler Worship*. University of California Press, 1946.

———. "*Pro Patria Mori* in Medieval Political Thought." *The American Historical Review* 56, no. 3 (April 1951): 472–92.

———. *Selected Studies*. J. J. Augustin, 1965.

Karsenti, Bruno. *La question juive des modernes: Philosophie de l'émancipation*. PUF, 2017.

König-Pralong, Catherine. "L'empire de la doctrine. Théologie *versus* sens commun." In Philippe Genet, ed. *Vérité et crédibilité: construire la vérité dans le système de communication de l'Occident (XIIIe–XVIIIe siècle)*. Éditions de la Sorbonne, 2015.

La Boétie, Étienne de. *Discourse on Voluntary Servitude*. Translated by James B. Atkinson and David Sices. Hackett Pub. Co. Inc., 2012.

Lahire, Bernard. *La culture des individus: Dissonances culturelles et distinction de soi*. La Découverte, 2004.

Landi, Sandro. *Naissance de l'opinion publique dans l'Italie moderne: Sagesse du peuple et savoir de gouvernement de Machiavel aux Lumières*. PUR, 2006.

Lavocat, Françoise. *Fait et fiction: Pour une frontière*. Seuil, 2016.

Le Brun, Jacques. *Le pouvoir d'abdiquer: Essai dur la déchéance volontaire*. Gallimard, 2009.

Lefort, Claude. "Machiavelli and the *Verità Effetuale*." In *Writing: The Political Test*. Translated by David Ames Curtis. Duke University Press, 2000.

———. *Le travail de l'oeuvre Machiavel*. Gallimard, 1971.

Le Goff, Jacques. *Saint Louis*. Translated by Gareth Evan Gollrad. University of Notre Dame Press, 2009.

Leibniz, Gottfried Wilhelm, and Jakob Thomasius. *Correspondence 1663–1672*. Edited, translated, and annotated by Richard Bodéüs. J. Vrin, 1993.

Le Roy Ladurie, Emmanuel. *Montaillou: Cathars and Catholics in a French Village, 1294–1324*. Translated by Barbara Bray. Scolar, 1978.

Lestringant, Frank. *Une sainte horreur, ou le voyage en Eucharistie: XVIe–XVIIIe siècle*. Presses universitaires de France, 1996.

Levi, Jean. *La Chine romanesque: Fictions d'Orient et d'Occident*. Seuil, 1995.

Lévi-Straus, Claude. "A Lesson in Wisdom from Mad Cows." In *We Are All Cannibals and Other Essays*. Translated by Jane Marie Todd. Columbia University Press, 2016.

Libera, Alain de. *L'invention du sujet moderne: Cours du Collège de France 2013–2014*. Vrin, 2015.

Lignereux, Yann. *Les rois imaginaires: Une histoire visuelle de la monarchie de Charles VIII à Louis XIV*. PUR, 2016.

Loehr, Joël. "Pour une histoire litéraire au rebours." *Poétique: revue de théorie et d'analyse litéraire* 161 (2010): 37–62.

Machiavelli, Niccolò. *The Discourses*. In *The Essential Writings of Machiavelli*. Edited and translated by Peter Constantine. Random House, 2007.

———. *Discourses on Livy*. Translated by Julia Conaway Bondanella and Peter Bondanella. Oxford University Press, 1997.

———. *History of Florence and of the Affairs of Italy, from the Earliest Times to the Death of Lorenzo the Magnificent*. Harper, 1960.

———. *The Prince*. Edited by Quentin Skinner and Russell Price. Cambridge University Press, 1988.

———. *De principatibus/Le Prince*. Edited and translated by Jean-Louis Fournel and Jean-Claude Zancarini. PUF, 2000.

Malcolm, Noel. "The Title Page of *Leviathan*, Seen in a Curious Perspective." In *Aspects of Hobbes*. Oxford University Press, 2002.

Marin, Louis. *Portrait of the King*. Translated by Martha M. Houle. Macmillan Press, 1988.

Mariot, Nicolas. *Histoire d'un sacrifice: Robert, Alixe et la guerre (1914–1917)*. Seuil, 2017.

Marsilius of Padua. *Defender of the Peace*. Edited and translated by Annabel Brett. Cambridge University Press, 2005.

Maupassant, Guy de. *Strong as Death*. D. Biddle, 1899.

Mazel, Florian. In Philippe Genet, ed. *Vérité et crédibilité: construire la vérité dans le système de communication de l'Occident (XIIIe–XVIIIe siècle)*. Éditions de la Sorbonne, 2015.

Menegaldo, Silvère. "*Les faiz Neron le cruel homme*: La figure de Néron dans quelques textes français du Moyen Âge." In Denis Bjaï and Silvère Menegaldo, eds., *Figures du tyran antique au Moyen Âge et à la Renaissance*. Klincksieck, 2009.

Mercier, Louis-Sébastien. *Tableau de Paris*. Published in English as *Picture of Paris, Before and After the Revolution*. Translated by Wilfrid and Emilie Jackson. G. Routledge and Sons, Ltd, 1929.

Michelet, Jules. "Avenir! Avenir!" *Europe* 19, no. 73 (January 15, 1929): 6.

———. *History of the French Revolution*. Translated by Charles Cocks. University of Chicago Press, 1967.

Michon, Pierre. "Trois noms de bêtes pour W.B." In Pierre Michon, Guy Petitdemande, and Bruno Tackels. *Trois cailloux pour Walter Benjamin*. L'Arachnoïde, 2010.

Milner, Jean-Claude. *Harry Potter: À l'école des sciences morales et politiques*. PUF, 2014.

———. *Le sage trompeur: Libres raisonnements sur Spinoza et les Juifs*. Verdier, 2013.

Monod, Jean-Claude. *La querelle de la sécularisation: Théologie politique et philosophies de l'histoire de Hegel à Blumenberg*. Libr. philosophique J. Vrin, 2002.

Montaigne, Michel de. "On Cannibals." In *Essays*. Translated by Donald Frame. Franklin Library, 1979–1980.

Morel, Philippe. "Les têtes composées d'Arcimboldo, les grotesques et l'esthétique du paradoxe." In S. Ferino Pagden, ed. *Arcimboldo 1526–1593*. Skira, 2007.

Mussato, Albertino. *Humanist Tragedies*. Translated by Gary R. Grund. Harvard University Press, 2011.

Najemy, John. *Between Friends: Discourses of Power and Desire in the Machiavelli-Vettori Letters of 1513–1515*. Princeton University Press, 1993.

Naudé, Gabriel. *Considérations politiques sur les coups d'État*. Éditions de Paris, 1989.

Nodet, Étienne. *Historical Jesus?: Necessity and Limits of an Inquiry*. Translated by J. Edward Crowley. T&T Clark, 2008.

Oexle, Otto Gerhard. *L'historisme et débat: De Nietzsche à Kantorowicz*. Aubier, 2001.

———. *Political Thought and the Realities of Power in the Middle Ages*. Vandenhoek and Ruprecht, 1998.

Orwell, George. *Nineteen Eighty-Four*. Orion Publishing Group Ltd, 2021.

Ozouf, Mona. *Varenne: La mort de la royauté*. Gallimard, 2005.

Palmieri, Luca. *L'expérience d'un concept: Michel Foucault entre épistémologie et histoire*. Éditions de la Sorbonne, 2012.

Panofsky, Erwin. *Tomb Sculpture: Four Lectures on Its Changing Aspects from Ancient Egypt to Bernini*. Edited by H. W. Janson. H. N. Abrams, 1964.

Pastoureau, Michel. *The Bear: History of a Fallen King*. Translated by George Holoch. Belknap Press of Harvard University Press, 2011.

Pedrizet, Paul. *La Vierge de Miséricorde: Étude d'un thème iconographique*. A. Fontemoing, 1908.

Plutarch. *Plutarch's Lives*. 2 volumes. Modern Library, 2001.

Potte-Bonneville, Matthieu, ed. *Game of Thrones: Série noire*. Les prairies ordinaires, 2015.

Pysiak, Jerzy. "Philippe Auguste, roi des derniers temps." *Annales* (2002).

Quesnay, François. *The Economical Table*. University Press of the Pacific, 2004.

Recht, Roland. *Believing and Seeing: The Art of Gothic Cathedrals*. Translated by Mary Whittall. University of Chicago Press, 2008.

Revault d'Allones, Myriam. *Le miroir et la scène: Ce que peut la représentation politique*. Seuil, 2016.

Rigord. *The Deeds of Philip Augustus: An English Translation of Rigord's "Gesta Philippi Augusti."* Translated by Larry F. Field. Cornell University Press, 2022.

Robert, Aurélien. "Scepticisme ou renoncement au dogme? Interpréter l'Euchariste aux XIIIe et XIVe siècles." *Chôra. Revues d'études anciennes et médiévales* 6 (2008): 251–88.

Roman de Fauvel: In the Edition of Mesire Chaillou de Pesstain. Broude Bros., 1990.

Roose, Alexander. "*L'éloge de Néron* de Cardan: Un traité du soupçon, une utopie, une autobiographie." In Geneviève Goubier, Daniel Martin, and Bérengère Parmentier, eds. *Doute et imagination: Constructions du savoir de la Renaissance aux Lumières*. Classiques Garnier, 2011.

Rosanvallon, Pierre. *Le bon gouvernement*. Seuil, 2015.

Rosier-Catach, Irène. *La parole efficace: Signe, rituel, sacré*. Seuil, 2004.

Ryan, Marie Laure. *Possible Worlds, Artificial Intelligence, and Narrative Theory*. Indiana University Press, 1991.

Sabatier, Gérard. "Un morceau de roi: L'exhibition de la jambe sur les portraits des Bourbons, XVIIe–XVIIIe siècles." In Marcello Fantoni, ed. *I gesti del potere*. Le Cáriti, 2011.

Saint-Simon, Louis de Rouvroy, duc de. *La cour du régent*. Dent, c. 1908.

Schaeffer, Jean-Marie. *Why Fiction?* Translated by Dorrit Cohn. University of Nebraska Press, 2010.

Schefer, Jean-Louis. *L'hostie profanée: Histoire d'une fiction théologique*. P.O.L., 2007.

Schlanger, Judith E. *La mémoire des œuvres*. Verdier, 2008.

Schmitt, Carl. *The Leviathan in the State Theory of Thomas Hobbes: Meaning and Failure of a Political Symbol*. Translated by George Schwab and Erna Hilfstein. Greenwood Press, 1996.

———. *State, Movement, People: The Triadic Structure of the Political Unity: The Question of Legality*. Translated by Simona Draghici. Plutarch Press, 2001.

Shakespeare, William. *The Tragedy of King Richard the Second*. In *The Riverside Shakespeare*. Houghton Mifflin, 1974.

Shapin, Steven, and Simon Schaffer. *Leviathan and the Air-Pump: Hobbes, Boyle, and the Experimental Life*. Princeton University Press, 1985.

Skinner, Quentin. *Hobbes and Republican Liberty*. Cambridge University Press, 2008.

———. "Truth and the Historian." A lecture delivered at St. Mary, University of London in 2011. Available online at https://www.youtube.com/watch?v=EjM5qg-u-LA

Sollers, Philippe. "Logique de la fiction." In *Logique de la fiction et autres textes*. Éditions Cécile Defaut, 2005.

Spector, Céline. *Éloges de l'injustice: La philosophie face à la déraison.* Éditions du Seuil, 2016.

Sublet, Jacqueline. *Les trois vies du Sultan Baïbars.* Imprimerie Nationale, 1992.

Suetonius Tranquillus, C. *The Lives of the Caesars.* 2 volumes. Translated by J. C. Rolfe. Harvard University Press, Loeb Classical Library, 1913.

Supiot, Alain. *Le gouvernement par les nombres: Cours au Collège de France (2012–2014).* Fayard, 2015.

Tacitus, Cornelius. *The Annals and the Histories.* Translated by Alfred John Church and William Jackson Brodribb. Encyclopaedia Britannica, 1955.

Thomas, Yan. *Les opérations du droit.* Seuil, 2011.

Thomas Aquinas. *Première question disputée. La vérité (De veritate).* Translated by C. Brouwer and M. Peeters. Vrin, 2002.

Trump, Donald J., with Tony Schwartz. *Trump: The Art of the Deal.* Random House, 1988.

Twain, Mark. *The Diary of Adam and Eve.* Modern Library, 1996 [1904].

Vasari, Giorgio. *The Lives of the Most Excellent Painters, Sculptors, and Architects.* Edited by Philip Jacks. Translated by Gaston du C. de Vere. Modern Library, 2006.

———. *Vasari on Technique, Being the Introduction to the Three Arts of Design, Architecture, Sculpture and Painting, Prefixed to the Lives of the Most Excellent Painters, Sculptors, and Architects.* Edited G. Baldwin Brown. Translated by Louisa S. Maclehose. J. M. Dent & Co., 1907.

Villani, Giovanni. *Nuova Cronica.* Edited by Giuseppe Porta. Fondazione Pietro Bembo, 1991.

Viner, Katharine. "How Technology Disrupted the Truth." *The Guardian*, July 12, 2016, available at https://www.theguardian.com/media/2016/jul/12/how-technology-disrupted-the-truth

Wanegffelen, Thierry. "La controverse entre Robert Céneau et Martin Bucer sur l'Eucharistie (septembre 1534–janvier 1535)." *Revue d'histoire de l'Église de France* 77–199 (1991): 341–49.

William of Malmesbury. *The Chronicles of the Kings of England*. Edited by J. A. Giles. Henry G. Bohn, 1847.

———. *The Deeds of the Bishops of England (Gesta pontificum Anglorum)*. Translated by David Preest. Boydell Press, 2002.

IMAGE CREDITS

iv	Wikipedia Commons
7	World History Archive / Alamy Stock Photo
9	The Picture Art Collection / Alamy Stock Photo
10	Charles Chaplin, Buster Keaton in the 1952 United Artists film *Limelight.* © Roy Export S.A.S.
15	Web Gallery of Art
16	Web Gallery of Art
19	Wikipedia Commons
20	Web Gallery of Art
122	Wikipedia Commons
146–9	Web Gallery of Art
174	Web Gallery of Art
176	Internet Archive
179	Internet Archive
182	Wikipedia Commons
186	CanalBlog
188–9	Wikipedia Commons
191	Wikipedia Commons
192	Wikipedia Commons
194	Library of Congress
195	Wikipedia Commons
201	Wikipedia Commons

203 Wikipedia Commons
204 Internet Archive
206 Division of Rare and Manuscript Collections,
Cornell University Library
208 Wikipedia Commons
210 Wikipedia Commons
211 Houghton Library, Harvard University
212 [upper] Library of Congress
212 [lower] Ohio State University
218 [inset] Wikipedia Commons
218 [letter] The History Collection / Alamy Stock Photo
223 Beinecke Rare Book and Manuscript Library, Yale University Library
230 The Picture Art Collection / Alamy Stock Photo
231 Wikipedia Commons
233 Statens Museum for Kunst, Copenhagen, Denmark
239 Museo Galileo, Institute and Museum of the History of Science
251 Web Gallery of Art
252 Heritage Image Partnership Ltd / Alamy Stock Photo
257 Centre Historique des Archives Nationales, Paris, France /
Archives Charmet / Bridgeman Images
258 Wikipedia Commons
261 Wikipedia Commons
265 The Metropolitan Museum of Art, Harris Brisbane Dick Fund, 1935
266 Wikipedia Commons
268 Wikipedia Commons
270 Internet Archive
271 The Metropolitan Museum of Art, The Elisha Whittelsey Collection,
The Elisha Whittelsey Fund, 1959
272 Wikipedia Commons
273 © 2025 The Andy Warhol Foundation for the Visual Arts, Inc. /
Licensed by Artists Rights Society (ARS), New York.
Randy Duchaine / Alamy Stock Photo
274 Christophe Meneboeuf, Wikipedia Commons
275 The Bodleian Libraries, University of Oxford
277 Web Gallery of Art
352 Bibliothèque nationale de France, Manuscrit Français 146,
illumination from folio 11, recto